THE
VAMPRESS GIRLS

City of the Lost Souls

THE
VAMPRESS GIRLS

City of the Lost Souls

JACY NOVA and NICK NOVA

KENSINGTON PUBLISHING CORP.
http://www.kensingtonbooks.com

KENSINGTON BOOKS are published by

Kensington Publishing Corp.
850 Third Avenue
New York, NY 10022

All Kensington titles, imprints, and distributed lines are available at
special quantity discounts for bulk purchases for sales promotions,
premiums, fund-raising, educational or institutional use.

Special book excerpts or customized printings can also be created to
fit specific needs. For details, write or phone the office of the
Kensington Special Sales Manager: Kensington Publishing Corp., 850
Third Avenue, New York, NY 10022. Attn: Special Sales Department.
Phone: 1-800-221-2647.

ISBN-13: 978-0-7582-2528-3
ISBN-10: 0-7582-2528-8

First Kensington Trade Paperback Printing: May 2008
10 9 8 7 6 5 4 3 2 1

Printed in the United States of America

Jacy Nova

This book is dedicated to Nik and Boris,
the two muses in my life. Much love.
A special thanks to June Clark and the Kensington team.

Nick Nova

This book is dedicated to my Mom, Dad, Grandma,
Nessa, Todd, Derek, and Greg.

LOVE

TRIBE: VAMPIRE

ZODIAC SIGN: CANCER

TITLE: HIGH PRIESTESS OF THE VAMPIRE CLAN

THE MOTHER OF THE VAMPRESS GIRLS SHE IS THE SOLE PROTECTOR OF THE DREAMERS AND THE VAMPRESS CODE. DO NOT BE FOOLED BY HER KIND AND LOVING HEART: SHE IS CONSIDERED ONE OF THE MOST POWERFUL VAMPIRES TO WALK THE EARTH.

SHADE

TRIBE: DEMON

ZODIAC SIGN: SCORPIO

TITLE: HIGH PRIEST OF THE DEMON CLAN

A FALLEN VAMPIRE. HIS GREED AND LUST TO POSSESS THE VAMPRESS CODE CONSUMES HIM. WOMEN FIND IT HARD TO RESIST HIS MAGNETIC CHARMS. INTENSELY SECRETIVE, HE IS AN INTIMIDATING FORCE AMONG THE DEMONS.

PASSION

TRIBE: VAMPIRE

ZODIAC SIGN: LEO

TITLE: THE VAMPRESS
GIRLS

INSTRUMENT: VOCALS

THE OLDEST OF THE
FOUR SISTERS, PASSION
ENJOYS BEING THE
CENTER OF ATTENTION.
SHE IS CREATIVE AND
PASSIONATE. QUITE THE
FASIONISTA. SHE IS
CONSIDERED THE HEART
BREAKER OF THE GIRLS.

SWEET

TRIBE: VAMPIRE

ZODIAC SIGN: PISCES

TITLE: THE VAMPRESS
GIRLS

INSTRUMENT: DRUMS

AN OLD SOUL, SWEET IS
SHY AND QUIET. HER
UNCANNY PSYCHIC
ABILITIES COME IN HANDY
WHEN PROTECTING THE
WORLD FROM THE DREAM
SUCKING DEMONS AND
THE WITCHES.

RAVEN

TRIBE: VAMPIRE

ZODIAC SIGN: TAURUS

TITLE: THE VAMPRESS GIRLS

INSTRUMENT: GUITARS

THE MOST OUTSPOKEN OF THE GIRLS. RAVEN IS PERSISTANT AND DETERMINED IN ACHIEVING HER GOAL. DESPITE HER WICKED SENSE OF HUMOR, SHE'S A HOPELESS ROMANTIC AND IS WAITING FOR 'THE ONE' TO SWEEP HER OFF HER FEET.

PAGE

TRIBE: VAMPIRE

ZODIAC SIGN: VIRGO

TITLE: THE VAMPRESS GIRLS

INSTRUMENT: BASS

THE RESIDENT FAMILY GEEK, PAGE IS SENSITIVE AND SUPER-SMART. MORE OF A HOMEBODY, HER KEEN INTUITION OFTEN KEEPS THE GIRLS OUT OF STICKY SITUATIONS.

BRANDY

TRIBE: DEMON

ZODIAC SIGN: SAGITTARIUS

TITLE: THE DEMON GIRLS

INSTRUMENT: LEAD VOCALS

BRANDY IS A FREE SPIRIT WHO NEVER TAKES NO FOR AN ANSWER. FUN LOVING AND ALWAYS OUT-SPOKEN, SHE IS FIERCELY INDEPENDENT AND DETERMINED TO TAKE THE BAND TO NUMBER ONE ON THE CHARTS.

JADE

TRIBE: DEMON

ZODIAC SIGN: ARIES

TITLE: THE DEMON GIRLS

INSTRUMENT: BASS

JADE'S NON-STOP ENERGY IS CENTRAL TO THE PUNK SOUND OF HER BAND. HER BIG EGO CAN BE OVERBEARING AT TIMES. HER ARCH NEMESIS IS RAVEN, WHO STOLE HER MAN DAMIEN. WHAT REVENGE WILL SHE BESTOW ON THE VAMPRESS GIRLS?

EVE

TRIBE: DEMON

ZODIAC SIGN: AQUARIUS

TITLE: THE DEMON GIRLS

INSTRUMENT: GUITARS

EVE PRIDES HERSELF ON BEING UNIQUE AND UNCONVENTIONAL. SHE IS ORIGINAL IN CREATIVE EXPRESSION AND GETS BORED EASILY. SHE IS INTENSELY JEALOUS OF THE VAMPRESS GIRLS SUCCESS.

SPAZ

TRIBE: DEMON

ZODIAC SIGN: GEMINI

TITLE: THE DEMON GIRLS

INSTRUMENT: DRUMS

SPAZ LOVES TO TALK AND HAS A GREAT SENSE OF HUMOR. THE IMPULSIVE MEMBER OF THE GROUP, SHE HAS A SECRET CRUSH ON SHADE. SHE IS JADE'S SIDEKICK IN WREAKING HAVOC IN THE VAMPRESS GIRLS LIVES.

LUCY FUR

TRIBE: DEMON

ZODIAC SIGN: CAPRICORN

TITLE: PRINCESS OF DARKNESS.

AN EXTRAORDINARY BUSINESS WOMAN. LUCY FUR IS SUPER CONFIDENT AND IS CALCULATING IN HER WAYS. CUNNING AND SMART, SHE IS SHADE'S GIRLFRIEND. TOGETHER THEY ARE BOTH DETERMINED TO POSSESS THE VAMPRESS CODE.

DAMIEN

TRIBE: DEMON

ZODIAC SIGN: LIBRA

TITLE: PRINCE OF DARKNESS

DAMIEN IS LUCY'S BROTHER AND HEIR TO THE THRONE OF THE DEMON EMPIRE. HE IS OUTWARDLY CHARMING AND FRIENDLY. BUT IS MADE OF STEEL UNDERNEATH. WILL RAVEN'S LOVE MELT HIS HEART OF STONE?

THE VAMPRESS GIRLS

City of the Lost Souls

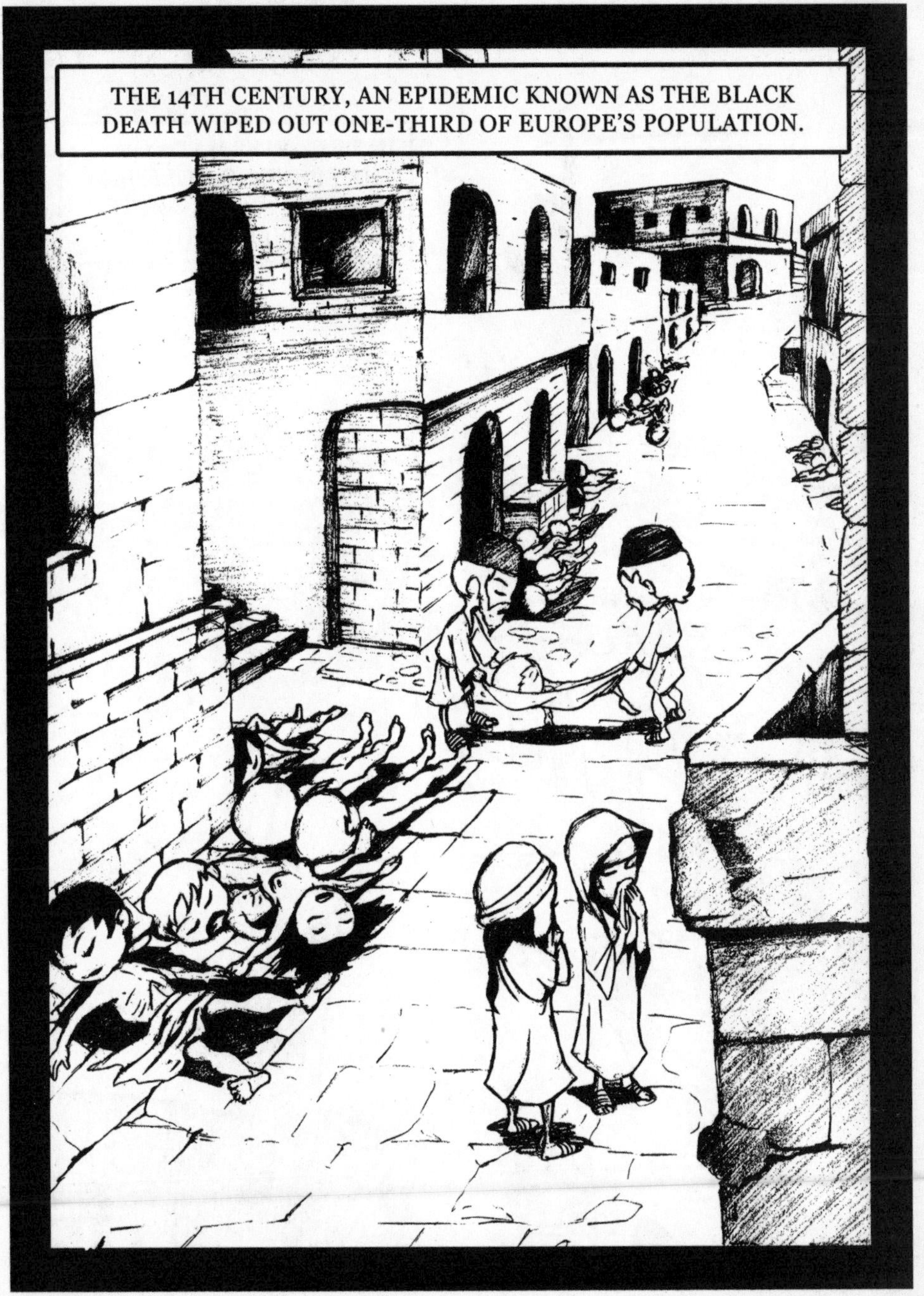
THE 14TH CENTURY, AN EPIDEMIC KNOWN AS THE BLACK DEATH WIPED OUT ONE-THIRD OF EUROPE'S POPULATION.

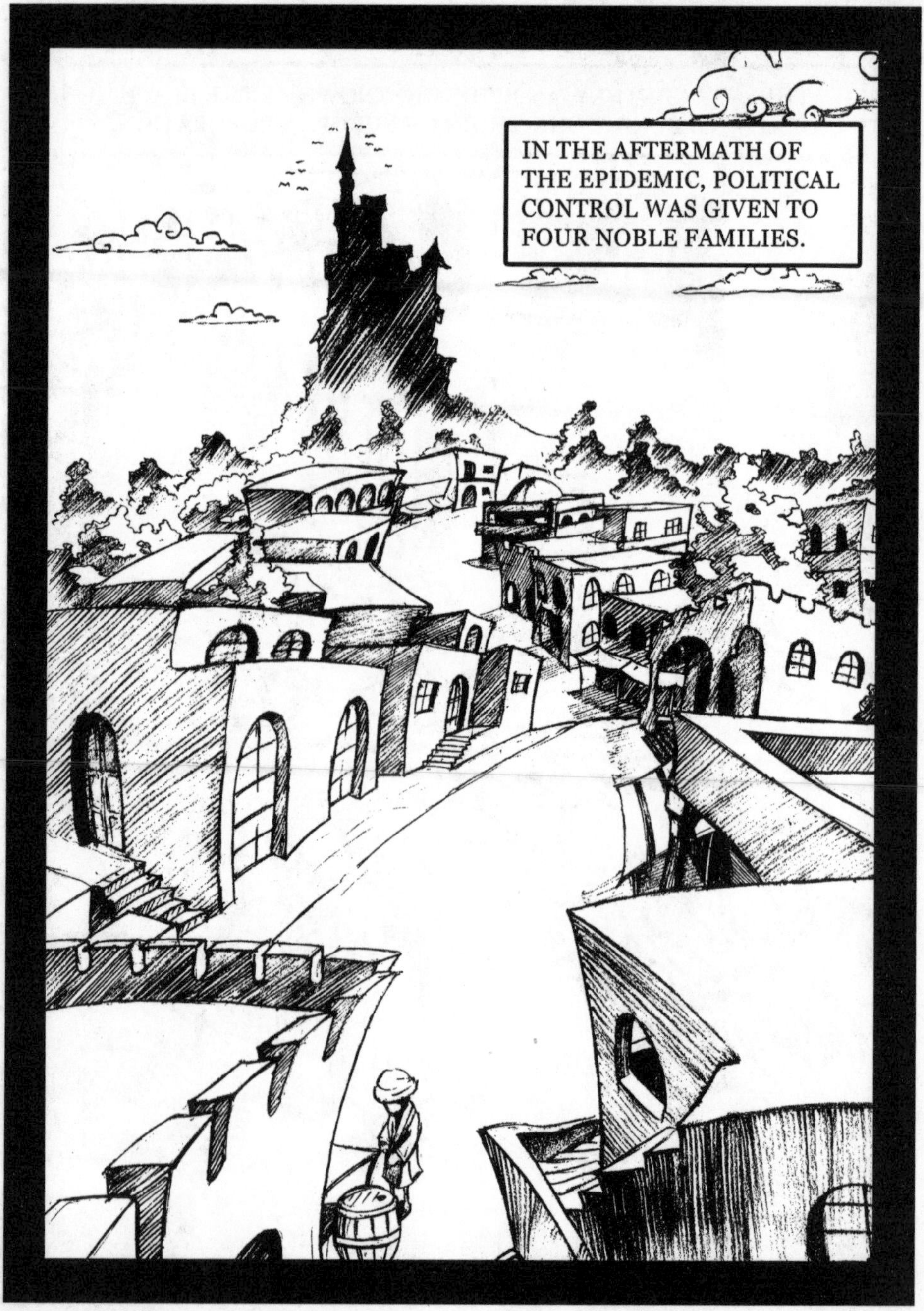
IN THE AFTERMATH OF THE EPIDEMIC, POLITICAL CONTROL WAS GIVEN TO FOUR NOBLE FAMILIES.

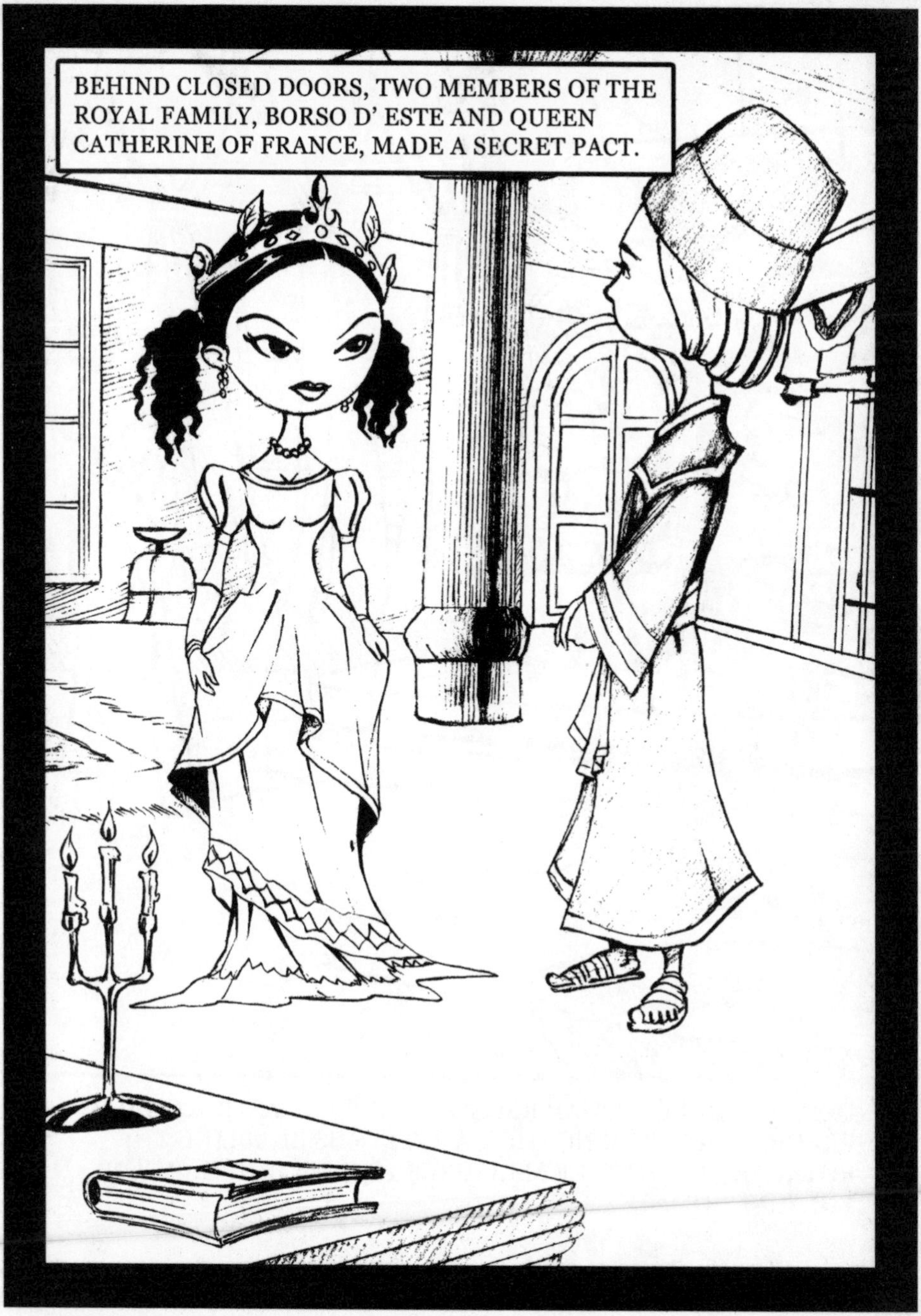
BEHIND CLOSED DOORS, TWO MEMBERS OF THE ROYAL FAMILY, BORSO D' ESTE AND QUEEN CATHERINE OF FRANCE, MADE A SECRET PACT.

QUEEN CATHERINE HAD RECEIVED SEVERAL ASTROLOGICAL
PREDICTIONS FROM NOSTRADAMUS, THUS ENABLING THE
ROYAL FAMILY TO TAKE MEASURES TO MAINTAIN HARMONY IN
THE KINGDOM.

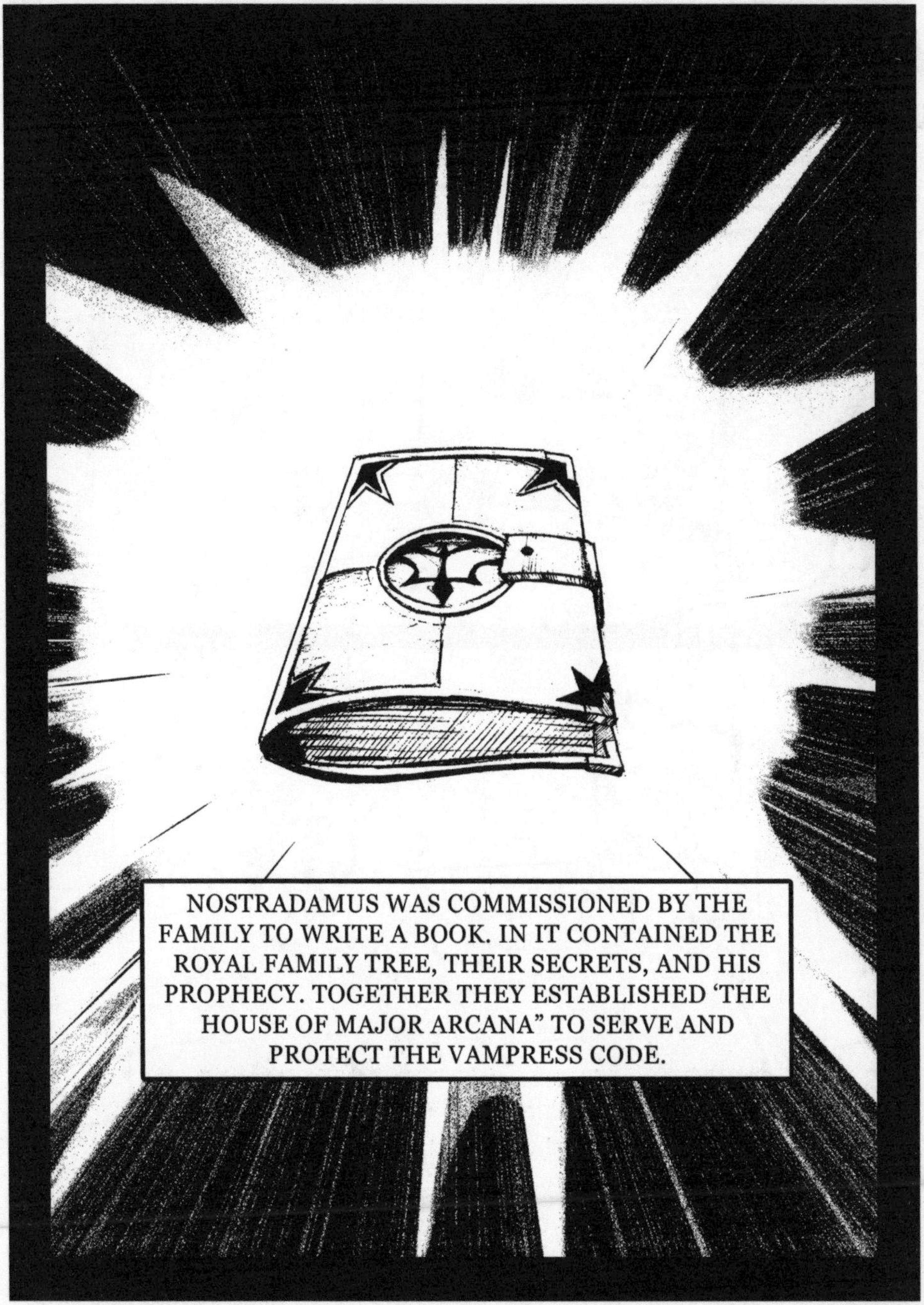
NOSTRADAMUS WAS COMMISSIONED BY THE FAMILY TO WRITE A BOOK. IN IT CONTAINED THE ROYAL FAMILY TREE, THEIR SECRETS, AND HIS PROPHECY. TOGETHER THEY ESTABLISHED 'THE HOUSE OF MAJOR ARCANA" TO SERVE AND PROTECT THE VAMPRESS CODE.

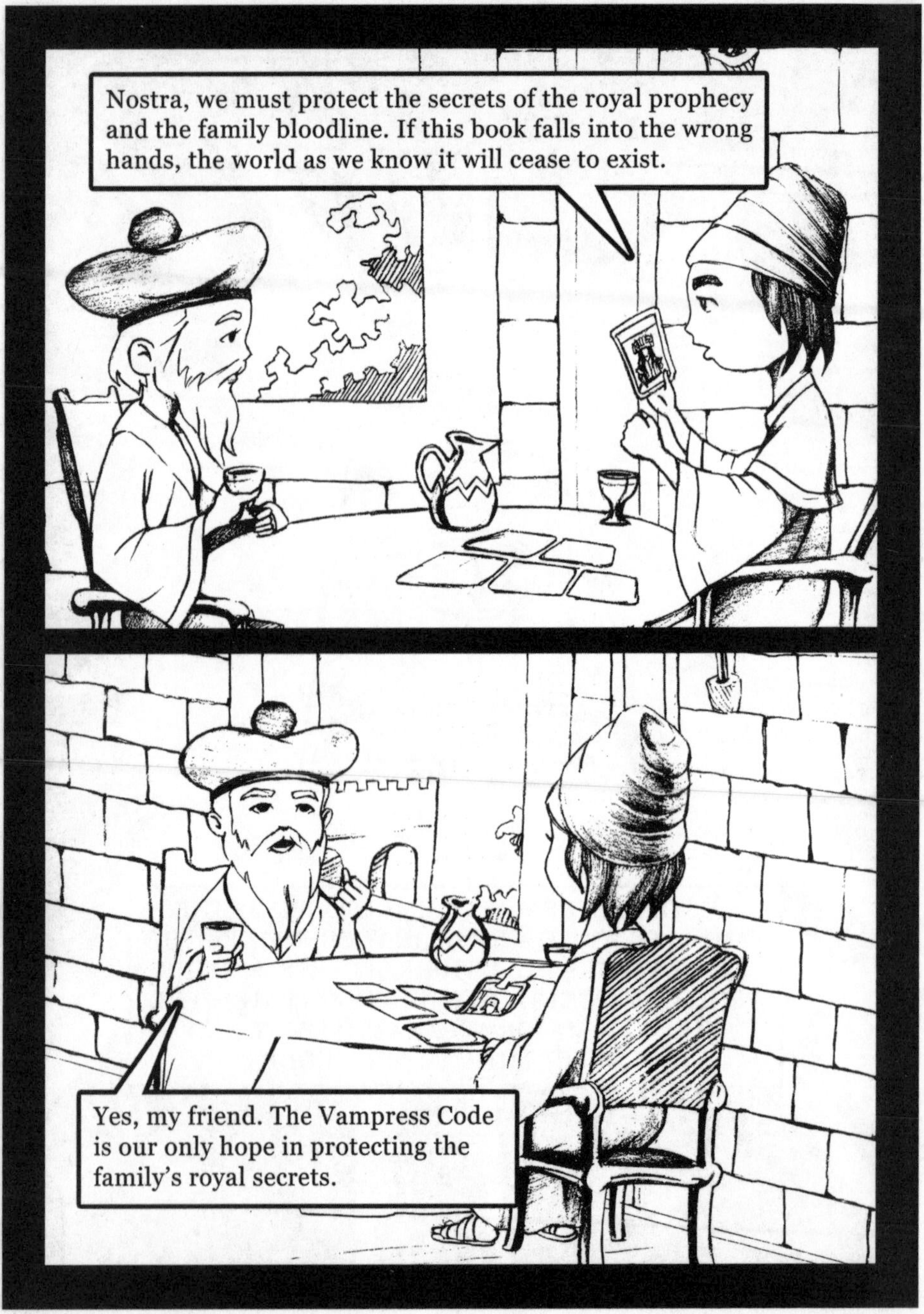
Nostra, we must protect the secrets of the royal prophecy and the family bloodline. If this book falls into the wrong hands, the world as we know it will cease to exist.
Yes, my friend. The Vampress Code is our only hope in protecting the family's royal secrets.

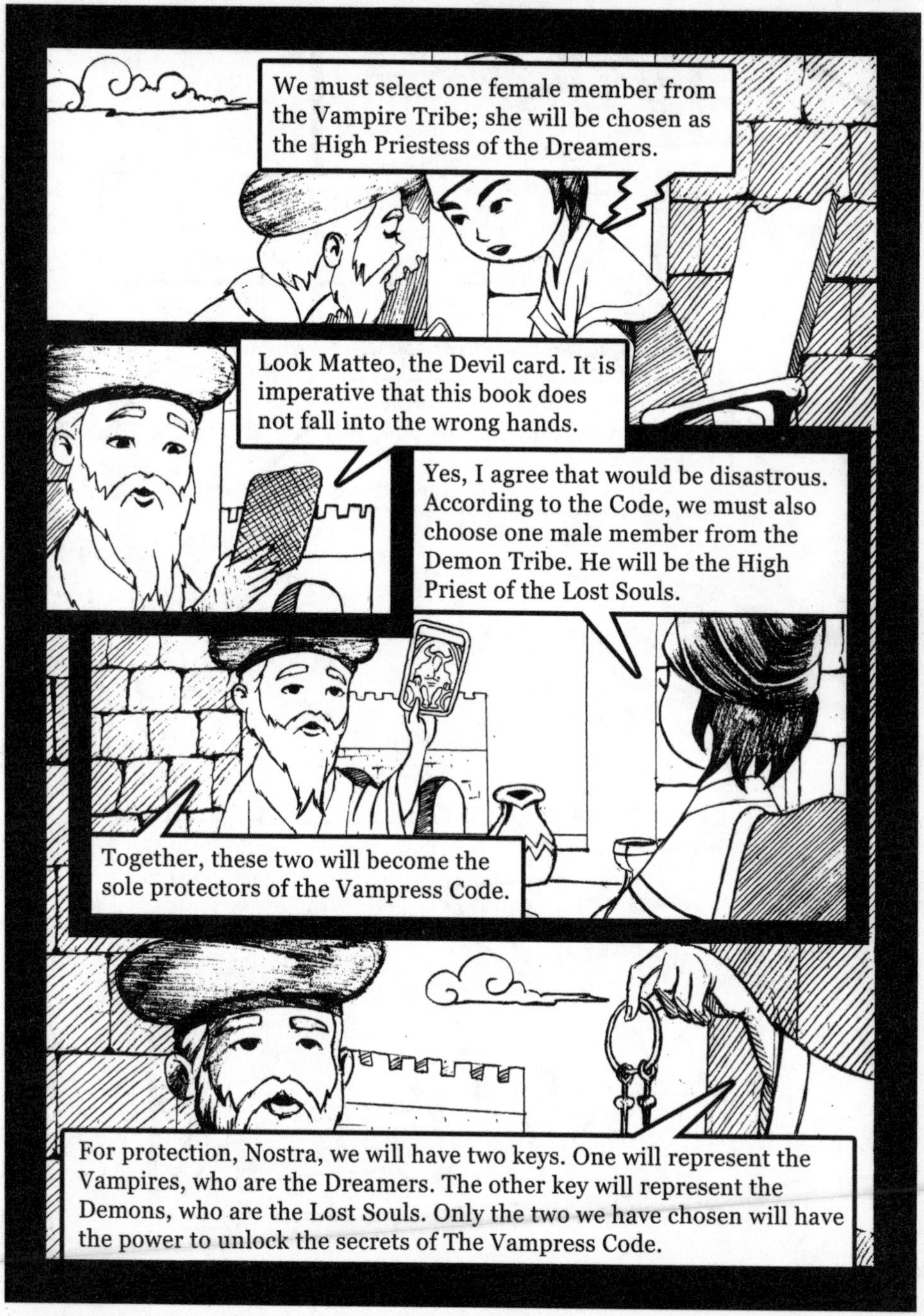

We must select one female member from the Vampire Tribe; she will be chosen as the High Priestess of the Dreamers.
Look Matteo, the Devil card. It is imperative that this book does not fall into the wrong hands.
Yes, I agree that would be disastrous. According to the Code, we must also choose one male member from the Demon Tribe. He will be the High Priest of the Lost Souls.
Together, these two will become the sole protectors of the Vampress Code.
For protection, Nostra, we will have two keys. One will represent the Vampires, who are the Dreamers. The other key will represent the Demons, who are the Lost Souls. Only the two we have chosen will have the power to unlock the secrets of The Vampress Code.

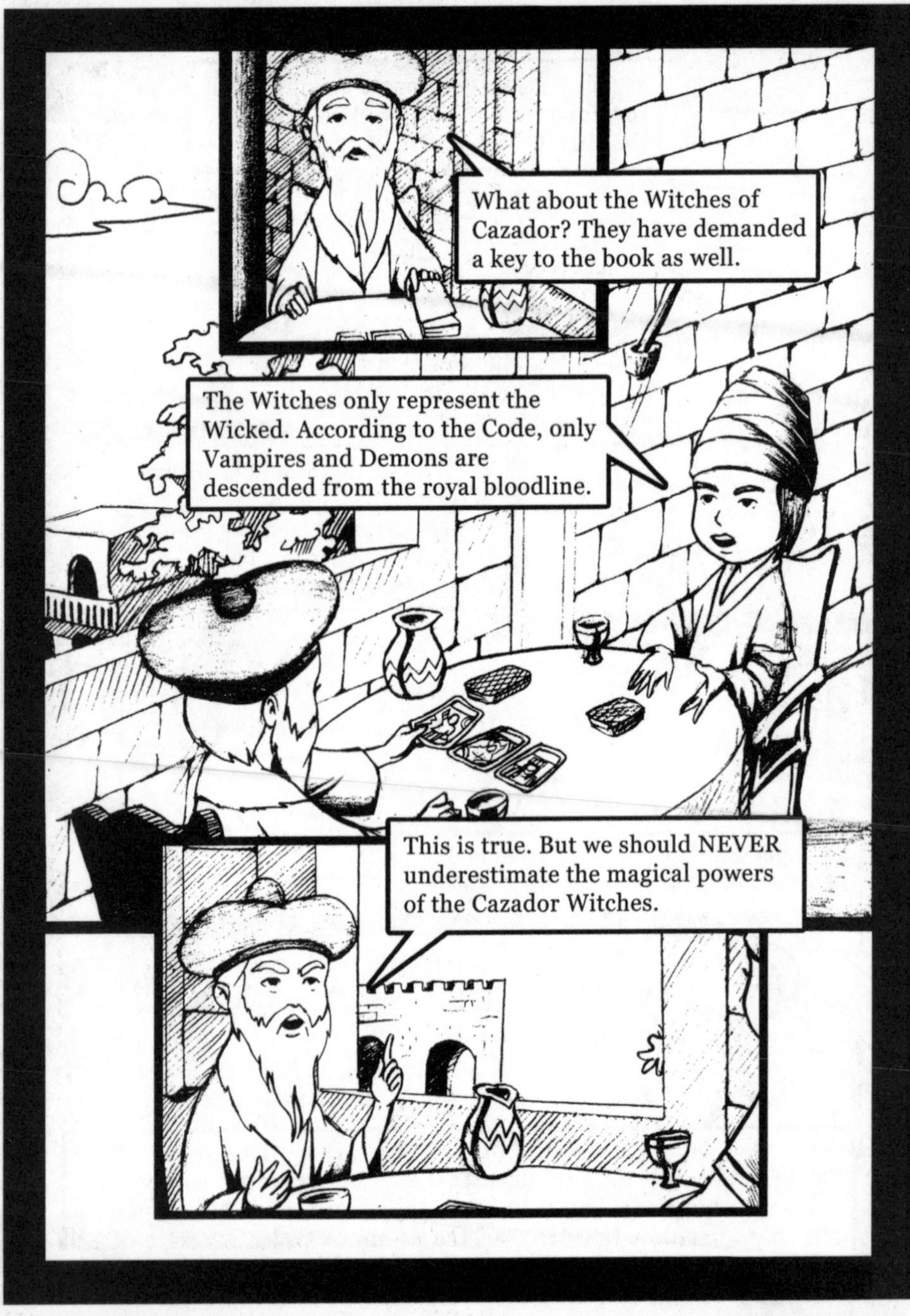
What about the Witches of Cazador? They have demanded a key to the book as well.
The Witches only represent the Wicked. According to the Code, only Vampires and Demons are descended from the royal bloodline.
This is true. But we should NEVER underestimate the magical powers of the Cazador Witches.

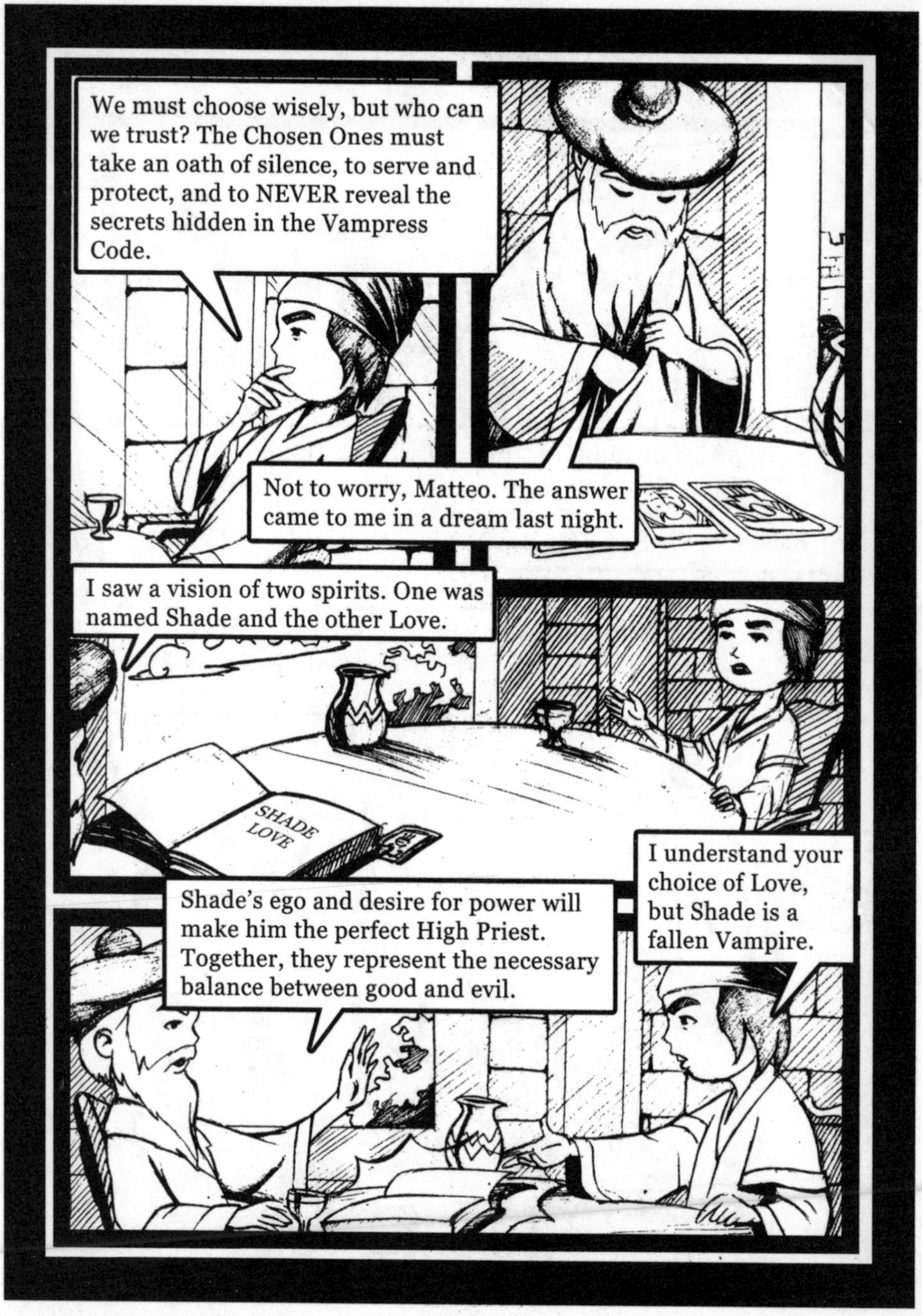
We must choose wisely, but who can we trust? The Chosen Ones must take an oath of silence, to serve and protect, and to NEVER reveal the secrets hidden in the Vampress Code.
Not to worry, Matteo. The answer came to me in a dream last night.
I saw a vision of two spirits. One was named Shade and the other Love.
SHADE
LOVE
Shade's ego and desire for power will make him the perfect High Priest. Together, they represent the necessary balance between good and evil.
I understand your choice of Love, but Shade is a fallen Vampire.

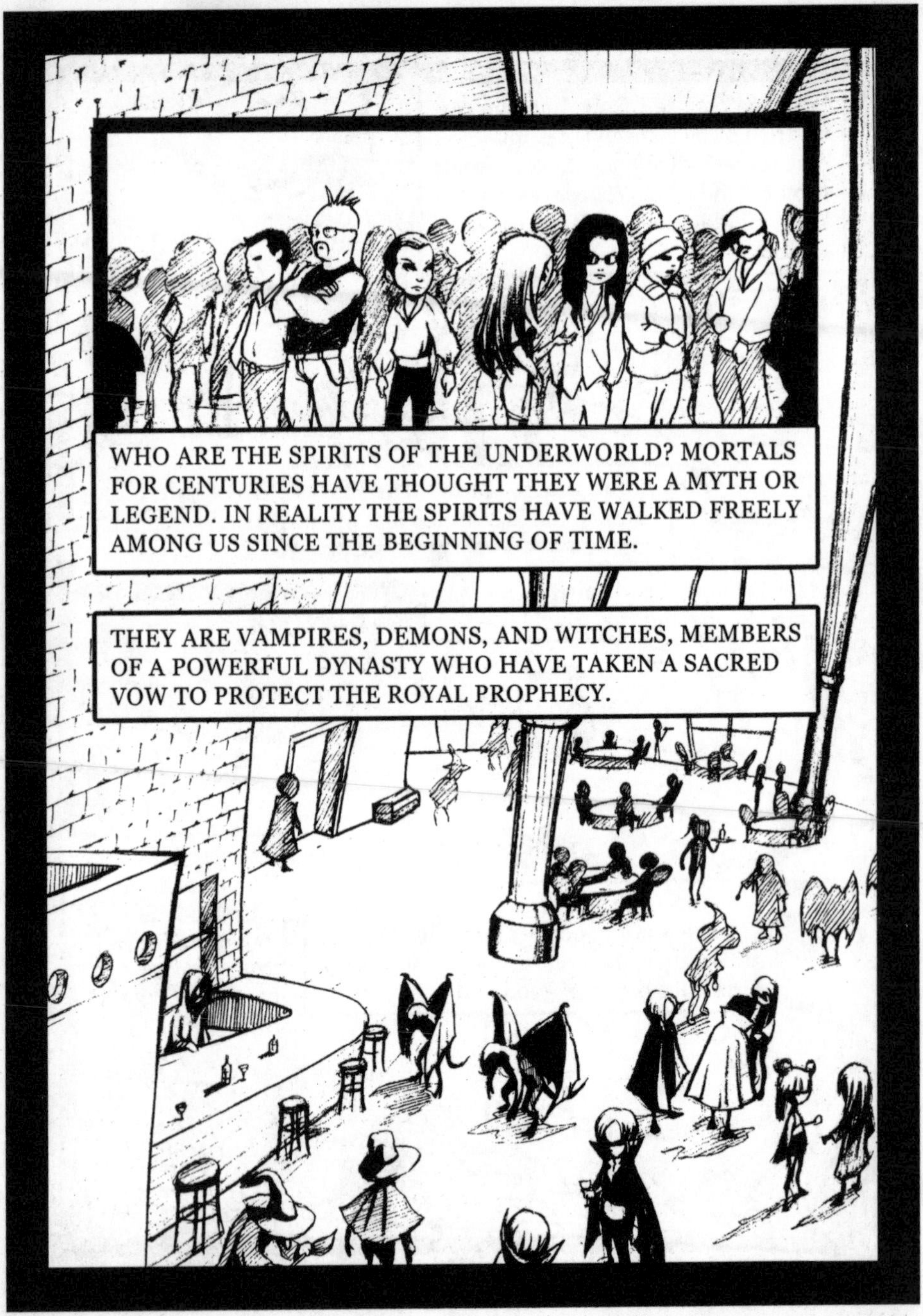
WHO ARE THE SPIRITS OF THE UNDERWORLD? MORTALS FOR CENTURIES HAVE THOUGHT THEY WERE A MYTH OR LEGEND. IN REALITY THE SPIRITS HAVE WALKED FREELY AMONG US SINCE THE BEGINNING OF TIME.
THEY ARE VAMPIRES, DEMONS, AND WITCHES, MEMBERS OF A POWERFUL DYNASTY WHO HAVE TAKEN A SACRED VOW TO PROTECT THE ROYAL PROPHECY.

THE ANCIENT BOOK CONTAINED THE ROYAL FAMILY TREE, AND THE SPIRAL OF KNOWLEDGE. ACCORDING TO PROPHECY, IF THE VAMPRESS CODE WAS EVER REVEALED, THE GATES OF HEAVEN AND HELL WOULD OPEN, AND THE WORLD WOULD BE THROWN INTO CHAOS.

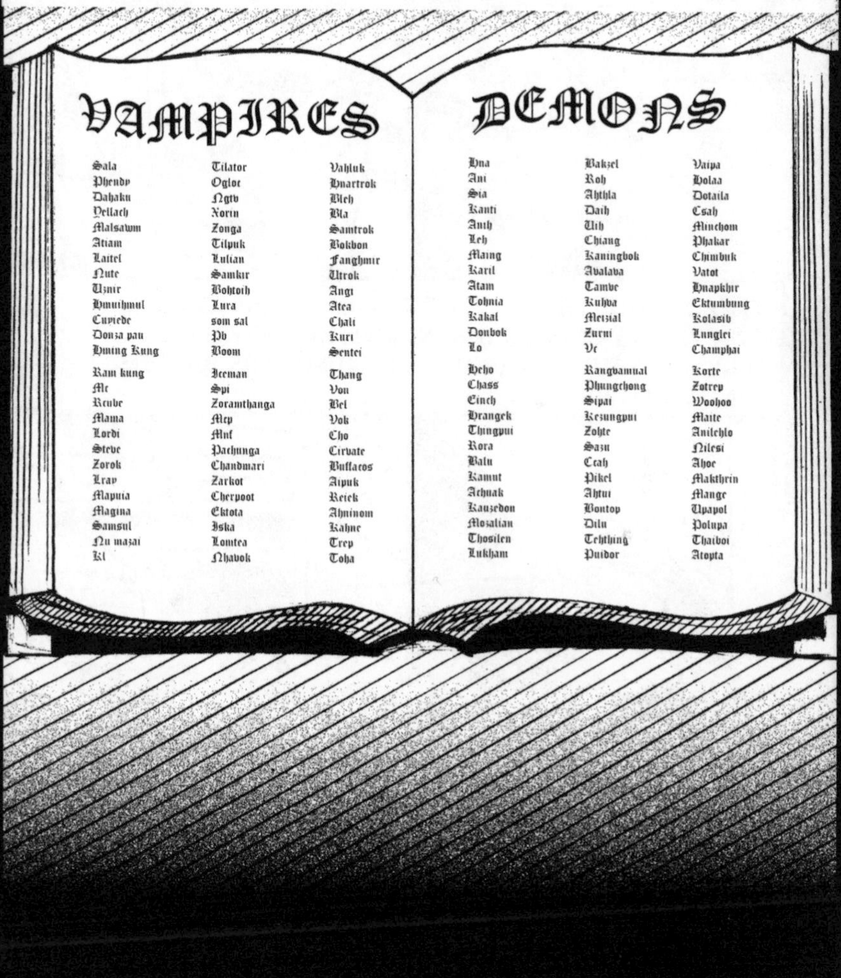
VAMPIRES
Sala
Phendy
Dahaku
Yellach
Malsawm
Atiam
Laitel
Nute
Uznir
Hmuihmul
Cuyiede
Donza pau
Hming Kung
Ram kung
Me
Reube
Mama
Lordi
Steve
Zorok
Lray
Mapuia
Magina
Samsul
Nu mazai
Kl
Tilator
Ogloe
Ngtv
Xorin
Zonga
Tilpuk
Lulian
Samkir
Bohtoih
Lura
som sal
Pb
Boom
Iceman
Spi
Zoramthanga
Mep
Muf
Pachunga
Chandmari
Zarkot
Cherpoot
Ektota
Iska
Lomtea
Nhavok
Vahluk
Hnartrok
Bleh
Bla
Samtrok
Bokbon
Fanghmir
Utrok
Angi
Atea
Chali
Kuri
Sentei
Thang
Von
Bel
Vok
Cho
Cirvate
Buffacos
Aipuk
Reiek
Ahninom
Kahne
Trep
Toha
DEMONS
Hna
Ani
Sia
Kanti
Anih
Leh
Maing
Karil
Atam
Tohnia
Kakal
Donbok
Lo
Heho
Chass
Einch
Hrangek
Thingpui
Rora
Balu
Kamut
Achuak
Kauzedon
Mozalian
Thosilen
Lukham
Bakzel
Roh
Ahthla
Daih
Uih
Chiang
Kaningbok
Avalava
Tambe
Kuhva
Meizial
Zurni
Ve
Rangvamual
Phungchong
Sipai
Kezungpui
Zohte
Sazu
Ceah
Pikel
Ahtui
Bontop
Dilu
Tehthing
Puidor
Vaipa
Holaa
Dotaila
Csah
Minchom
Phakar
Chimbuk
Vatot
Hnapkhir
Ektumbung
Kolasib
Lunglei
Champhai
Korte
Zotrep
Woohoo
Maite
Anilchlo
Nilesi
Ahoe
Makthrin
Mange
Upapol
Polupa
Thaiboi
Atopta

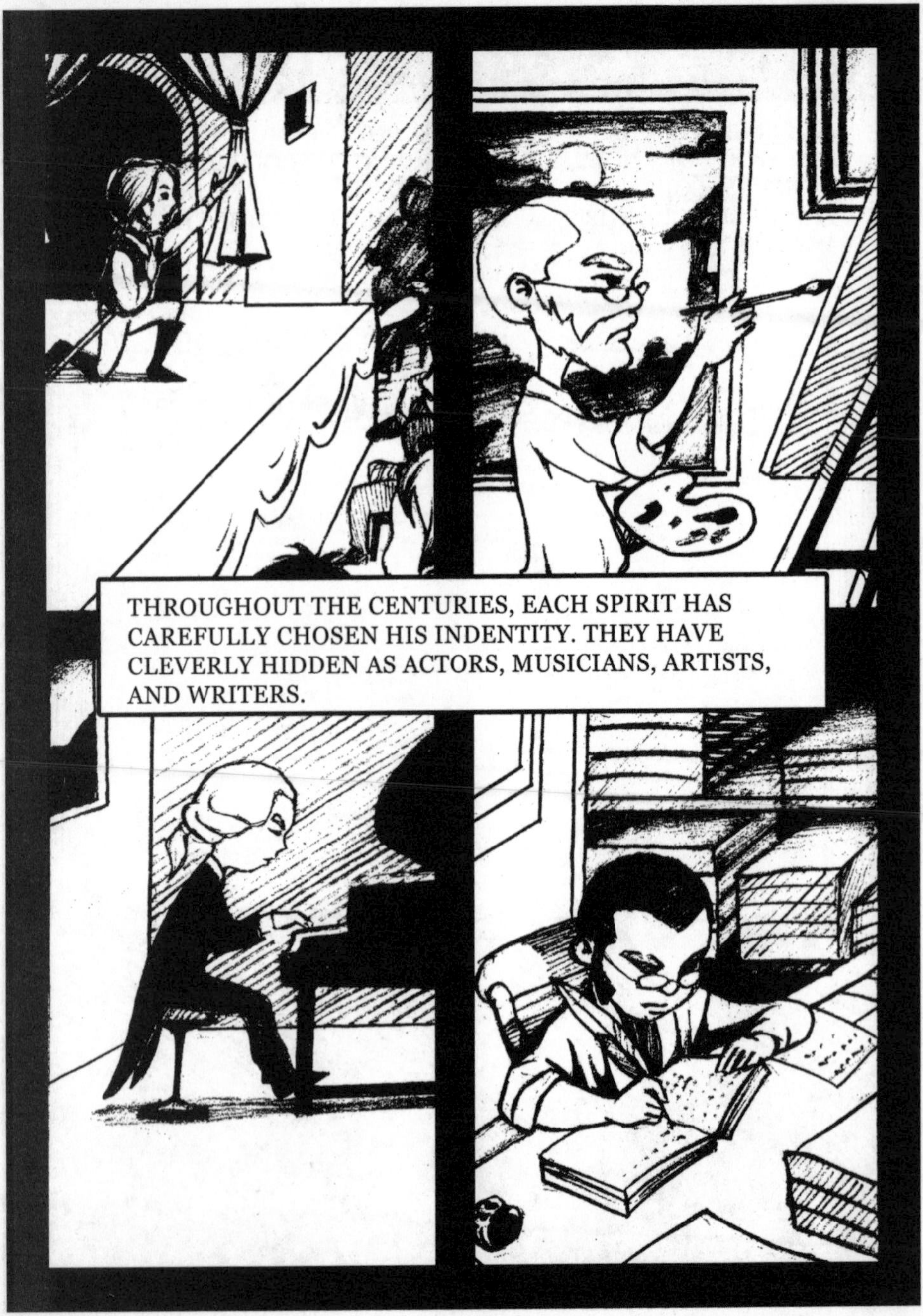
THROUGHOUT THE CENTURIES, EACH SPIRIT HAS CAREFULLY CHOSEN HIS INDENTITY. THEY HAVE CLEVERLY HIDDEN AS ACTORS, MUSICIANS, ARTISTS, AND WRITERS.

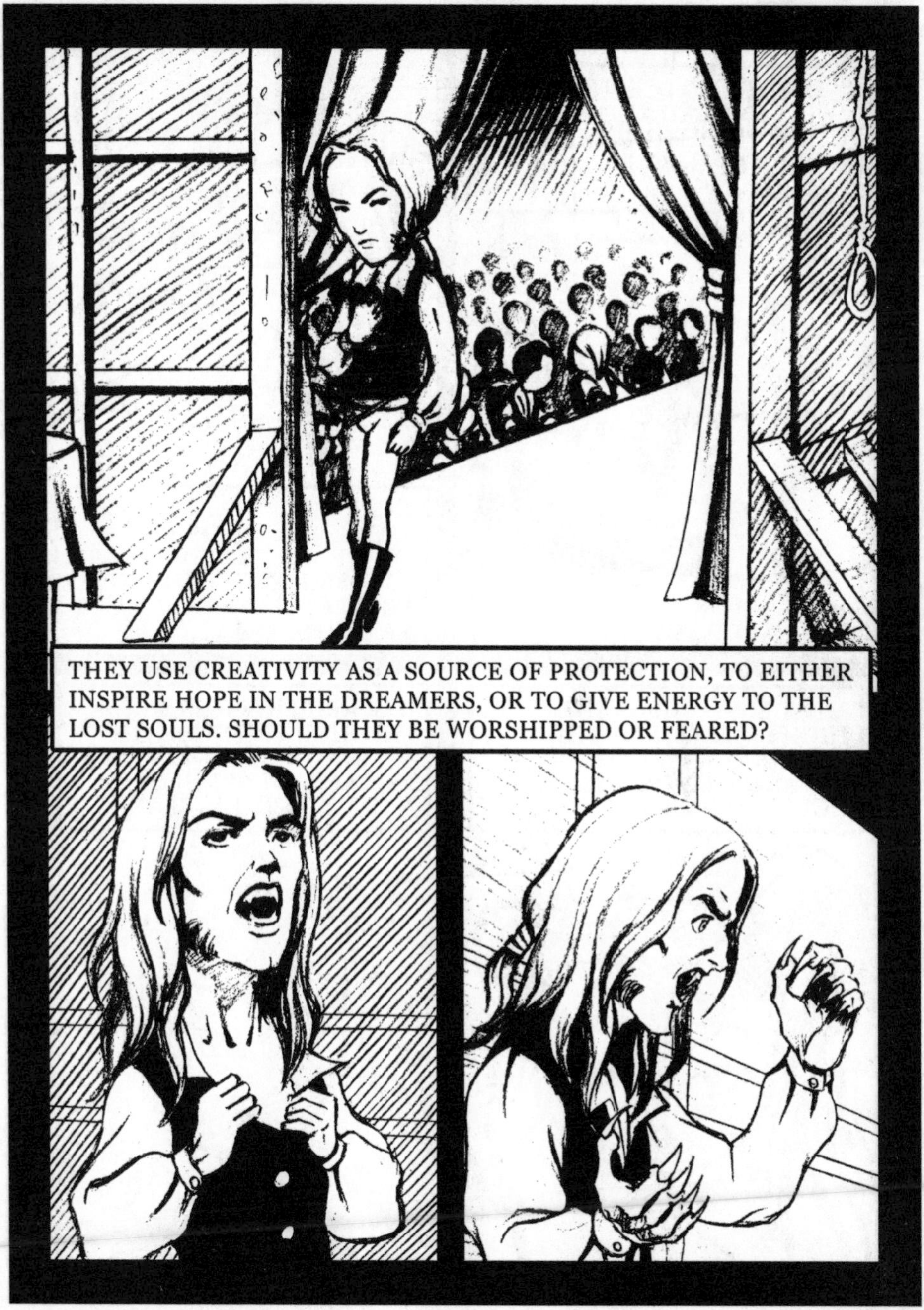
THEY USE CREATIVITY AS A SOURCE OF PROTECTION, TO EITHER INSPIRE HOPE IN THE DREAMERS, OR TO GIVE ENERGY TO THE LOST SOULS. SHOULD THEY BE WORSHIPPED OR FEARED?

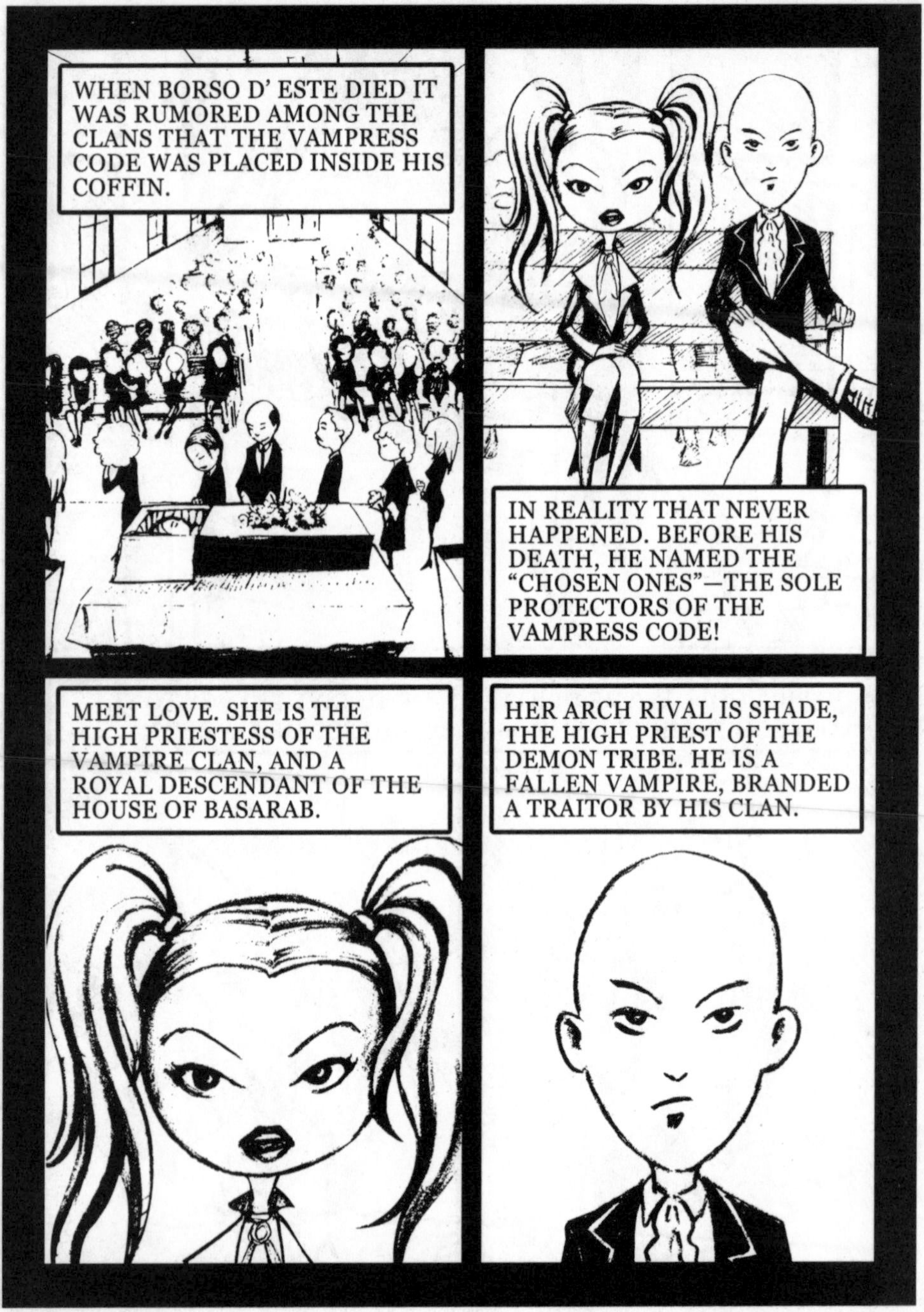
WHEN BORSO D' ESTE DIED IT WAS RUMORED AMONG THE CLANS THAT THE VAMPRESS CODE WAS PLACED INSIDE HIS COFFIN.
IN REALITY THAT NEVER HAPPENED. BEFORE HIS DEATH, HE NAMED THE "CHOSEN ONES"—THE SOLE PROTECTORS OF THE VAMPRESS CODE!
MEET LOVE. SHE IS THE HIGH PRIESTESS OF THE VAMPIRE CLAN, AND A ROYAL DESCENDANT OF THE HOUSE OF BASARAB.
HER ARCH RIVAL IS SHADE, THE HIGH PRIEST OF THE DEMON TRIBE. HE IS A FALLEN VAMPIRE, BRANDED A TRAITOR BY HIS CLAN.

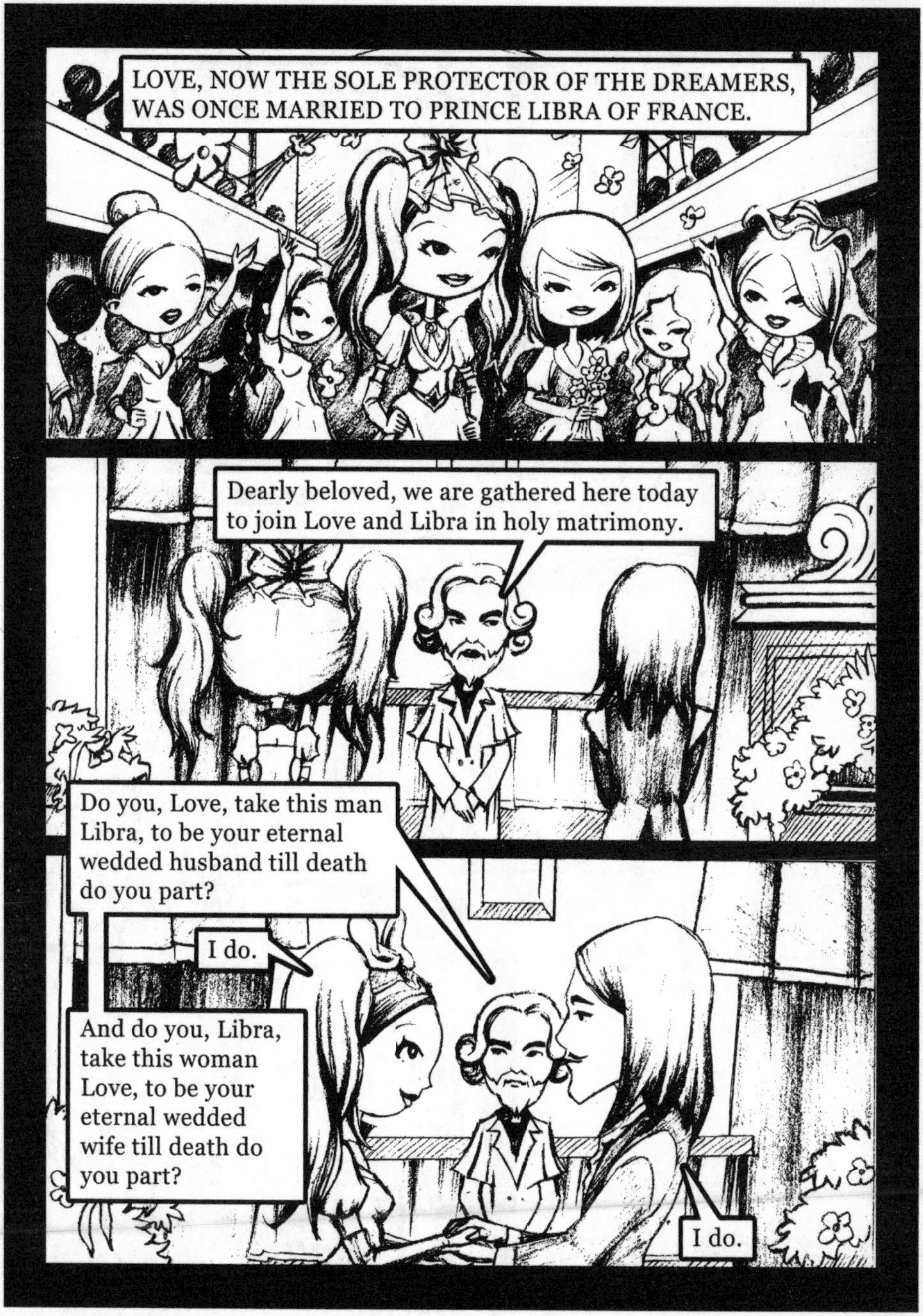
LOVE, NOW THE SOLE PROTECTOR OF THE DREAMERS, WAS ONCE MARRIED TO PRINCE LIBRA OF FRANCE.
Dearly beloved, we are gathered here today to join Love and Libra in holy matrimony.
Do you, Love, take this man Libra, to be your eternal wedded husband till death do you part?
I do.
And do you, Libra, take this woman Love, to be your eternal wedded wife till death do you part?
I do.

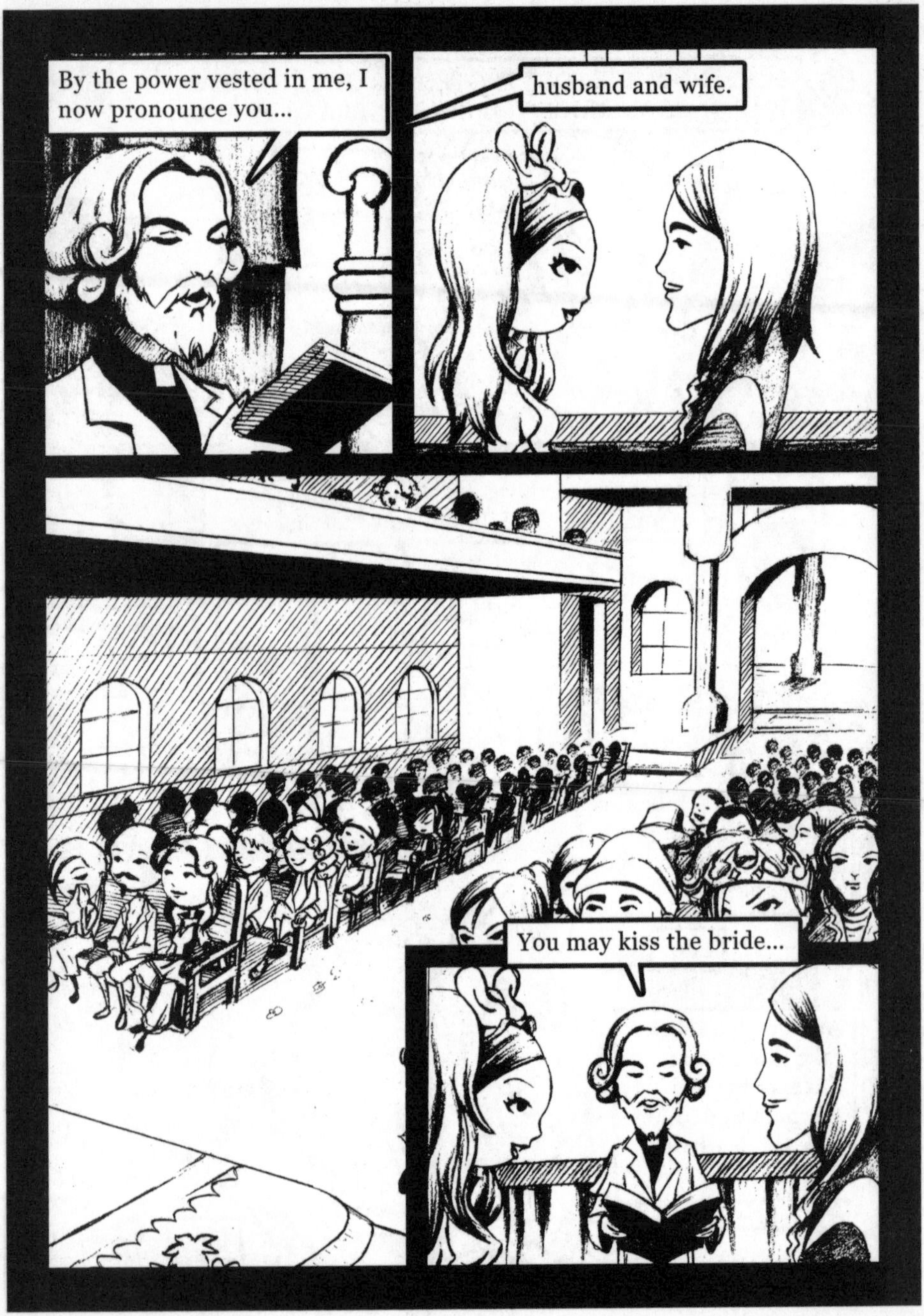
By the power vested in me, I now pronounce you...
husband and wife.
You may kiss the bride...

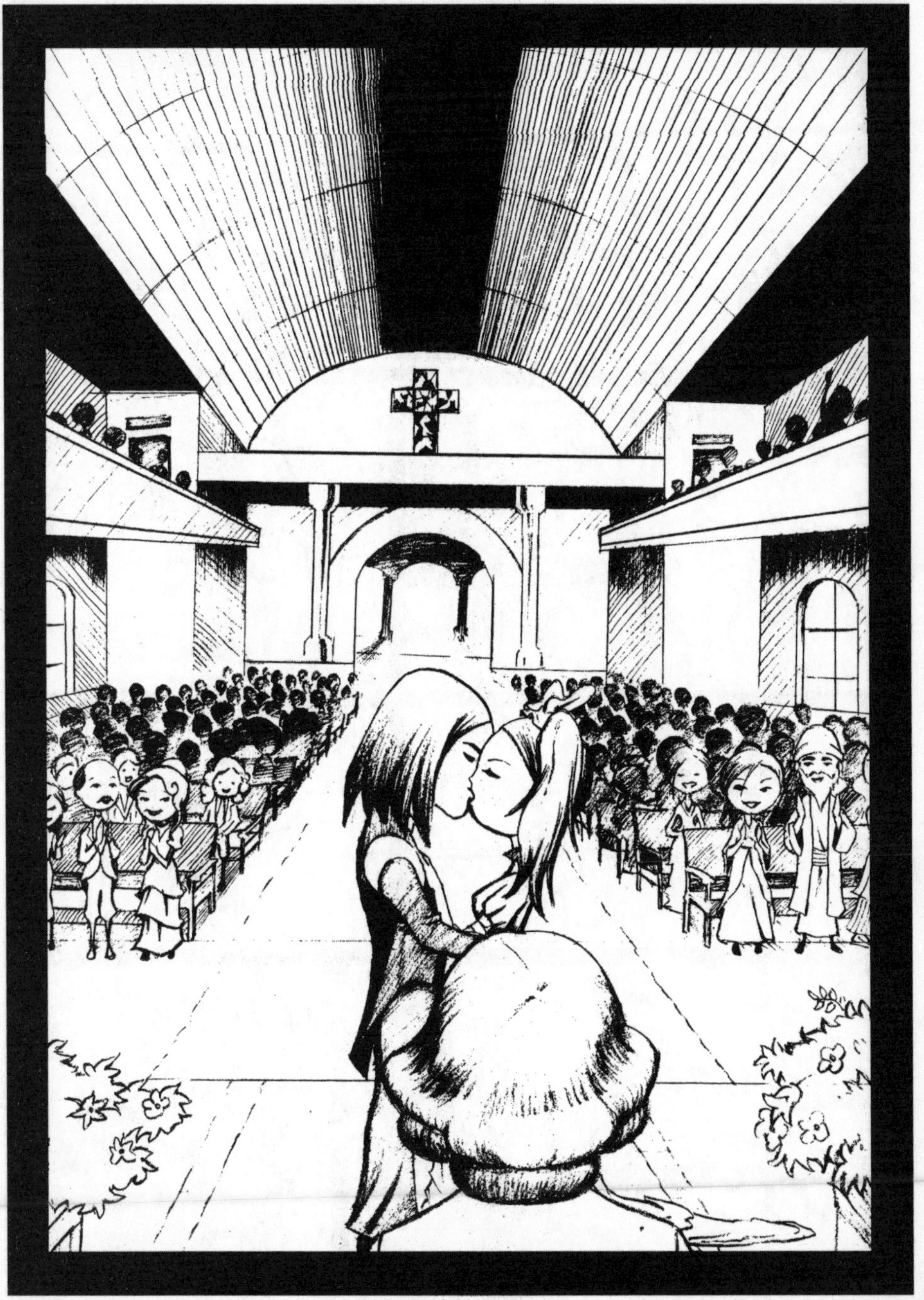

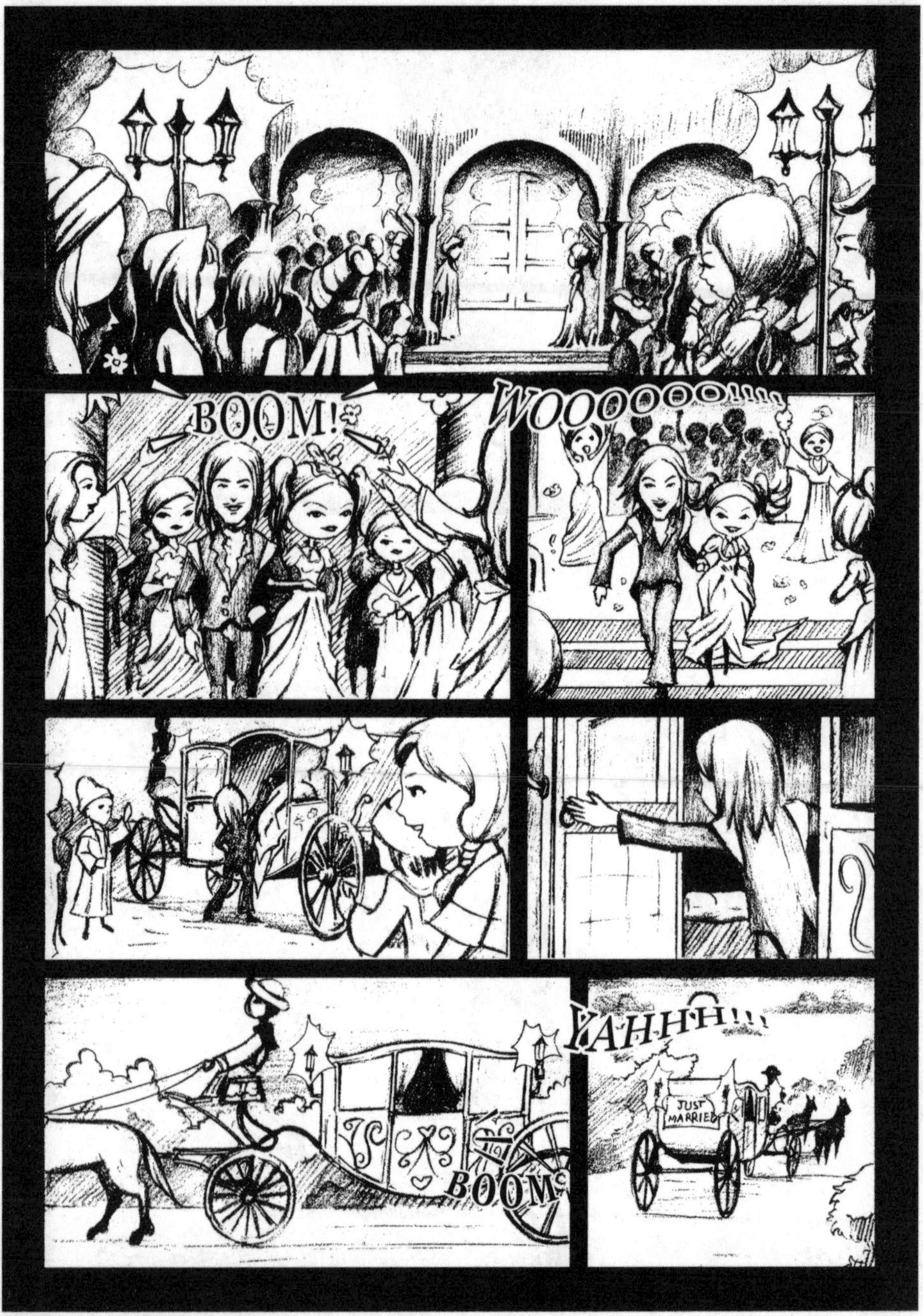
BOOM!
WOOOOOO!!!!
BOOM
YAHHH!!!
JUST MARRIED

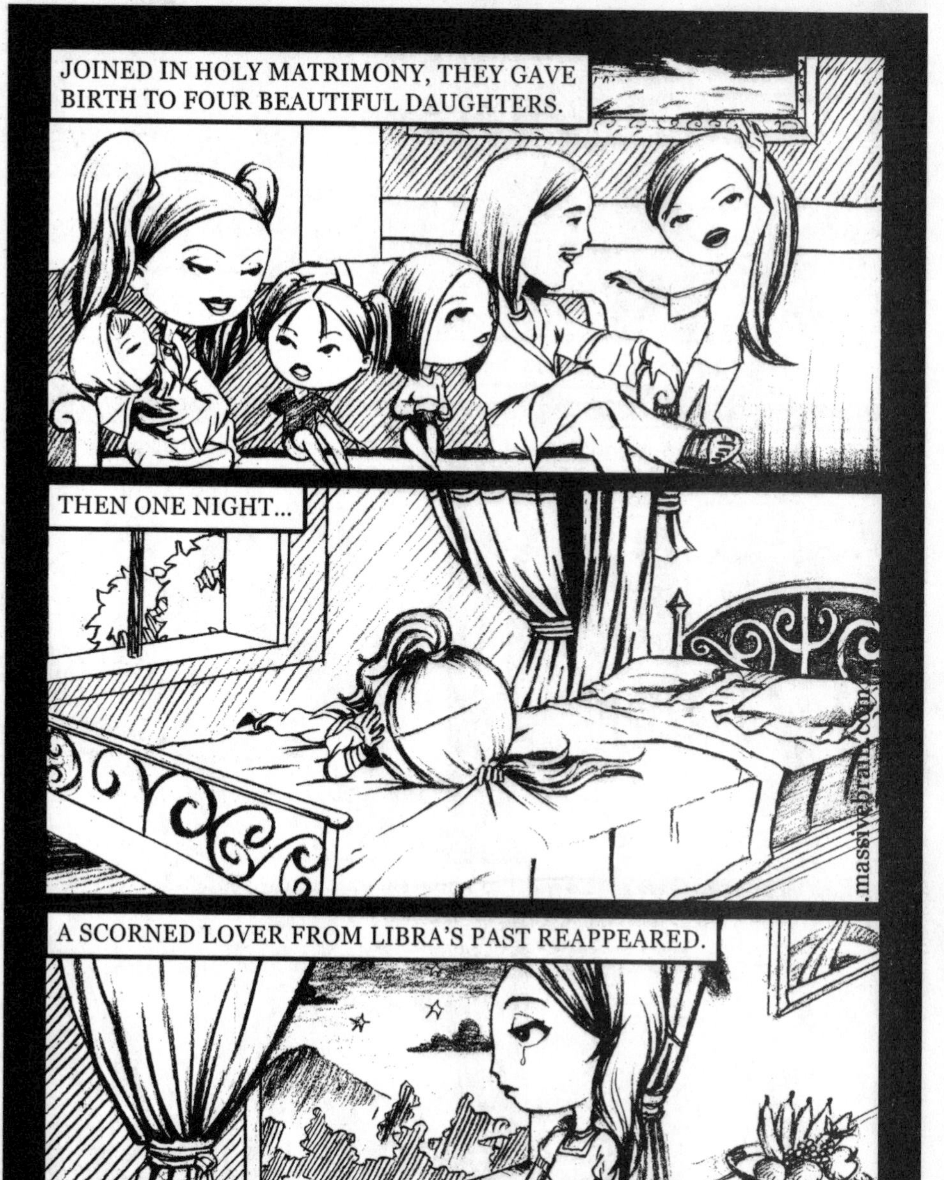
JOINED IN HOLY MATRIMONY, THEY GAVE BIRTH TO FOUR BEAUTIFUL DAUGHTERS.
THEN ONE NIGHT...
massivebrain.com
A SCORNED LOVER FROM LIBRA'S PAST REAPPEARED.

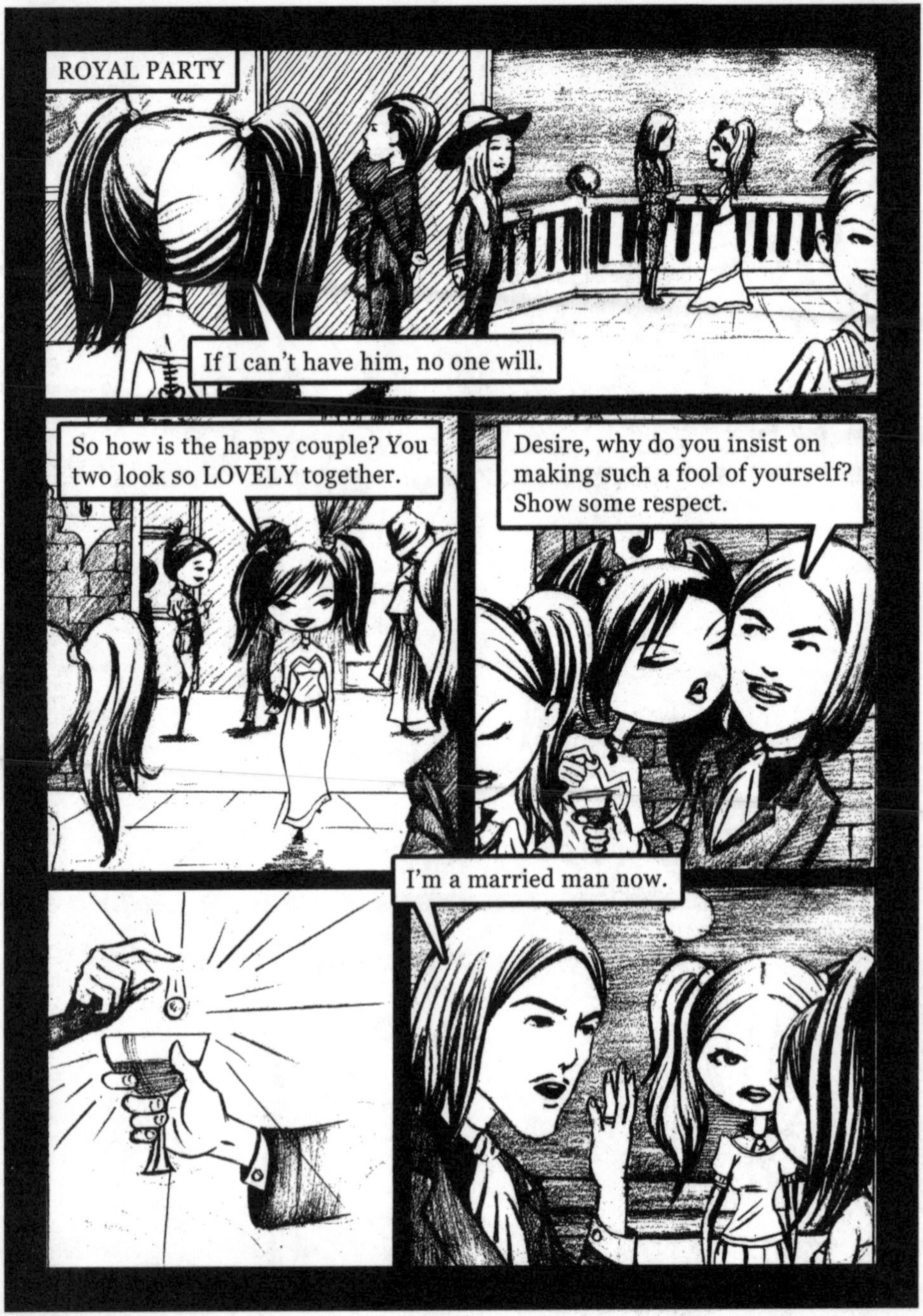
ROYAL PARTY
If I can't have him, no one will.
So how is the happy couple? You two look so LOVELY together.
Desire, why do you insist on making such a fool of yourself? Show some respect.
I'm a married man now.

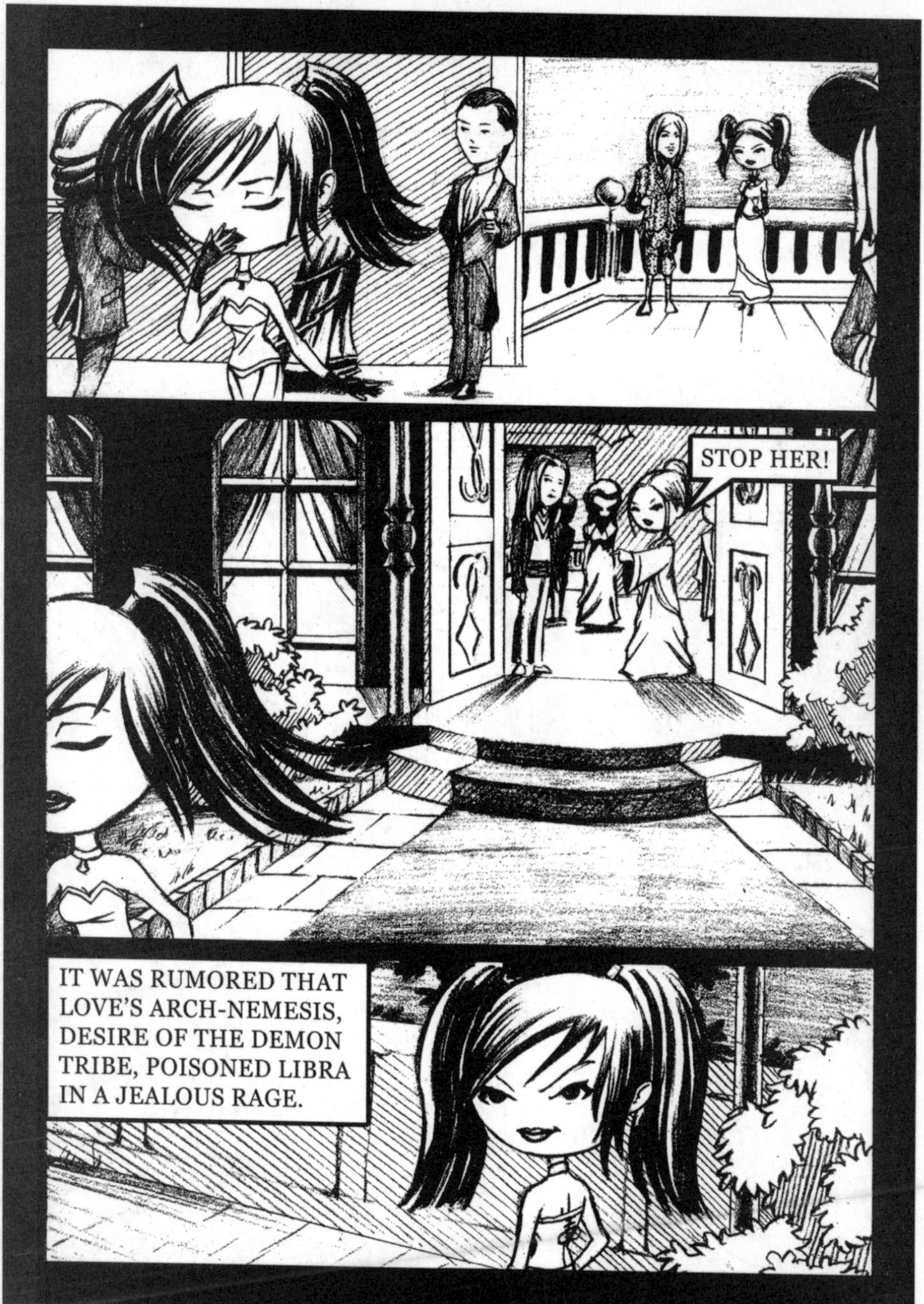
STOP HER!
IT WAS RUMORED THAT LOVE'S ARCH-NEMESIS, DESIRE OF THE DEMON TRIBE, POISONED LIBRA IN A JEALOUS RAGE.

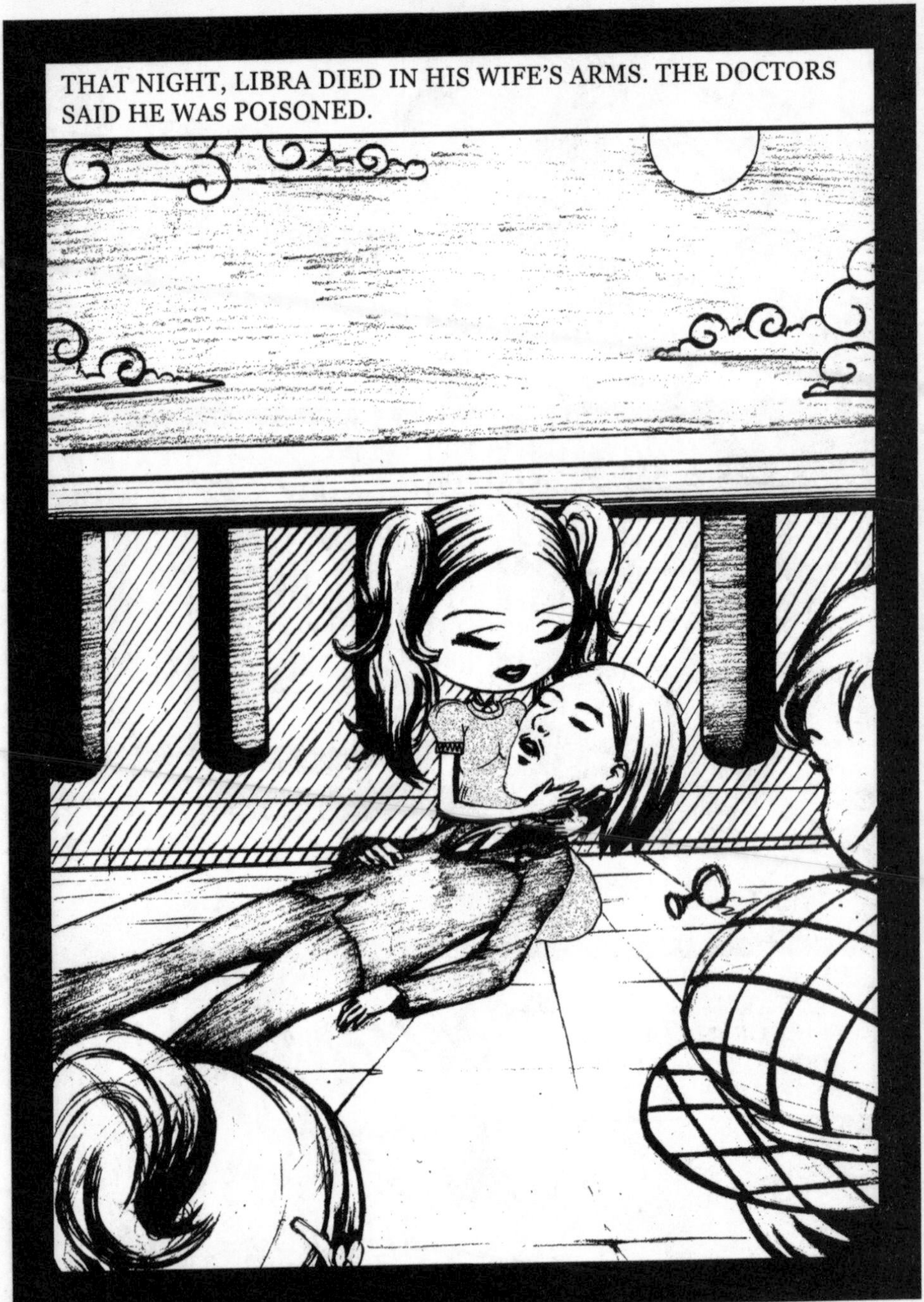
THAT NIGHT, LIBRA DIED IN HIS WIFE'S ARMS. THE DOCTORS SAID HE WAS POISONED.

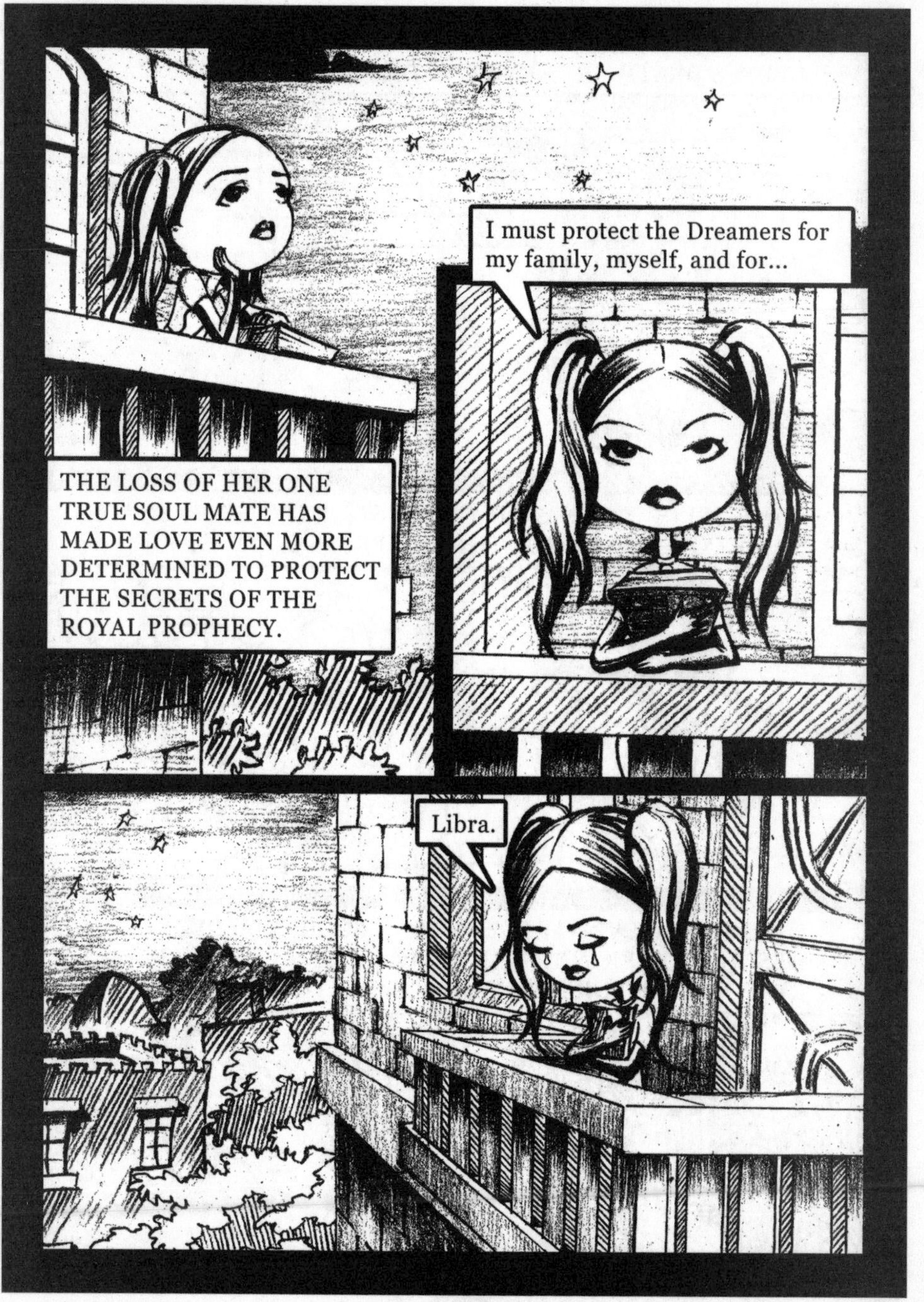
THE LOSS OF HER ONE TRUE SOUL MATE HAS MADE LOVE EVEN MORE DETERMINED TO PROTECT THE SECRETS OF THE ROYAL PROPHECY.
I must protect the Dreamers for my family, myself, and for...
Libra.

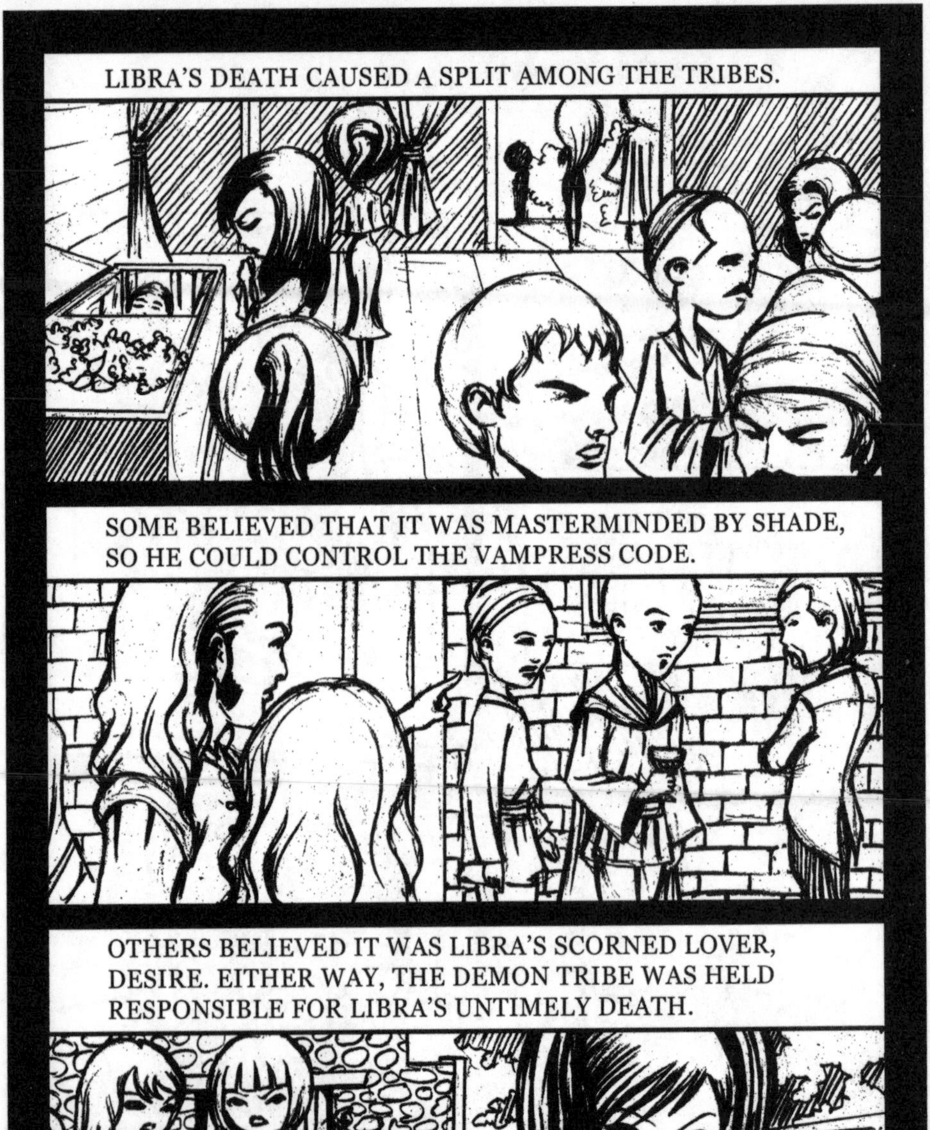
LIBRA'S DEATH CAUSED A SPLIT AMONG THE TRIBES.
SOME BELIEVED THAT IT WAS MASTERMINDED BY SHADE, SO HE COULD CONTROL THE VAMPRESS CODE.
OTHERS BELIEVED IT WAS LIBRA'S SCORNED LOVER, DESIRE. EITHER WAY, THE DEMON TRIBE WAS HELD RESPONSIBLE FOR LIBRA'S UNTIMELY DEATH.

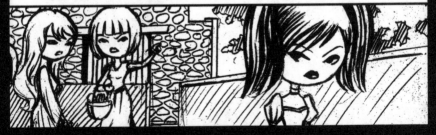

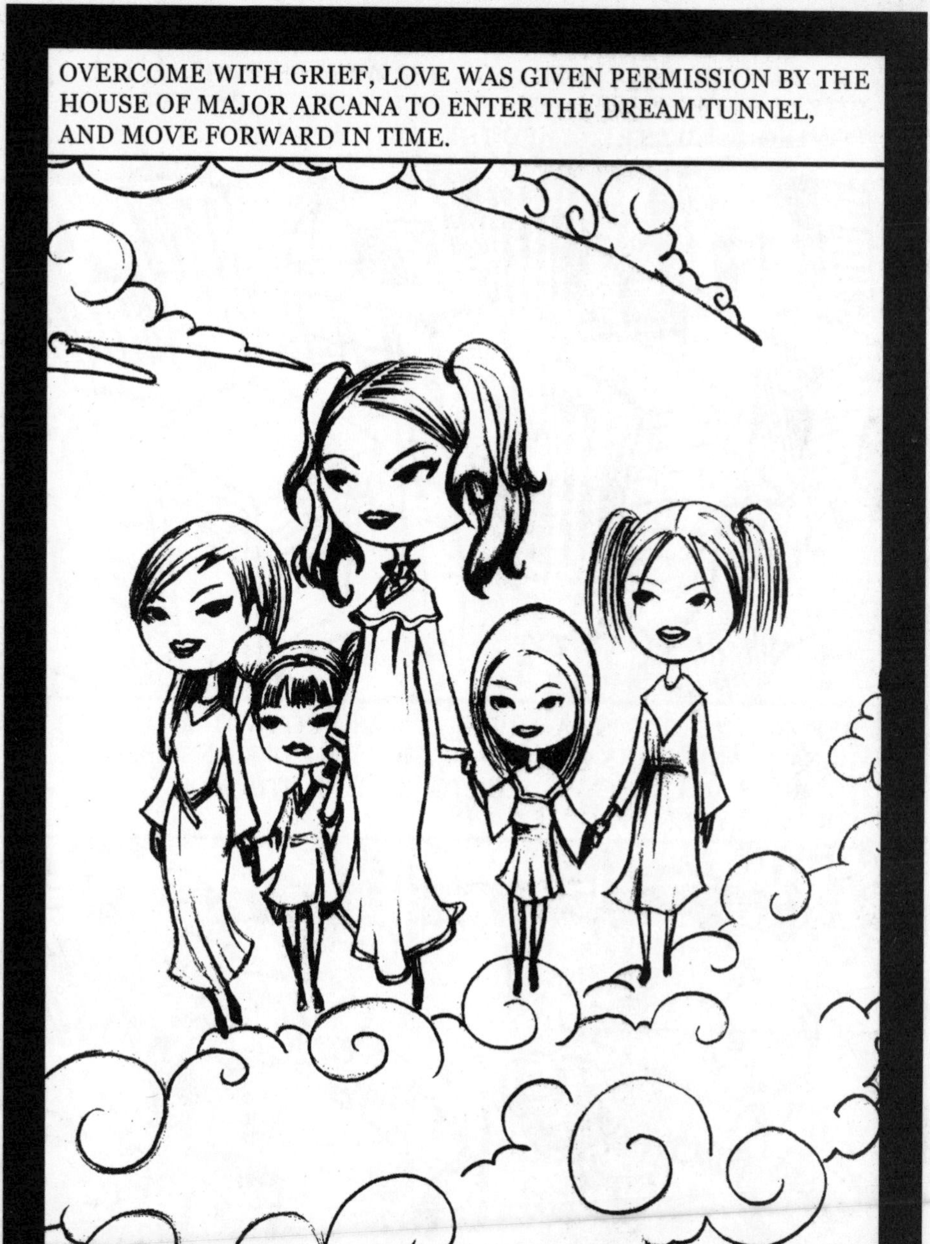
OVERCOME WITH GRIEF, LOVE WAS GIVEN PERMISSION BY THE HOUSE OF MAJOR ARCANA TO ENTER THE DREAM TUNNEL, AND MOVE FORWARD IN TIME.

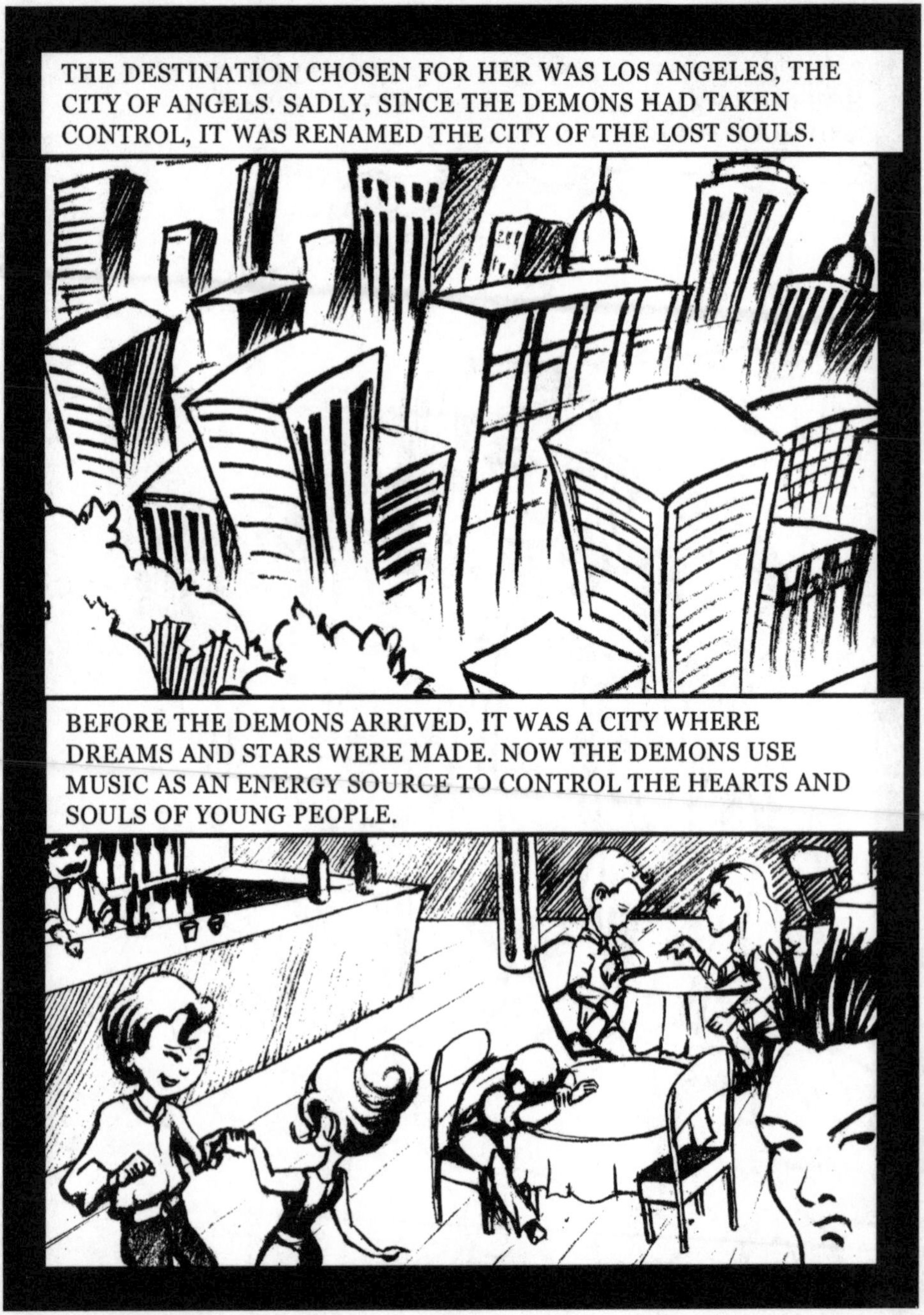
THE DESTINATION CHOSEN FOR HER WAS LOS ANGELES, THE CITY OF ANGELS. SADLY, SINCE THE DEMONS HAD TAKEN CONTROL, IT WAS RENAMED THE CITY OF THE LOST SOULS.
BEFORE THE DEMONS ARRIVED, IT WAS A CITY WHERE DREAMS AND STARS WERE MADE. NOW THE DEMONS USE MUSIC AS AN ENERGY SOURCE TO CONTROL THE HEARTS AND SOULS OF YOUNG PEOPLE.

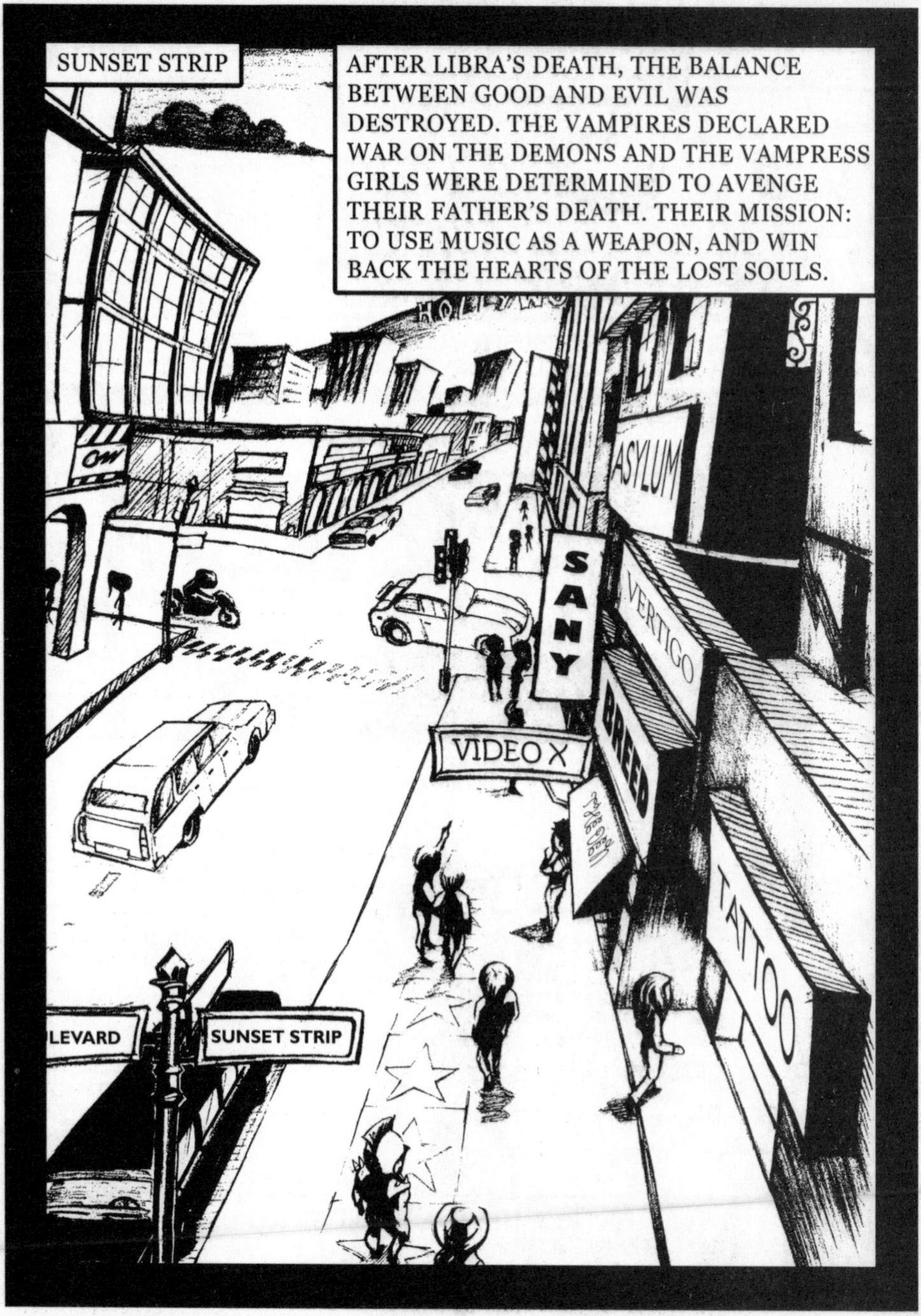
SUNSET STRIP
AFTER LIBRA'S DEATH, THE BALANCE BETWEEN GOOD AND EVIL WAS DESTROYED. THE VAMPIRES DECLARED WAR ON THE DEMONS AND THE VAMPRESS GIRLS WERE DETERMINED TO AVENGE THEIR FATHER'S DEATH. THEIR MISSION: TO USE MUSIC AS A WEAPON, AND WIN BACK THE HEARTS OF THE LOST SOULS.
ASYLUM
SANY
VERTIGO
BREED
VIDEO X
TATTOO
LEVARD
SUNSET STRIP

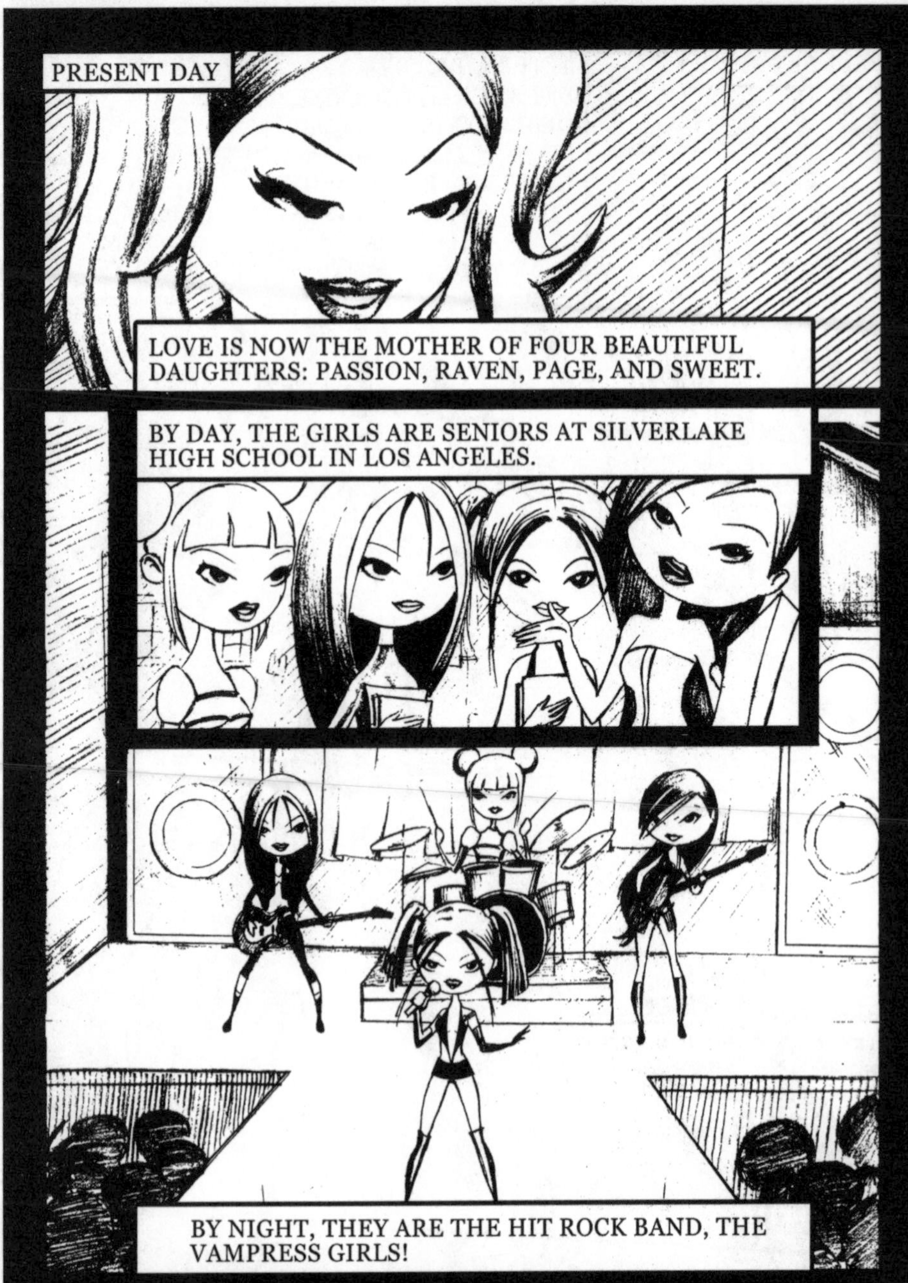
PRESENT DAY
LOVE IS NOW THE MOTHER OF FOUR BEAUTIFUL DAUGHTERS: PASSION, RAVEN, PAGE, AND SWEET.
BY DAY, THE GIRLS ARE SENIORS AT SILVERLAKE HIGH SCHOOL IN LOS ANGELES.
BY NIGHT, THEY ARE THE HIT ROCK BAND, THE VAMPRESS GIRLS!

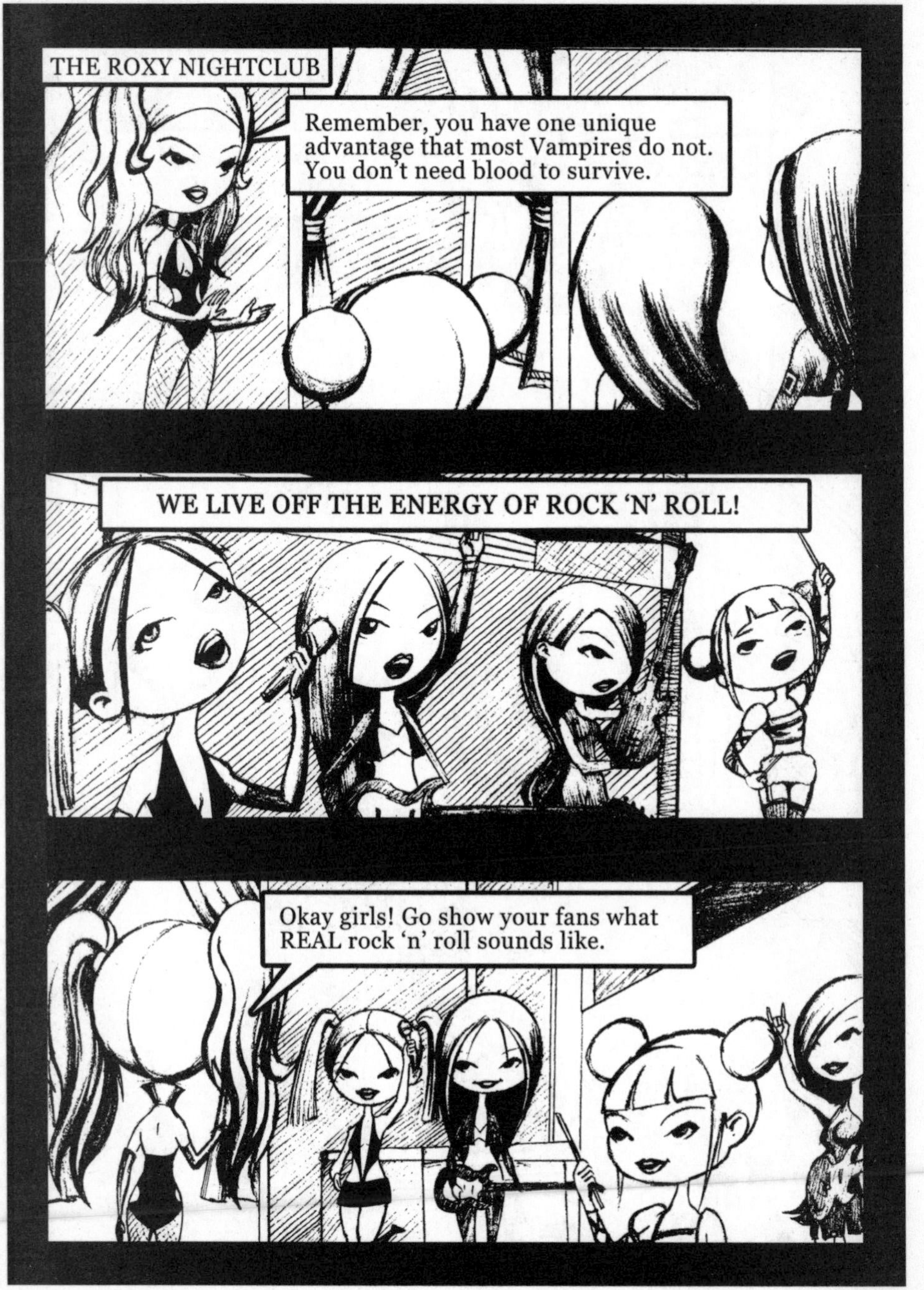
THE ROXY NIGHTCLUB
Remember, you have one unique advantage that most Vampires do not. You don't need blood to survive.
WE LIVE OFF THE ENERGY OF ROCK 'N' ROLL!
Okay girls! Go show your fans what REAL rock 'n' roll sounds like.

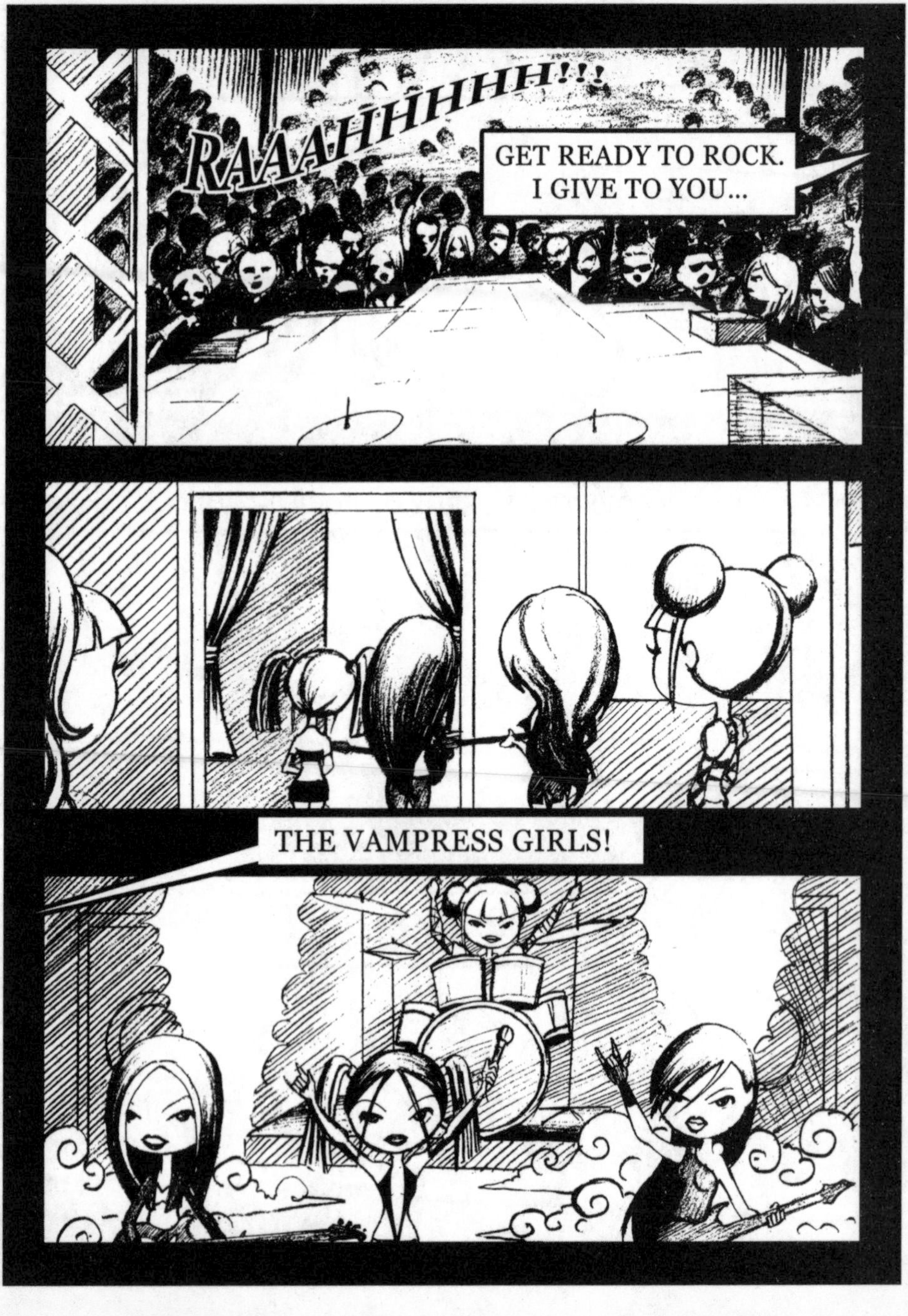
RAAAHHHHHH!!!
GET READY TO ROCK. I GIVE TO YOU...
THE VAMPRESS GIRLS!

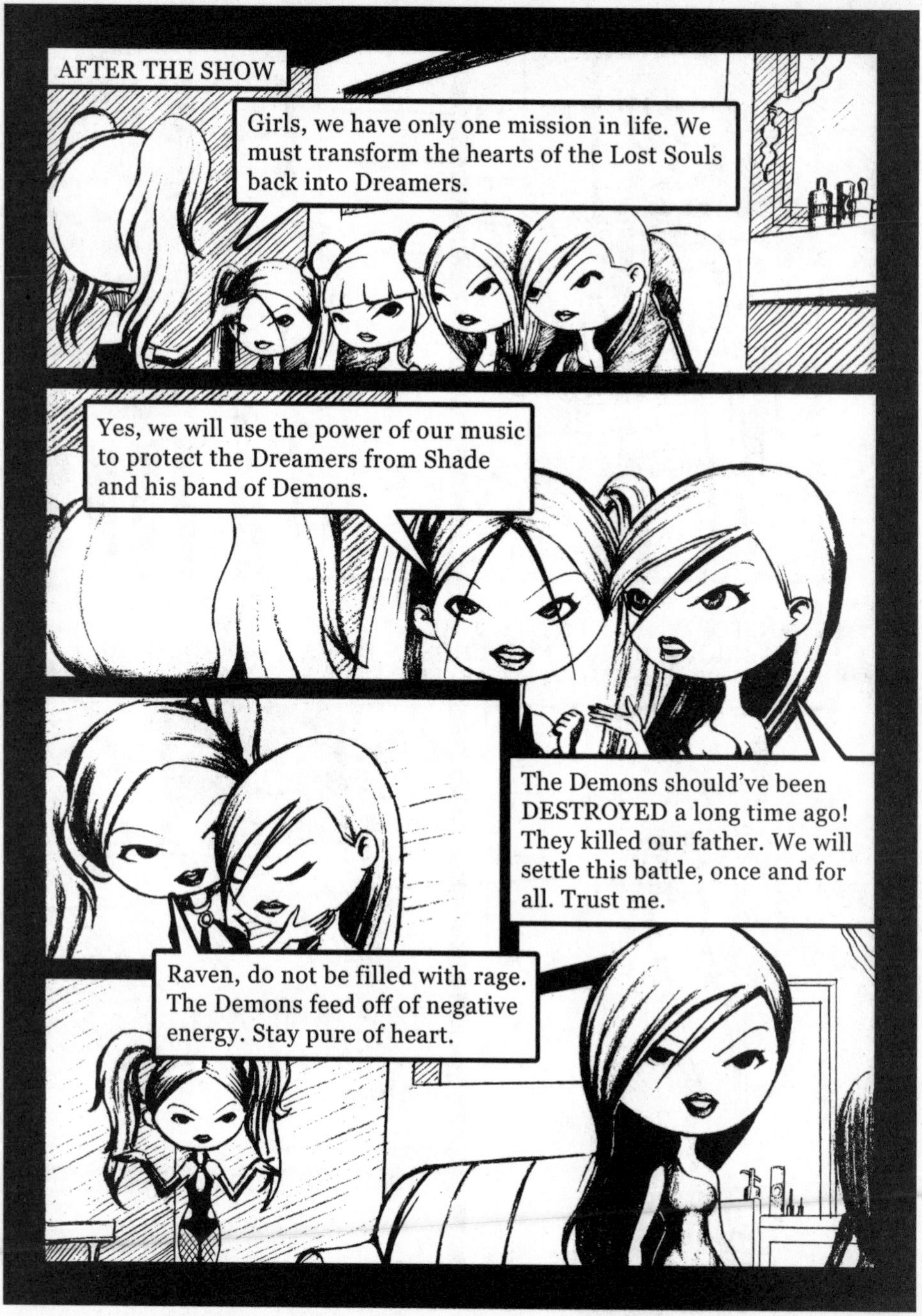
AFTER THE SHOW
Girls, we have only one mission in life. We must transform the hearts of the Lost Souls back into Dreamers.
Yes, we will use the power of our music to protect the Dreamers from Shade and his band of Demons.
The Demons should've been DESTROYED a long time ago! They killed our father. We will settle this battle, once and for all. Trust me.
Raven, do not be filled with rage. The Demons feed off of negative energy. Stay pure of heart.

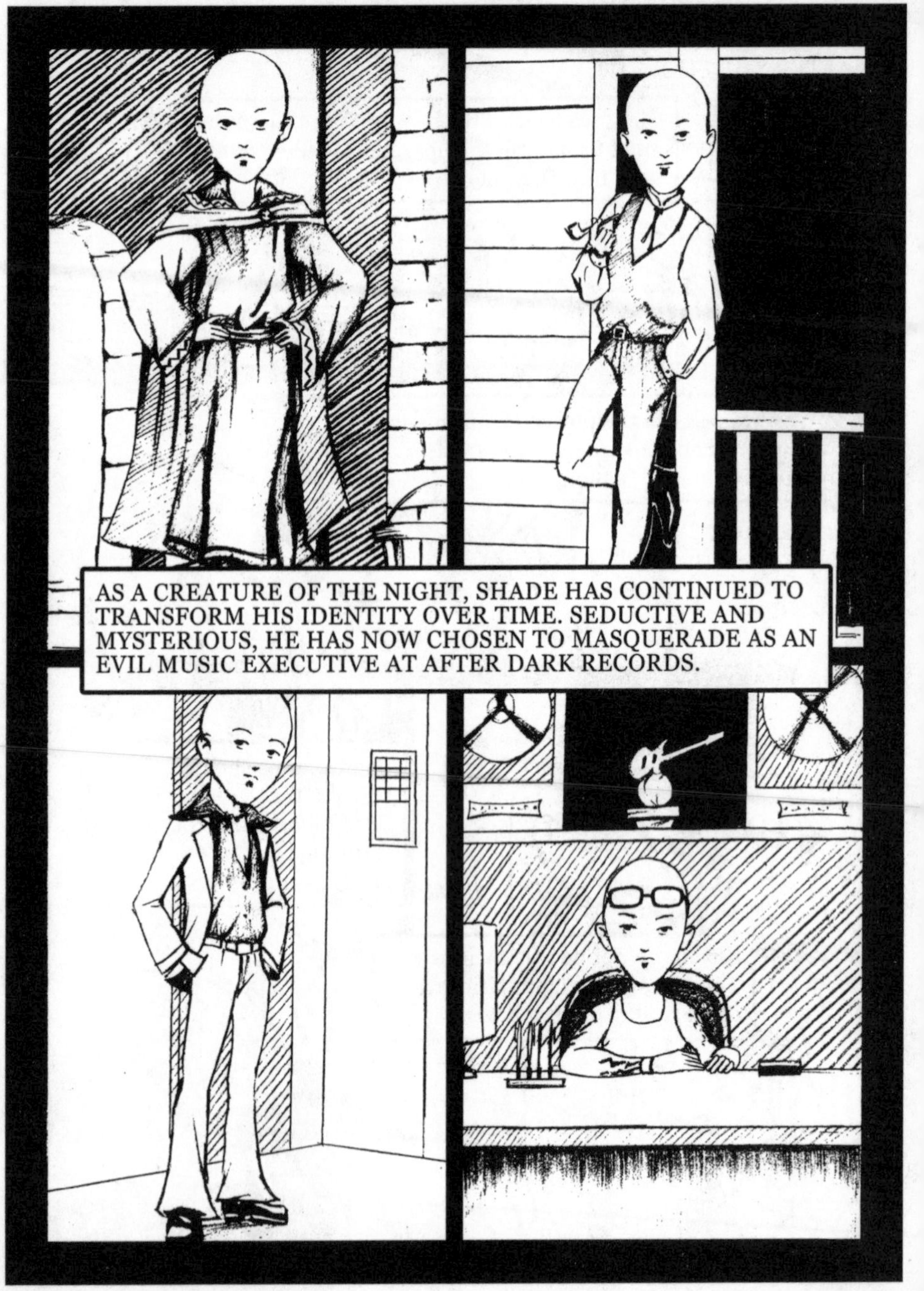
AS A CREATURE OF THE NIGHT, SHADE HAS CONTINUED TO TRANSFORM HIS IDENTITY OVER TIME. SEDUCTIVE AND MYSTERIOUS, HE HAS NOW CHOSEN TO MASQUERADE AS AN EVIL MUSIC EXECUTIVE AT AFTER DARK RECORDS.

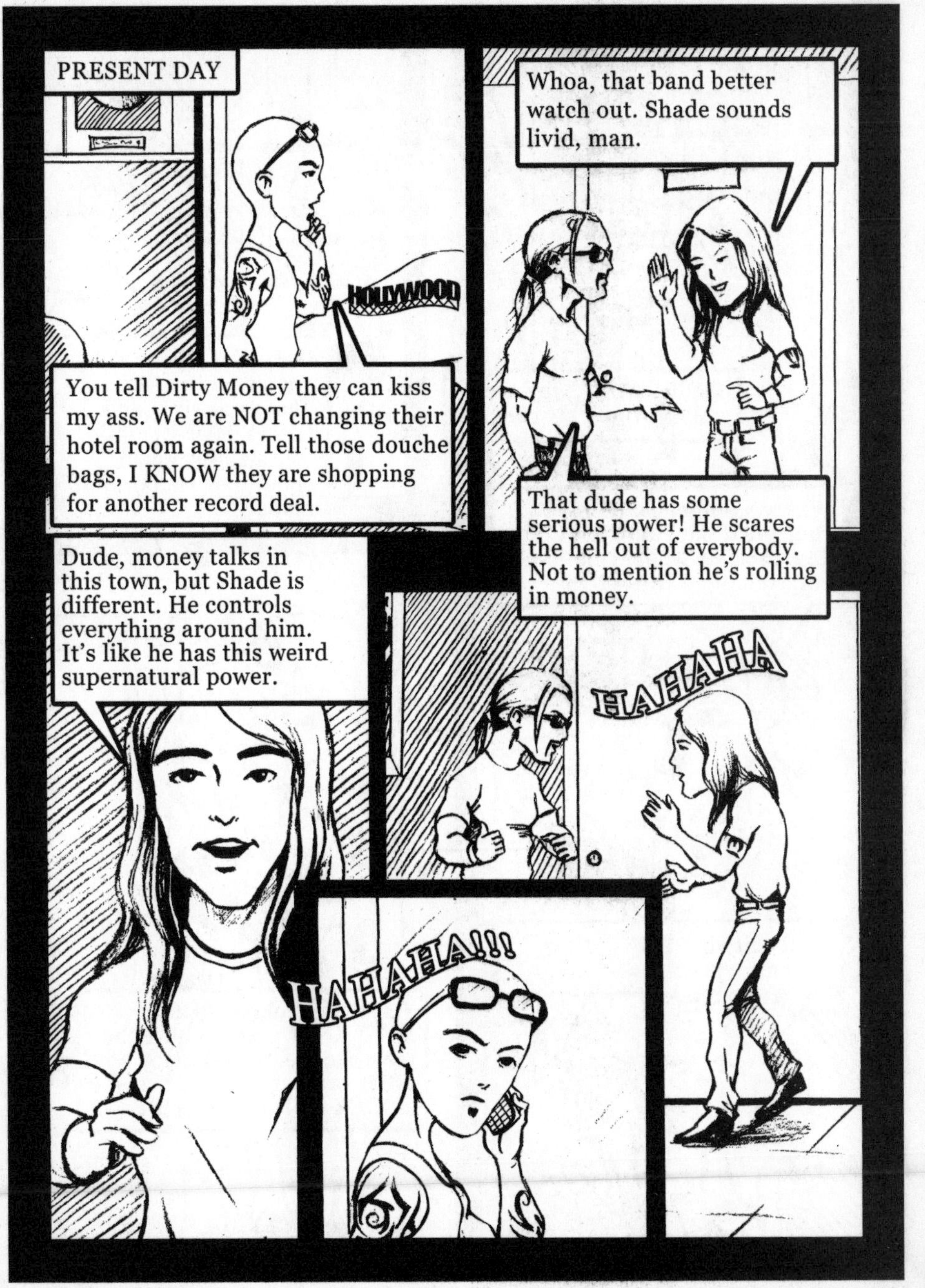
PRESENT DAY
HOLLYWOOD
You tell Dirty Money they can kiss my ass. We are NOT changing their hotel room again. Tell those douche bags, I KNOW they are shopping for another record deal.
Whoa, that band better watch out. Shade sounds livid, man.
That dude has some serious power! He scares the hell out of everybody. Not to mention he's rolling in money.
Dude, money talks in this town, but Shade is different. He controls everything around him. It's like he has this weird supernatural power.
HAHAHA
HAHAHA!!!

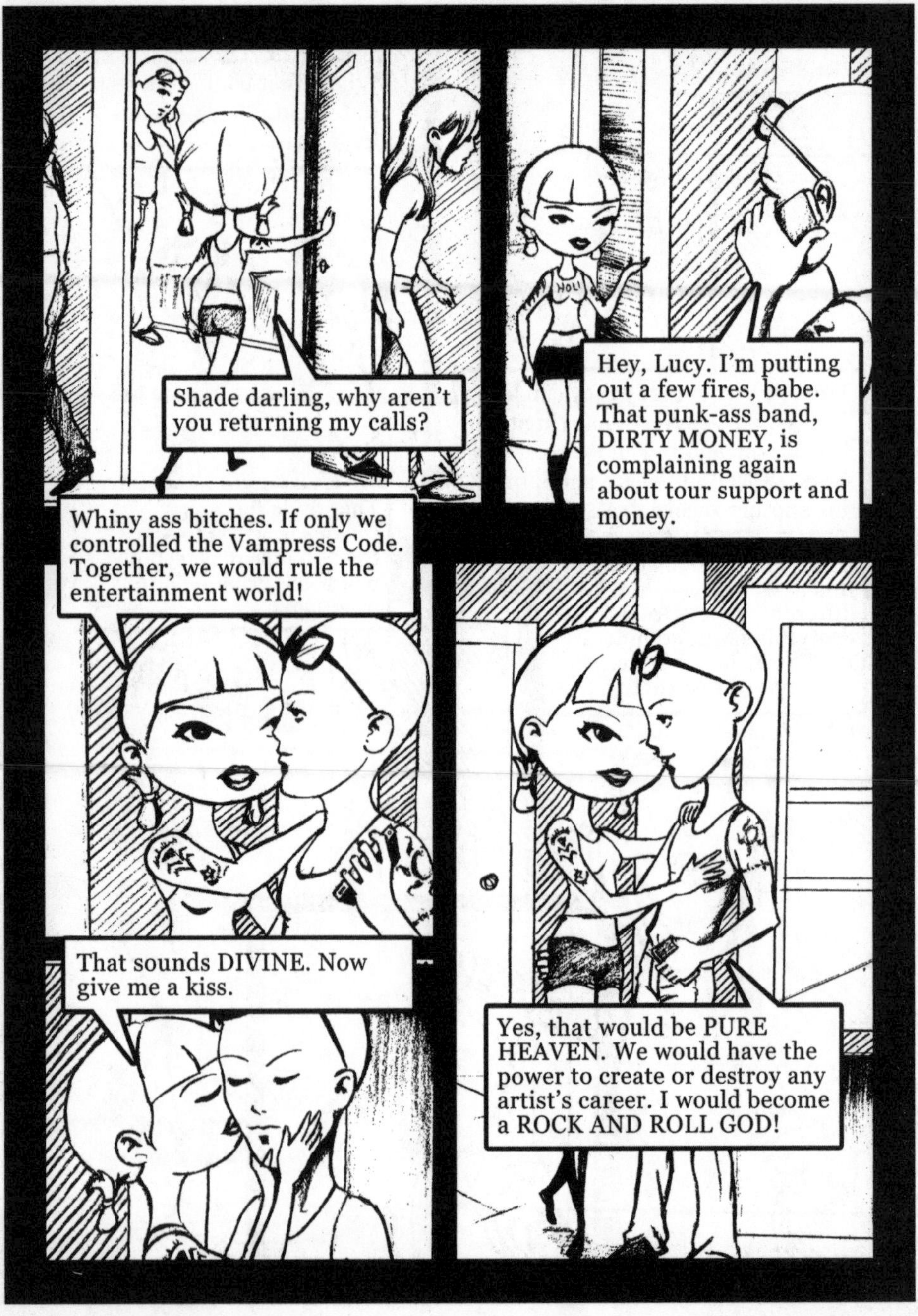
Shade darling, why aren't you returning my calls?
HOL
Hey, Lucy. I'm putting out a few fires, babe. That punk-ass band, DIRTY MONEY, is complaining again about tour support and money.
Whiny ass bitches. If only we controlled the Vampress Code. Together, we would rule the entertainment world!
That sounds DIVINE. Now give me a kiss.
Yes, that would be PURE HEAVEN. We would have the power to create or destroy any artist's career. I would become a ROCK AND ROLL GOD!

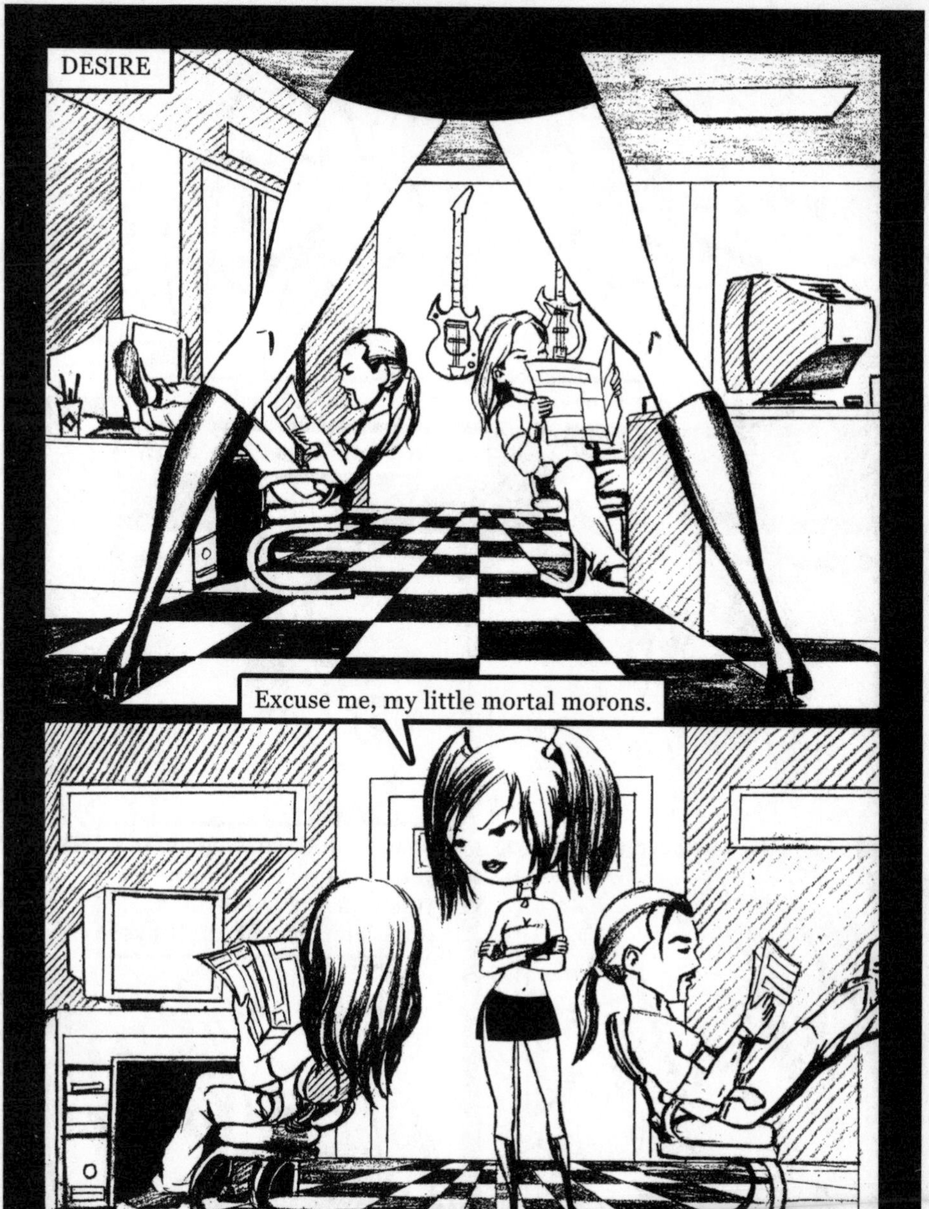
DESIRE
Excuse me, my little mortal morons.

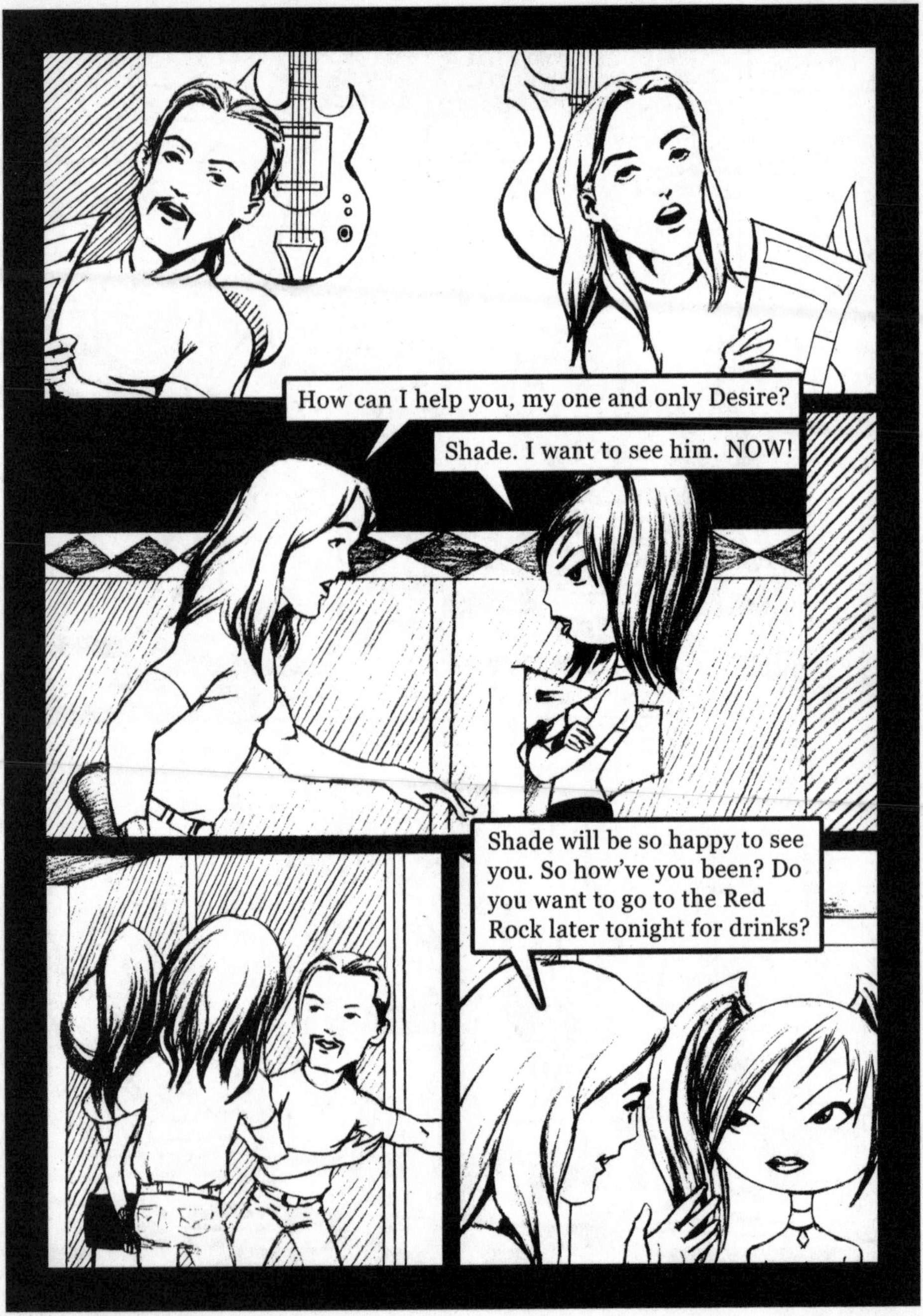
How can I help you, my one and only Desire?
Shade. I want to see him. NOW!
Shade will be so happy to see you. So how've you been? Do you want to go to the Red Rock later tonight for drinks?

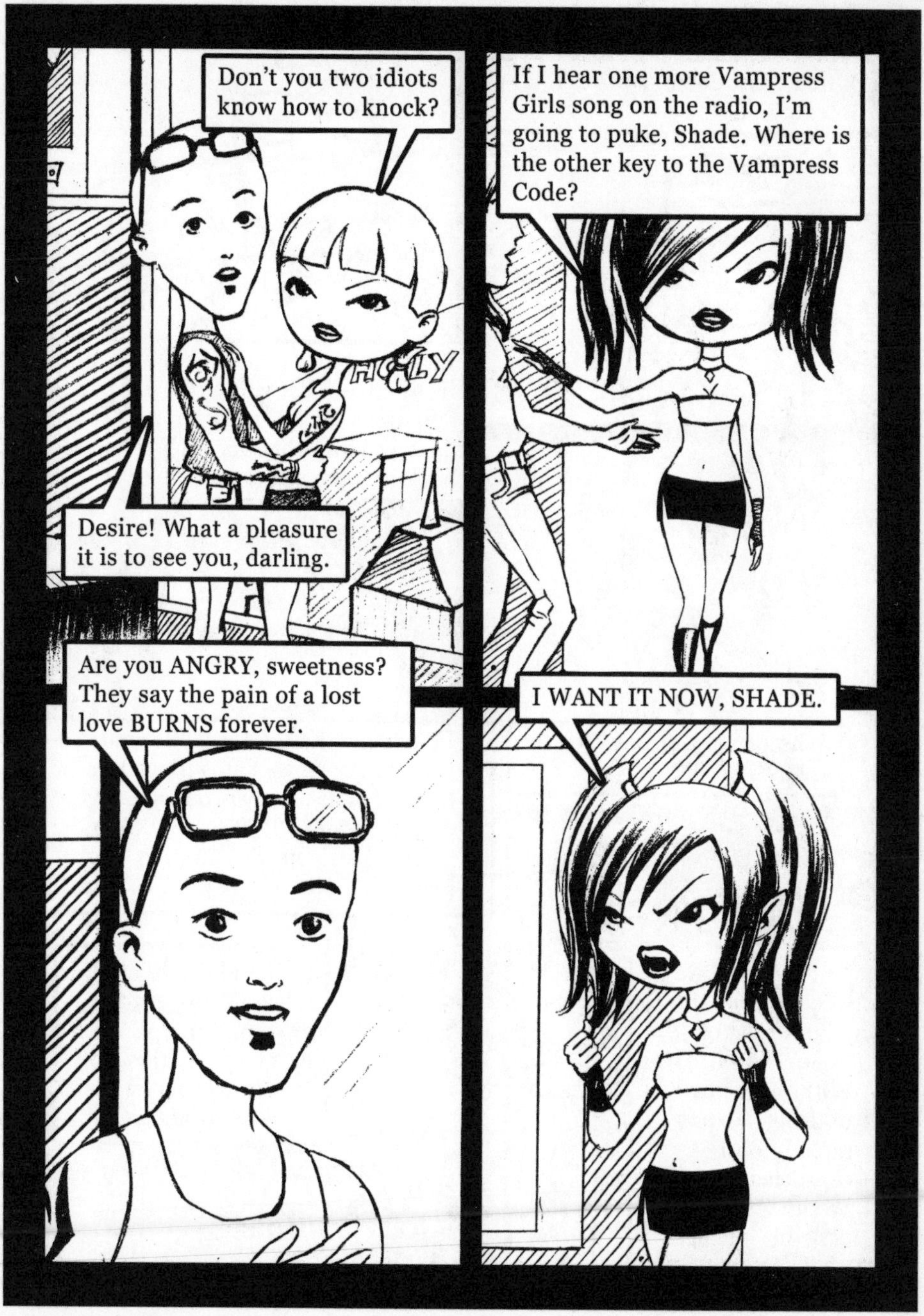
Don't you two idiots know how to knock?
Desire! What a pleasure it is to see you, darling.
If I hear one more Vampress Girls song on the radio, I'm going to puke, Shade. Where is the other key to the Vampress Code?
HOLLY
Are you ANGRY, sweetness? They say the pain of a lost love BURNS forever.
I WANT IT NOW, SHADE.

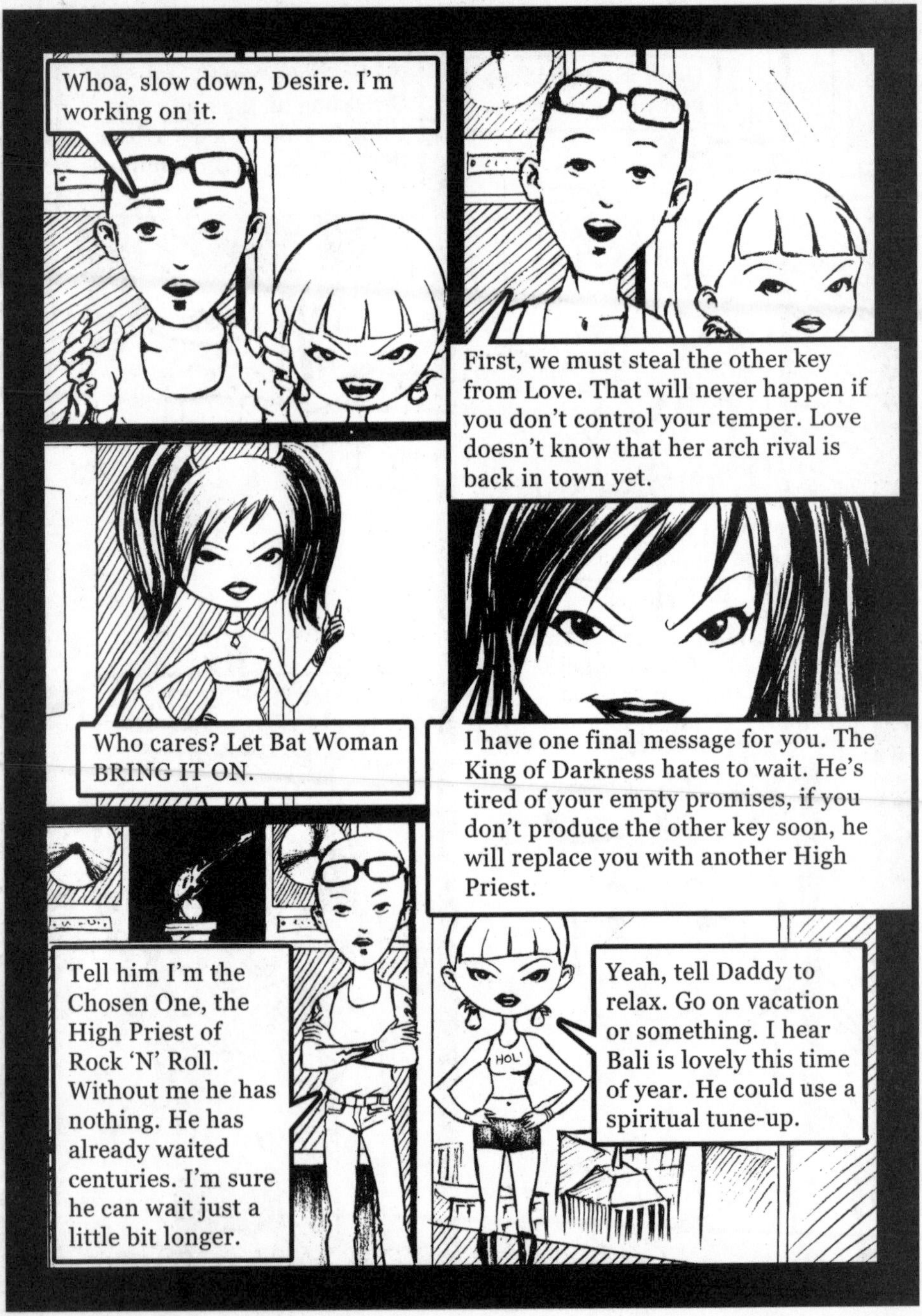
Whoa, slow down, Desire. I'm working on it.
First, we must steal the other key from Love. That will never happen if you don't control your temper. Love doesn't know that her arch rival is back in town yet.
Who cares? Let Bat Woman BRING IT ON.
I have one final message for you. The King of Darkness hates to wait. He's tired of your empty promises, if you don't produce the other key soon, he will replace you with another High Priest.
Tell him I'm the Chosen One, the High Priest of Rock 'N' Roll. Without me he has nothing. He has already waited centuries. I'm sure he can wait just a little bit longer.
HOLI
Yeah, tell Daddy to relax. Go on vacation or something. I hear Bali is lovely this time of year. He could use a spiritual tune-up.

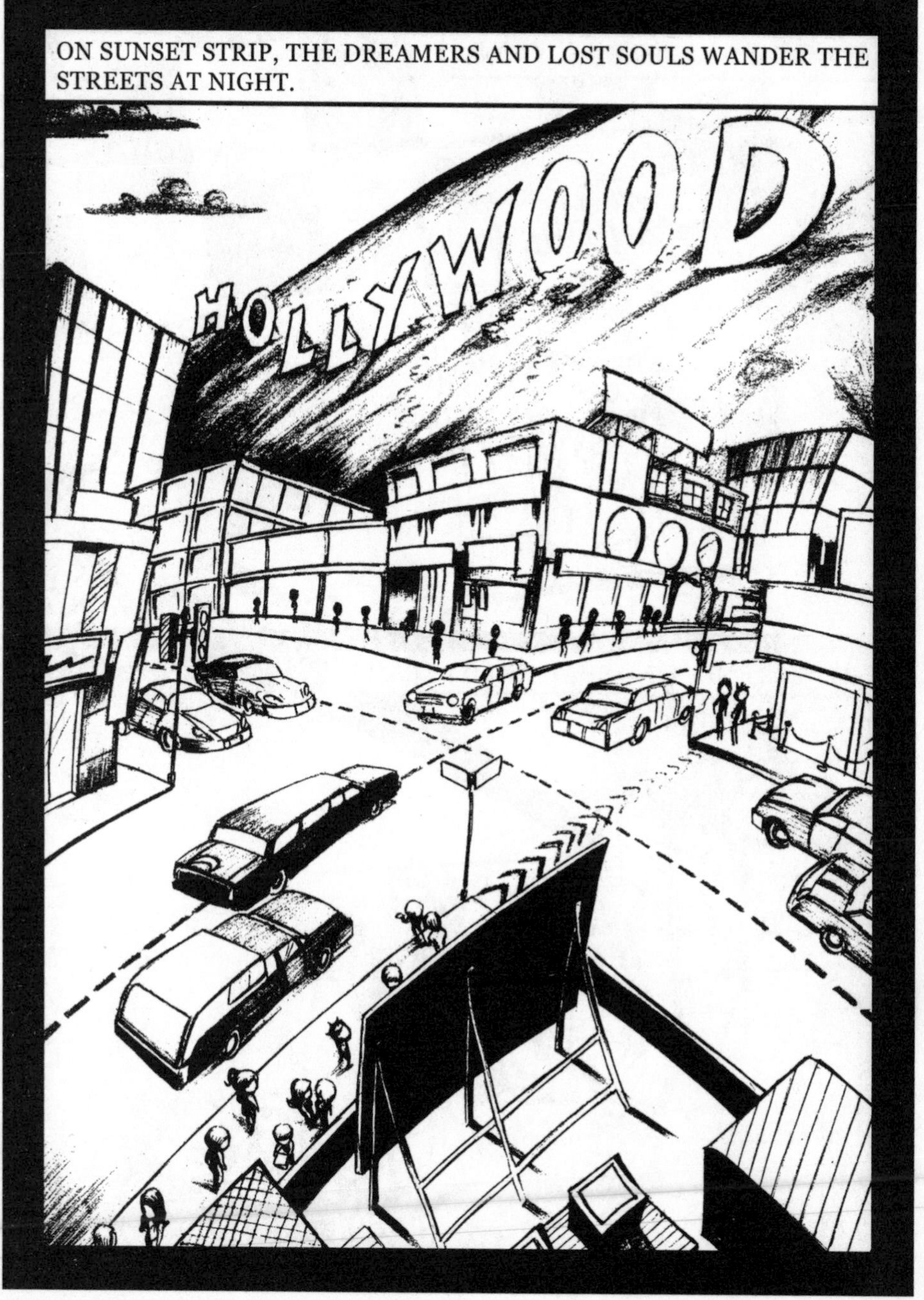
ON SUNSET STRIP, THE DREAMERS AND LOST SOULS WANDER THE STREETS AT NIGHT.
HOLLYWOOD

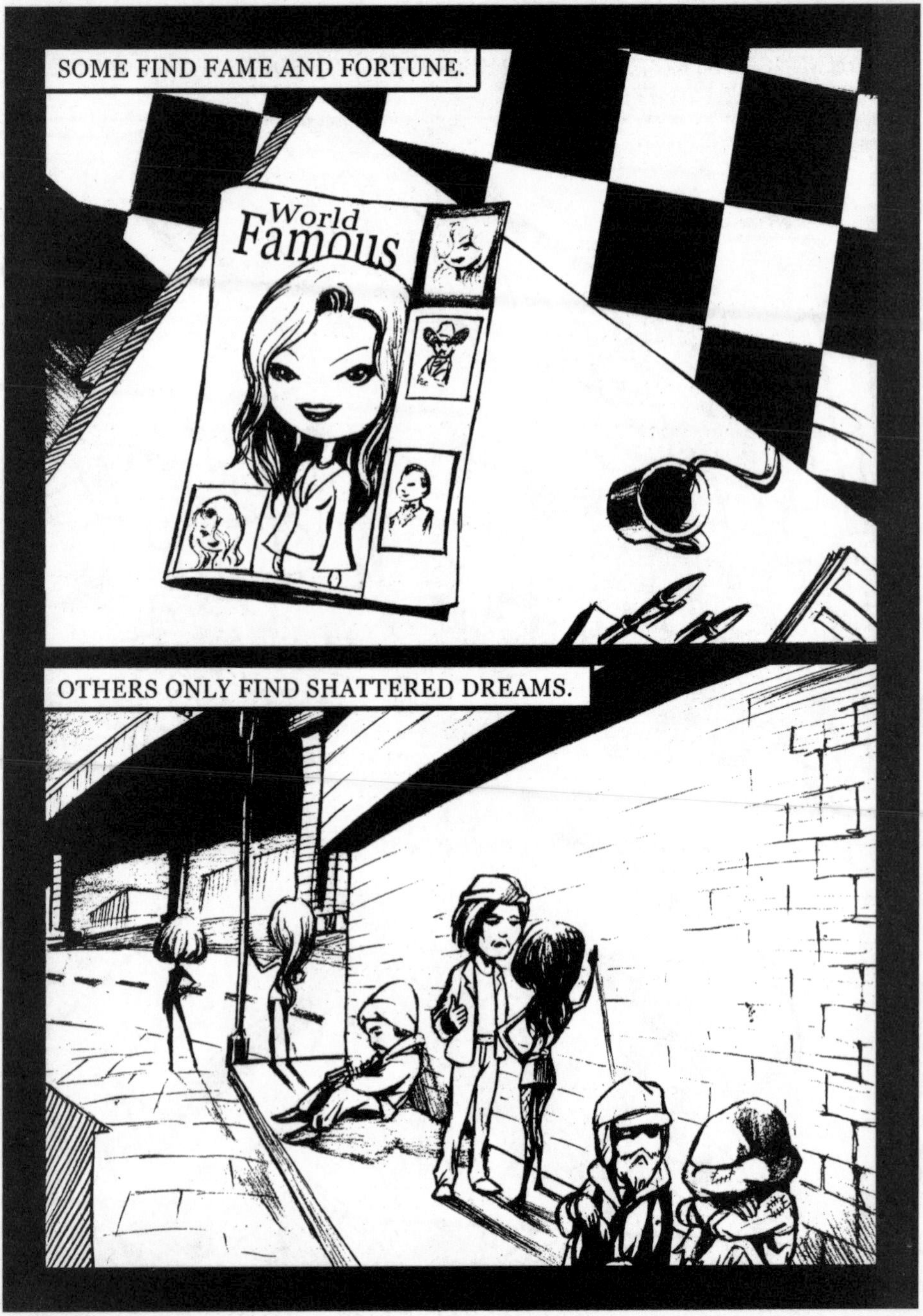
SOME FIND FAME AND FORTUNE.
World Famous
OTHERS ONLY FIND SHATTERED DREAMS.

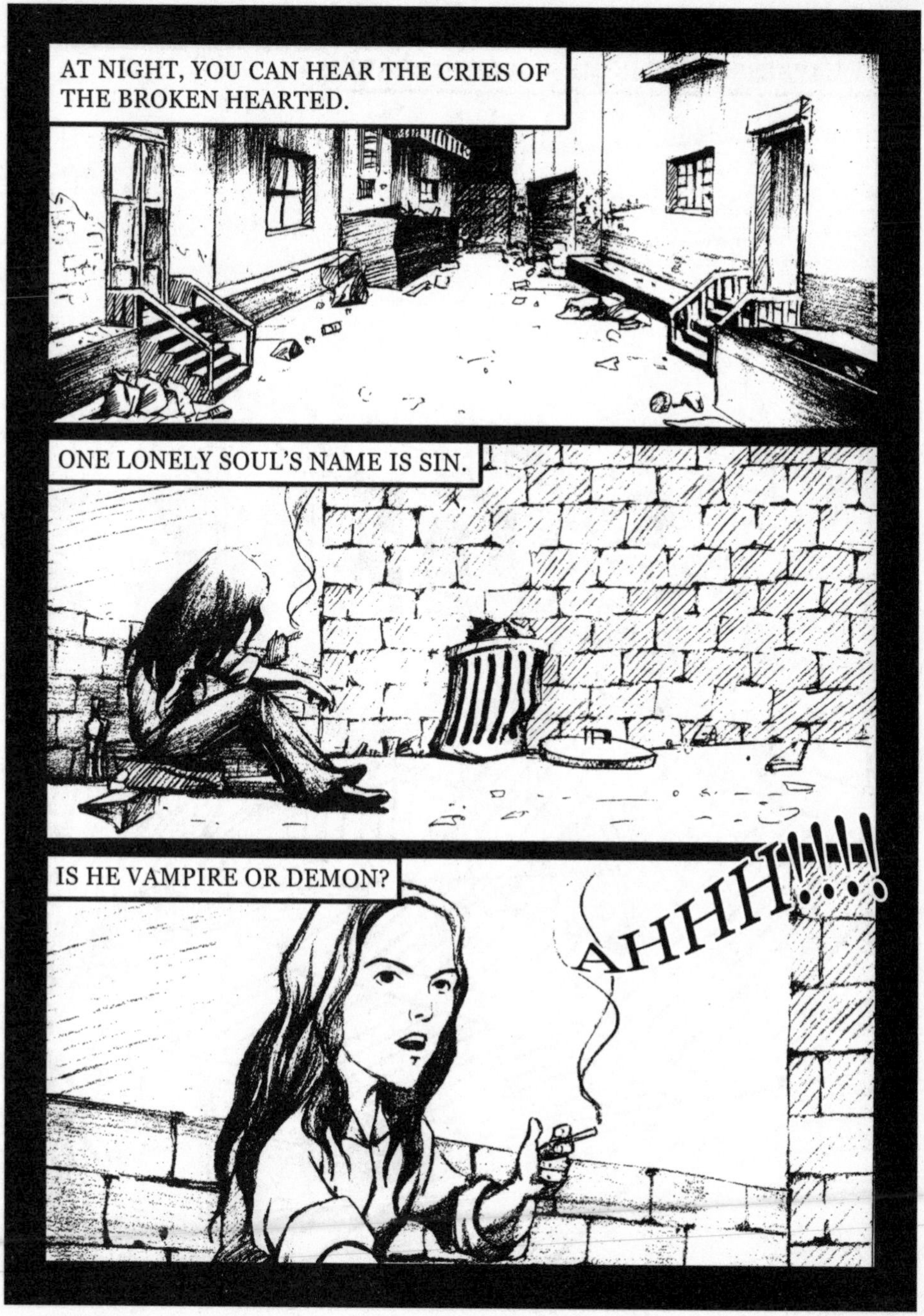
AT NIGHT, YOU CAN HEAR THE CRIES OF THE BROKEN HEARTED.
ONE LONELY SOUL'S NAME IS SIN.
IS HE VAMPIRE OR DEMON?
AHHH!!!!!

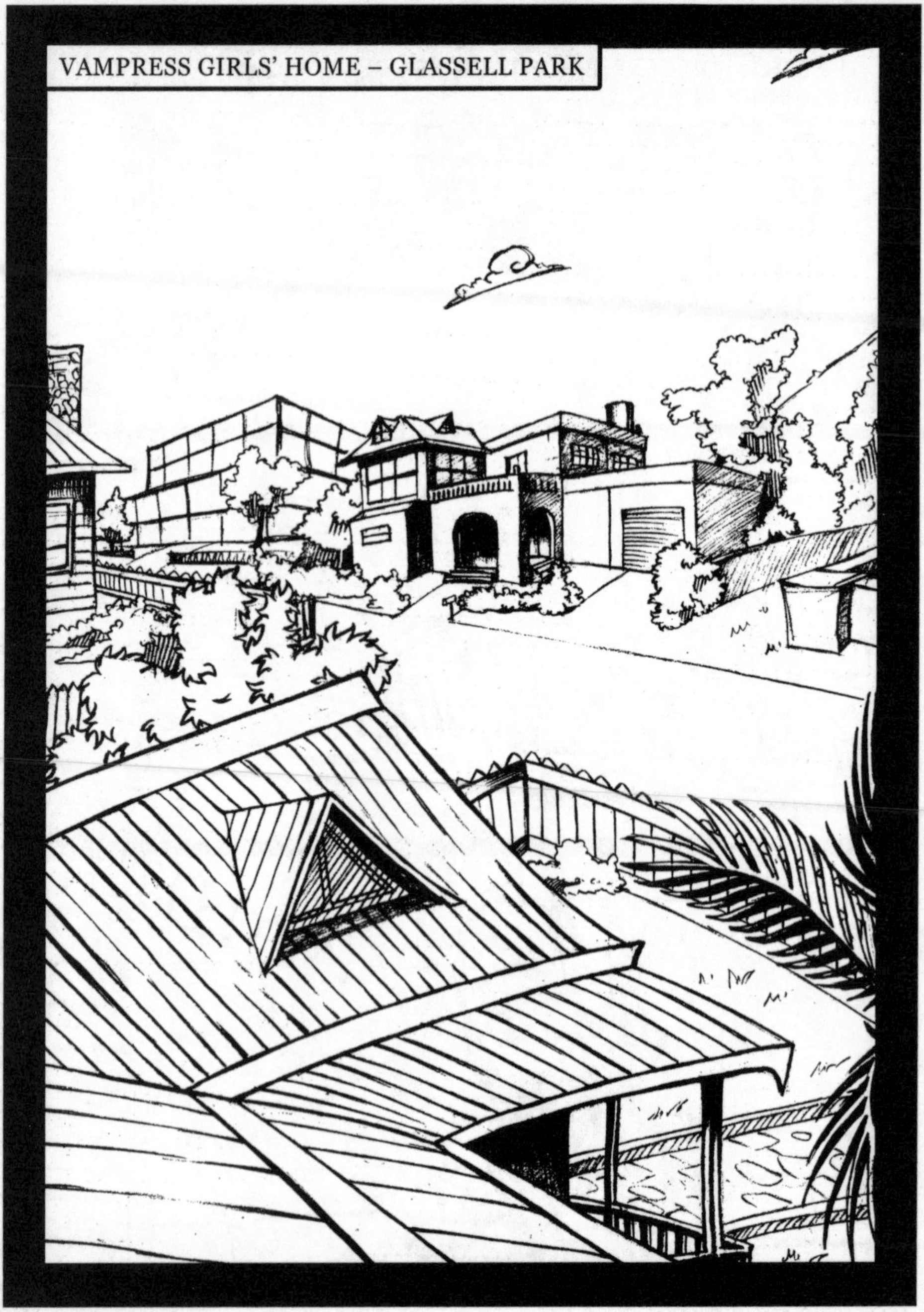
VAMPRESS GIRLS' HOME – GLASSELL PARK

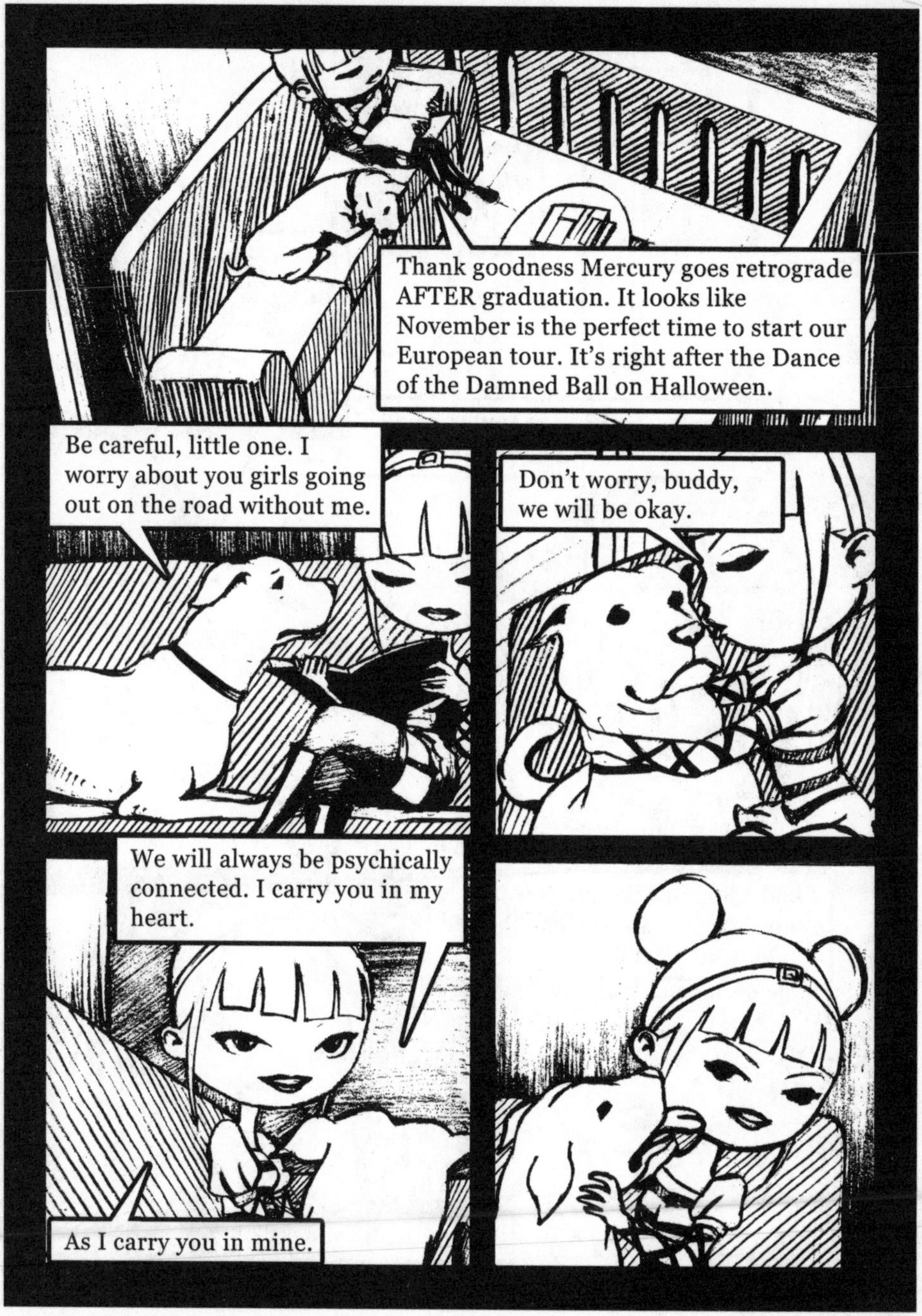

Thank goodness Mercury goes retrograde AFTER graduation. It looks like November is the perfect time to start our European tour. It's right after the Dance of the Damned Ball on Halloween.
Be careful, little one. I worry about you girls going out on the road without me.
Don't worry, buddy, we will be okay.
We will always be psychically connected. I carry you in my heart.
As I carry you in mine.

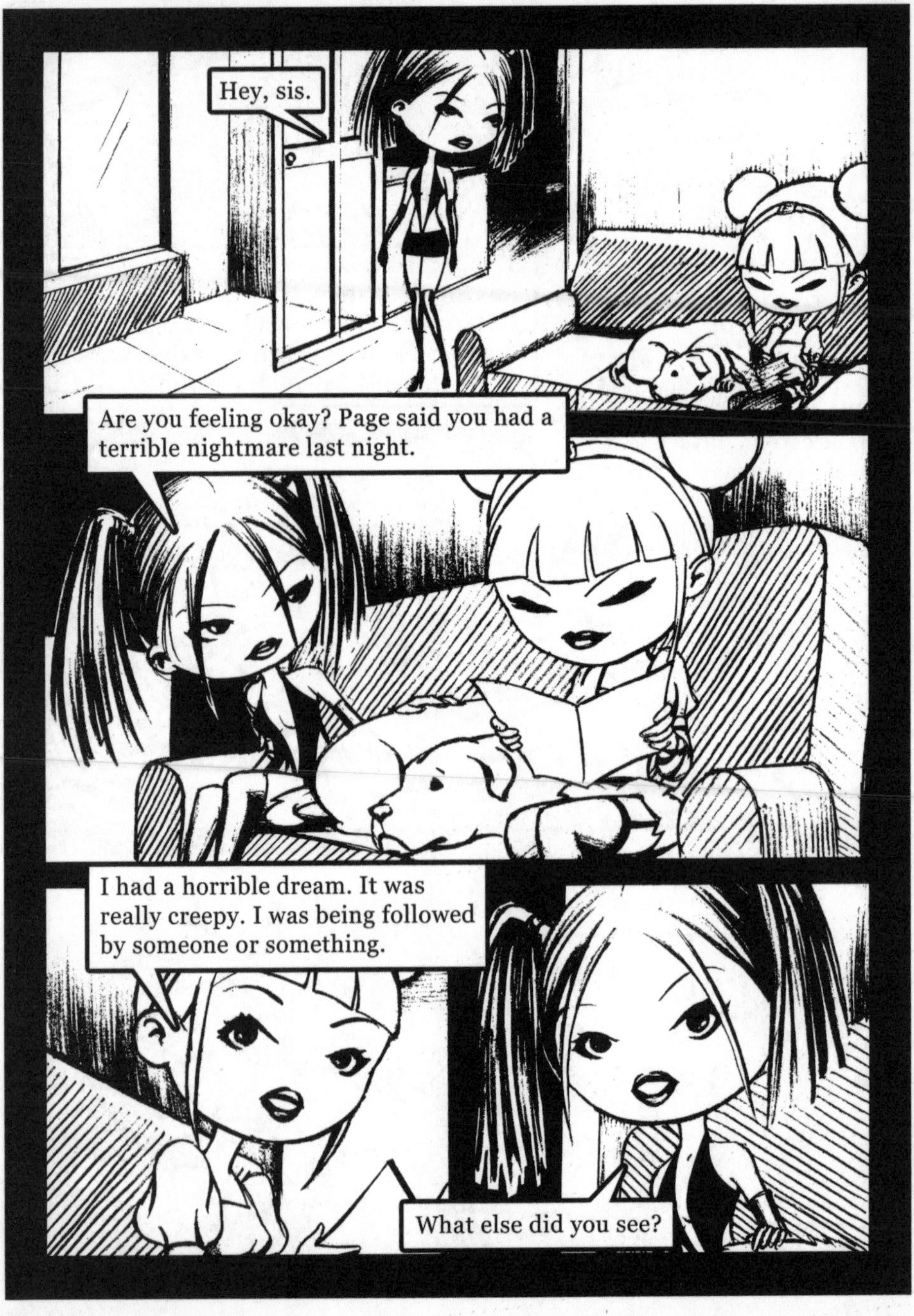
Hey, sis.
Are you feeling okay? Page said you had a terrible nightmare last night.
I had a horrible dream. It was really creepy. I was being followed by someone or something.
What else did you see?

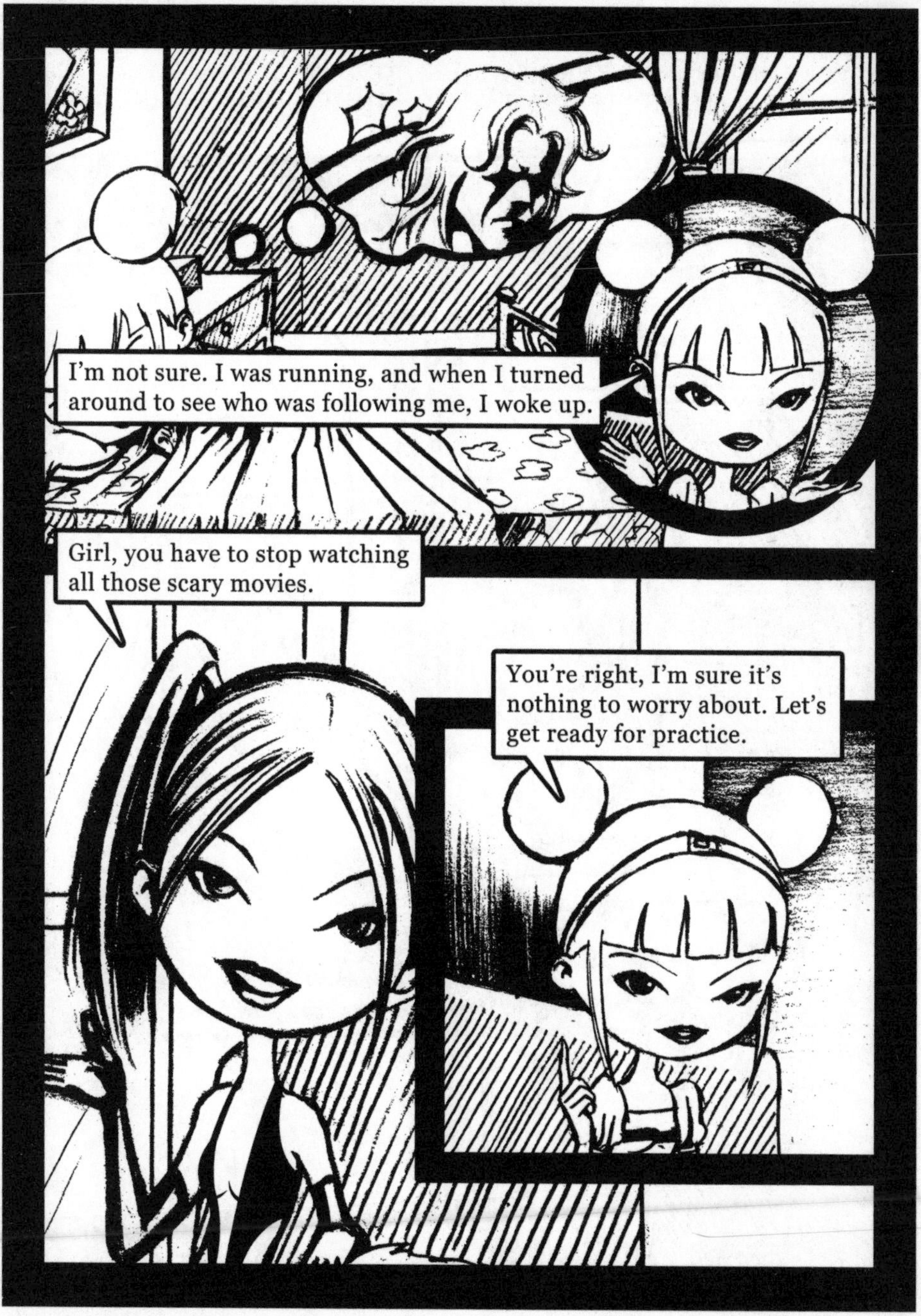
I'm not sure. I was running, and when I turned around to see who was following me, I woke up.
Girl, you have to stop watching all those scary movies.
You're right, I'm sure it's nothing to worry about. Let's get ready for practice.

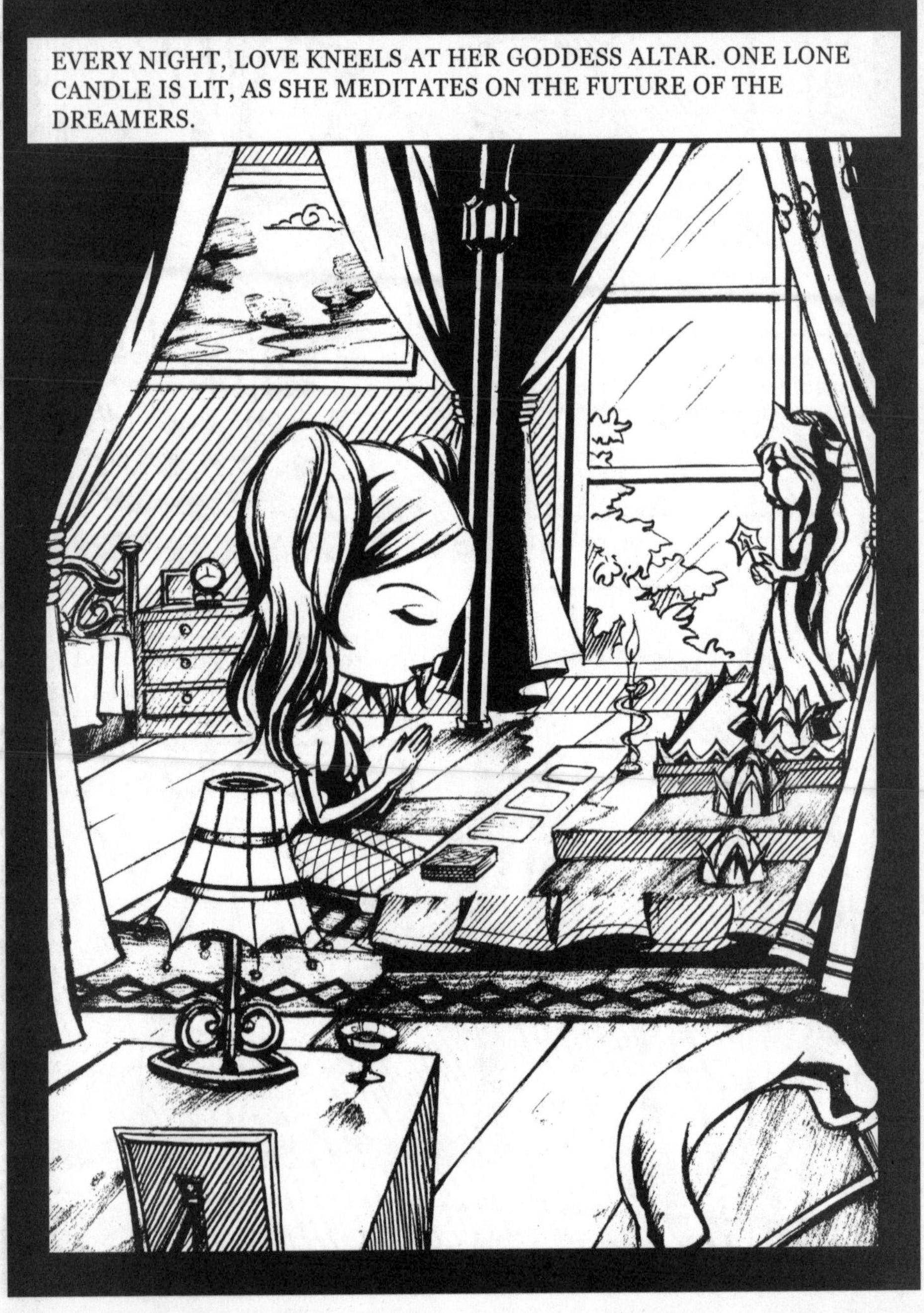
EVERY NIGHT, LOVE KNEELS AT HER GODDESS ALTAR. ONE LONE CANDLE IS LIT, AS SHE MEDITATES ON THE FUTURE OF THE DREAMERS.

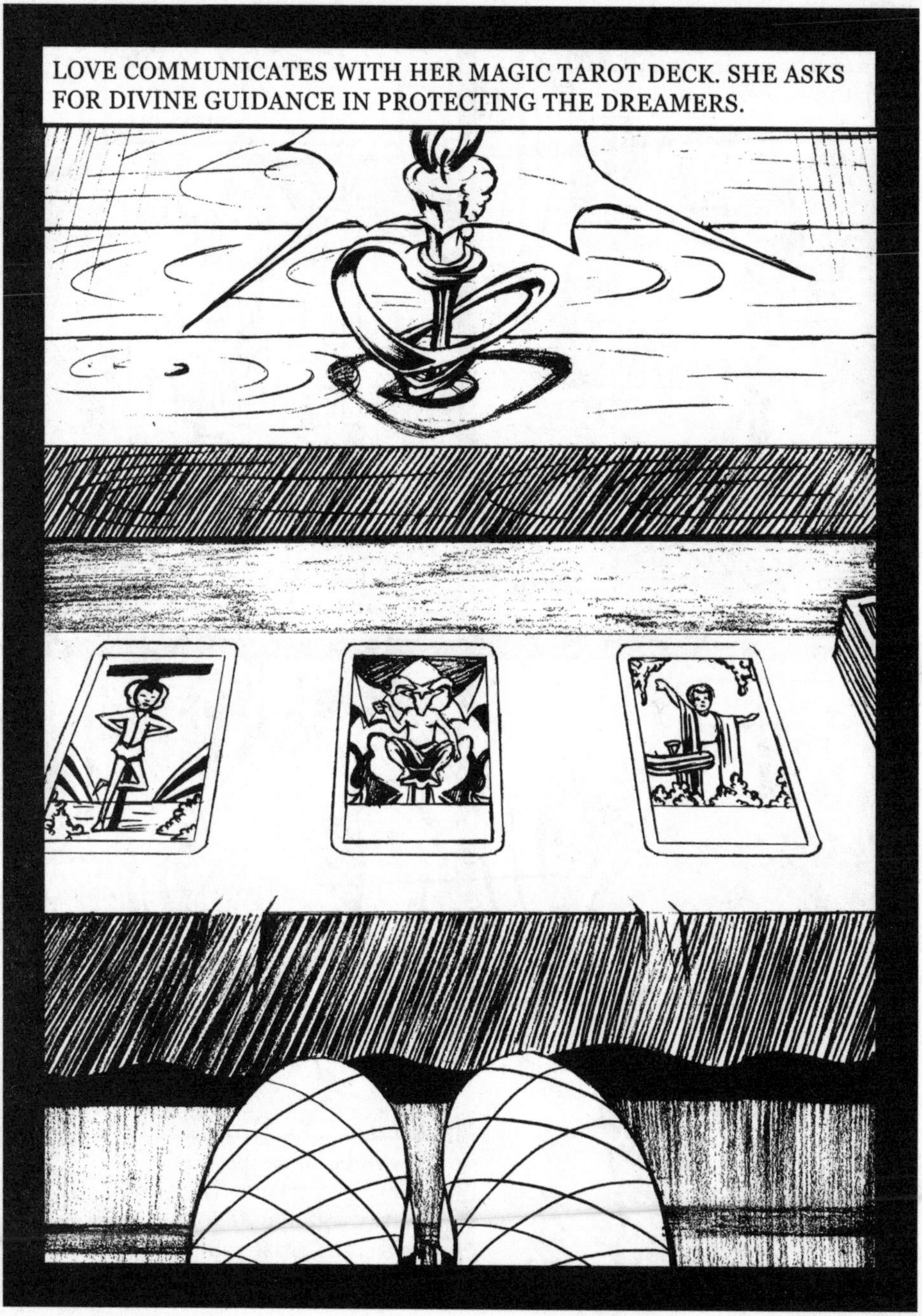
LOVE COMMUNICATES WITH HER MAGIC TAROT DECK. SHE ASKS FOR DIVINE GUIDANCE IN PROTECTING THE DREAMERS.

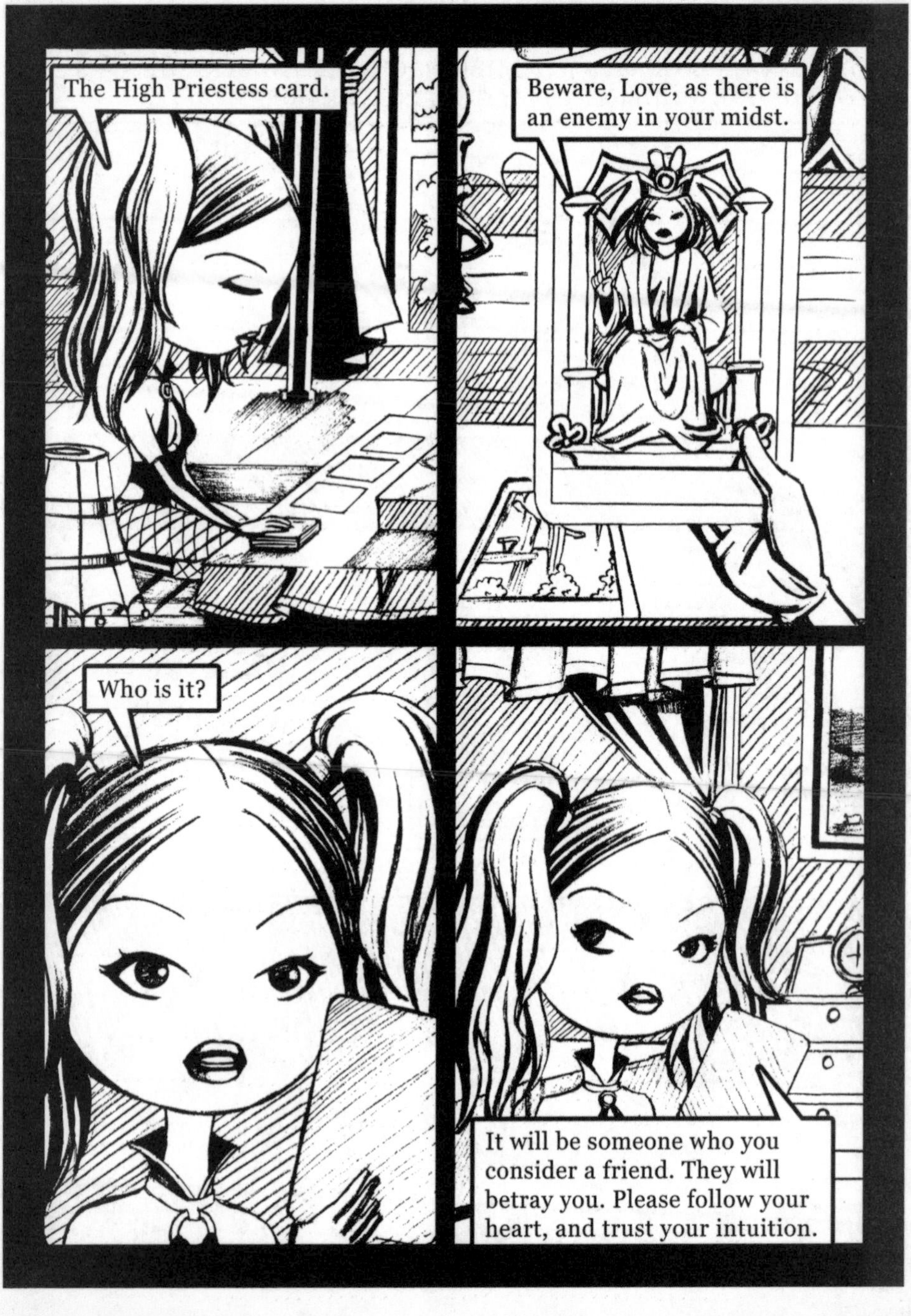
The High Priestess card.
Beware, Love, as there is an enemy in your midst.
Who is it?
It will be someone who you consider a friend. They will betray you. Please follow your heart, and trust your intuition.

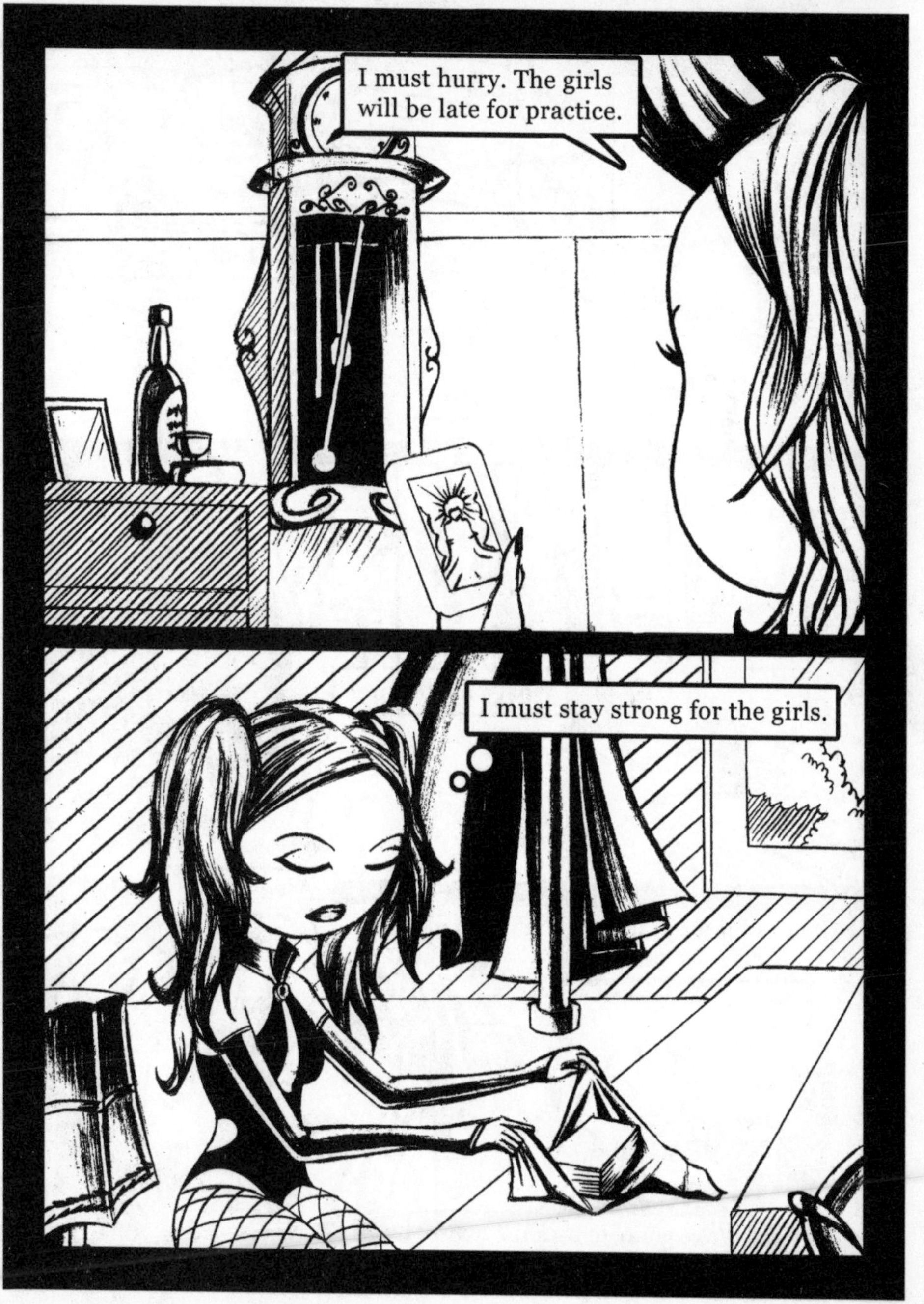
I must hurry. The girls will be late for practice.
I must stay strong for the girls.

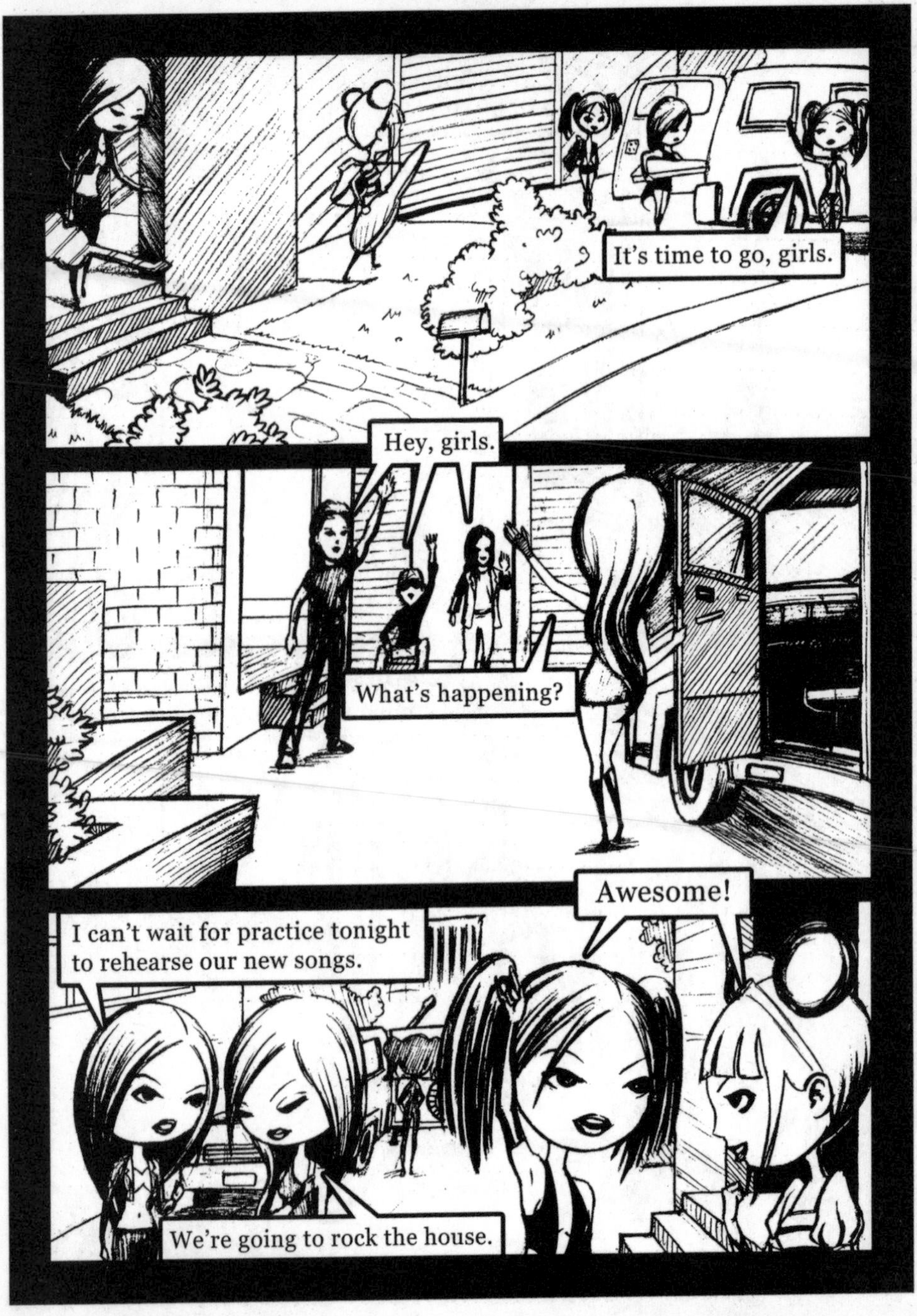
It's time to go, girls.
Hey, girls.
What's happening?
I can't wait for practice tonight to rehearse our new songs.
We're going to rock the house.
Awesome!

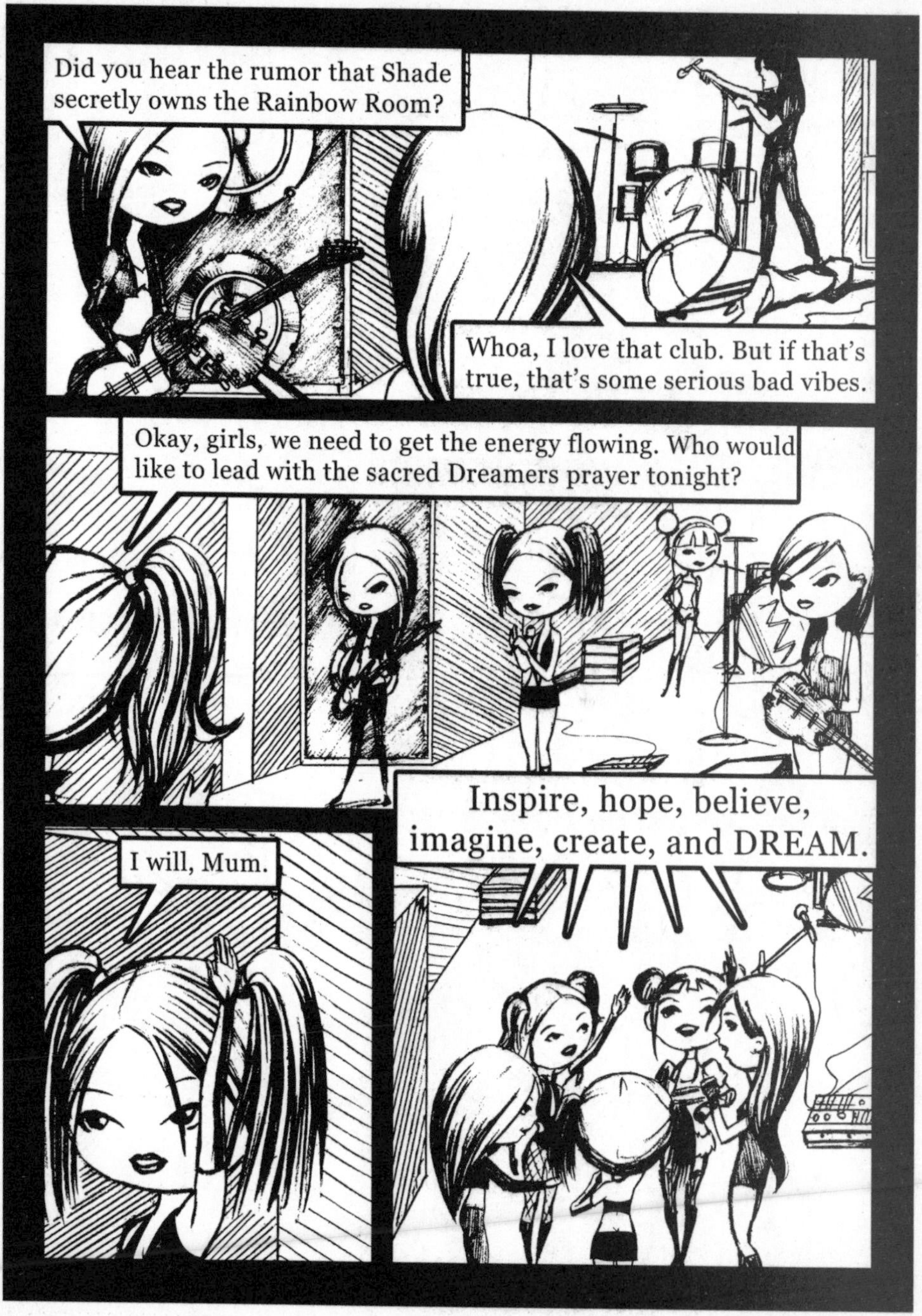
Did you hear the rumor that Shade secretly owns the Rainbow Room?
Whoa, I love that club. But if that's true, that's some serious bad vibes.
Okay, girls, we need to get the energy flowing. Who would like to lead with the sacred Dreamers prayer tonight?
I will, Mum.
Inspire, hope, believe, imagine, create, and DREAM.

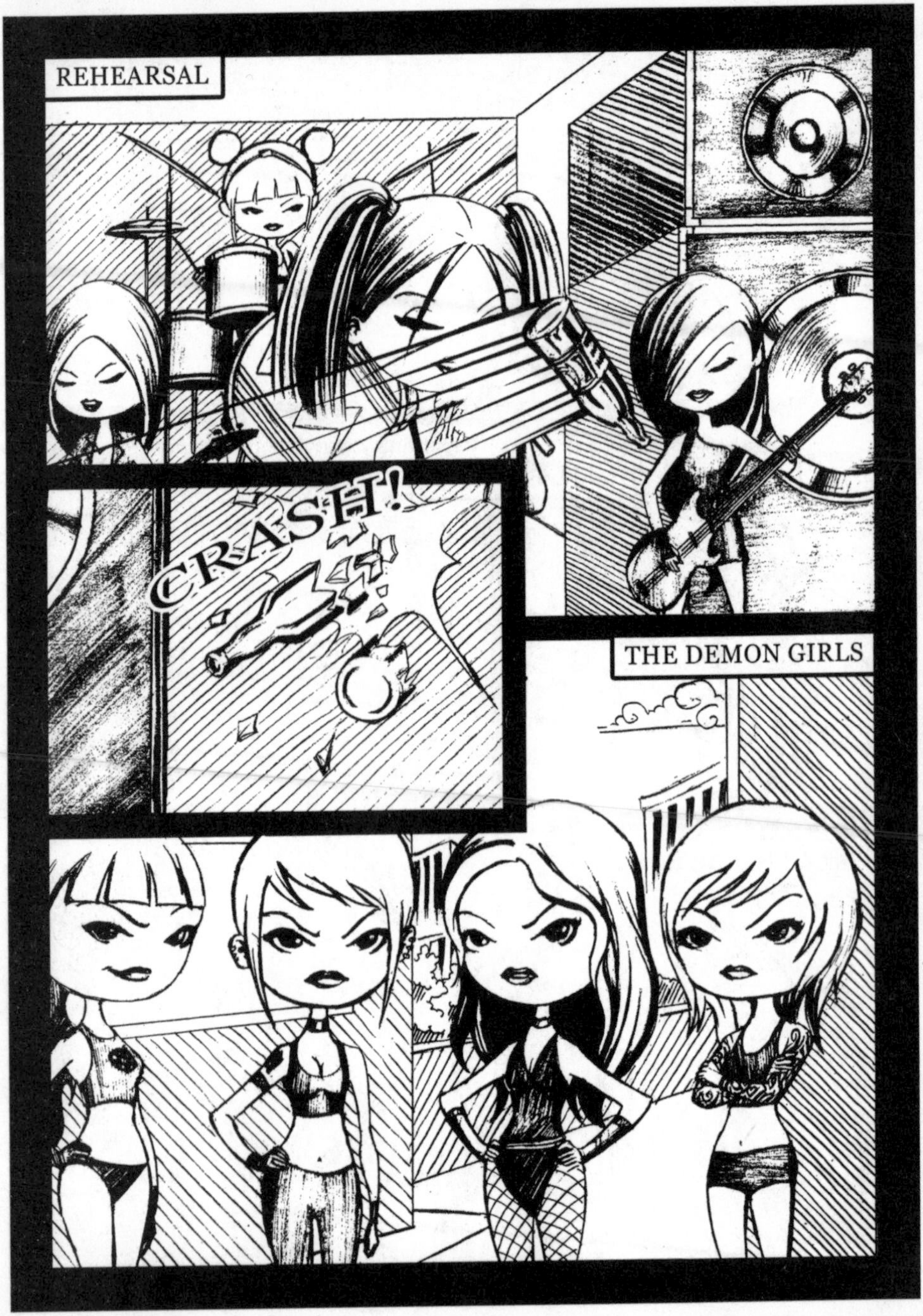
REHEARSAL
CRASH!
THE DEMON GIRLS

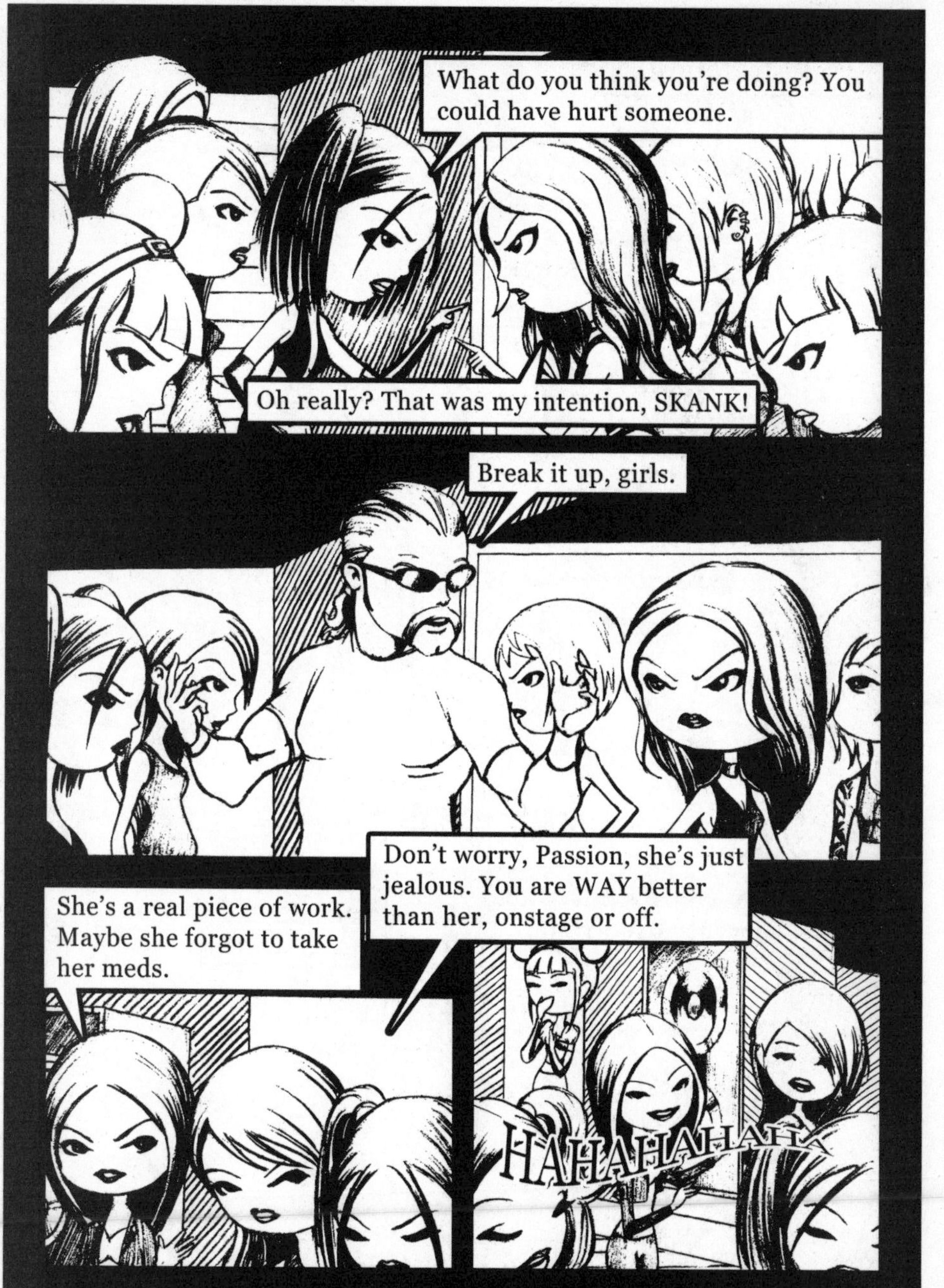
What do you think you're doing? You could have hurt someone.
Oh really? That was my intention, SKANK!
Break it up, girls.
She's a real piece of work. Maybe she forgot to take her meds.
Don't worry, Passion, she's just jealous. You are WAY better than her, onstage or off.
HAHAHAHAHA

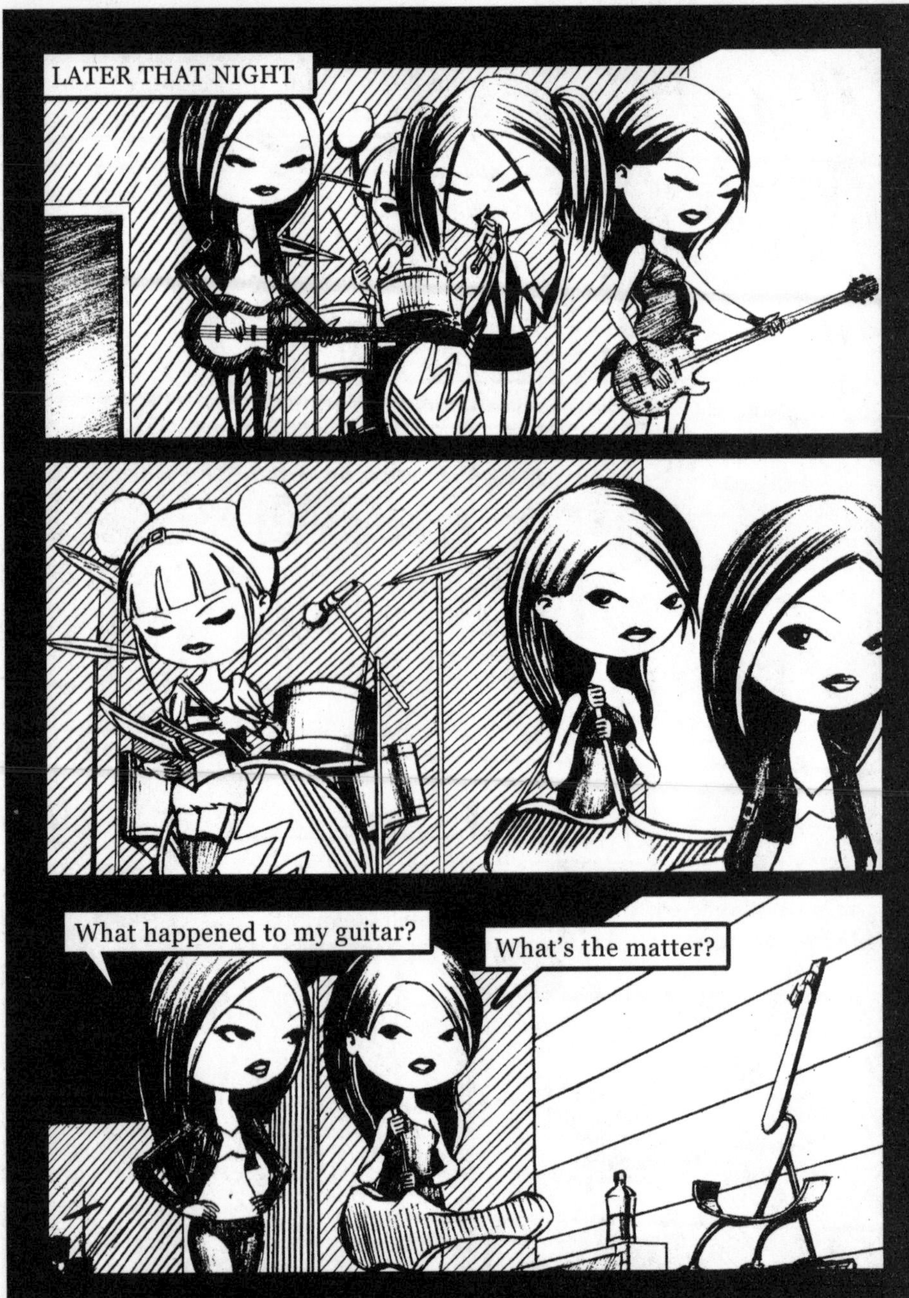
LATER THAT NIGHT
What happened to my guitar?
What's the matter?

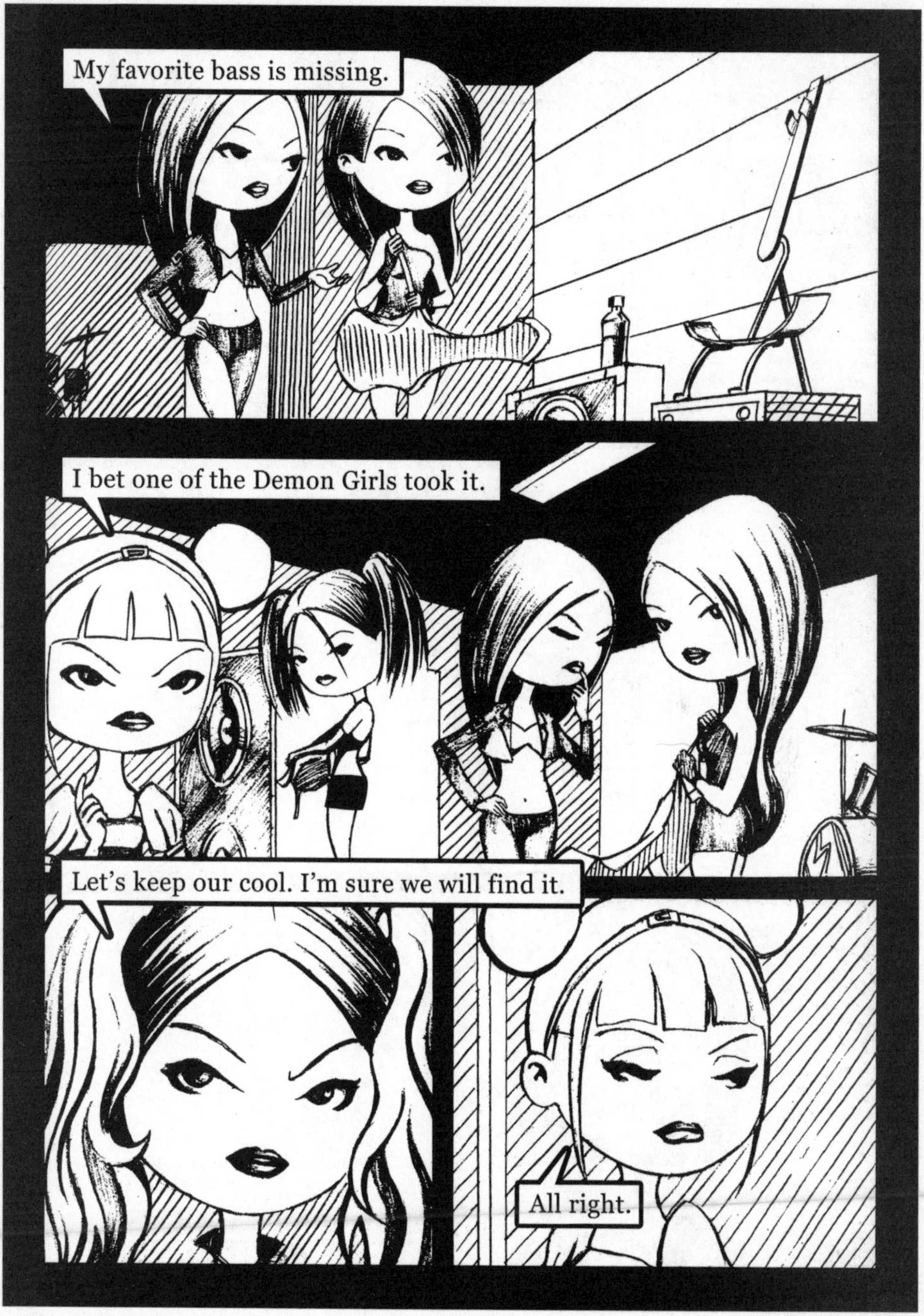
My favorite bass is missing.
I bet one of the Demon Girls took it.
Let's keep our cool. I'm sure we will find it.
All right.

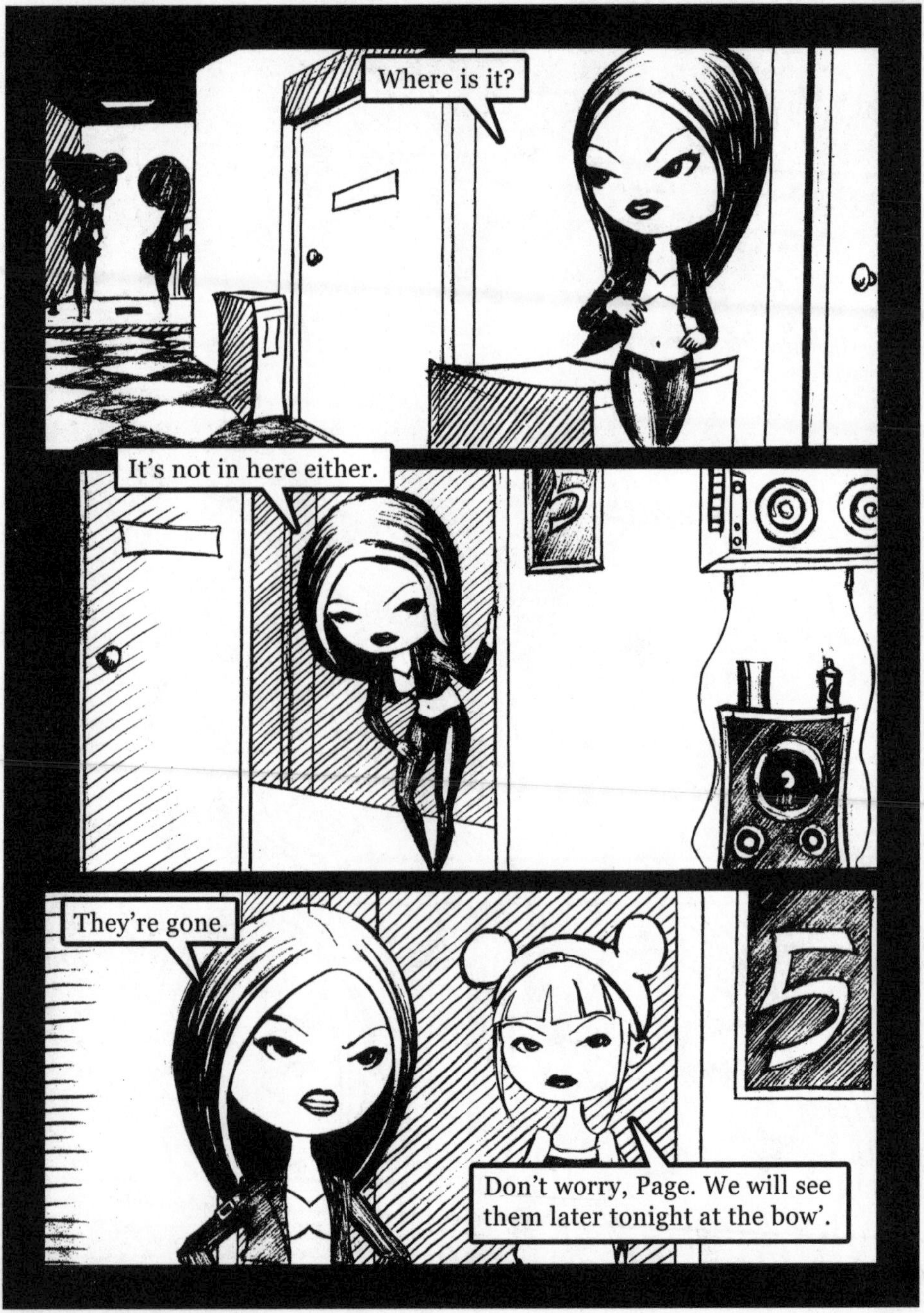
Where is it?
It's not in here either.
They're gone.
Don't worry, Page. We will see them later tonight at the bow'.

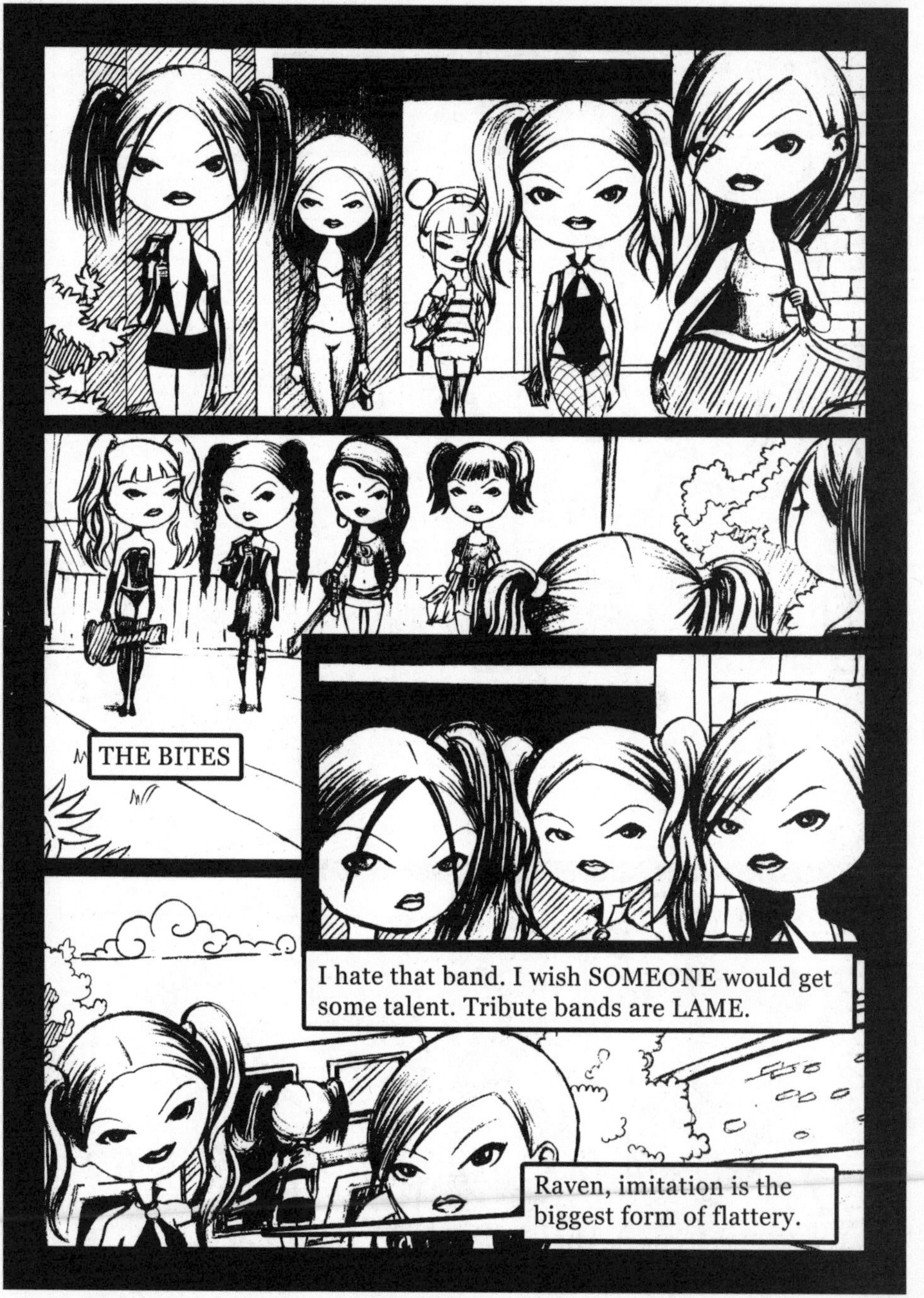
THE BITES
I hate that band. I wish SOMEONE would get some talent. Tribute bands are LAME.
Raven, imitation is the biggest form of flattery.

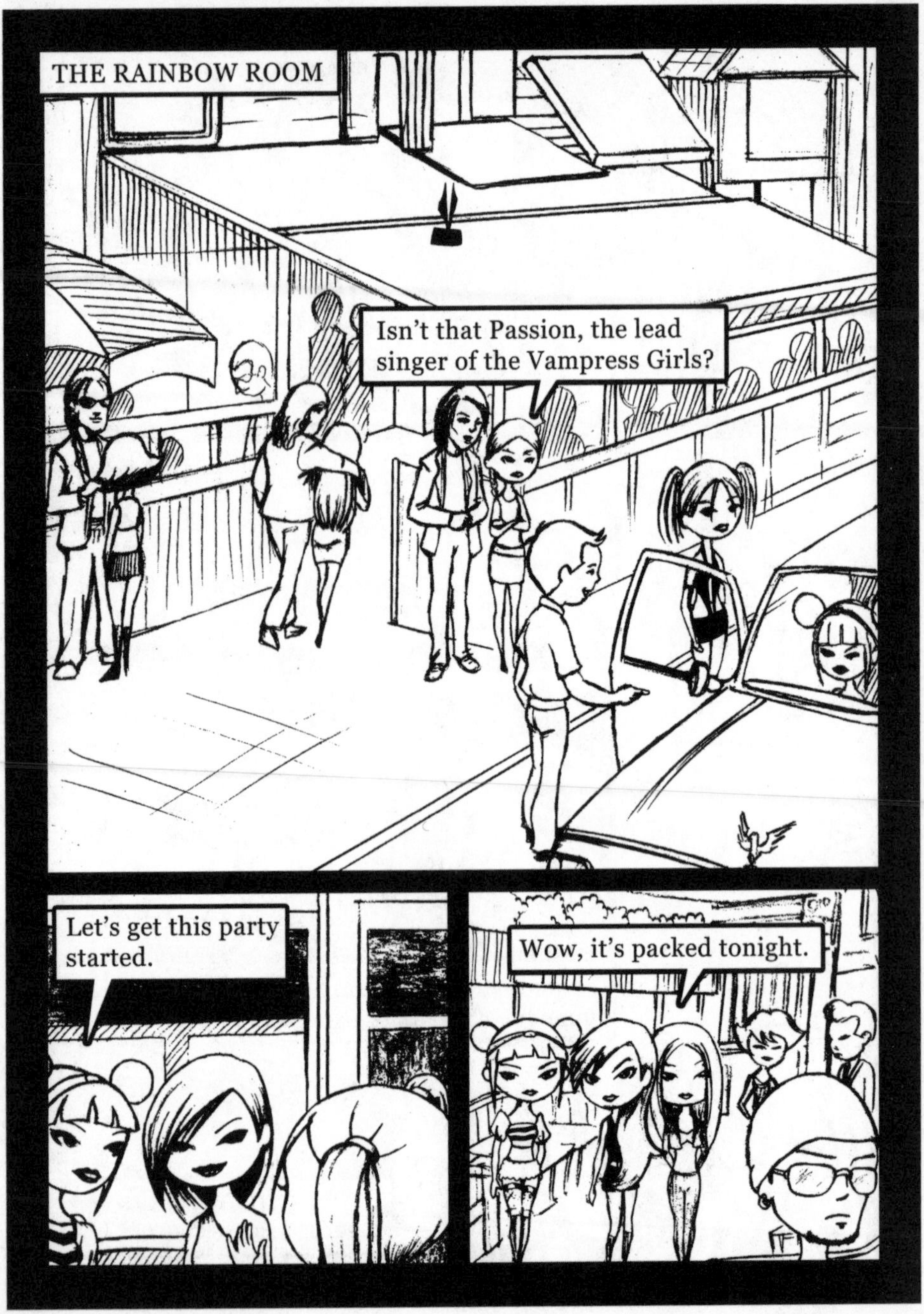
THE RAINBOW ROOM
Isn't that Passion, the lead singer of the Vampress Girls?
Let's get this party started.
Wow, it's packed tonight.

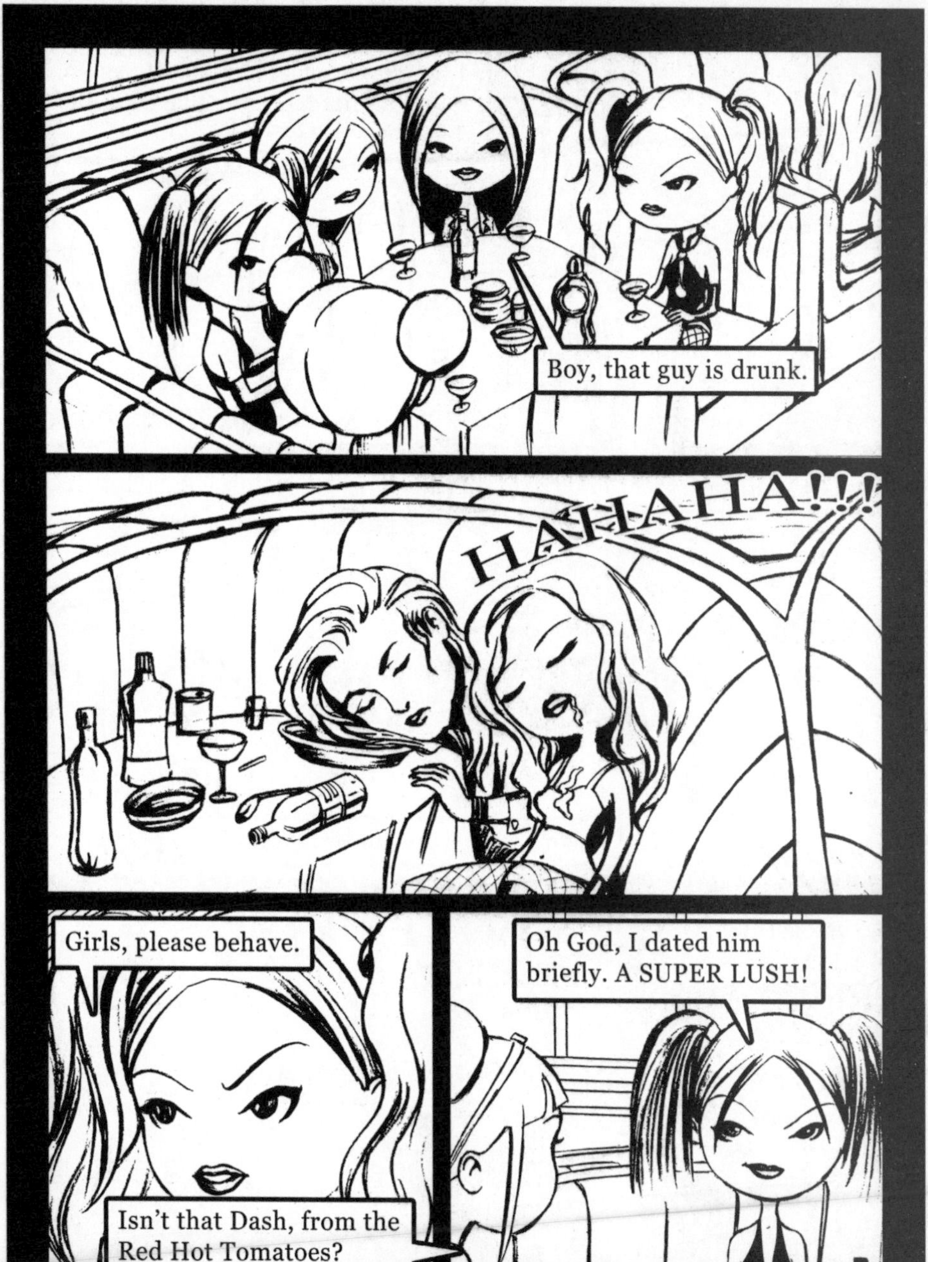
Boy, that guy is drunk.
HAHAHA!!!
Girls, please behave.
Isn't that Dash, from the Red Hot Tomatoes?
Oh God, I dated him briefly. A SUPER LUSH!

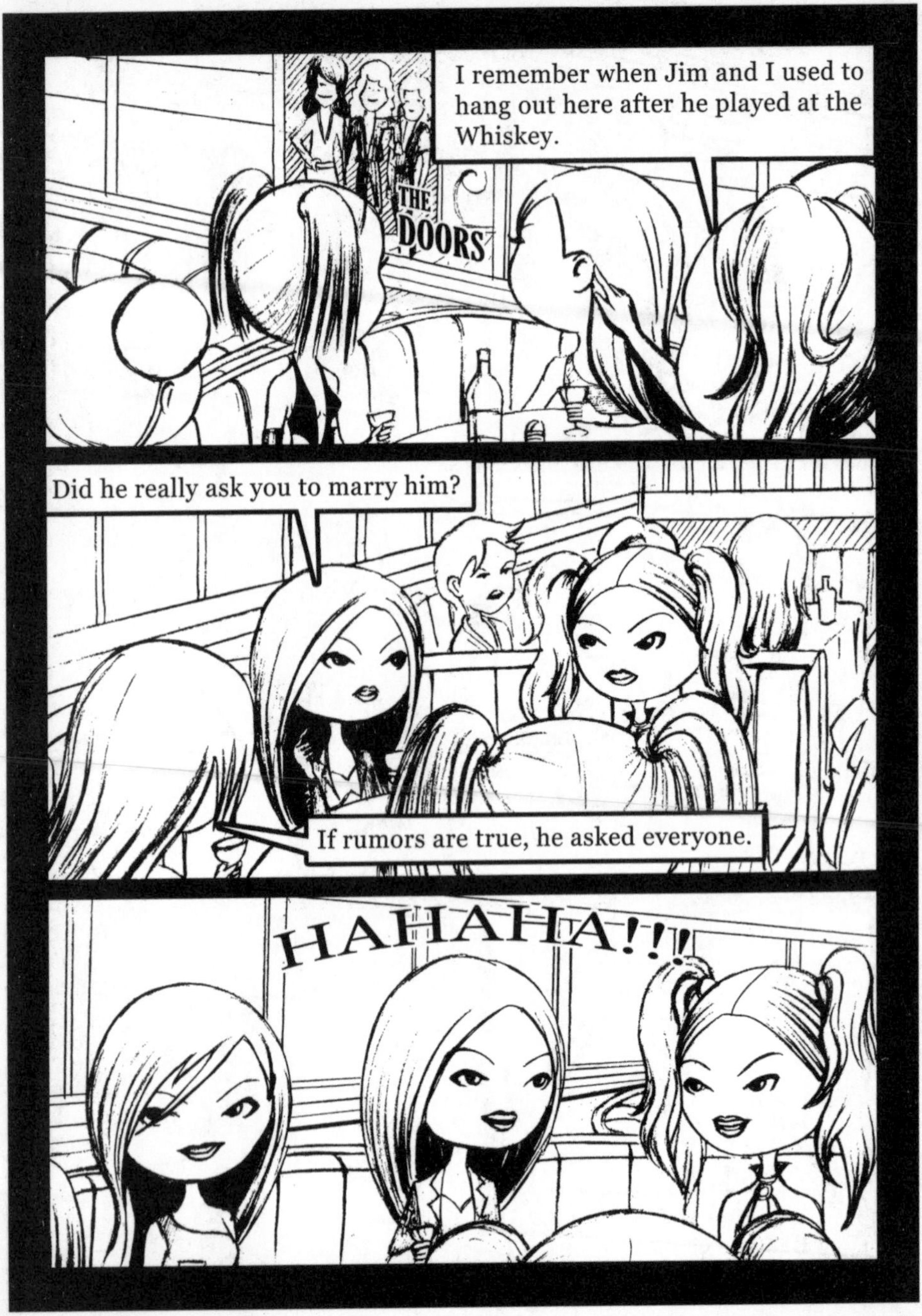
THE DOORS
I remember when Jim and I used to hang out here after he played at the Whiskey.
Did he really ask you to marry him?
If rumors are true, he asked everyone.
HAHAHA!!!

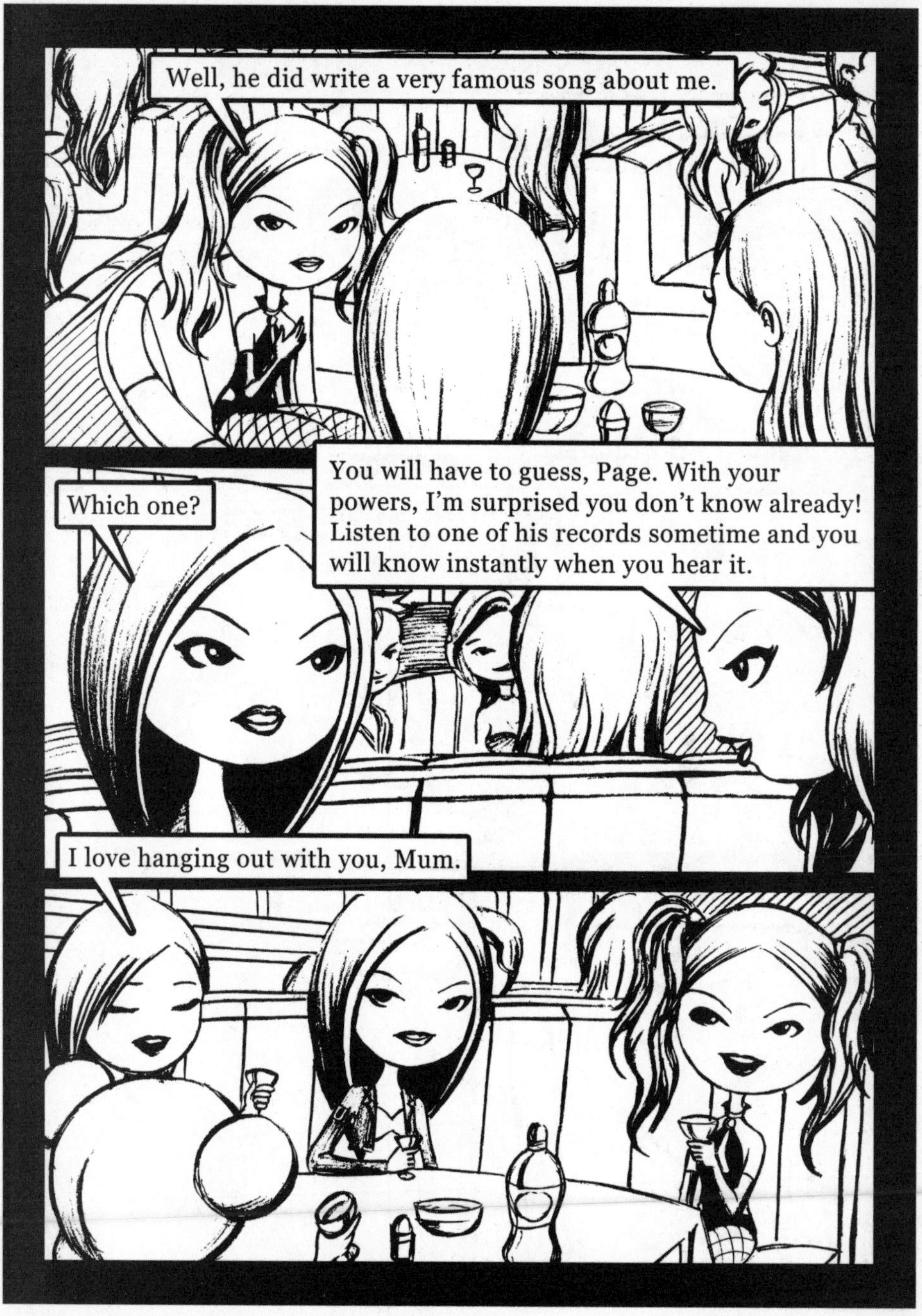
Well, he did write a very famous song about me.
Which one?
You will have to guess, Page. With your powers, I'm surprised you don't know already! Listen to one of his records sometime and you will know instantly when you hear it.
I love hanging out with you, Mum.

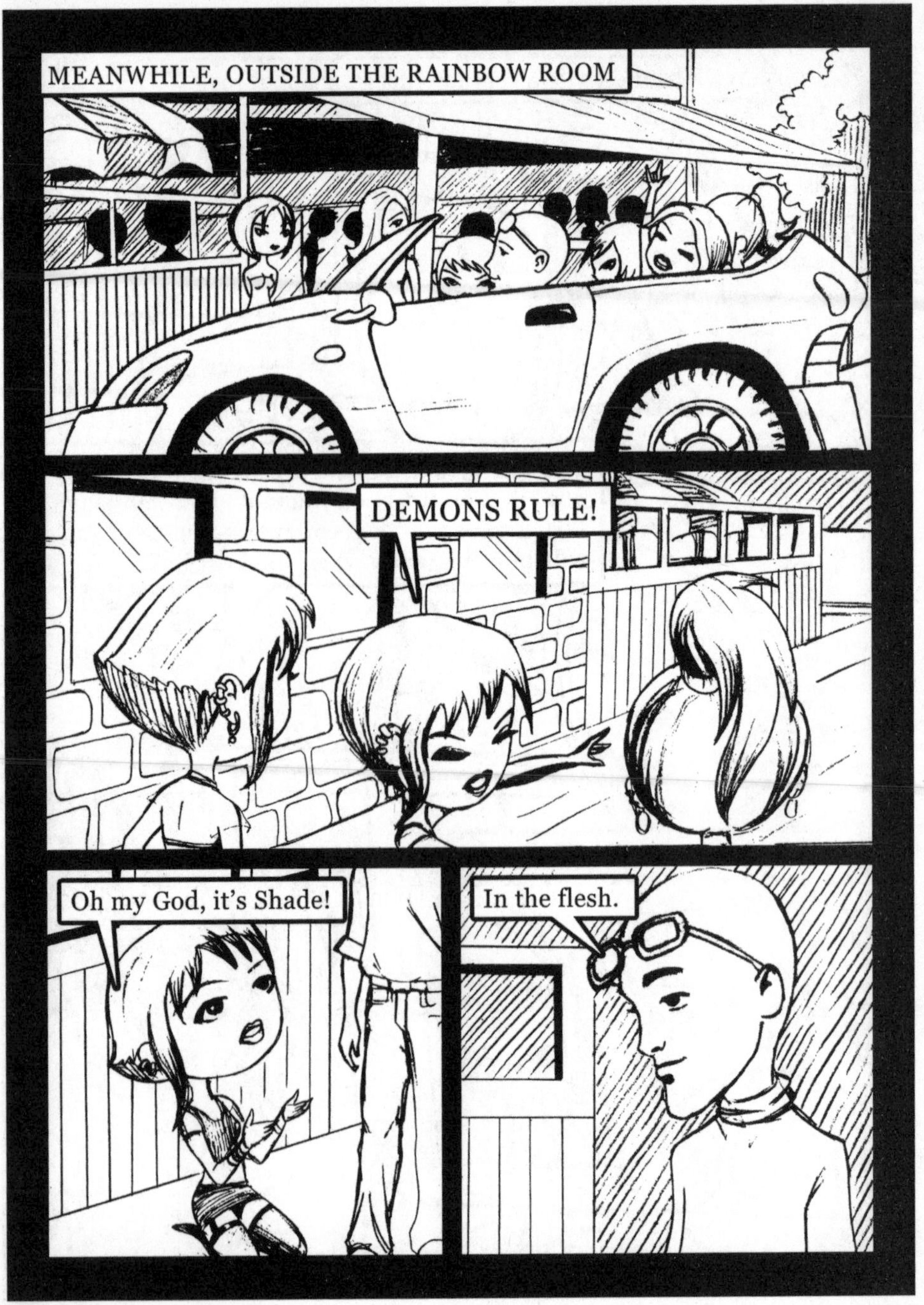
MEANWHILE, OUTSIDE THE RAINBOW ROOM
DEMONS RULE!
Oh my God, it's Shade!
In the flesh.

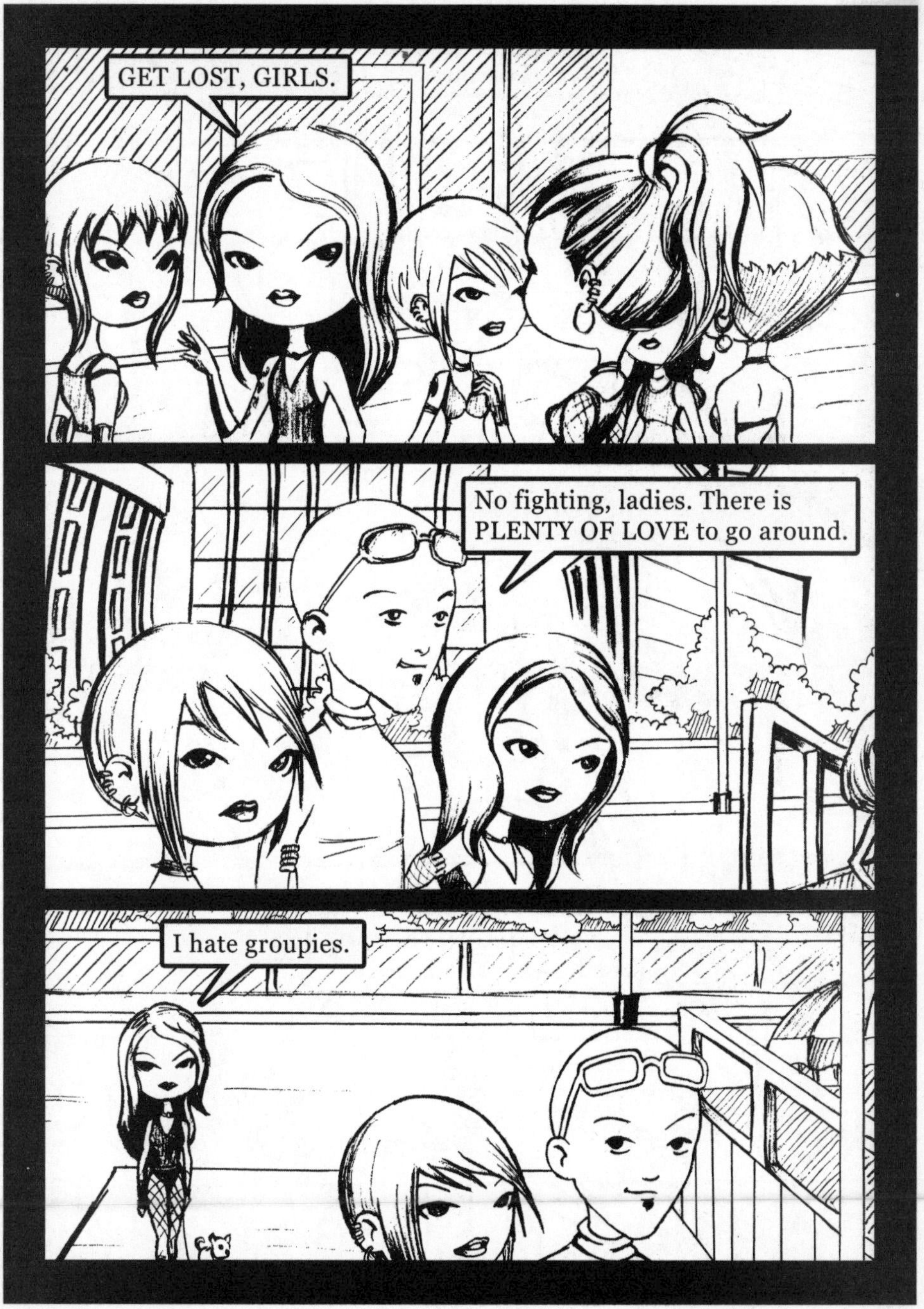
GET LOST, GIRLS.
No fighting, ladies. There is PLENTY OF LOVE to go around.
I hate groupies.

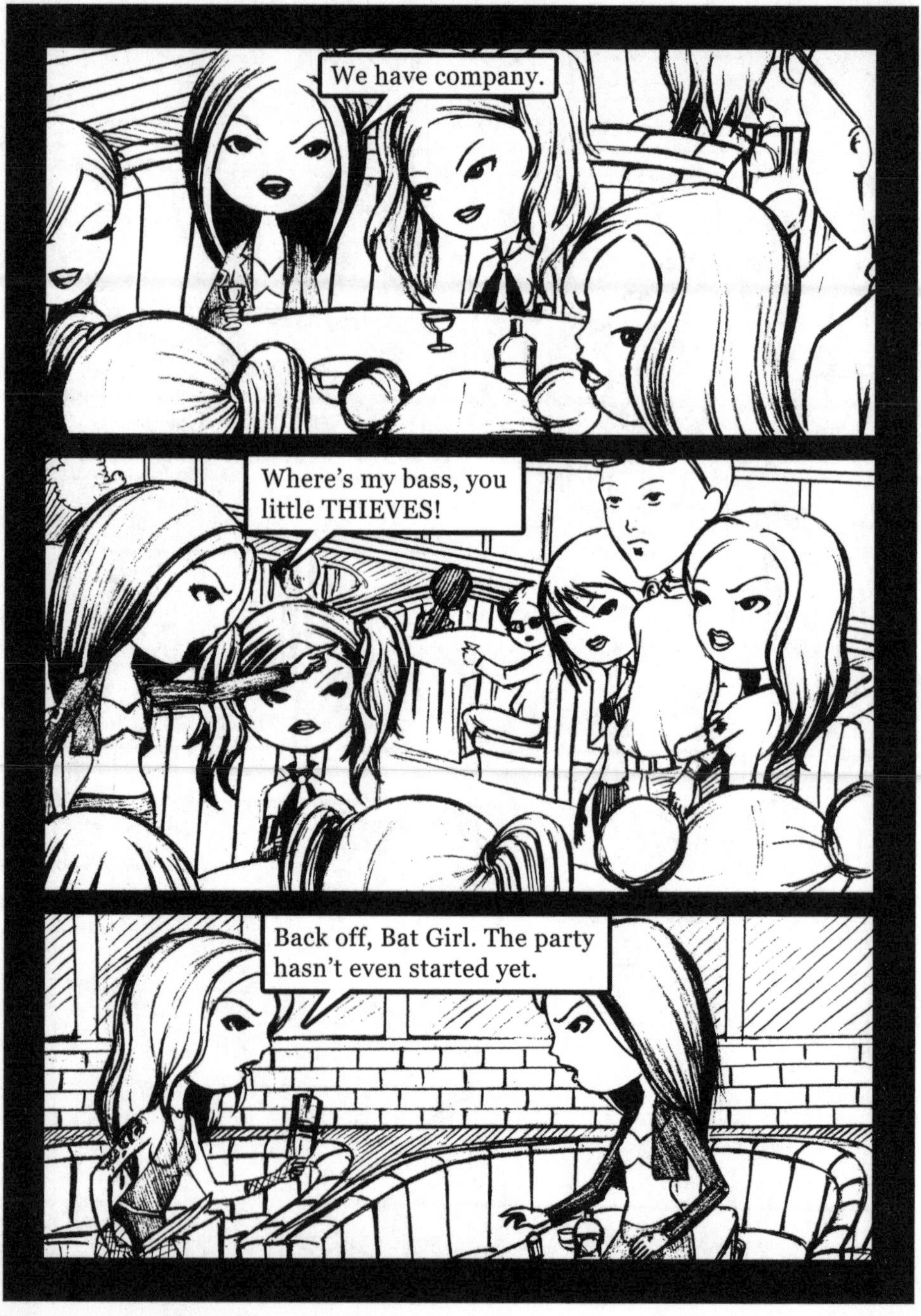
We have company.
Where's my bass, you little THIEVES!
Back off, Bat Girl. The party hasn't even started yet.

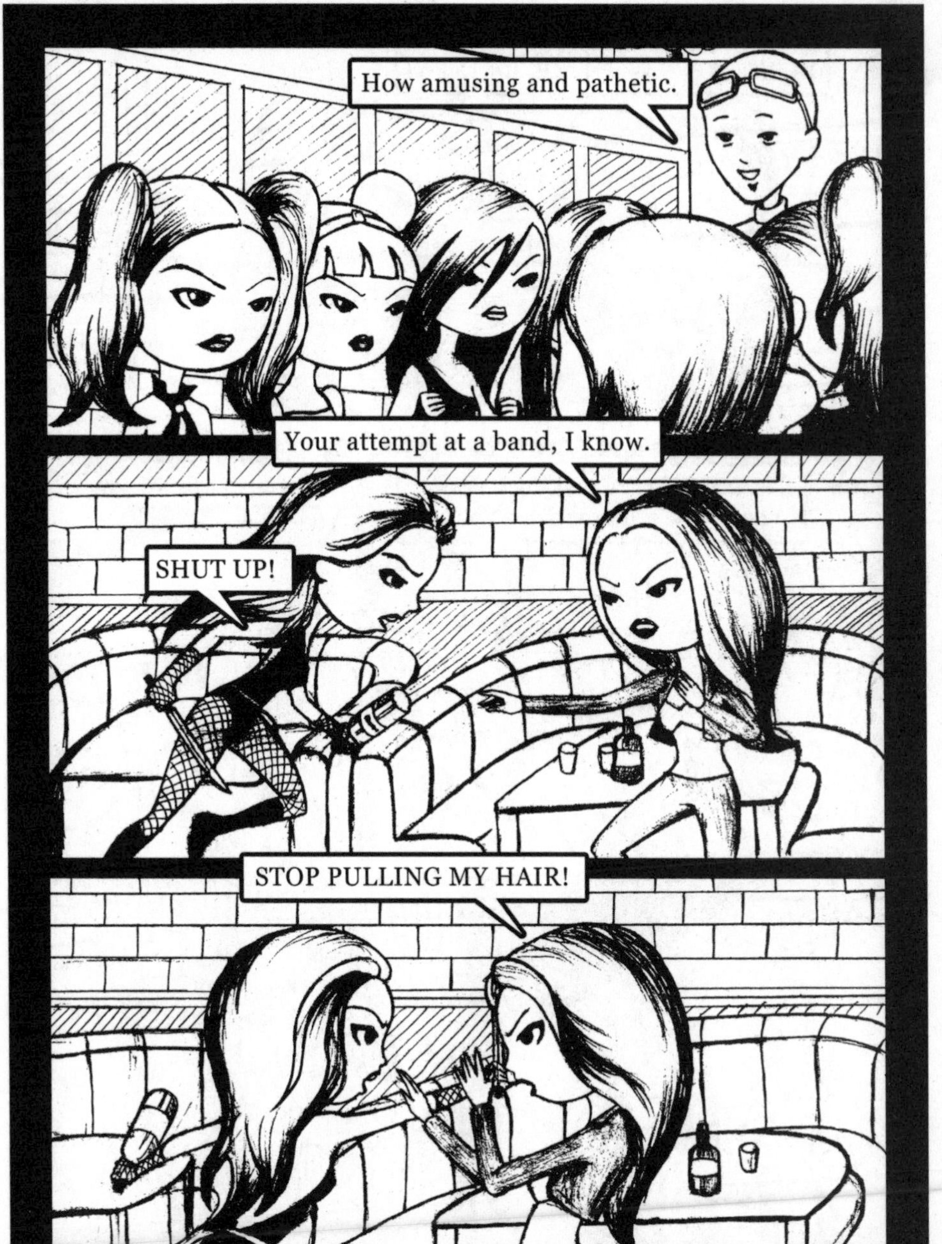
How amusing and pathetic.
Your attempt at a band, I know.
SHUT UP!
STOP PULLING MY HAIR!

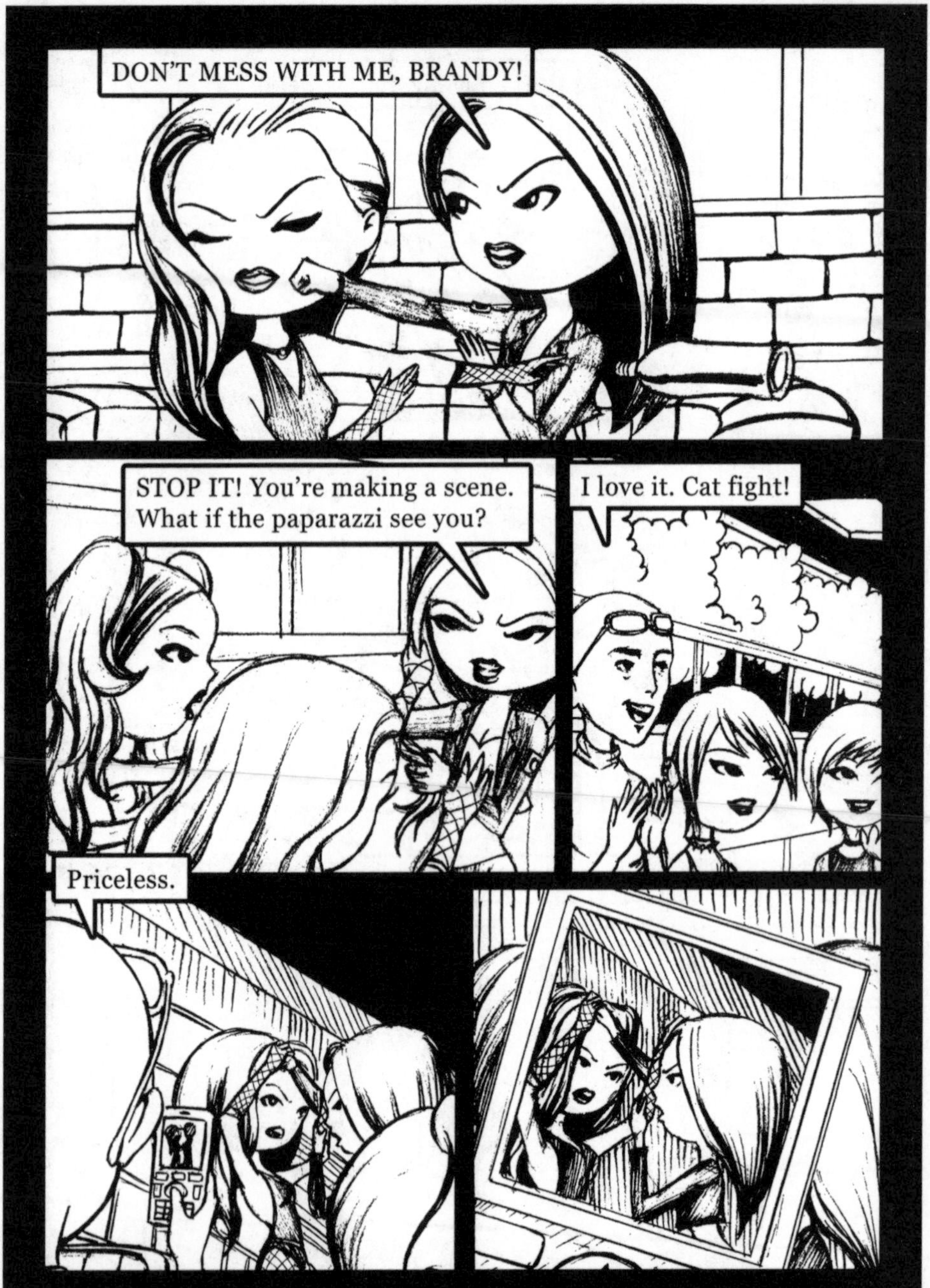
DON'T MESS WITH ME, BRANDY!
STOP IT! You're making a scene. What if the paparazzi see you?
I love it. Cat fight!
Priceless.

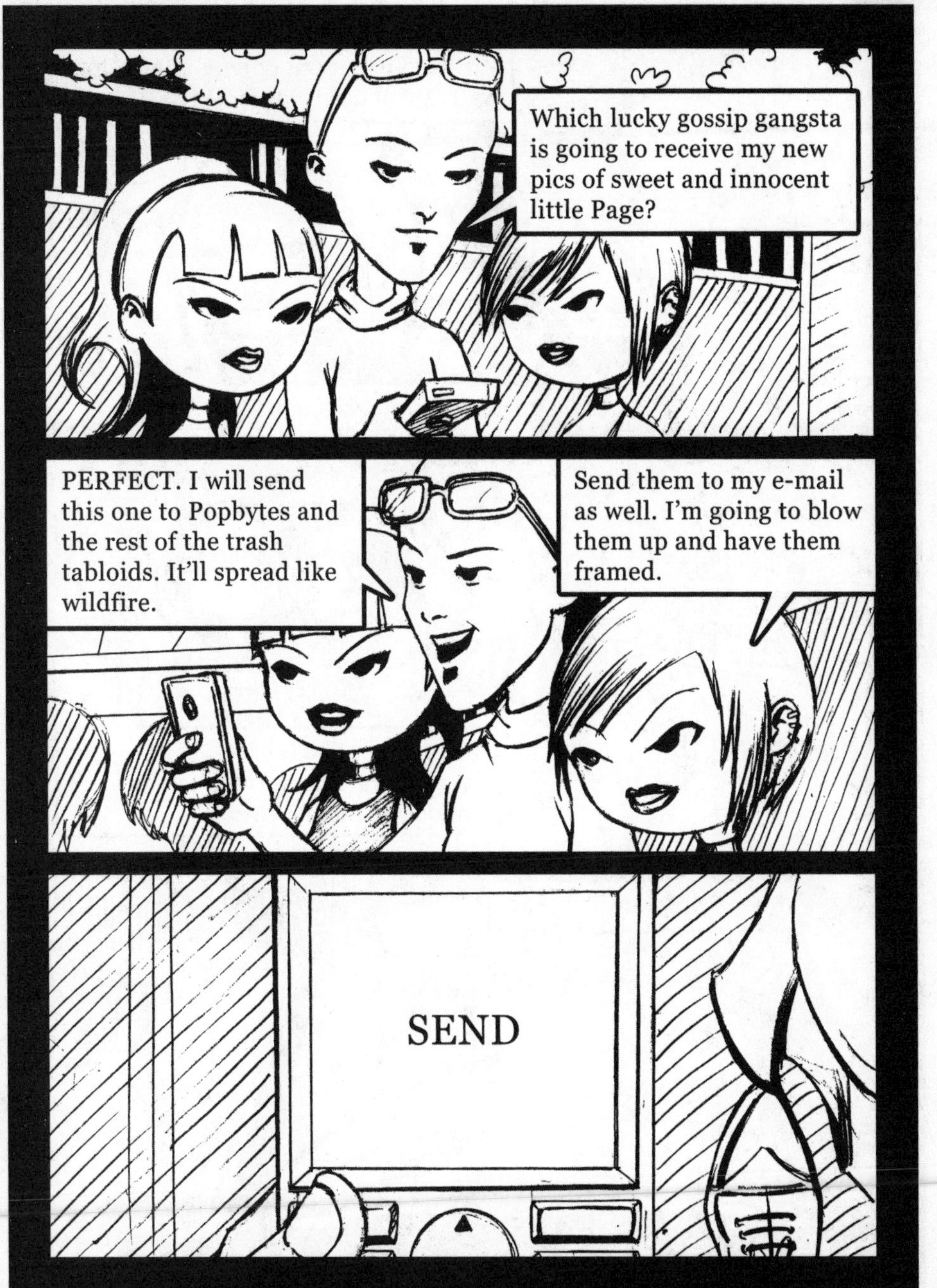
Which lucky gossip gangsta is going to receive my new pics of sweet and innocent little Page?
PERFECT. I will send this one to Popbytes and the rest of the trash tabloids. It'll spread like wildfire.
Send them to my e-mail as well. I'm going to blow them up and have them framed.
SEND

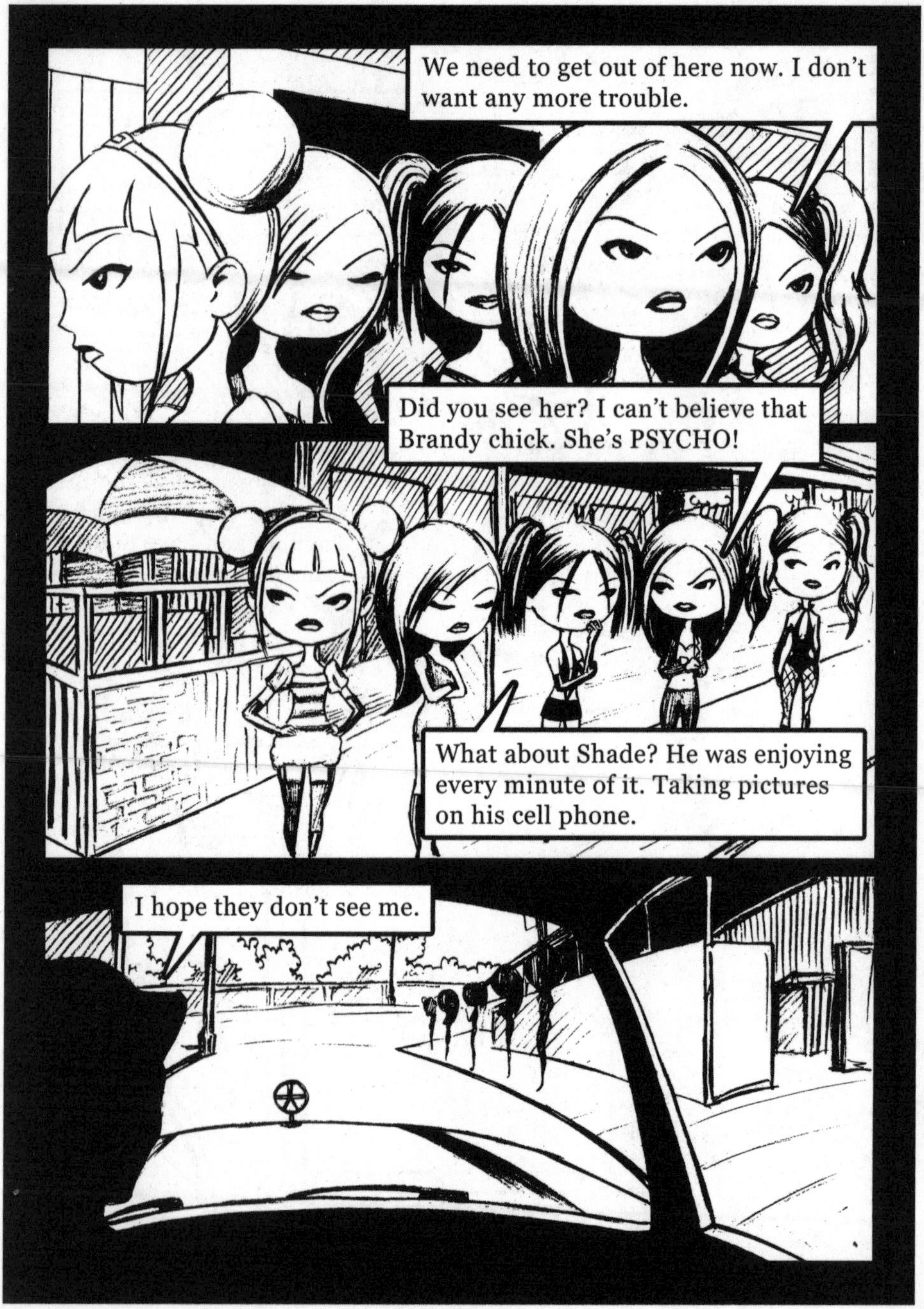
We need to get out of here now. I don't want any more trouble.
Did you see her? I can't believe that Brandy chick. She's PSYCHO!
What about Shade? He was enjoying every minute of it. Taking pictures on his cell phone.
I hope they don't see me.

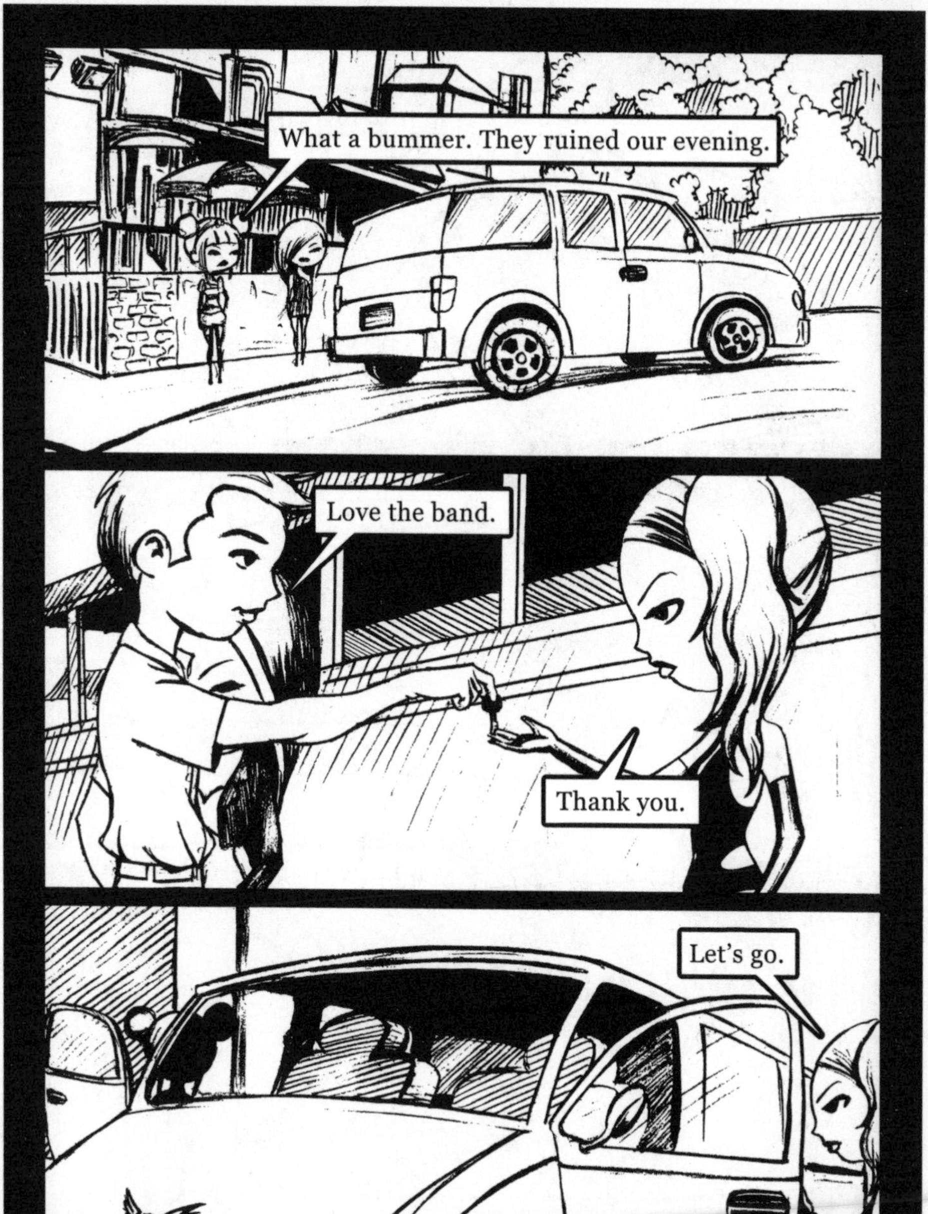
What a bummer. They ruined our evening.
Love the band.
Thank you.
Let's go.

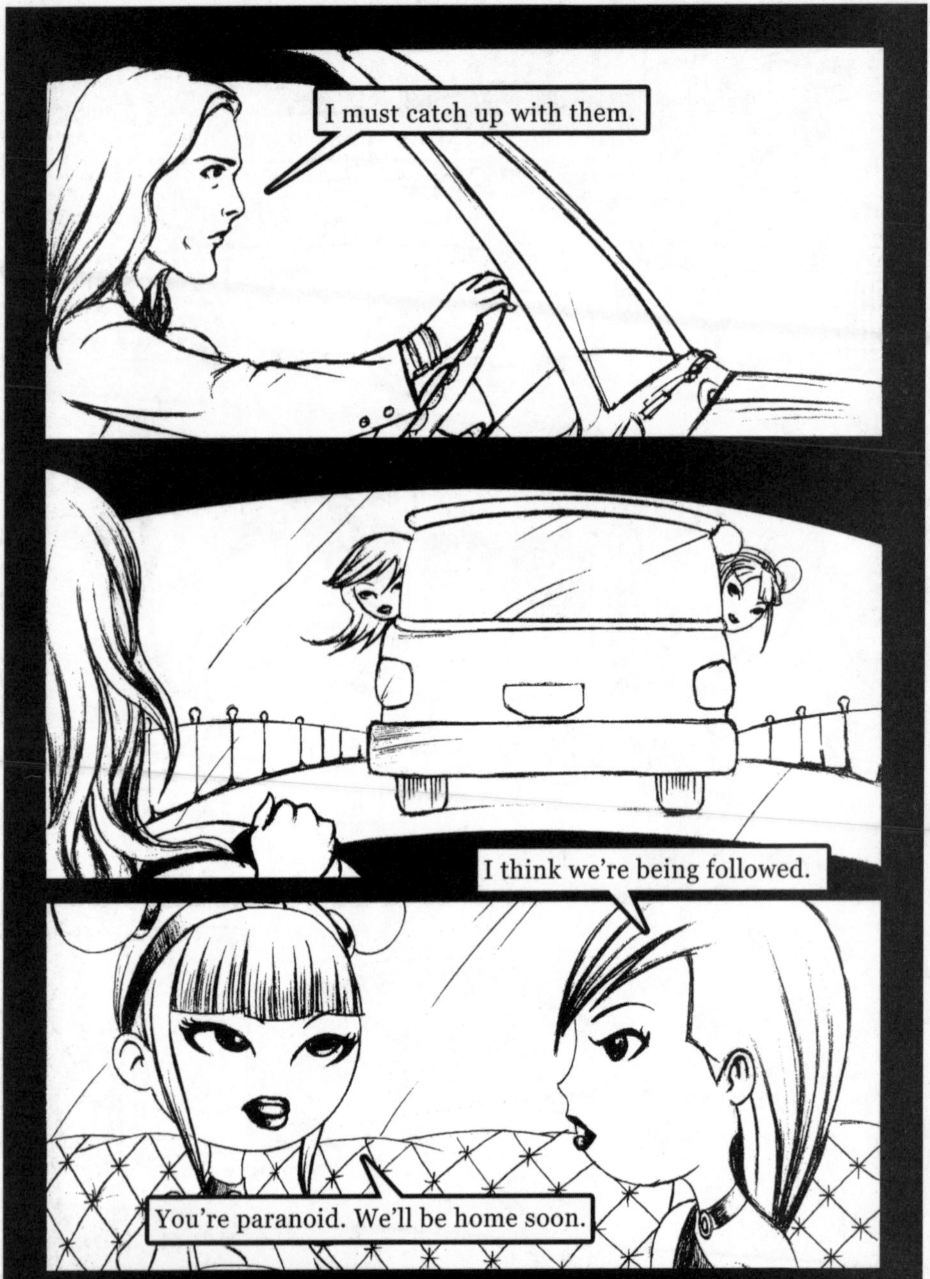
I must catch up with them.
I think we're being followed.
You're paranoid. We'll be home soon.

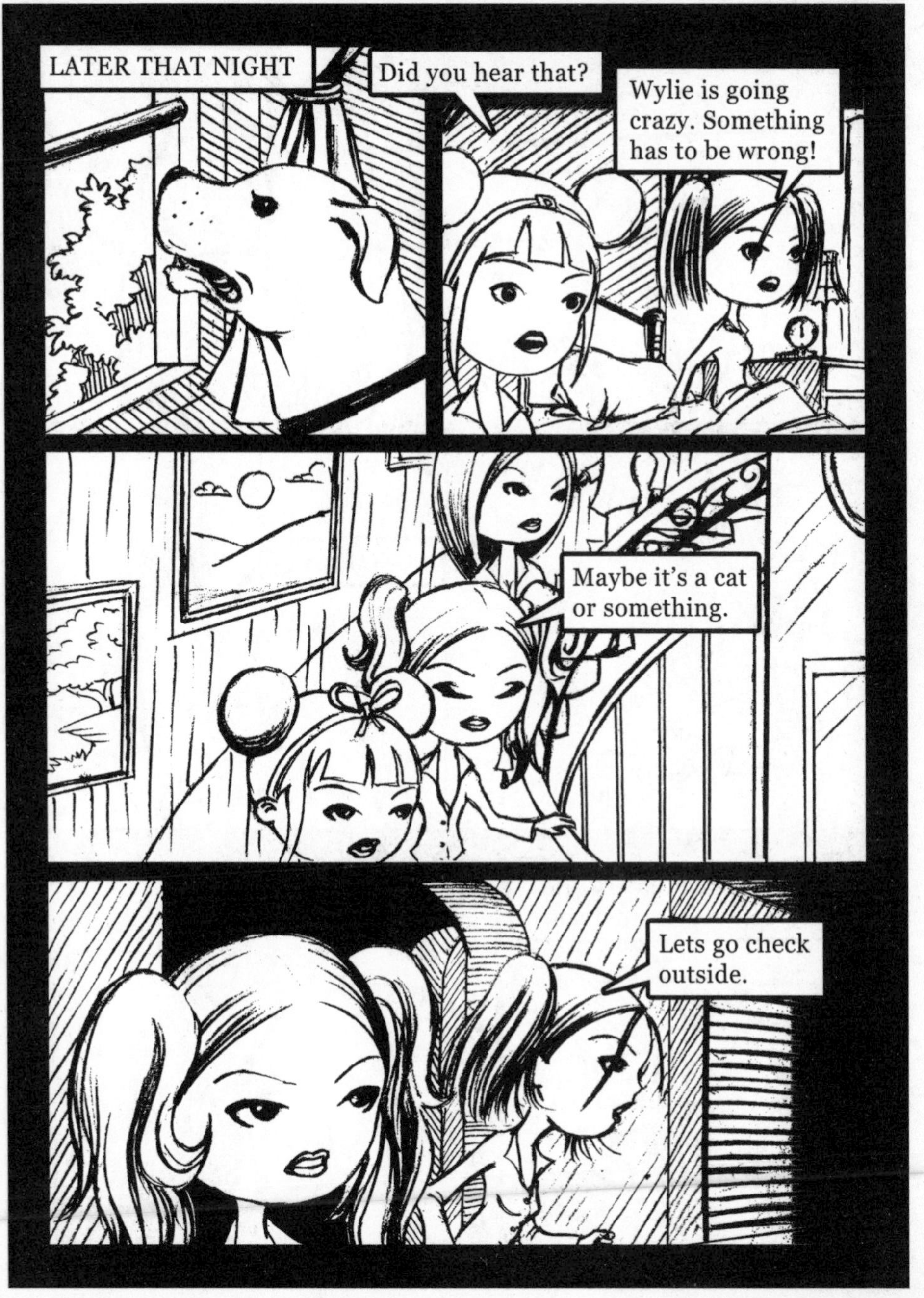
LATER THAT NIGHT
Did you hear that?
Wylie is going crazy. Something has to be wrong!
Maybe it's a cat or something.
Lets go check outside.

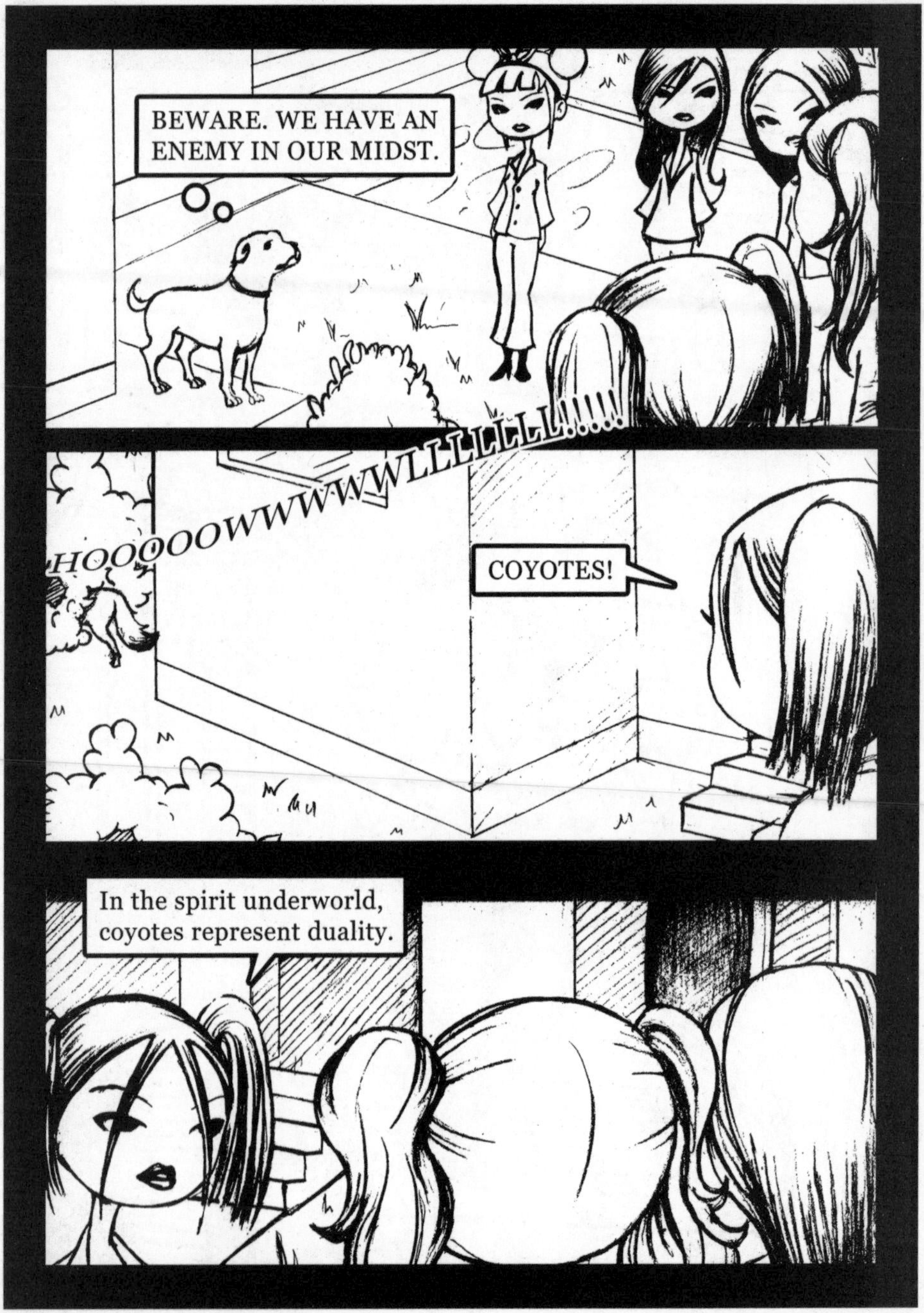
BEWARE. WE HAVE AN ENEMY IN OUR MIDST.
HOOOOOOWWWWWWLLLLLLL!!!!!!
COYOTES!
In the spirit underworld, coyotes represent duality.

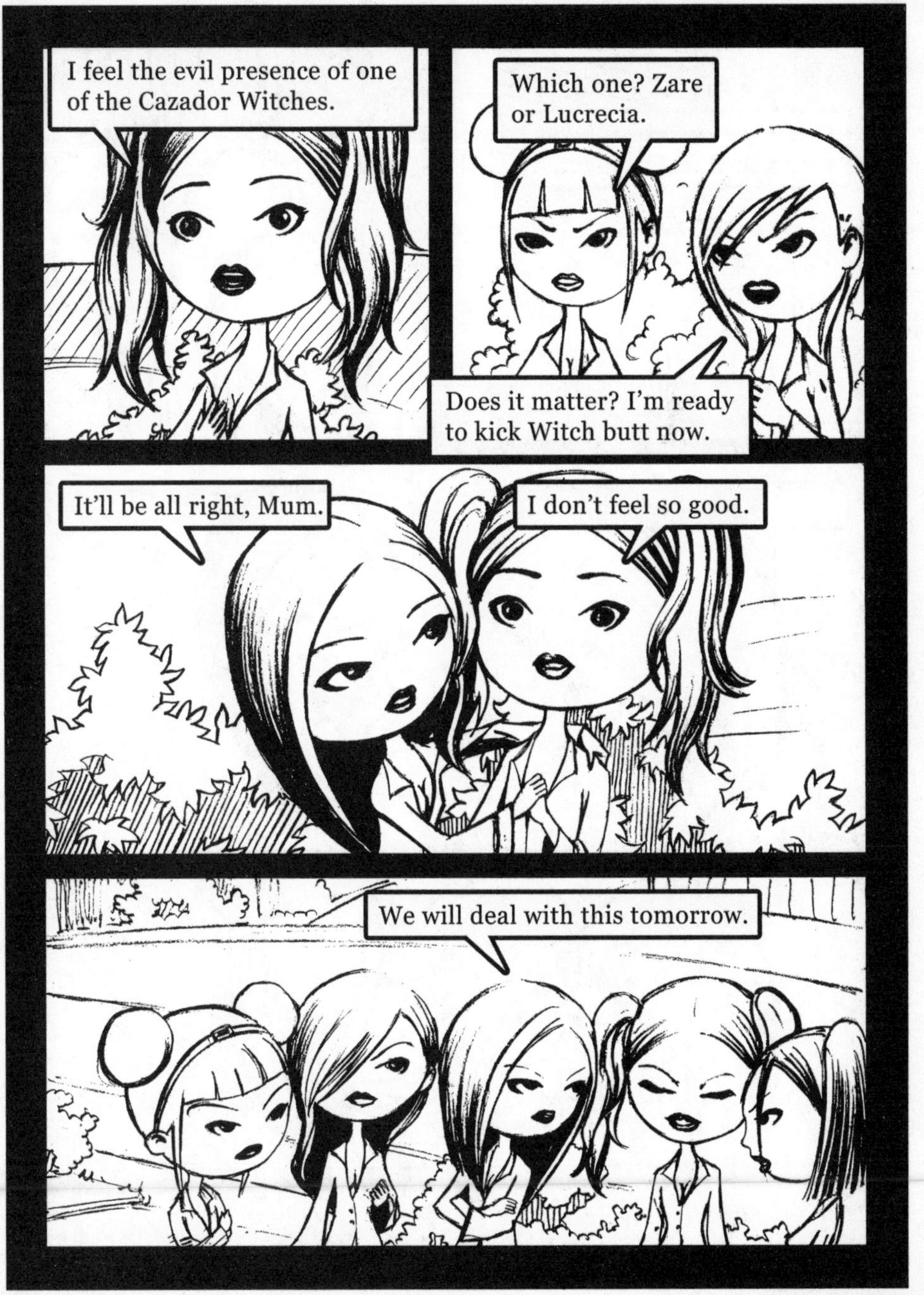
I feel the evil presence of one of the Cazador Witches.
Which one? Zare or Lucrecia.
Does it matter? I'm ready to kick Witch butt now.
It'll be all right, Mum.
I don't feel so good.
We will deal with this tomorrow.

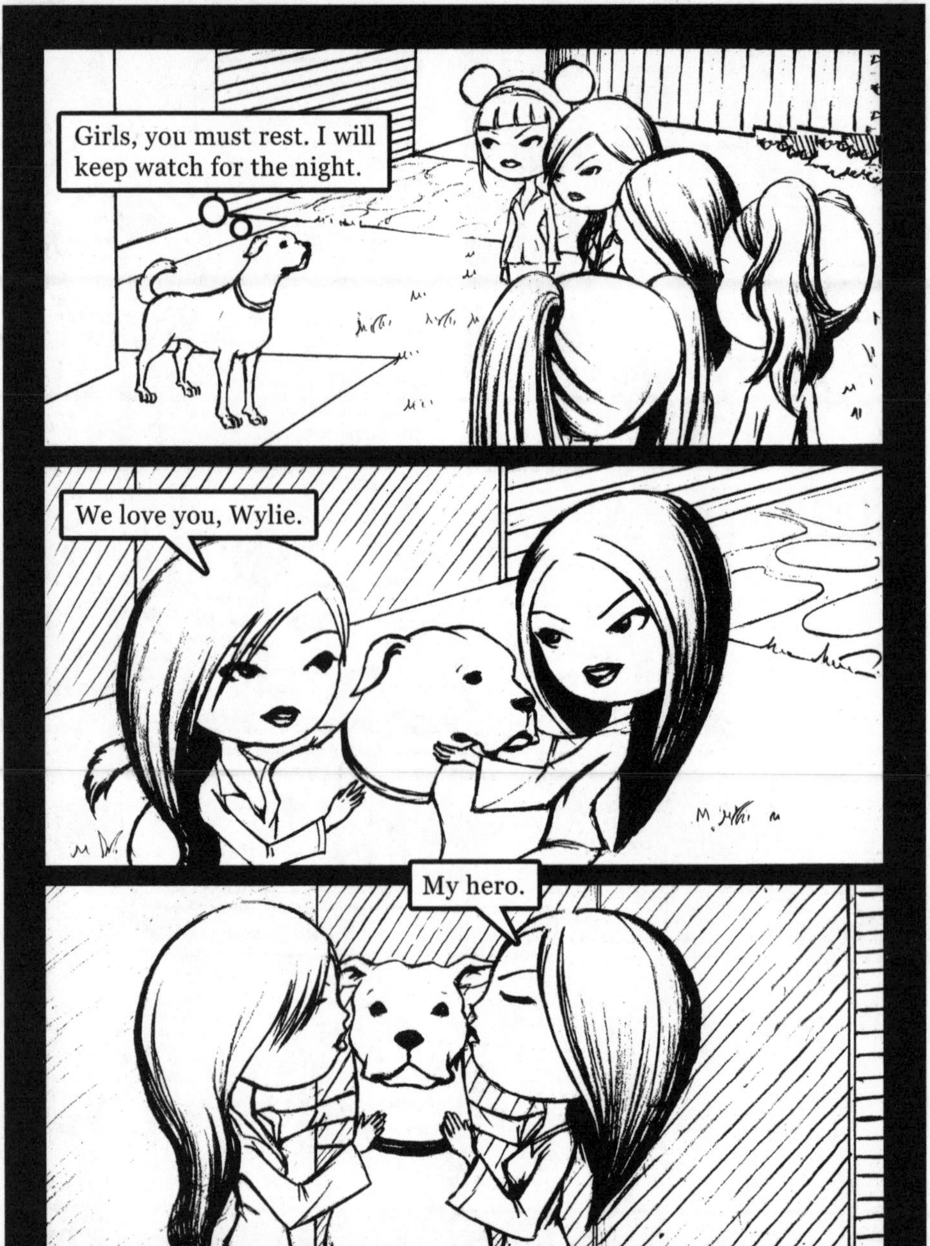
Girls, you must rest. I will keep watch for the night.
We love you, Wylie.
My hero.

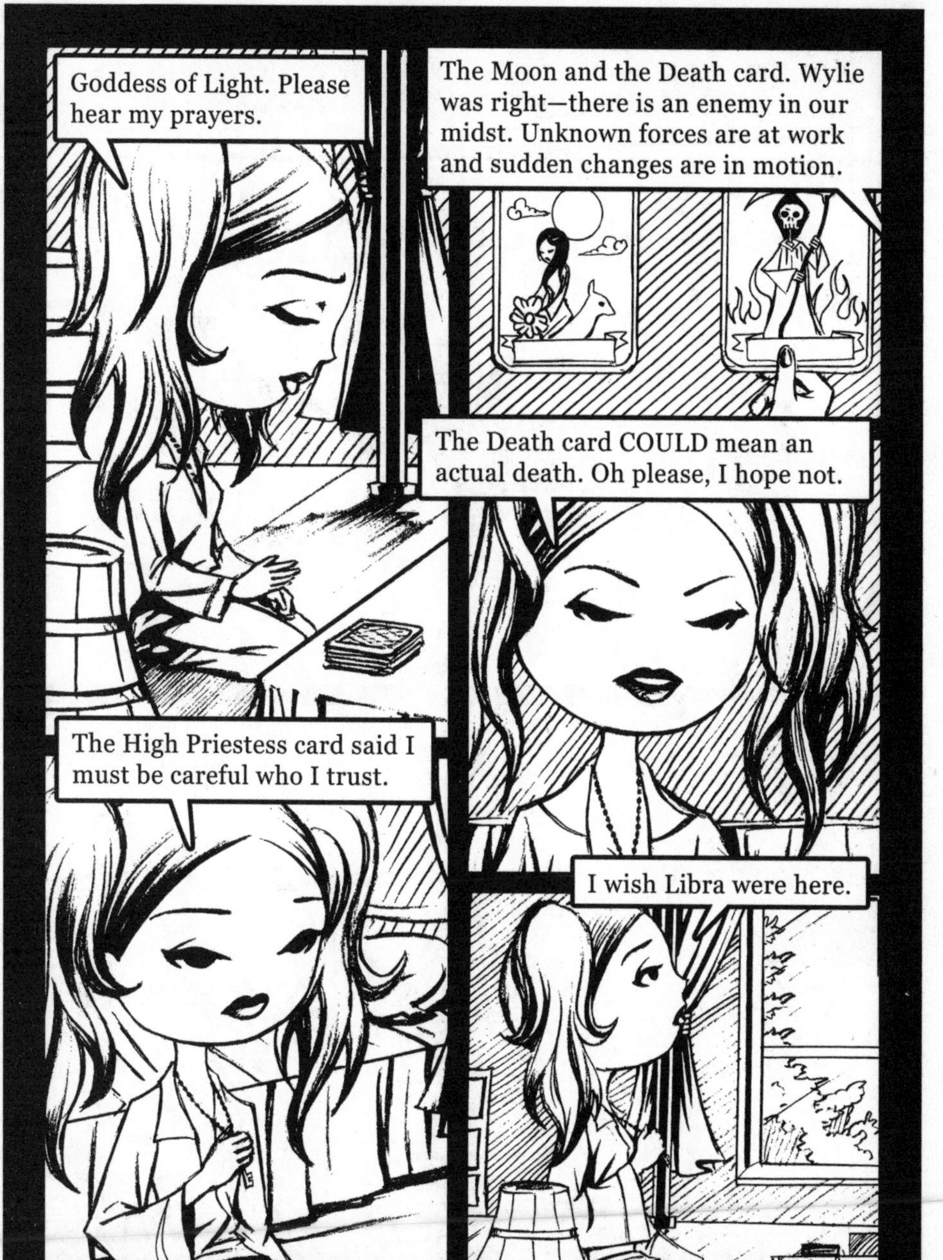
Goddess of Light. Please hear my prayers.
The Moon and the Death card. Wylie was right—there is an enemy in our midst. Unknown forces are at work and sudden changes are in motion.
The Death card COULD mean an actual death. Oh please, I hope not.
The High Priestess card said I must be careful who I trust.
I wish Libra were here.

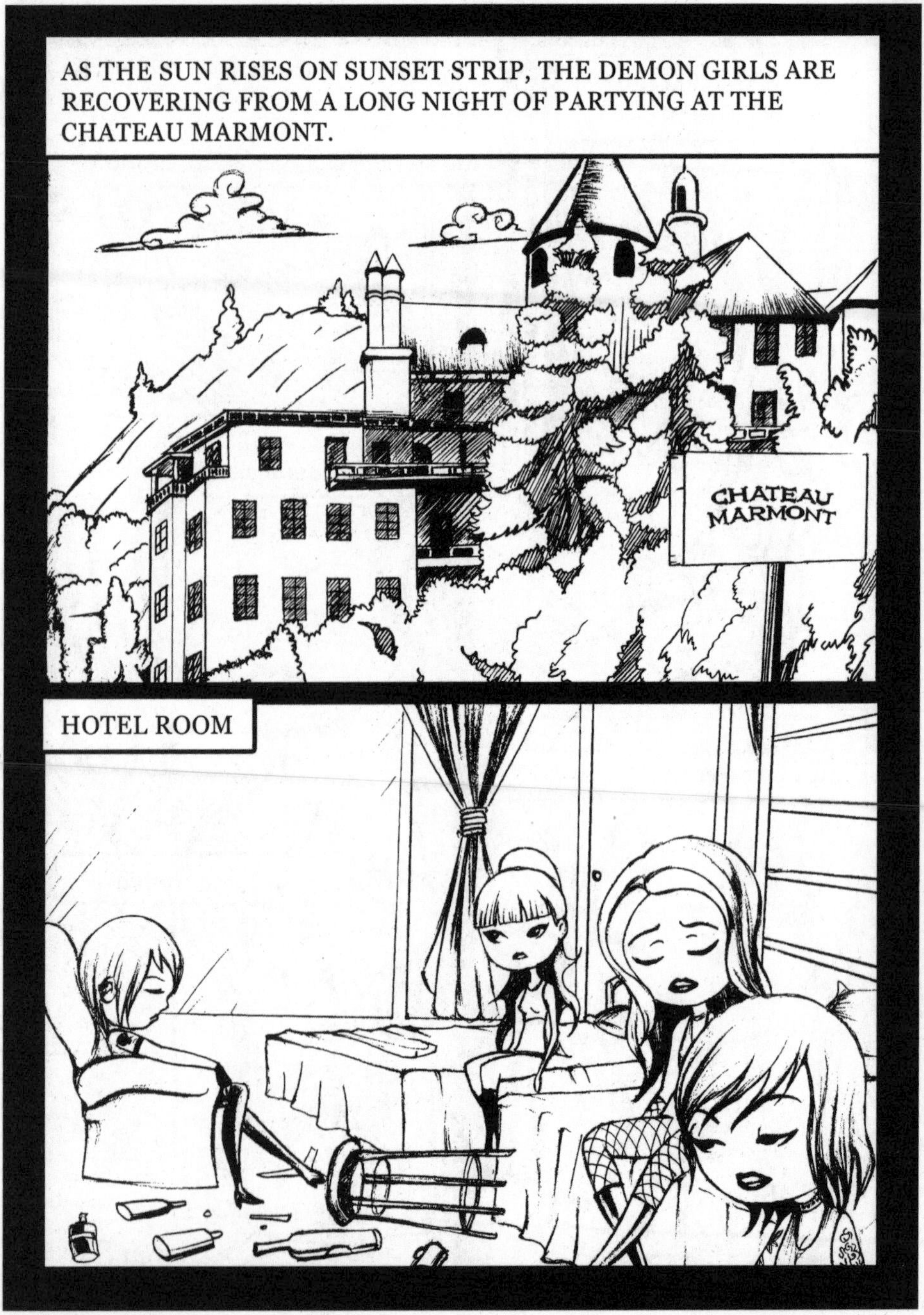
AS THE SUN RISES ON SUNSET STRIP, THE DEMON GIRLS ARE RECOVERING FROM A LONG NIGHT OF PARTYING AT THE CHATEAU MARMONT.
CHATEAU MARMONT
HOTEL ROOM

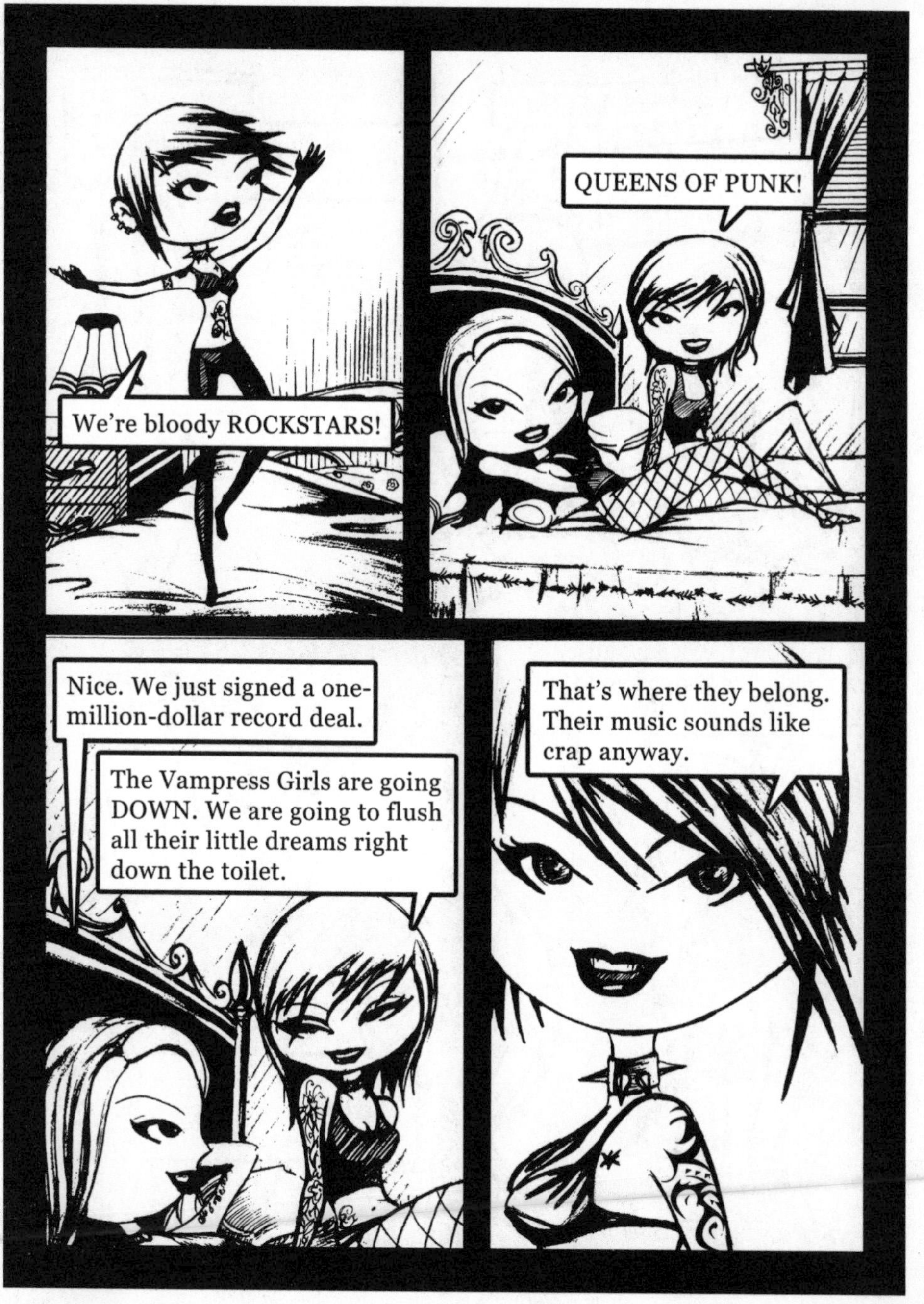
We're bloody ROCKSTARS!
QUEENS OF PUNK!
Nice. We just signed a one-million-dollar record deal.
The Vampress Girls are going DOWN. We are going to flush all their little dreams right down the toilet.
That's where they belong. Their music sounds like crap anyway.

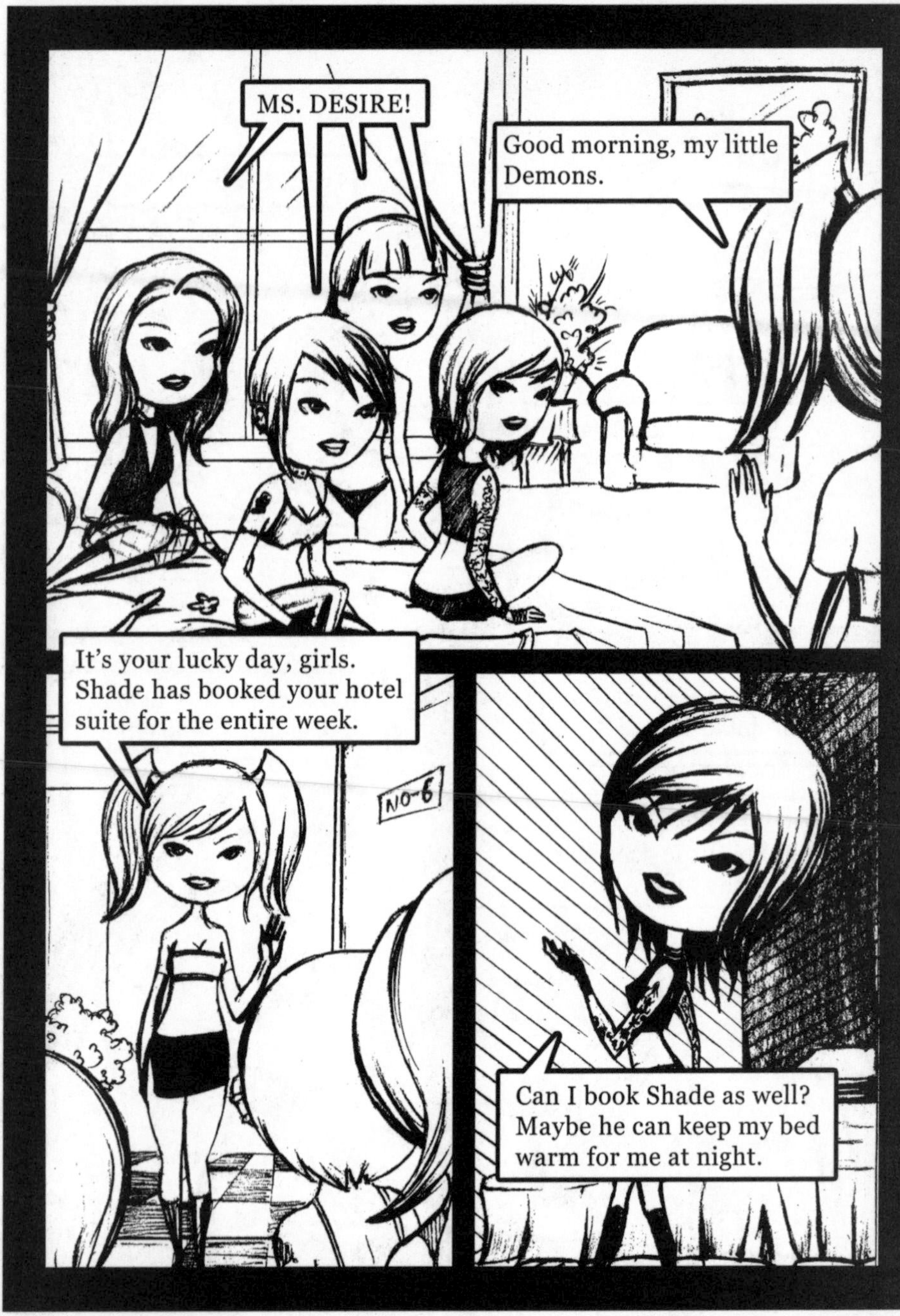
MS. DESIRE!
Good morning, my little Demons.
It's your lucky day, girls. Shade has booked your hotel suite for the entire week.
NO-6
Can I book Shade as well? Maybe he can keep my bed warm for me at night.

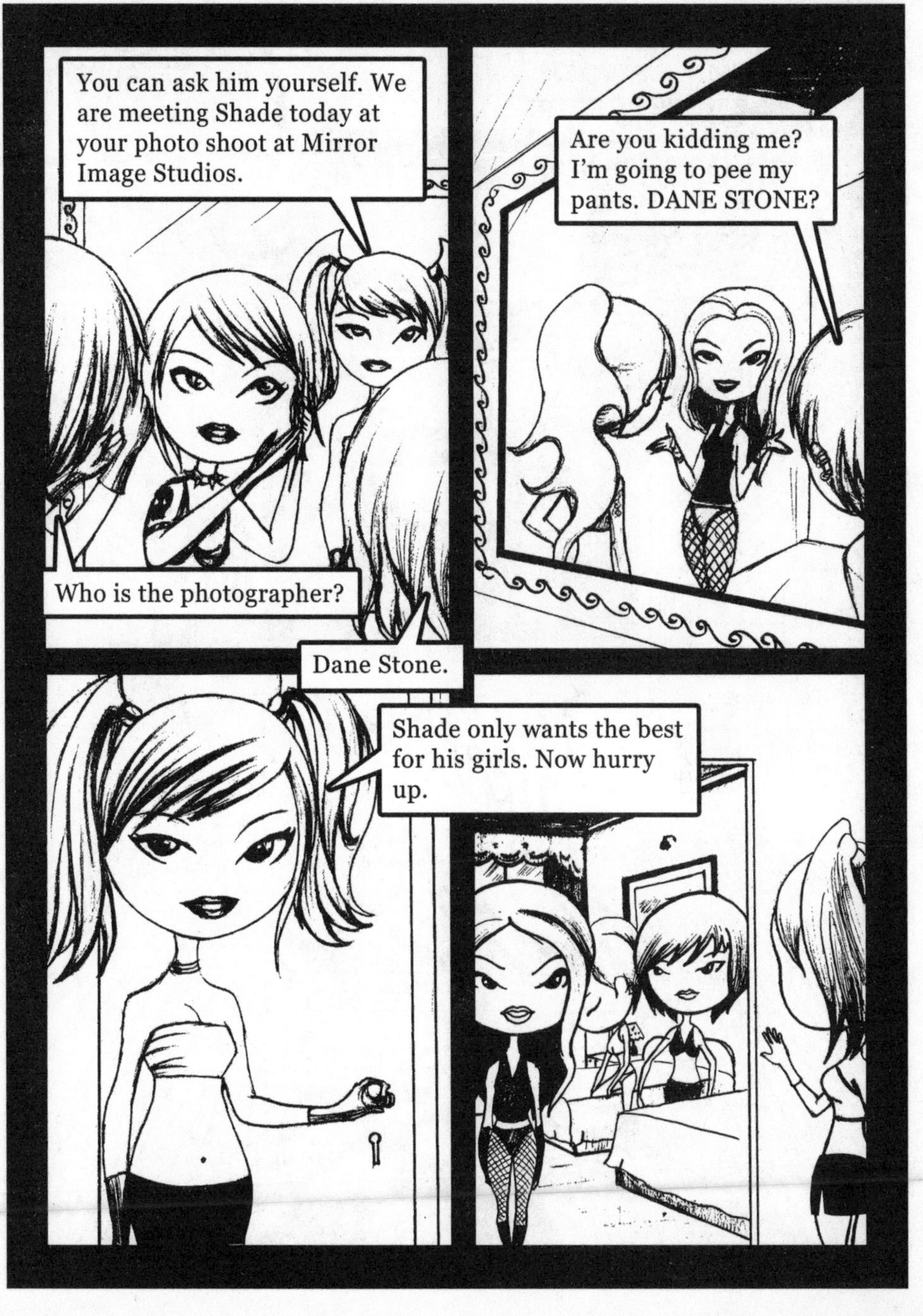
Who is the photographer?
You can ask him yourself. We are meeting Shade today at your photo shoot at Mirror Image Studios.
Are you kidding me? I'm going to pee my pants. DANE STONE?
Dane Stone.
Shade only wants the best for his girls. Now hurry up.

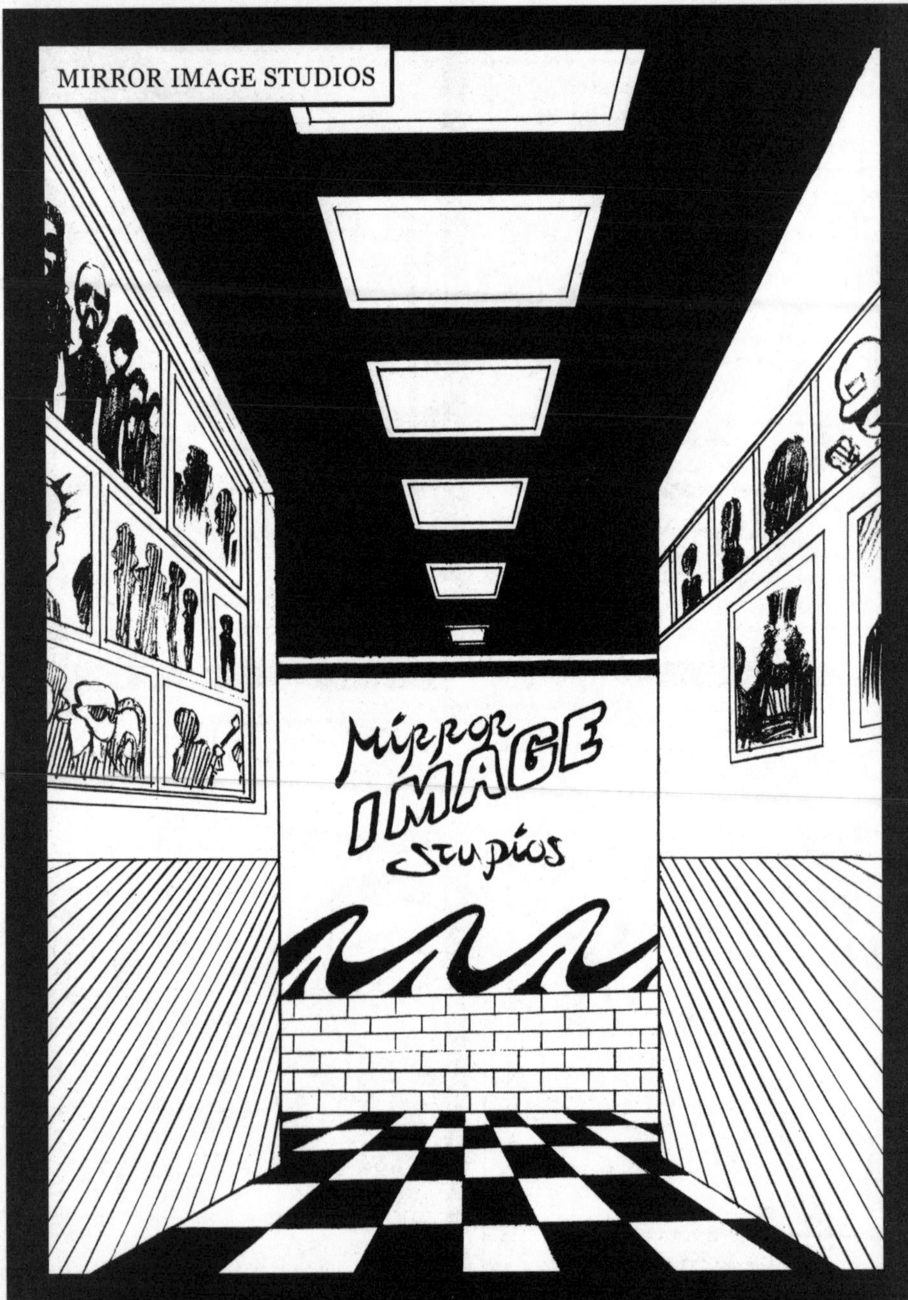
MIRROR IMAGE STUDIOS
Mirror
IMAGE
Studios

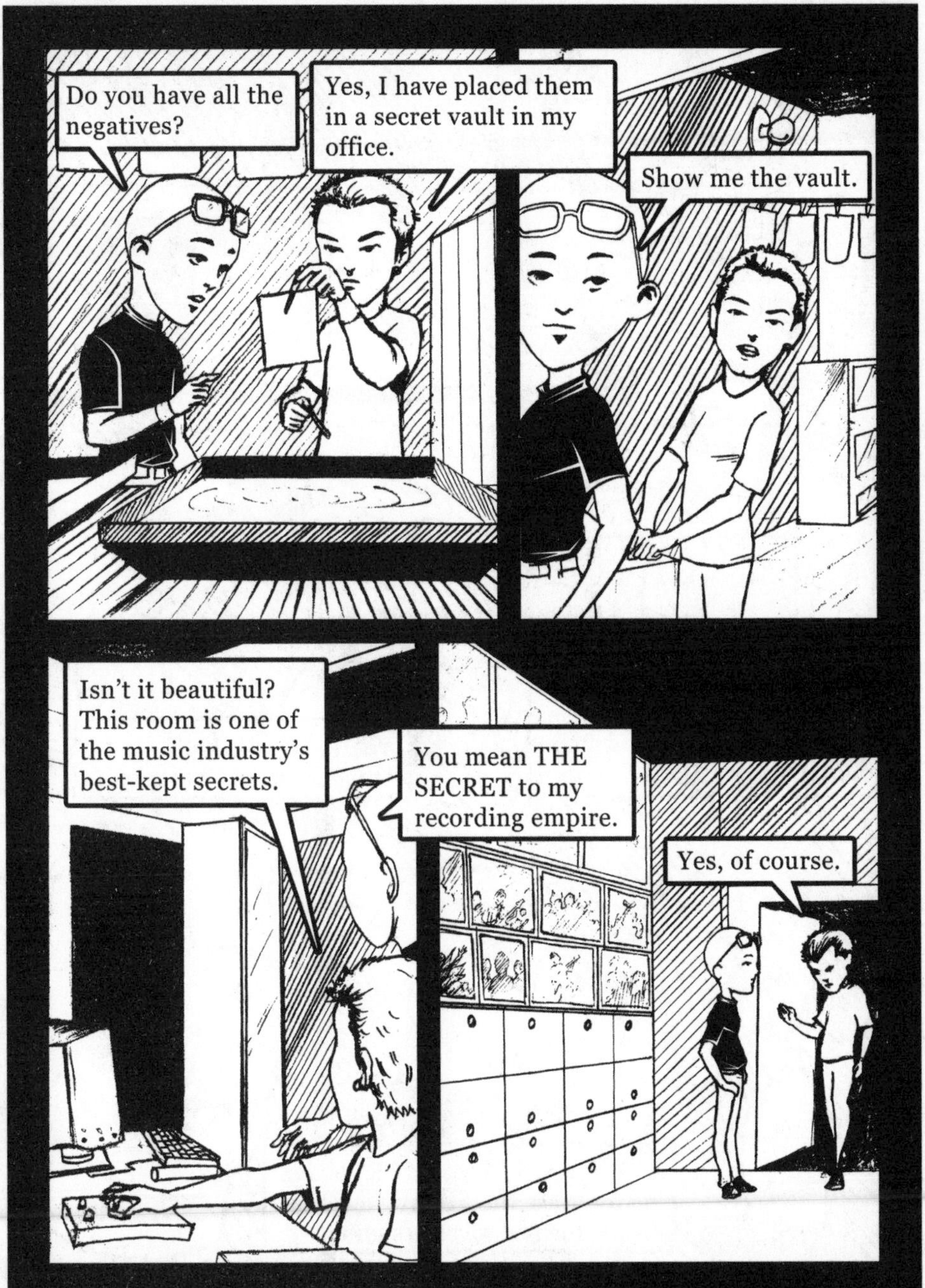
Do you have all the negatives?
Yes, I have placed them in a secret vault in my office.
Show me the vault.
Isn't it beautiful? This room is one of the music industry's best-kept secrets.
You mean THE SECRET to my recording empire.
Yes, of course.

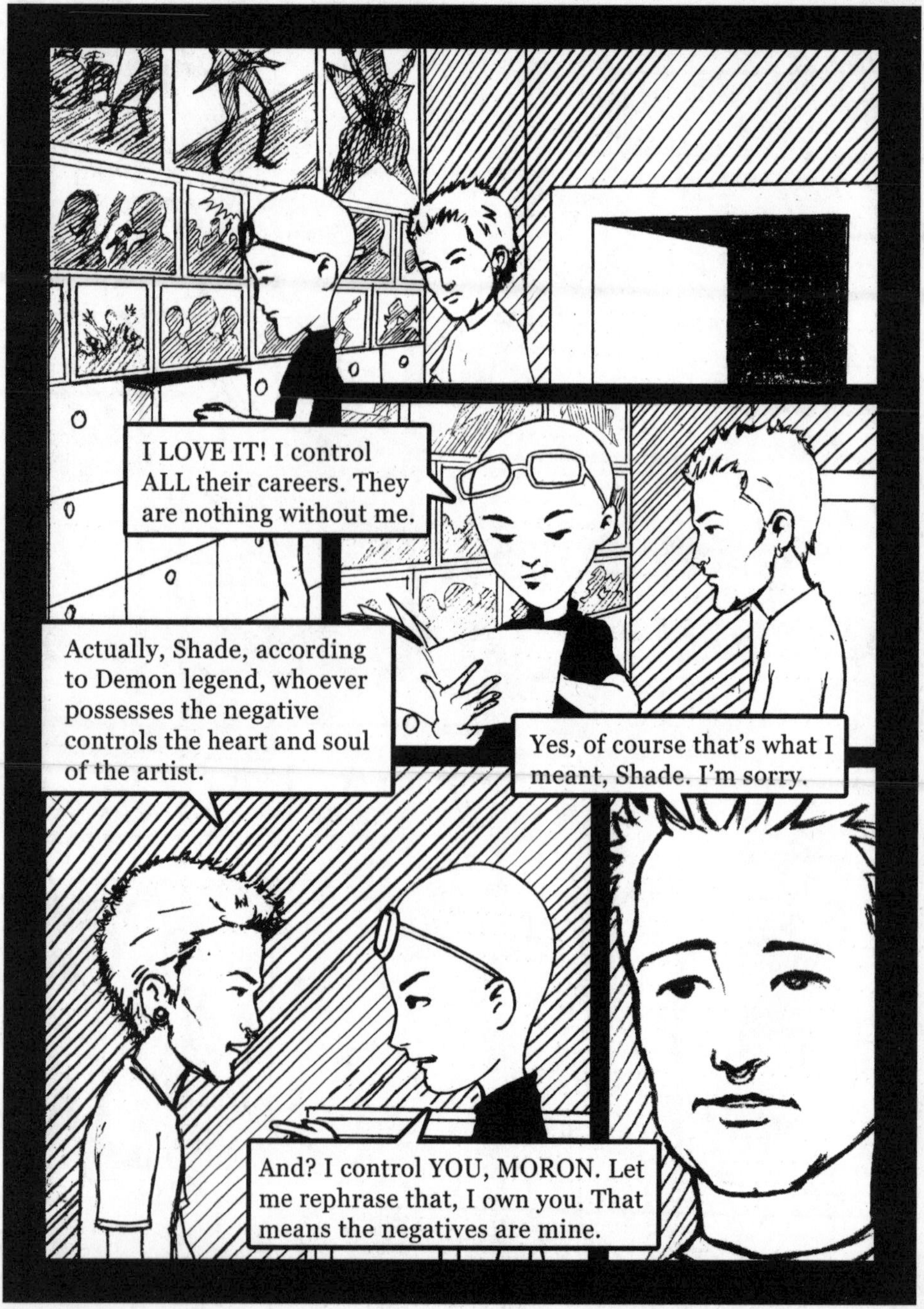
I LOVE IT! I control ALL their careers. They are nothing without me.
Actually, Shade, according to Demon legend, whoever possesses the negative controls the heart and soul of the artist.
Yes, of course that's what I meant, Shade. I'm sorry.
And? I control YOU, MORON. Let me rephrase that, I own you. That means the negatives are mine.

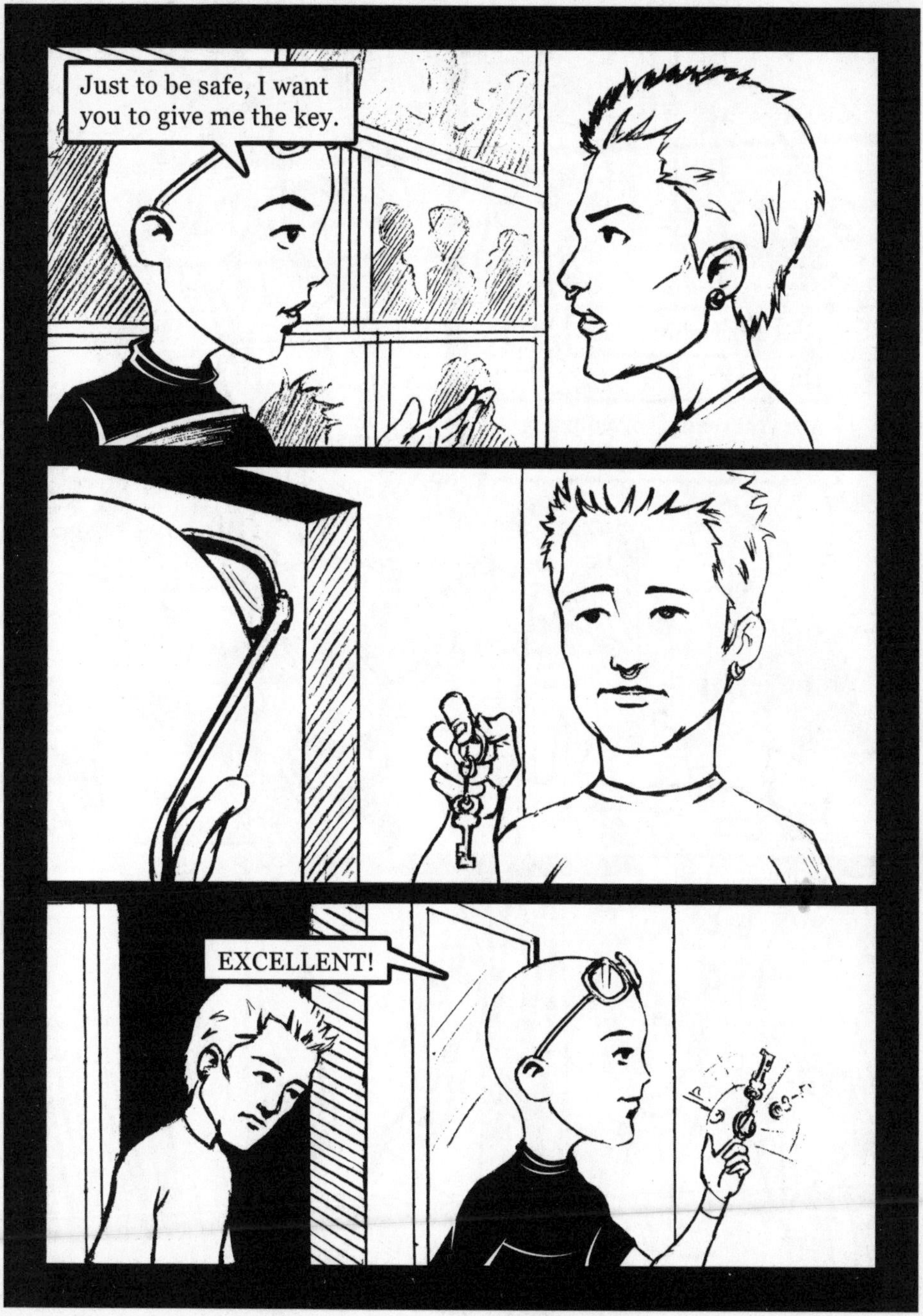
Just to be safe, I want you to give me the key.
EXCELLENT!

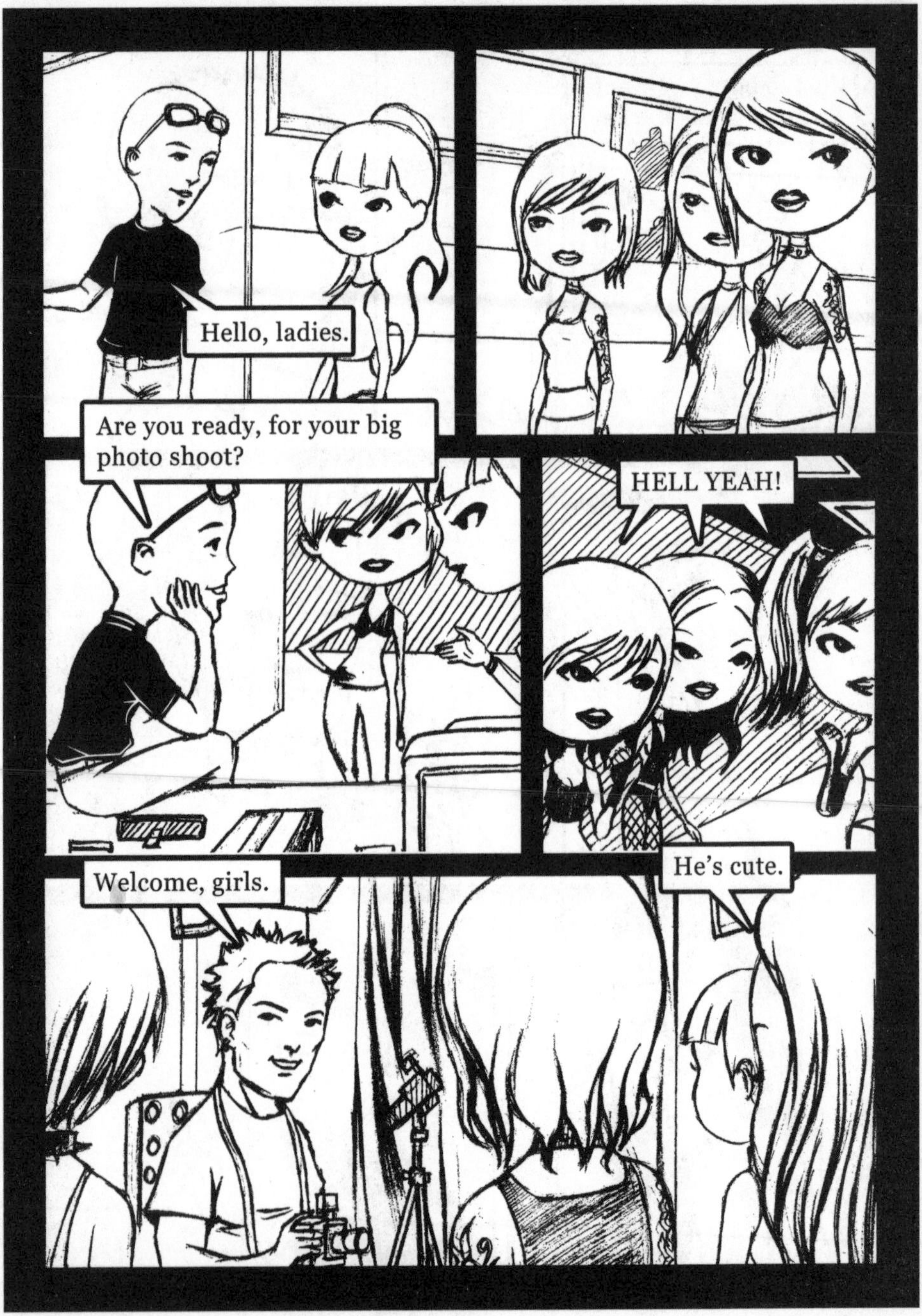
Hello, ladies.
Are you ready, for your big photo shoot?
HELL YEAH!
Welcome, girls.
He's cute.

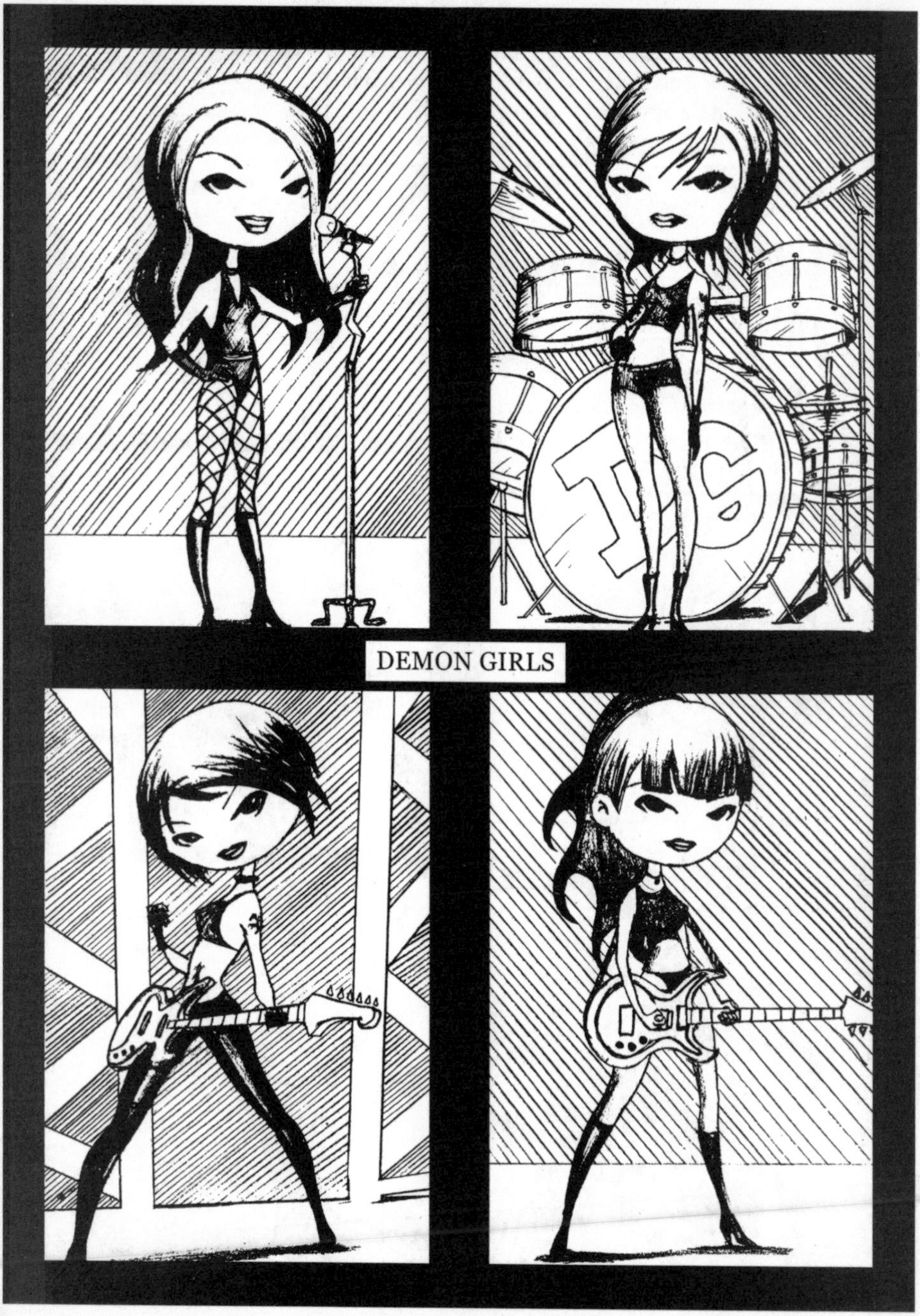
DG
DEMON GIRLS

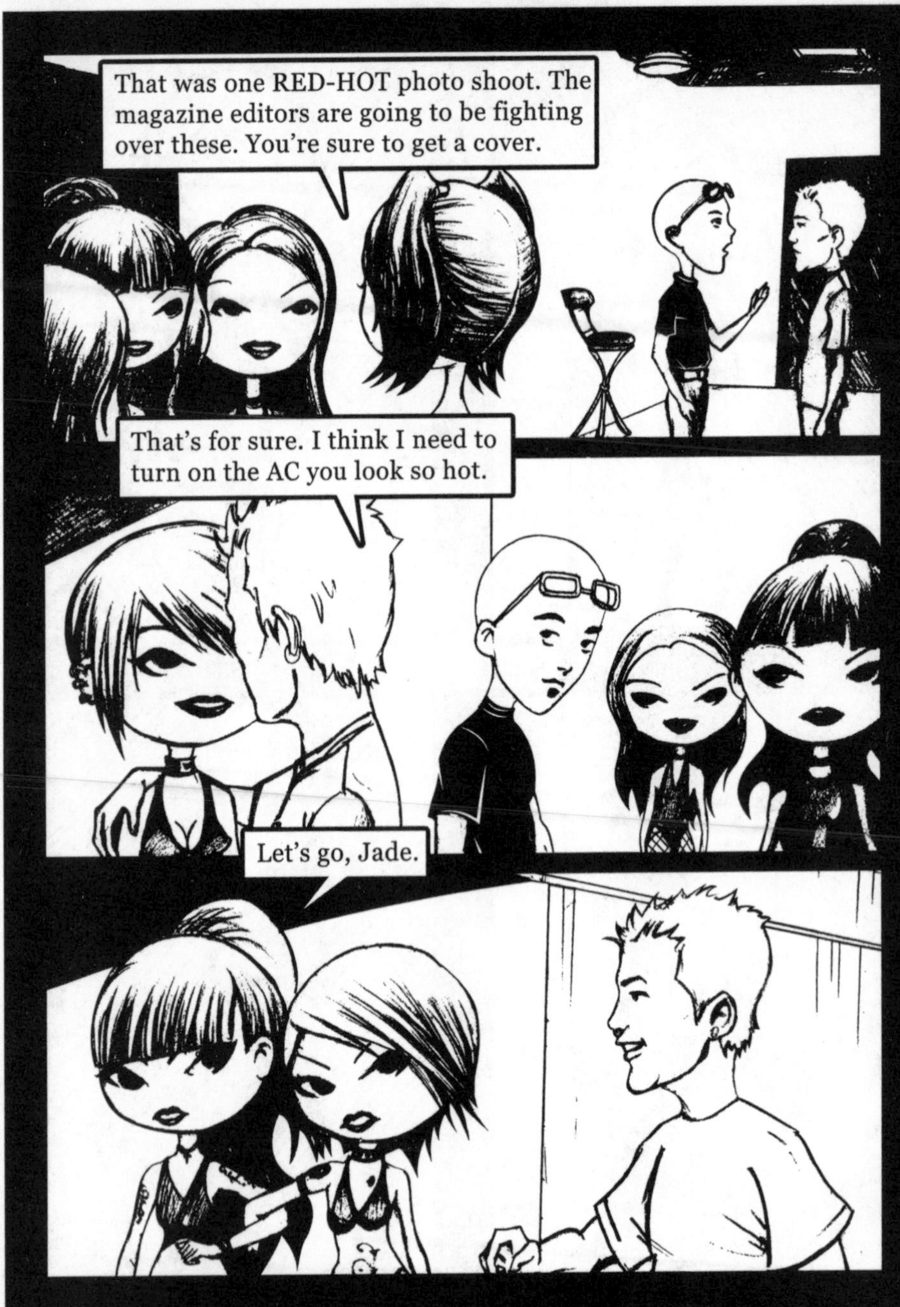
That was one RED-HOT photo shoot. The magazine editors are going to be fighting over these. You're sure to get a cover.
That's for sure. I think I need to turn on the AC you look so hot.
Let's go, Jade.

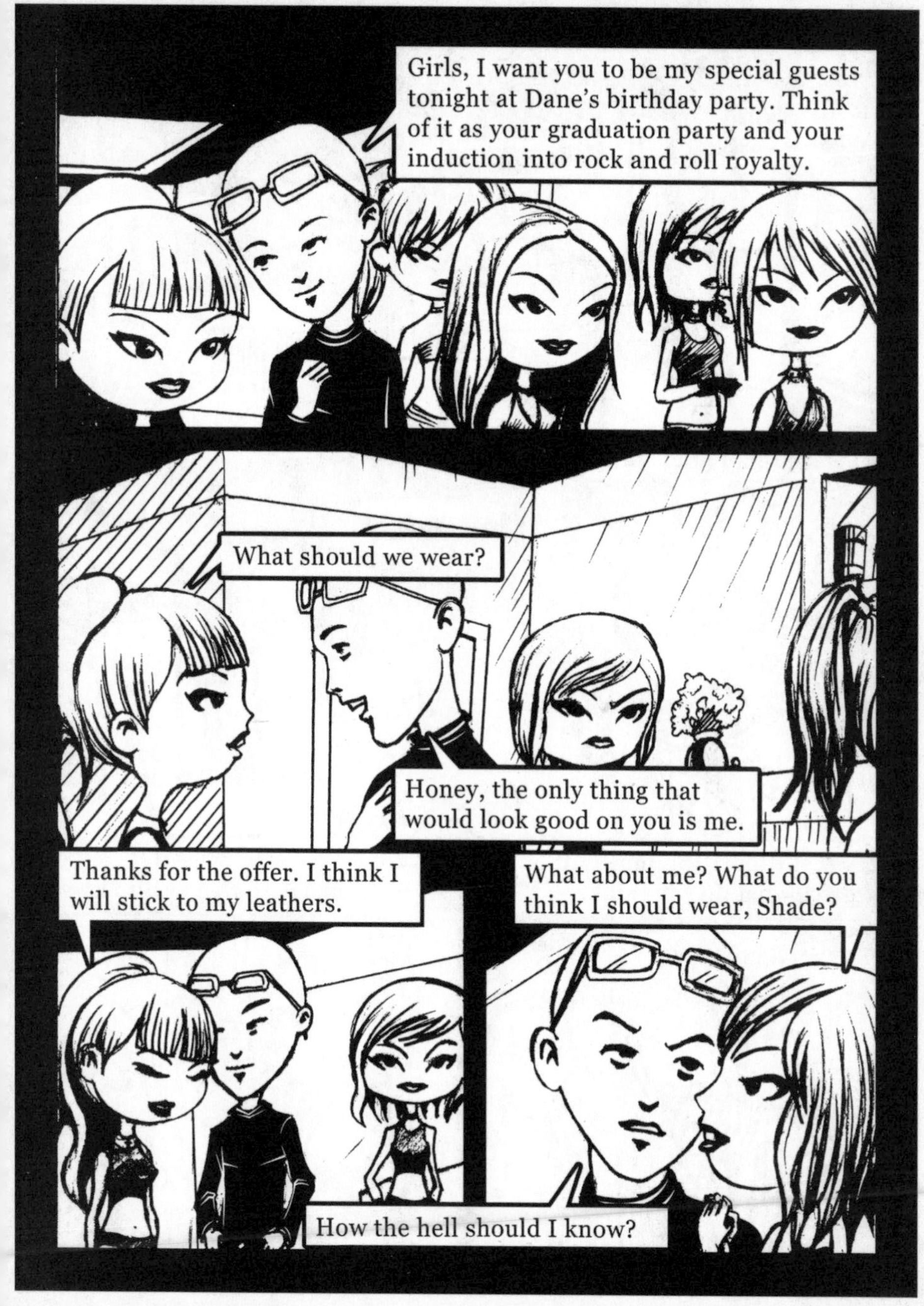
Girls, I want you to be my special guests tonight at Dane's birthday party. Think of it as your graduation party and your induction into rock and roll royalty.
What should we wear?
Honey, the only thing that would look good on you is me.
Thanks for the offer. I think I will stick to my leathers.
What about me? What do you think I should wear, Shade?
How the hell should I know?

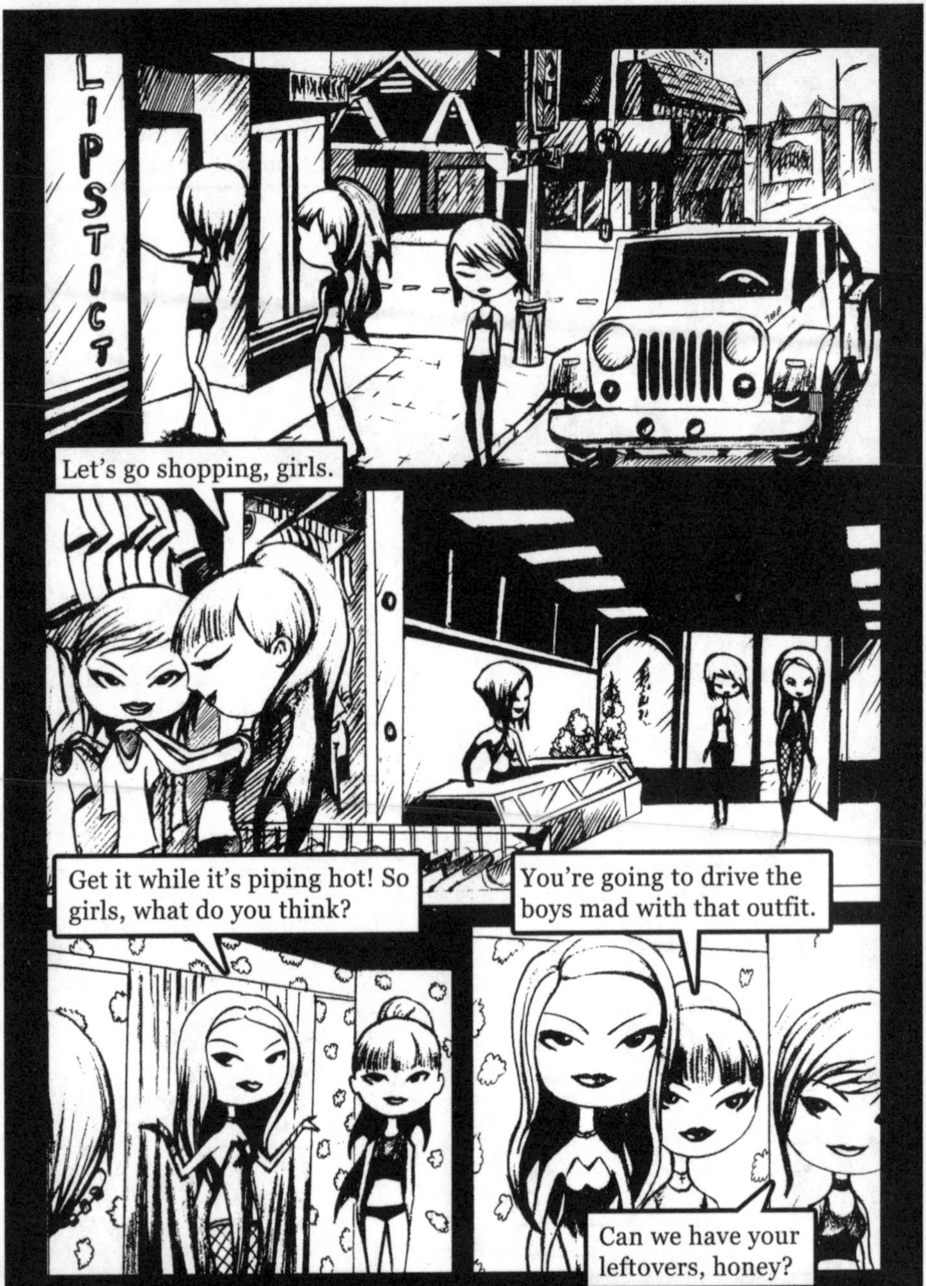
Let’s go shopping, girls.
Get it while it’s piping hot! So girls, what do you think?
You’re going to drive the boys mad with that outfit.
Can we have your leftovers, honey?

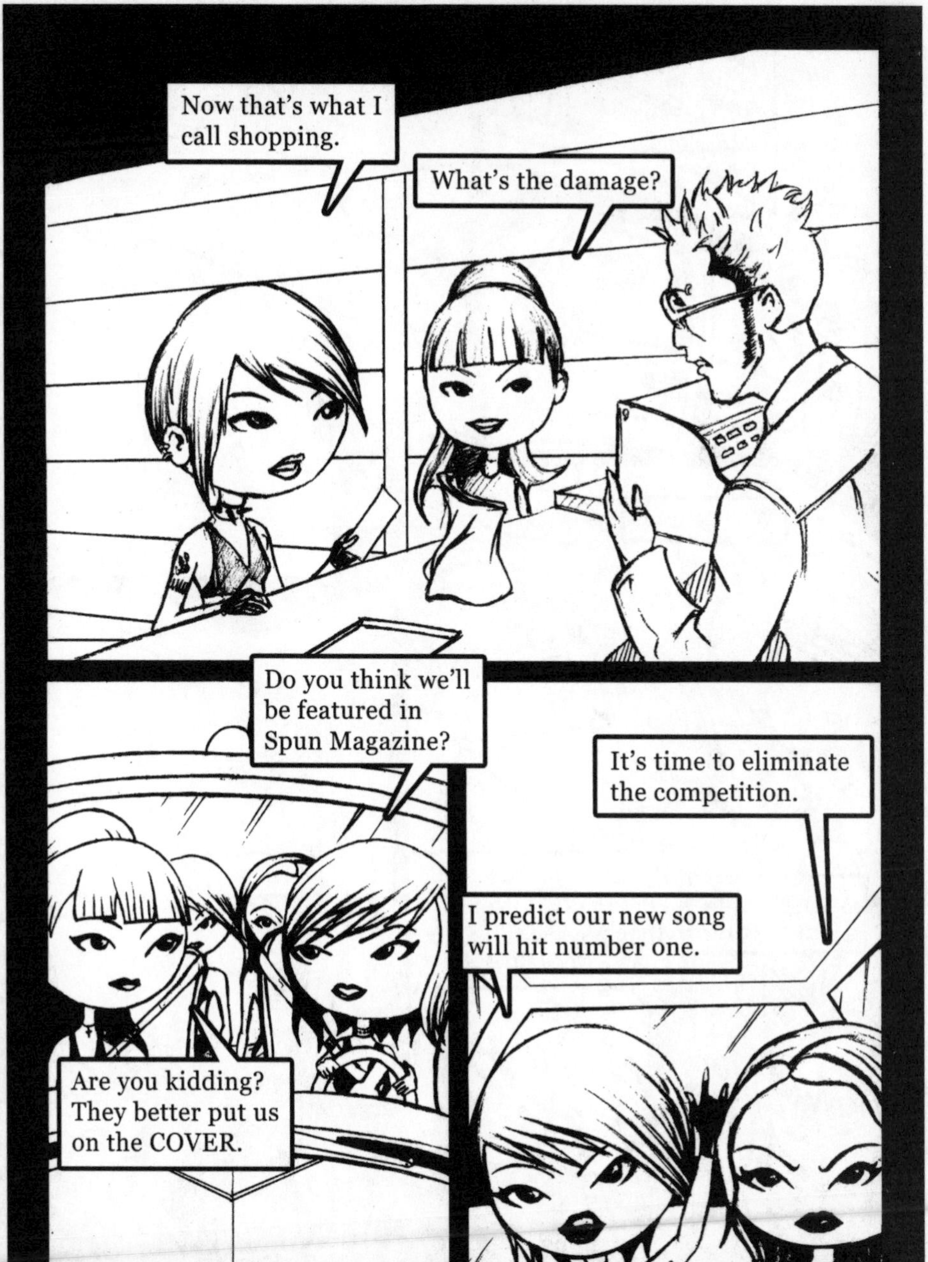
Now that's what I call shopping.
What's the damage?
Do you think we'll be featured in Spun Magazine?
Are you kidding? They better put us on the COVER.
It's time to eliminate the competition.
I predict our new song will hit number one.

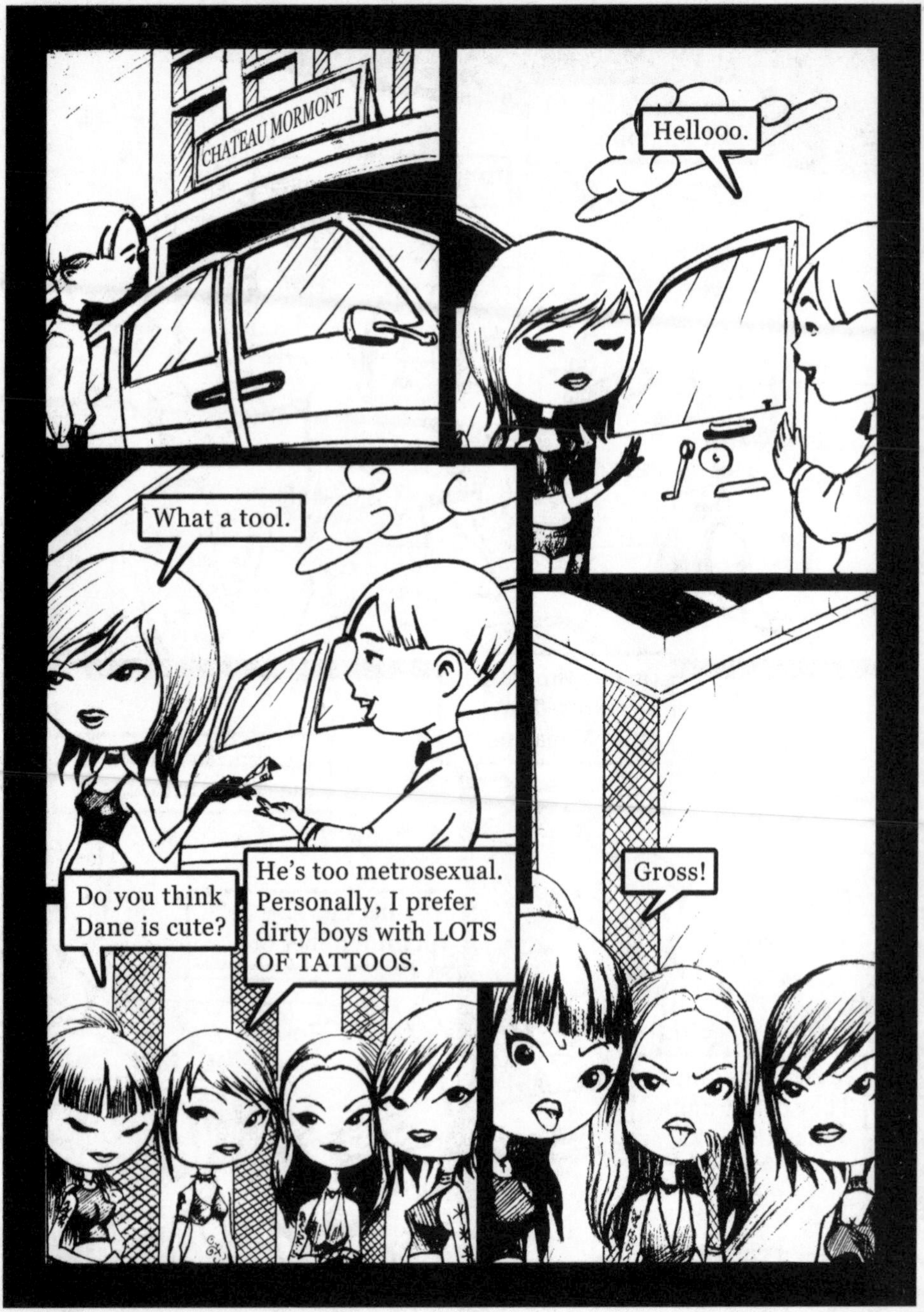
CHATEAU MORMONT
Hellooo.
What a tool.
Do you think Dane is cute?
He's too metrosexual. Personally, I prefer dirty boys with LOTS OF TATTOOS.
Gross!

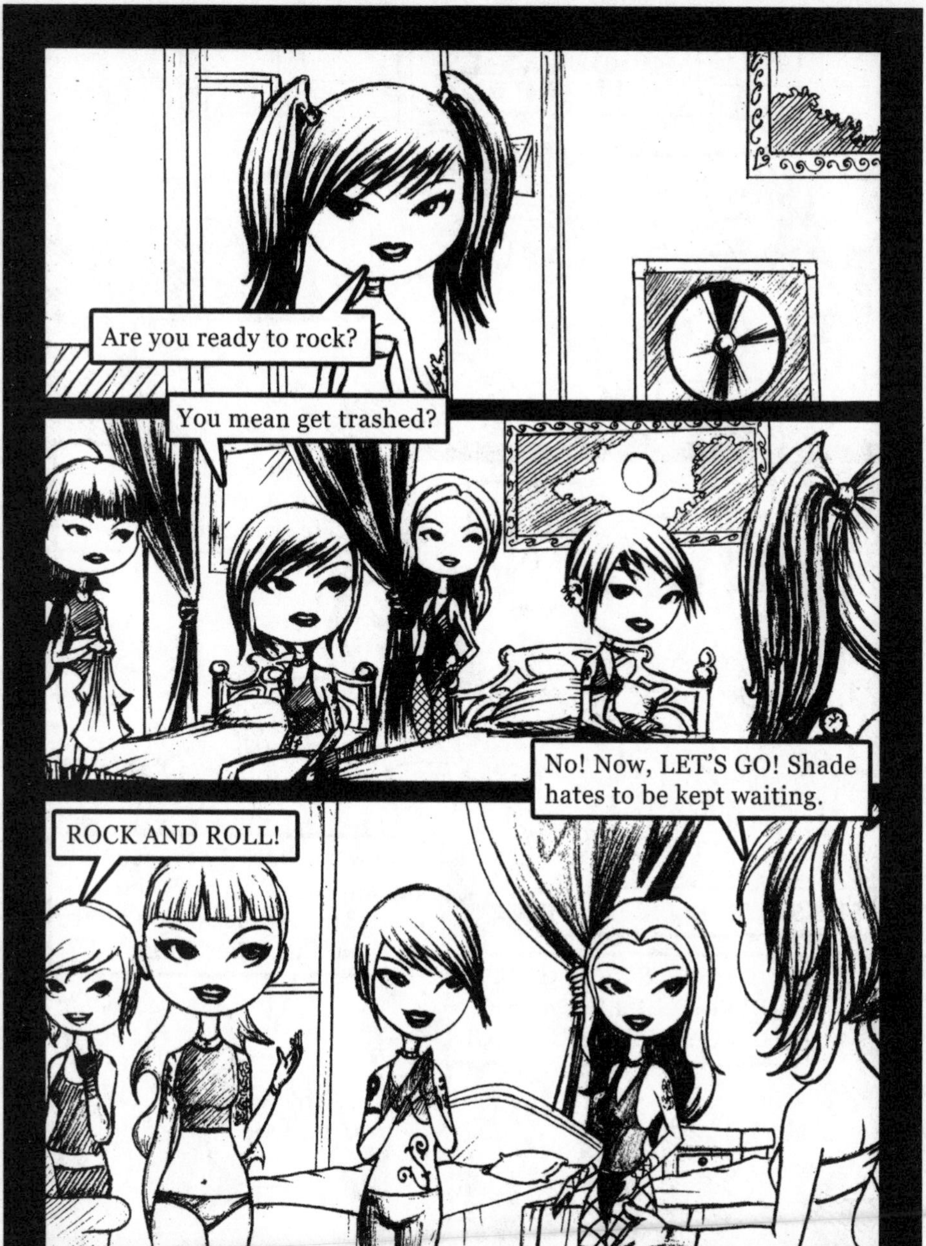
Are you ready to rock?
You mean get trashed?
No! Now, LET'S GO! Shade hates to be kept waiting.
ROCK AND ROLL!

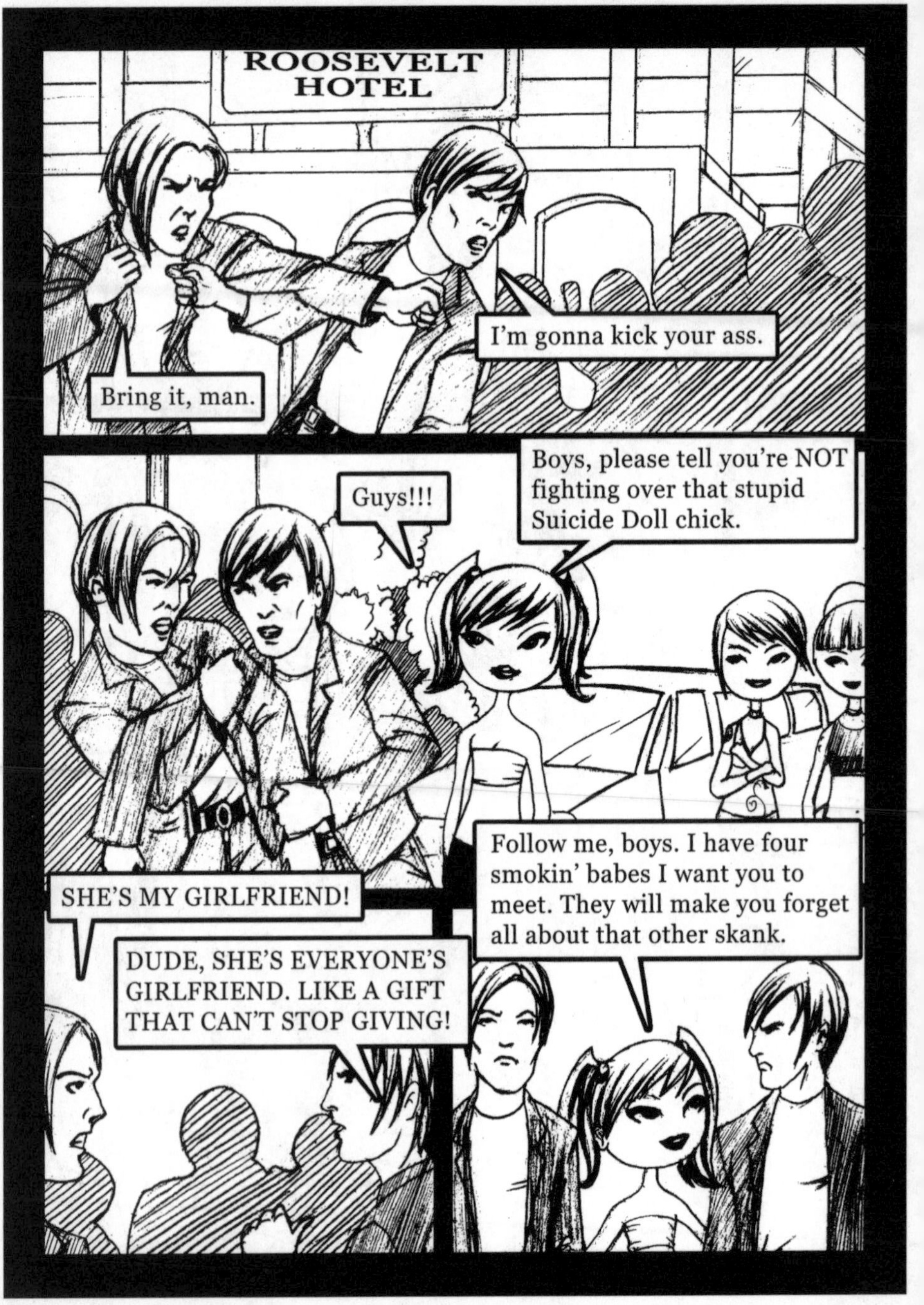
ROOSEVELT HOTEL
I'm gonna kick your ass.
Bring it, man.
Guys!!!
Boys, please tell you're NOT fighting over that stupid Suicide Doll chick.
SHE'S MY GIRLFRIEND!
DUDE, SHE'S EVERYONE'S GIRLFRIEND. LIKE A GIFT THAT CAN'T STOP GIVING!
Follow me, boys. I have four smokin' babes I want you to meet. They will make you forget all about that other skank.

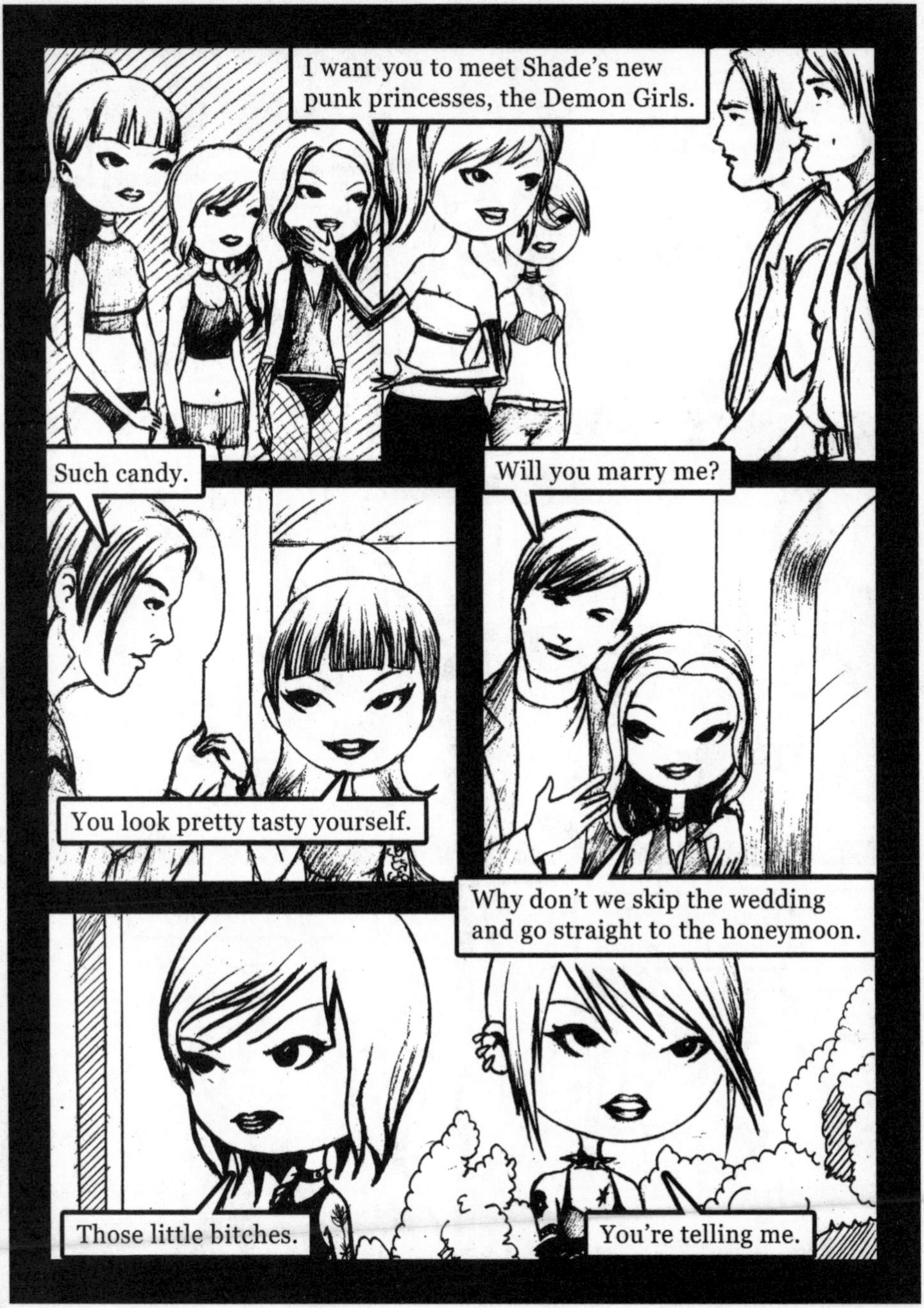
I want you to meet Shade's new punk princesses, the Demon Girls.
Such candy.
You look pretty tasty yourself.
Will you marry me?
Why don't we skip the wedding and go straight to the honeymoon.
Those little bitches.
You're telling me.

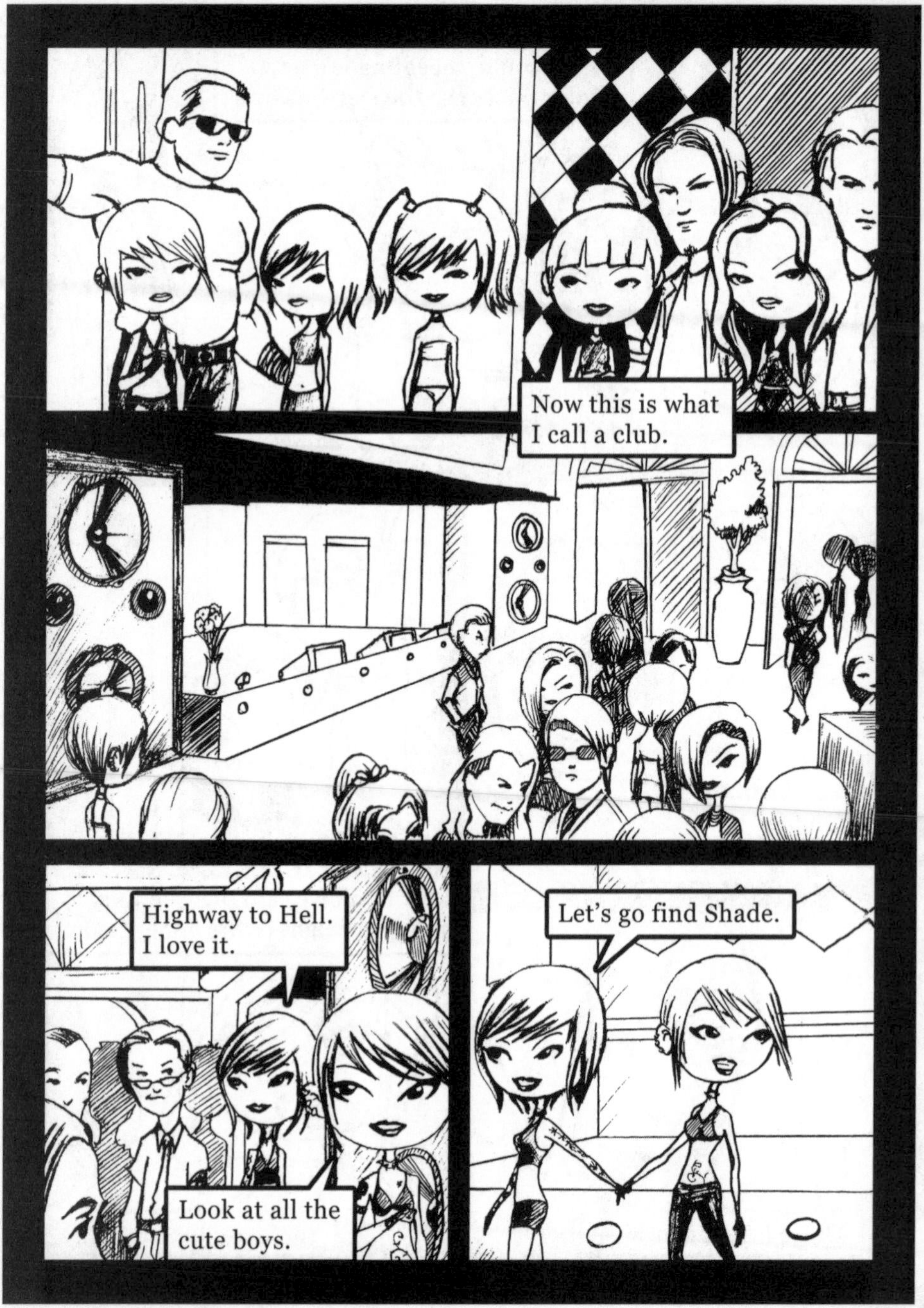
Now this is what I call a club.
Highway to Hell. I love it.
Look at all the cute boys.
Let's go find Shade.

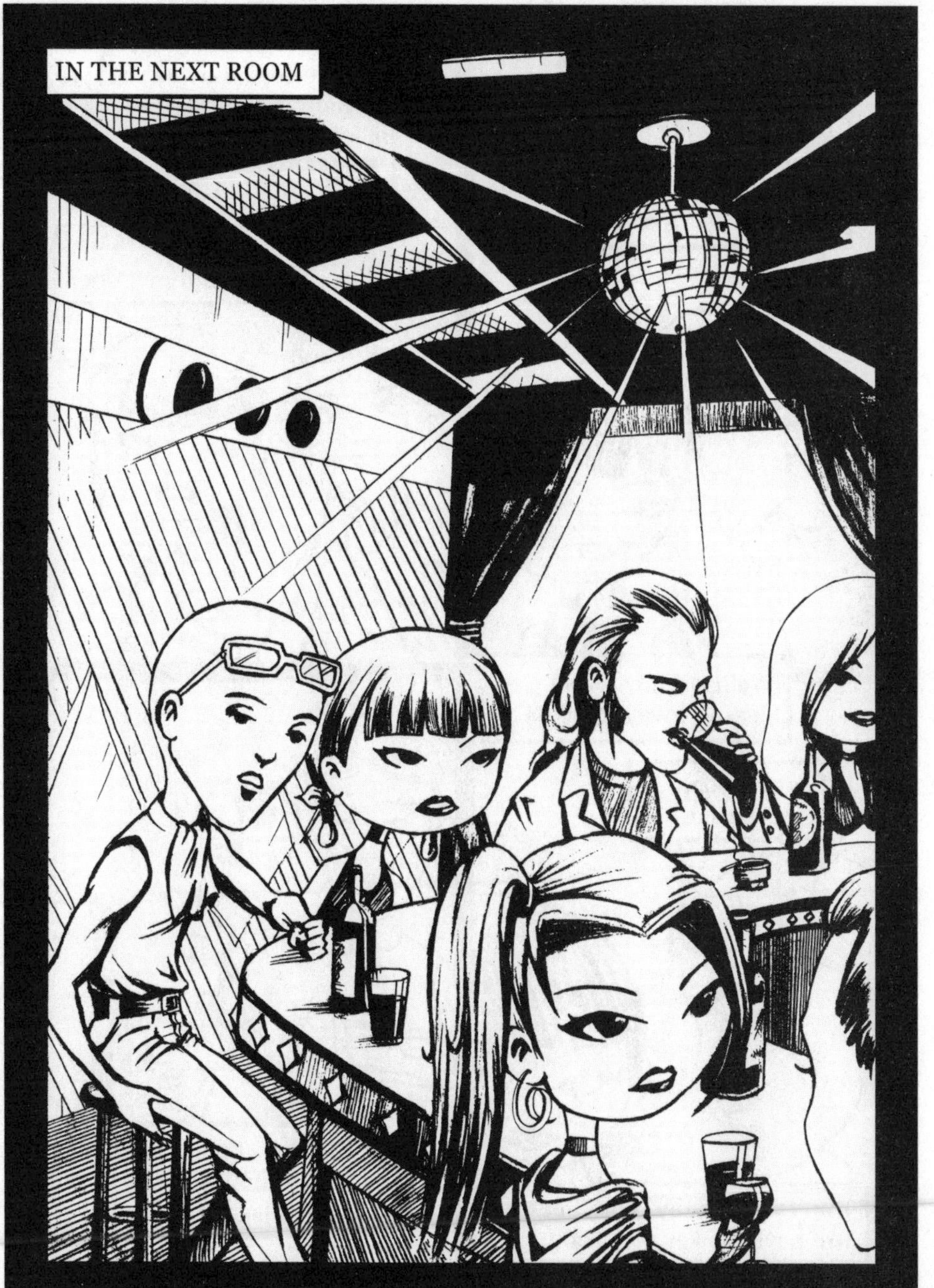
IN THE NEXT ROOM

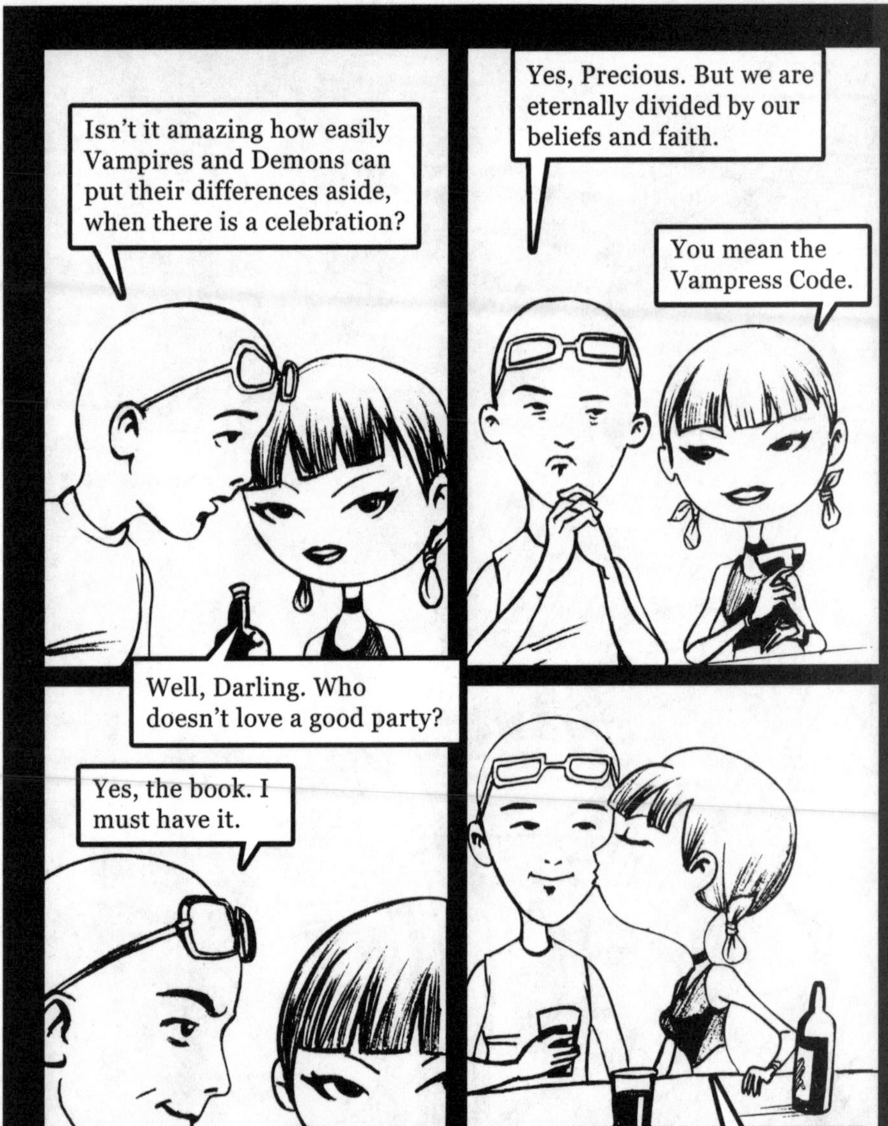
Isn't it amazing how easily Vampires and Demons can put their differences aside, when there is a celebration?
Well, Darling. Who doesn't love a good party?
Yes, Precious. But we are eternally divided by our beliefs and faith.
You mean the Vampress Code.
Yes, the book. I must have it.
Don't worry baby. I predict we will have the key very soon.
I know. I know. Soon everything will come into play.

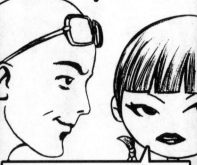

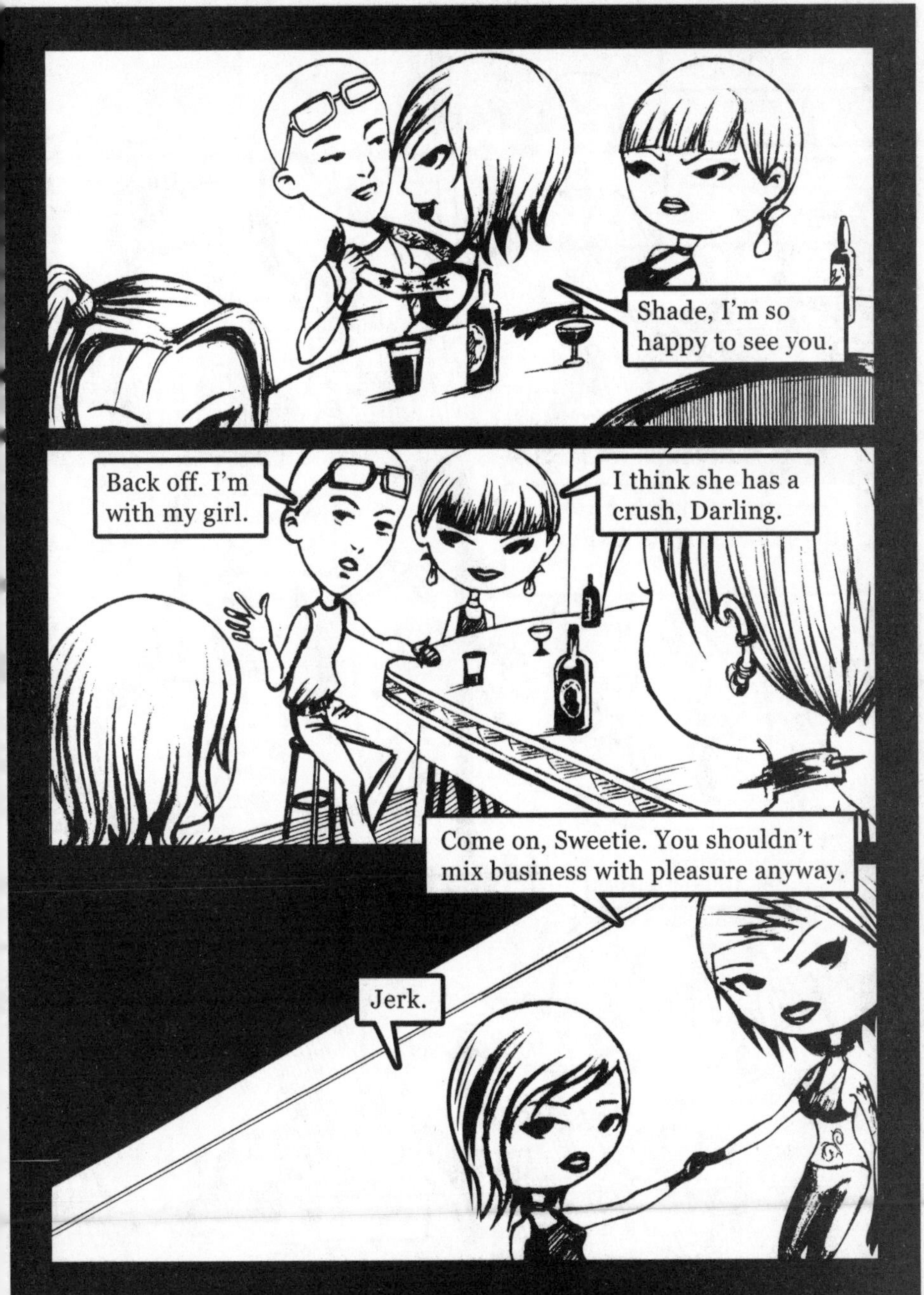
Shade, I'm so happy to see you.
Back off. I'm with my girl.
I think she has a crush, Darling.
Come on, Sweetie. You shouldn't mix business with pleasure anyway.
Jerk.

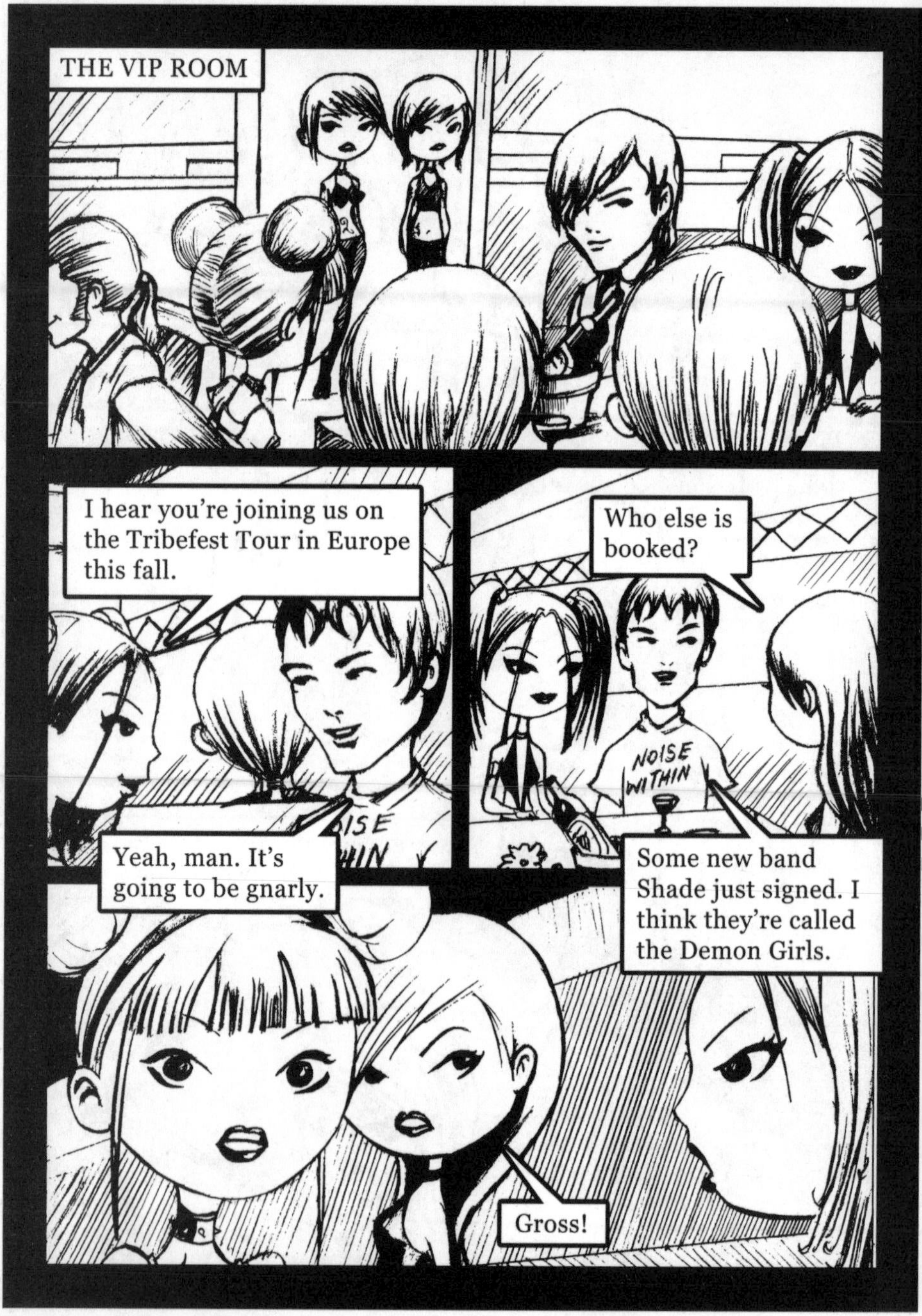
THE VIP ROOM
I hear you're joining us on the Tribefest Tour in Europe this fall.
Yeah, man. It's going to be gnarly.
Who else is booked?
NOISE WITHIN
Some new band Shade just signed. I think they're called the Demon Girls.
Gross!

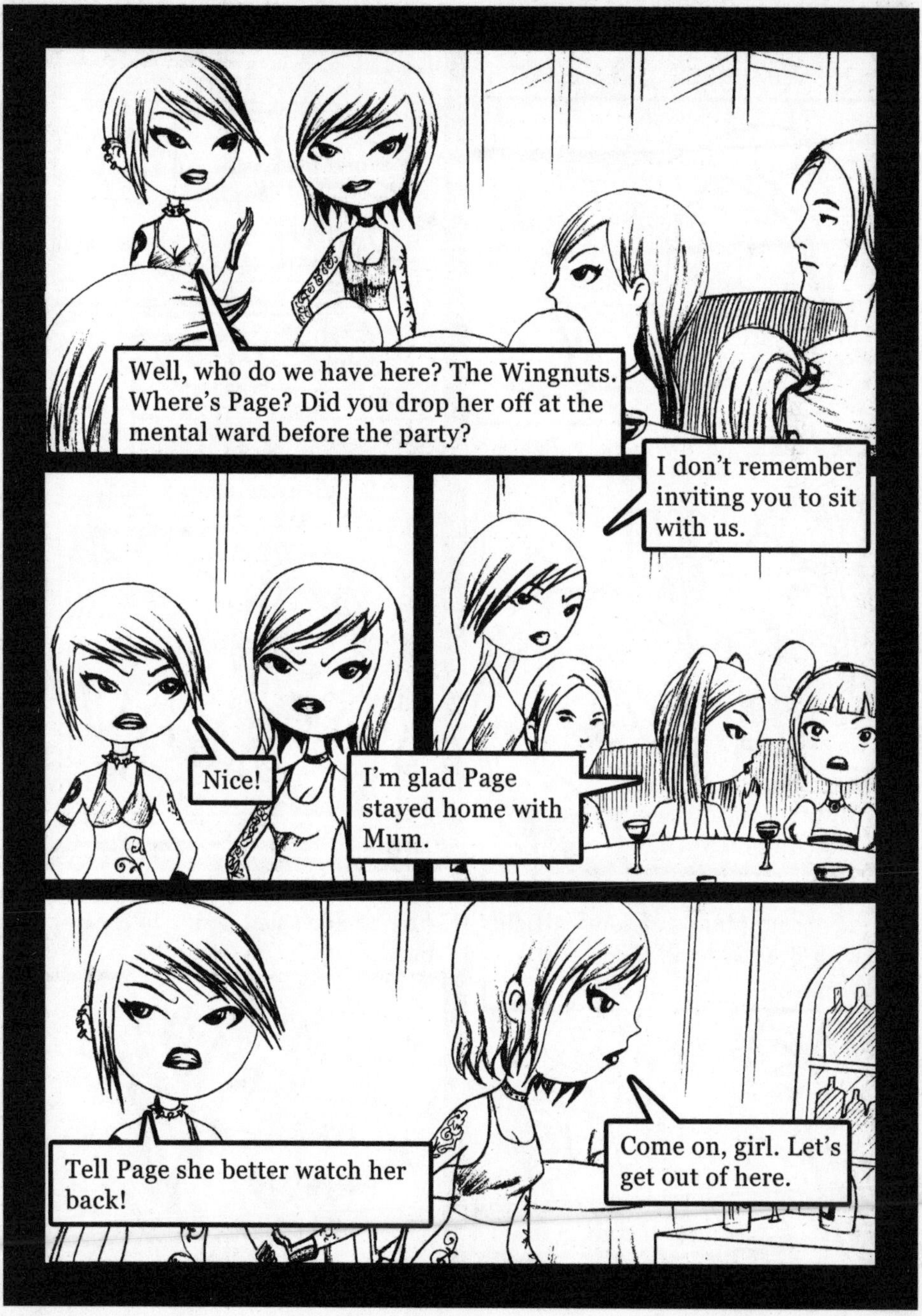
Well, who do we have here? The Wingnuts. Where's Page? Did you drop her off at the mental ward before the party?
Nice!
I'm glad Page stayed home with Mum.
I don't remember inviting you to sit with us.
Tell Page she better watch her back!
Come on, girl. Let's get out of here.

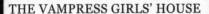

THE VAMPRESS GIRLS' HOUSE
POPBYTES.COM.
Wow!
Are you okay, Page?
Mum, have you seen these photos yet?
WHAT A JERK! Shade must have sent photos of your catfight with Brandy to all the gossip blogs.
I'm so embarrassed.
POPBYTES.CO
Don't worry. Everything will be fine. Shade's just trying to create buzz about his new band.

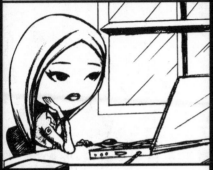

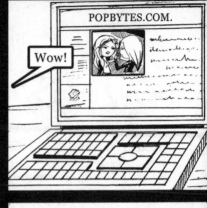

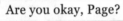

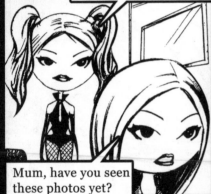

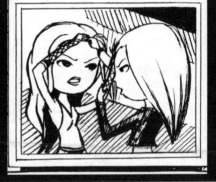

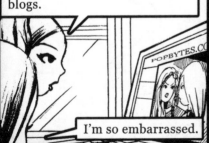

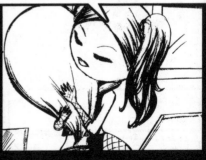

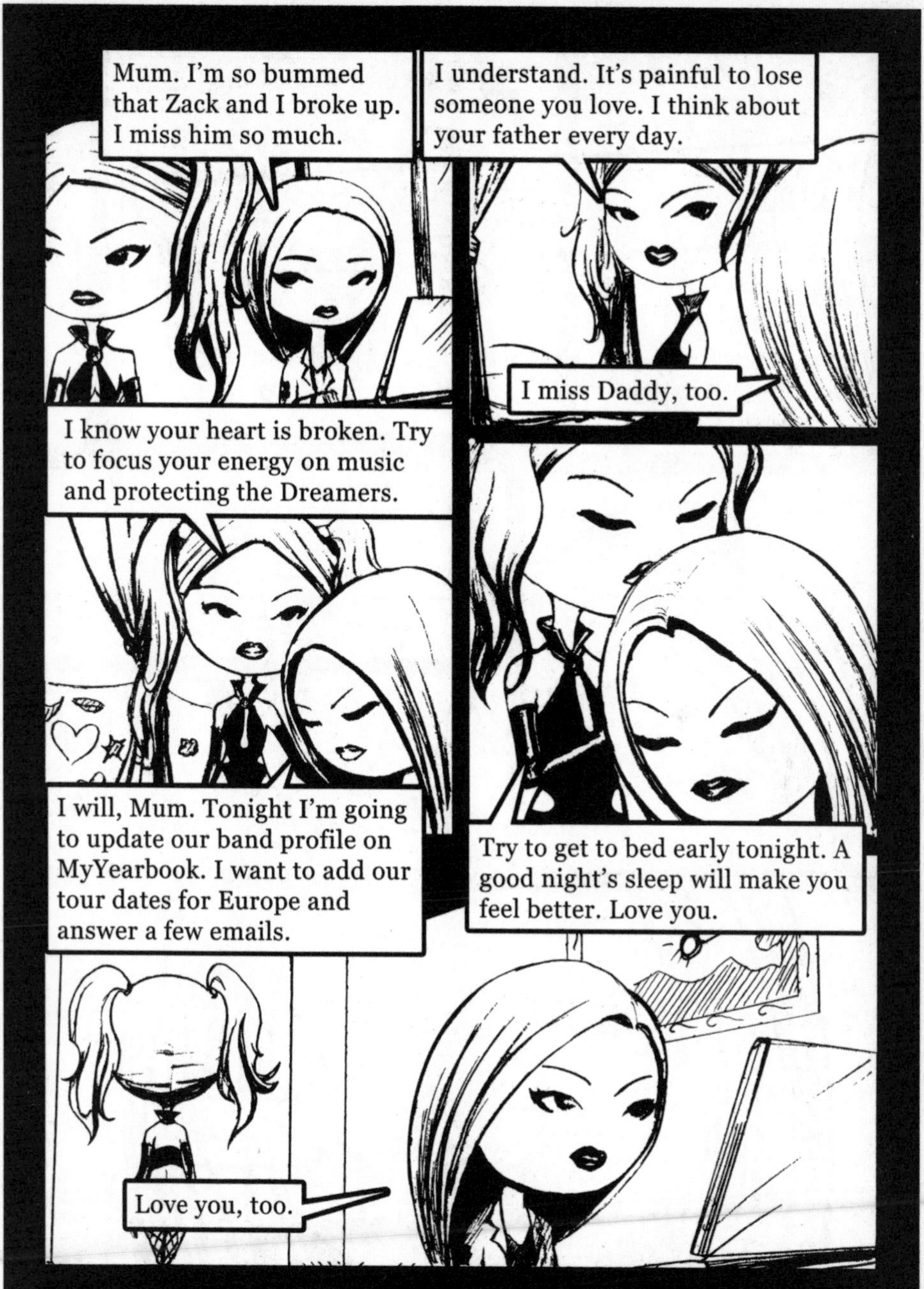
Mum. I'm so bummed that Zack and I broke up. I miss him so much.
I understand. It's painful to lose someone you love. I think about your father every day.
I miss Daddy, too.
I know your heart is broken. Try to focus your energy on music and protecting the Dreamers.
I will, Mum. Tonight I'm going to update our band profile on MyYearbook. I want to add our tour dates for Europe and answer a few emails.
Try to get to bed early tonight. A good night's sleep will make you feel better. Love you.
Love you, too.

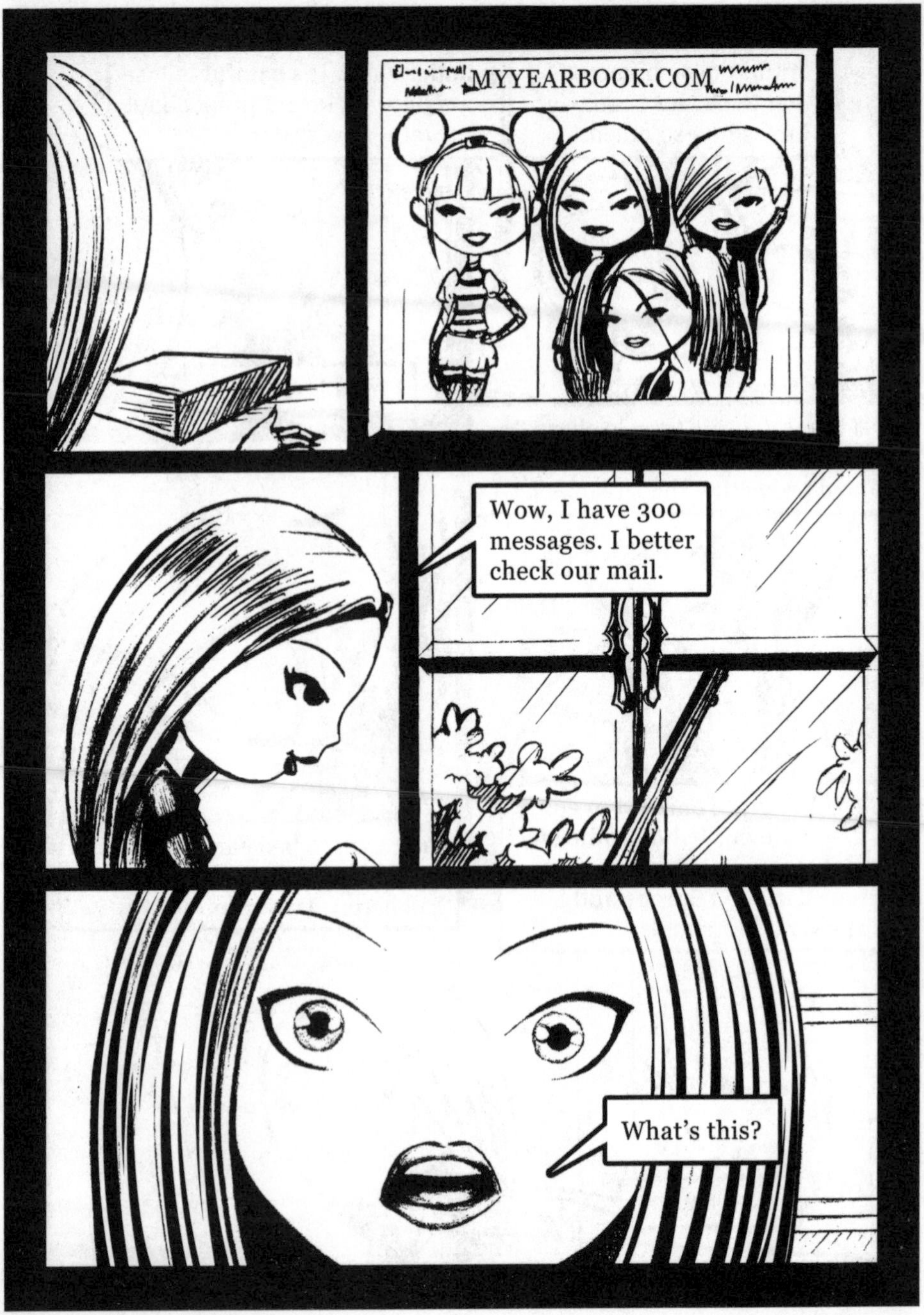
MYYEARBOOK.COM
Wow, I have 300 messages. I better check our mail.
What's this?

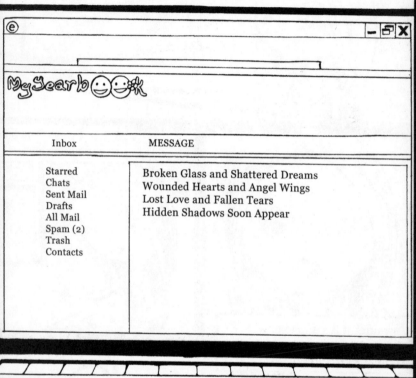

MySearbook

| Inbox | MESSAGE |

Starred
Chats
Sent Mail
Drafts
All Mail
Spam (2)
Trash
Contacts

Broken Glass and Shattered Dreams
Wounded Hearts and Angel Wings
Lost Love and Fallen Tears
Hidden Shadows Soon Appear

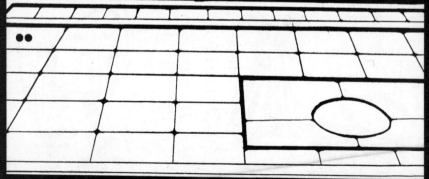

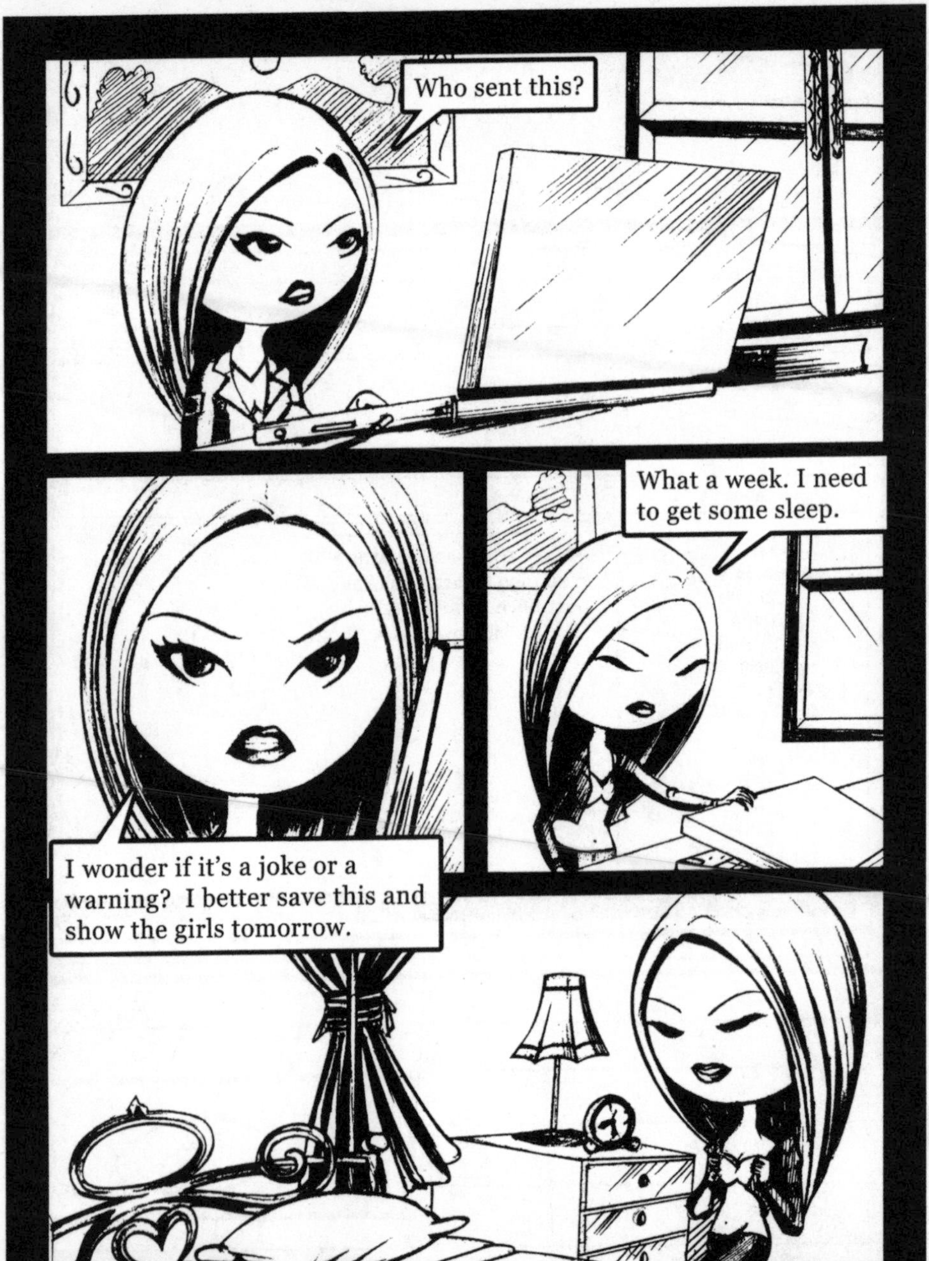
Who sent this?
I wonder if it's a joke or a warning? I better save this and show the girls tomorrow.
What a week. I need to get some sleep.

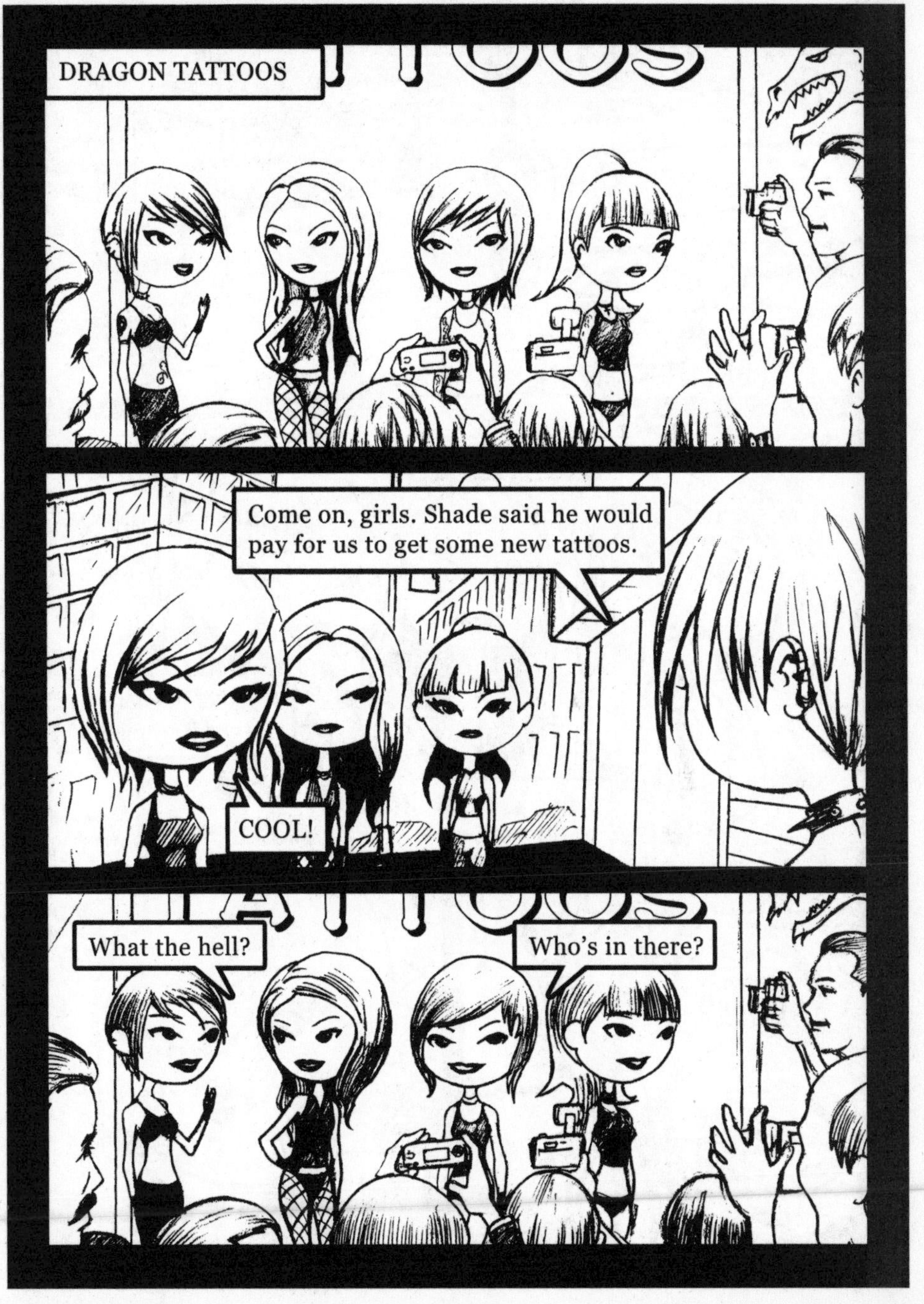
DRAGON TATTOOS
Come on, girls. Shade said he would pay for us to get some new tattoos.
COOL!
What the hell?
Who's in there?

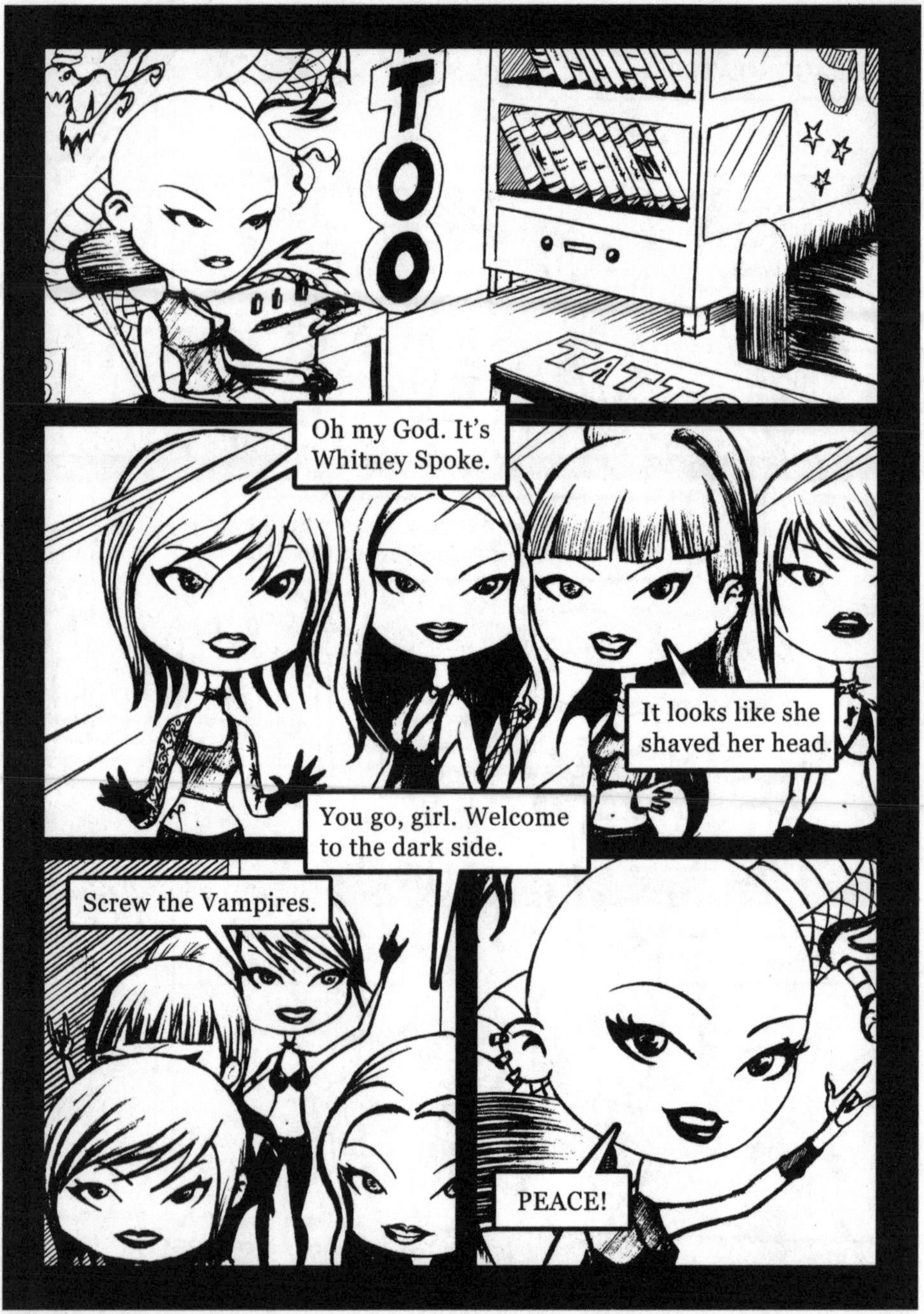
Oh my God. It's Whitney Spoke.
It looks like she shaved her head.
You go, girl. Welcome to the dark side.
Screw the Vampires.
PEACE!

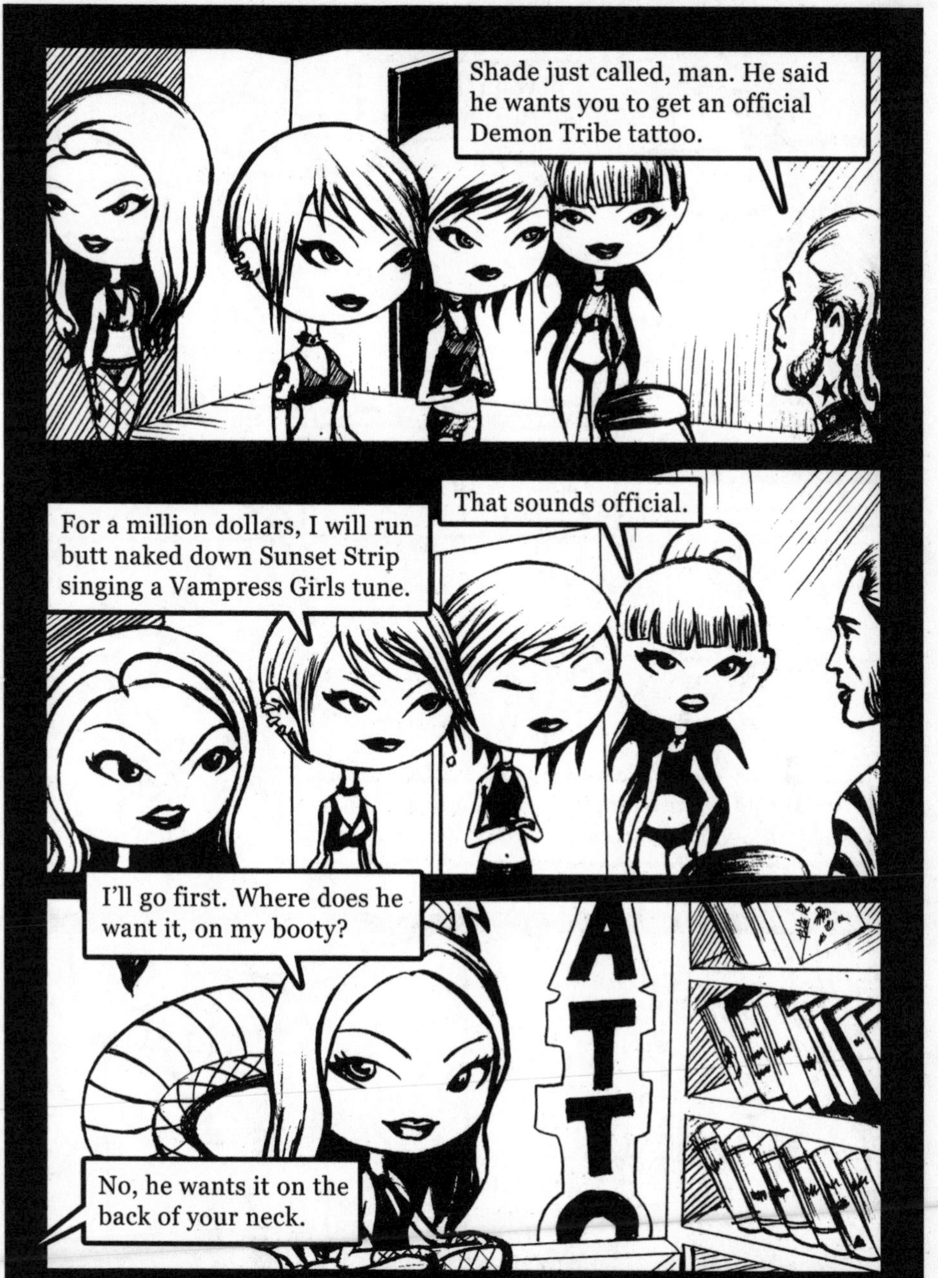
Shade just called, man. He said he wants you to get an official Demon Tribe tattoo.
For a million dollars, I will run butt naked down Sunset Strip singing a Vampress Girls tune.
That sounds official.
I'll go first. Where does he want it, on my booty?
ATTO
No, he wants it on the back of your neck.

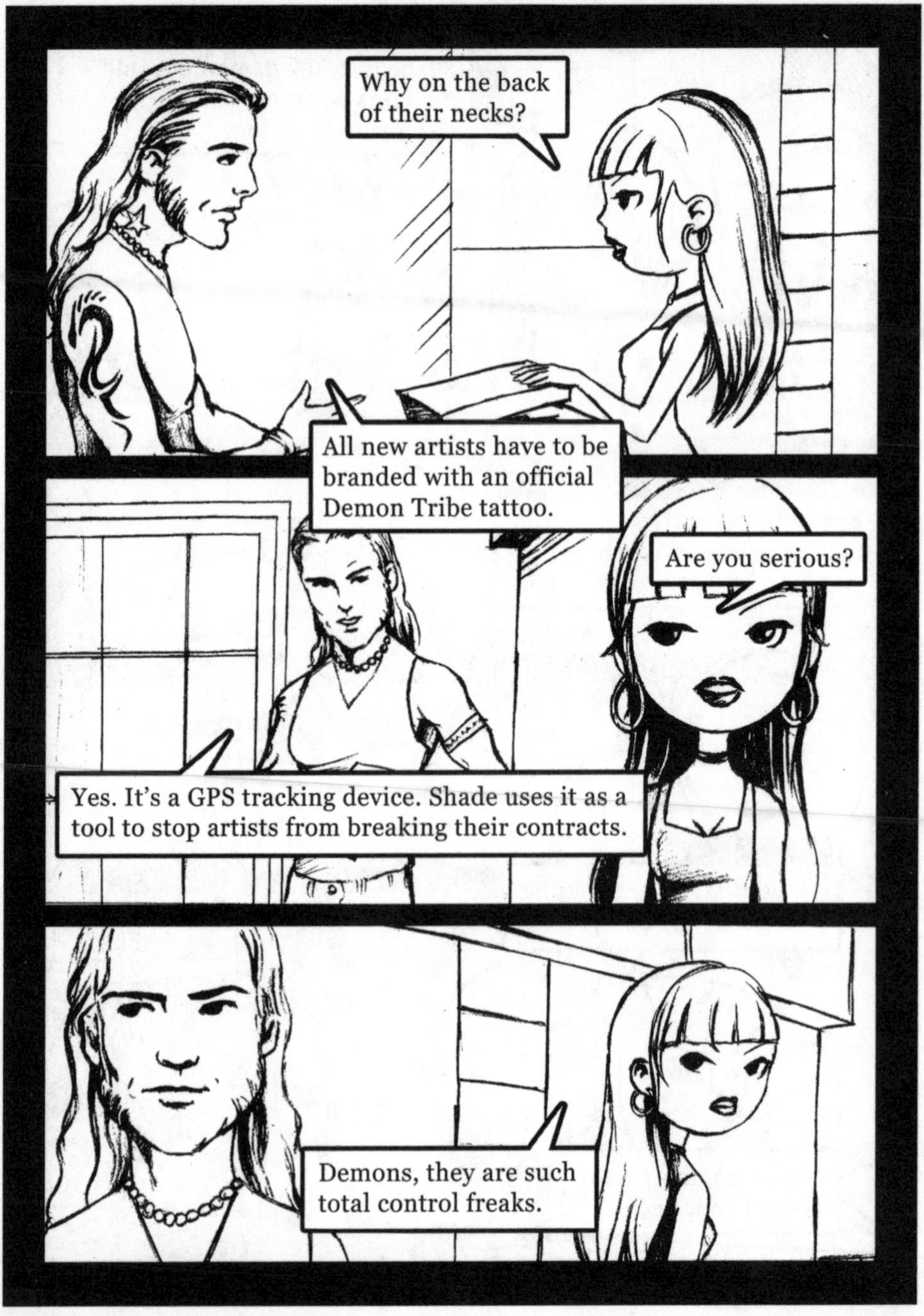
Why on the back of their necks?
All new artists have to be branded with an official Demon Tribe tattoo.
Are you serious?
Yes. It's a GPS tracking device. Shade uses it as a tool to stop artists from breaking their contracts.
Demons, they are such total control freaks.

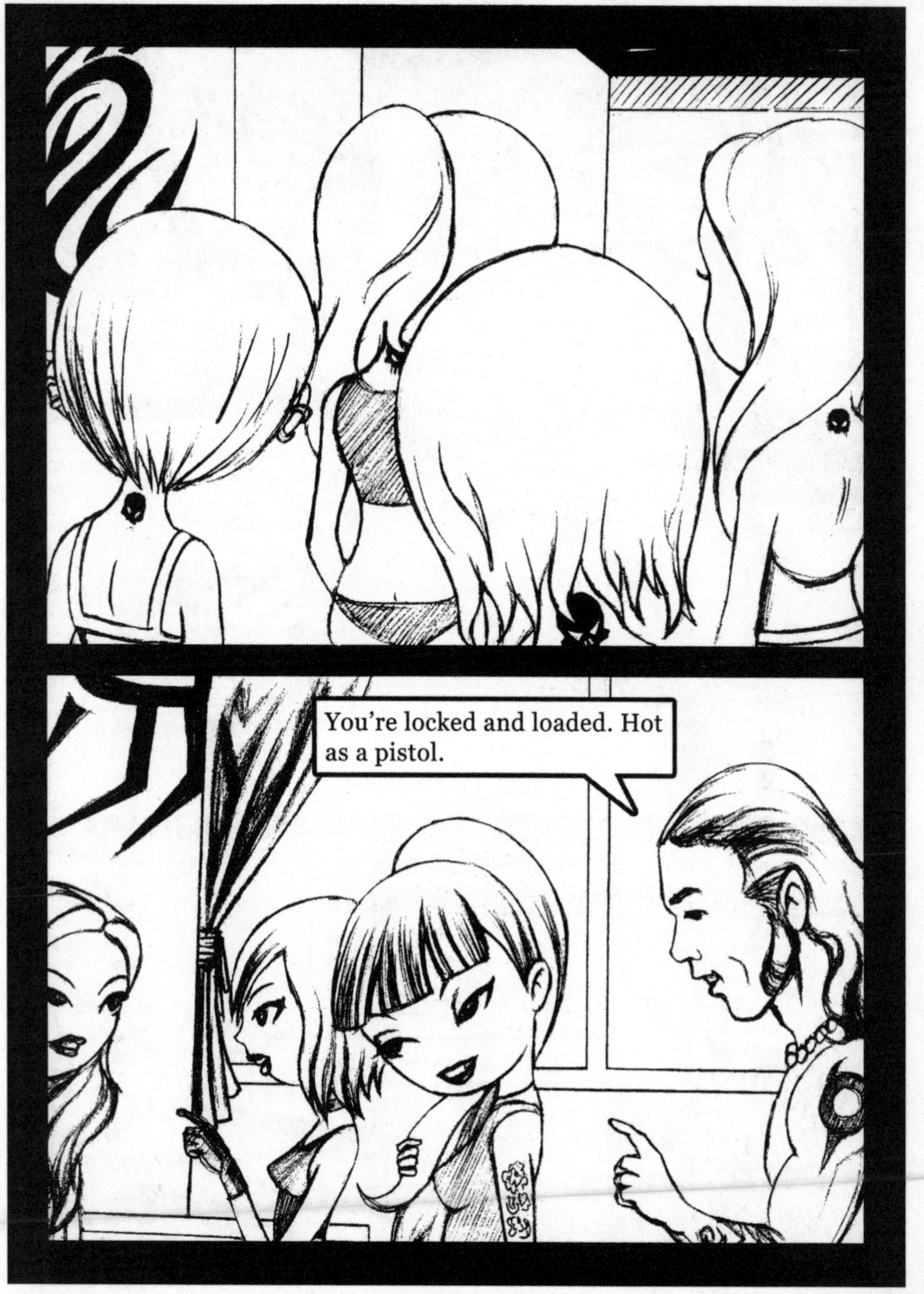
You're locked and loaded. Hot as a pistol.

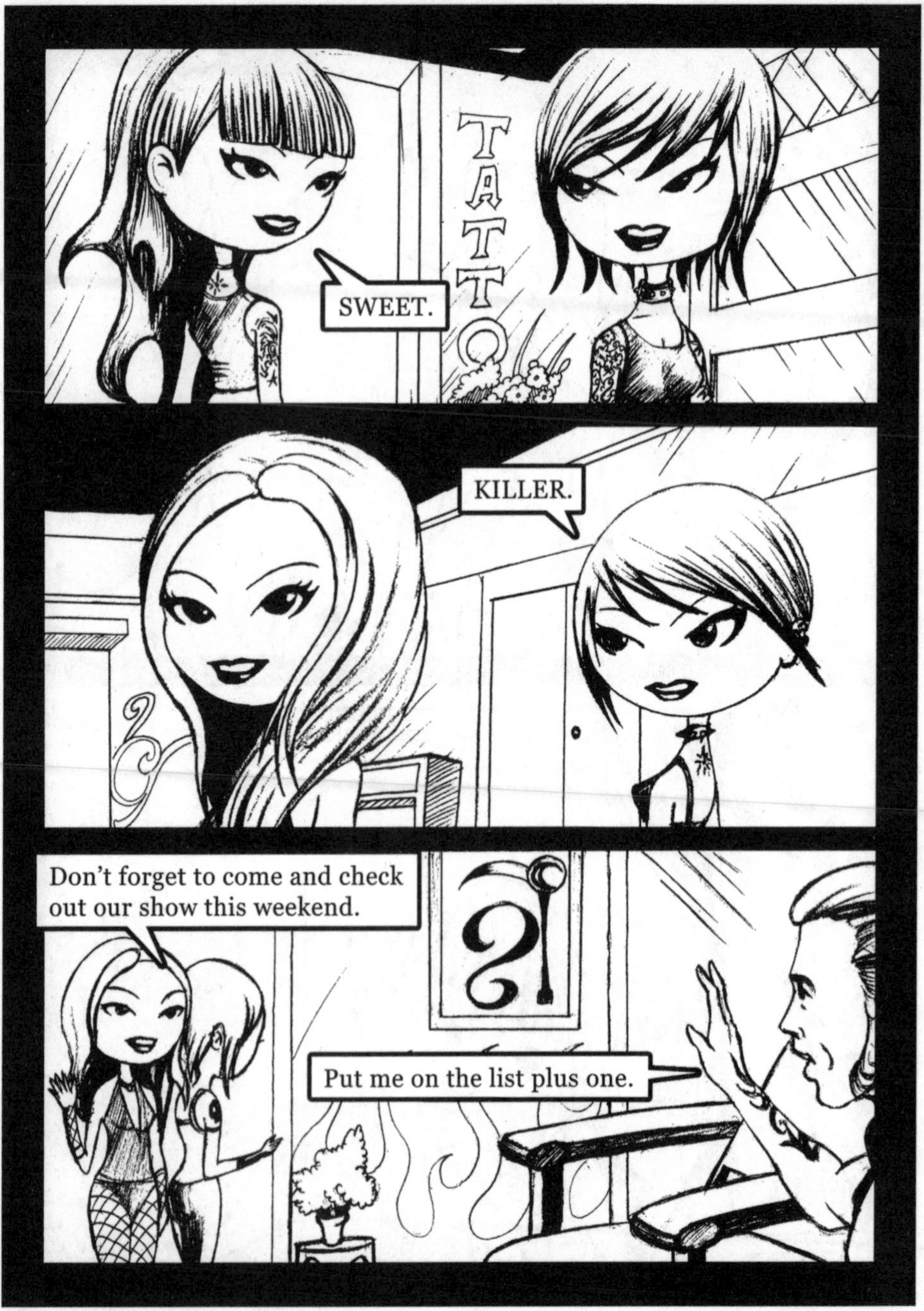
SWEET.
KILLER.
Don't forget to come and check out our show this weekend.
Put me on the list plus one.

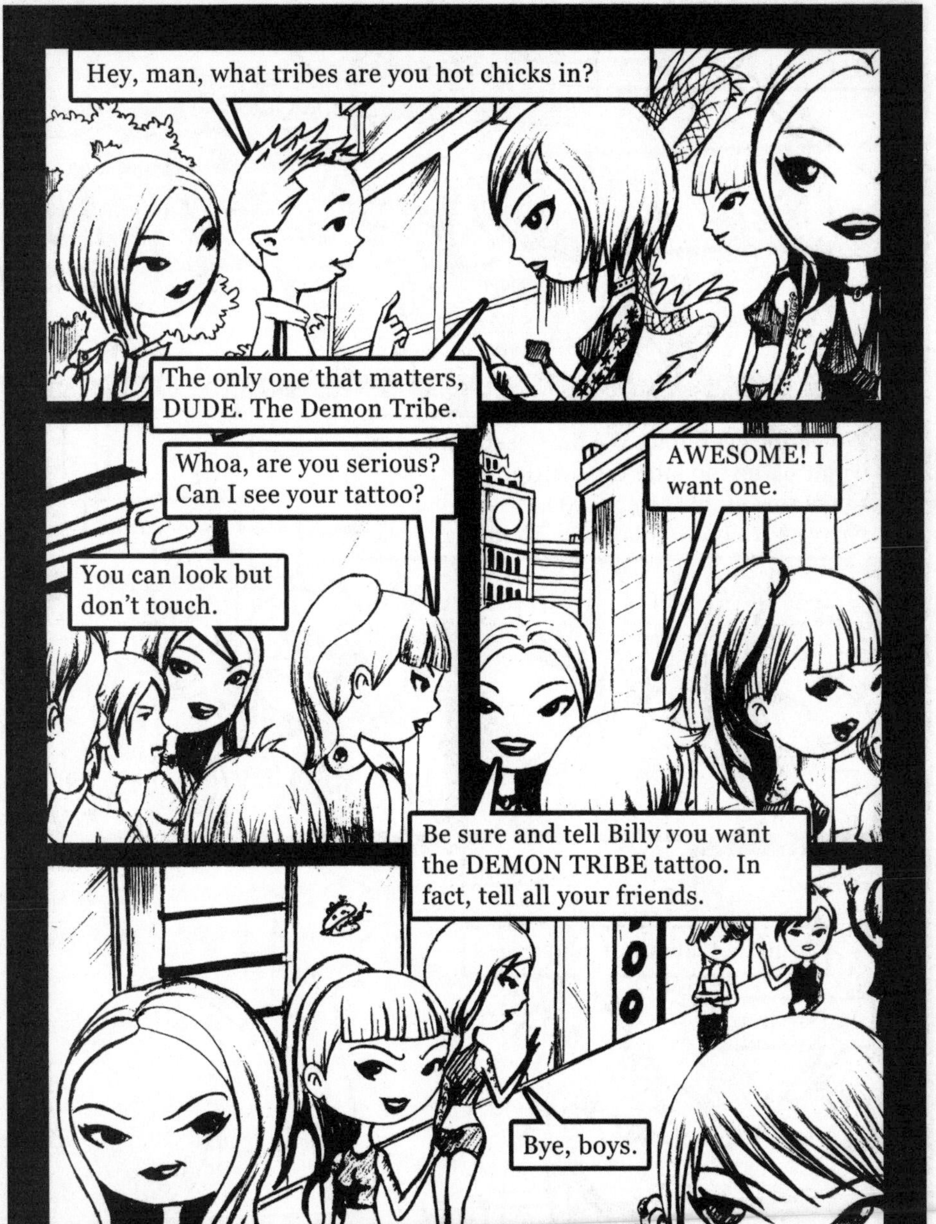
Hey, man, what tribes are you hot chicks in?
The only one that matters, DUDE. The Demon Tribe.
Whoa, are you serious? Can I see your tattoo?
You can look but don't touch.
AWESOME! I want one.
Be sure and tell Billy you want the DEMON TRIBE tattoo. In fact, tell all your friends.
Bye, boys.

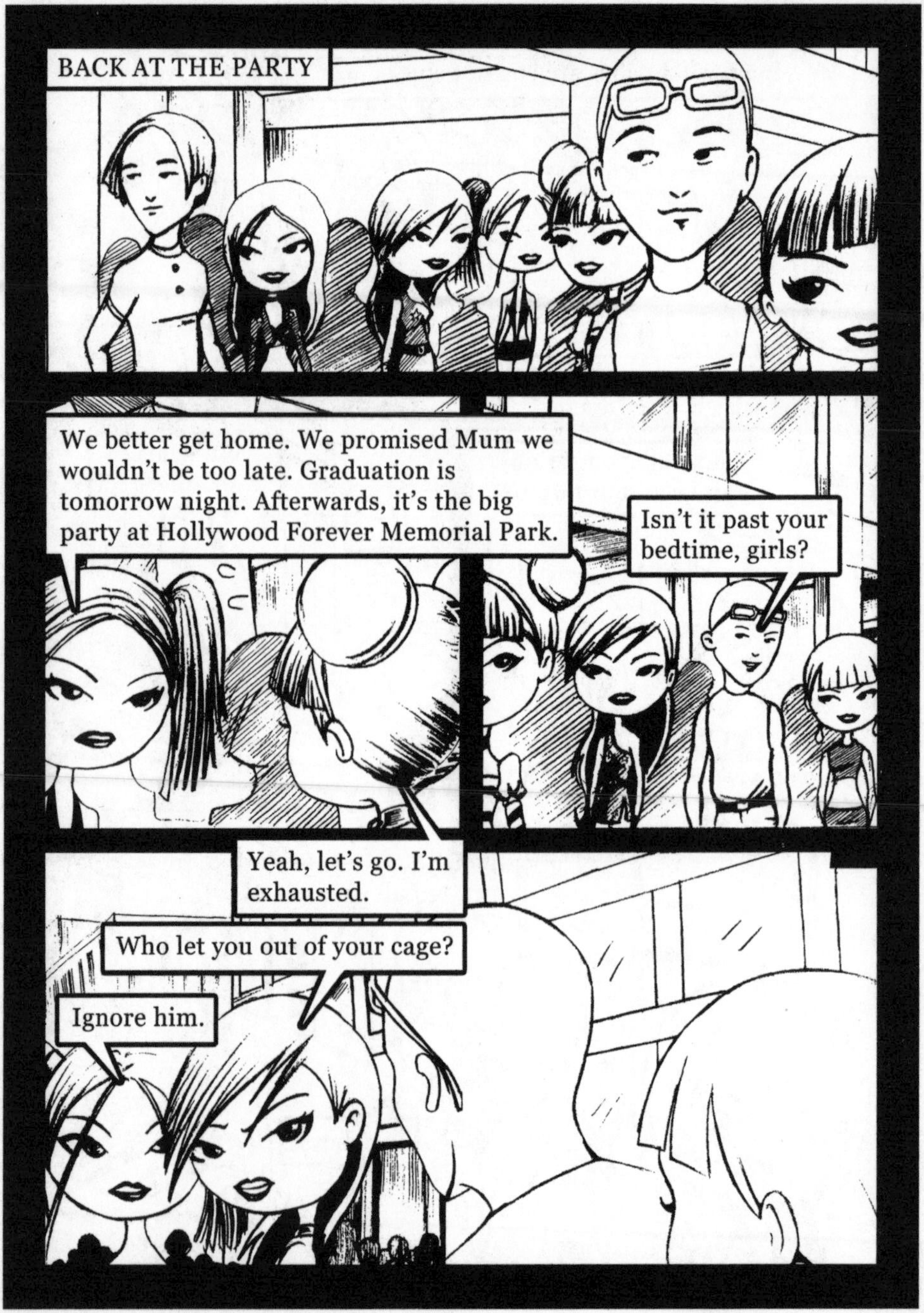
BACK AT THE PARTY
We better get home. We promised Mum we wouldn't be too late. Graduation is tomorrow night. Afterwards, it's the big party at Hollywood Forever Memorial Park.
Isn't it past your bedtime, girls?
Yeah, let's go. I'm exhausted.
Who let you out of your cage?
Ignore him.

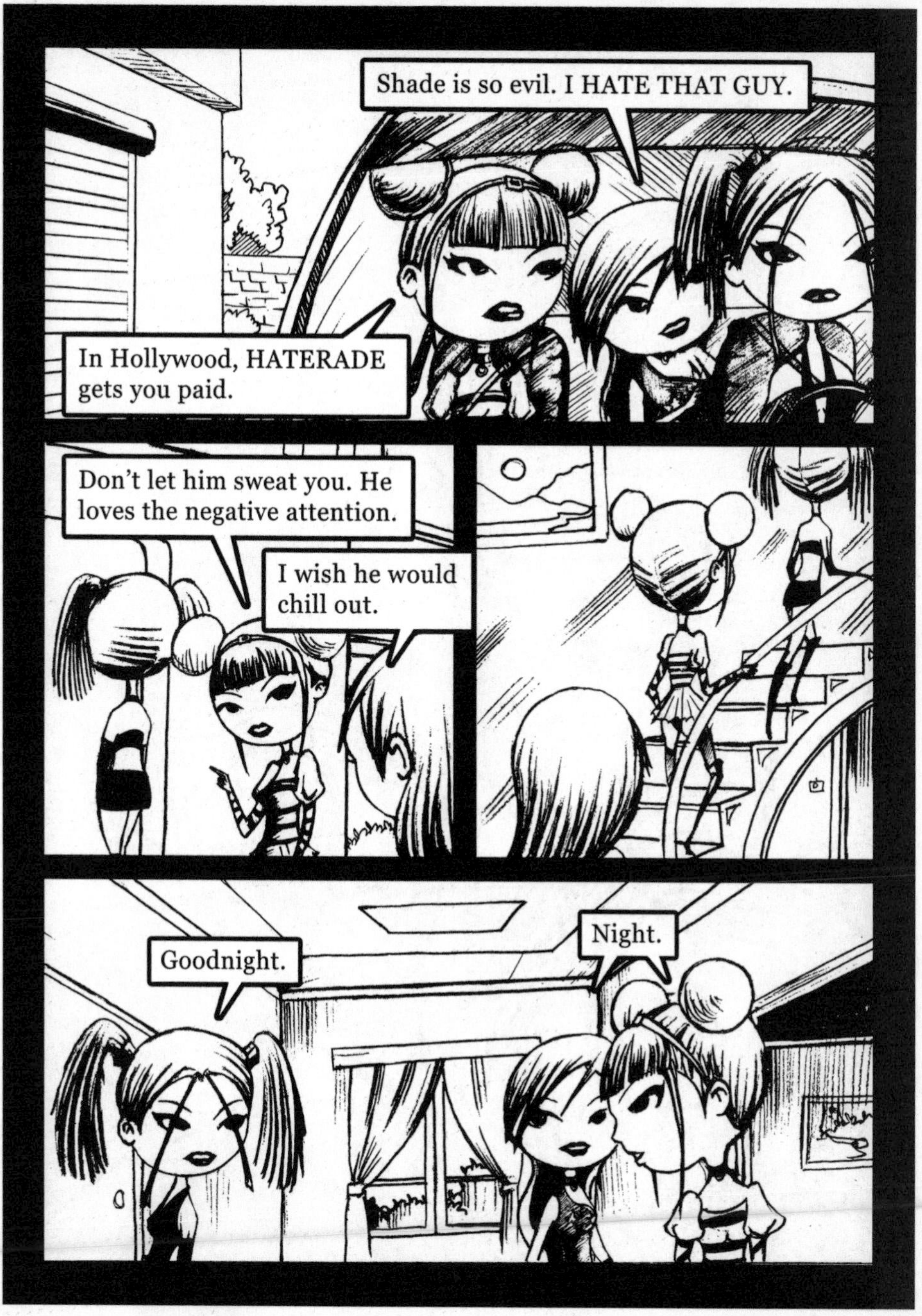
Shade is so evil. I HATE THAT GUY.
In Hollywood, HATERADE gets you paid.
Don't let him sweat you. He loves the negative attention.
I wish he would chill out.
Goodnight.
Night.

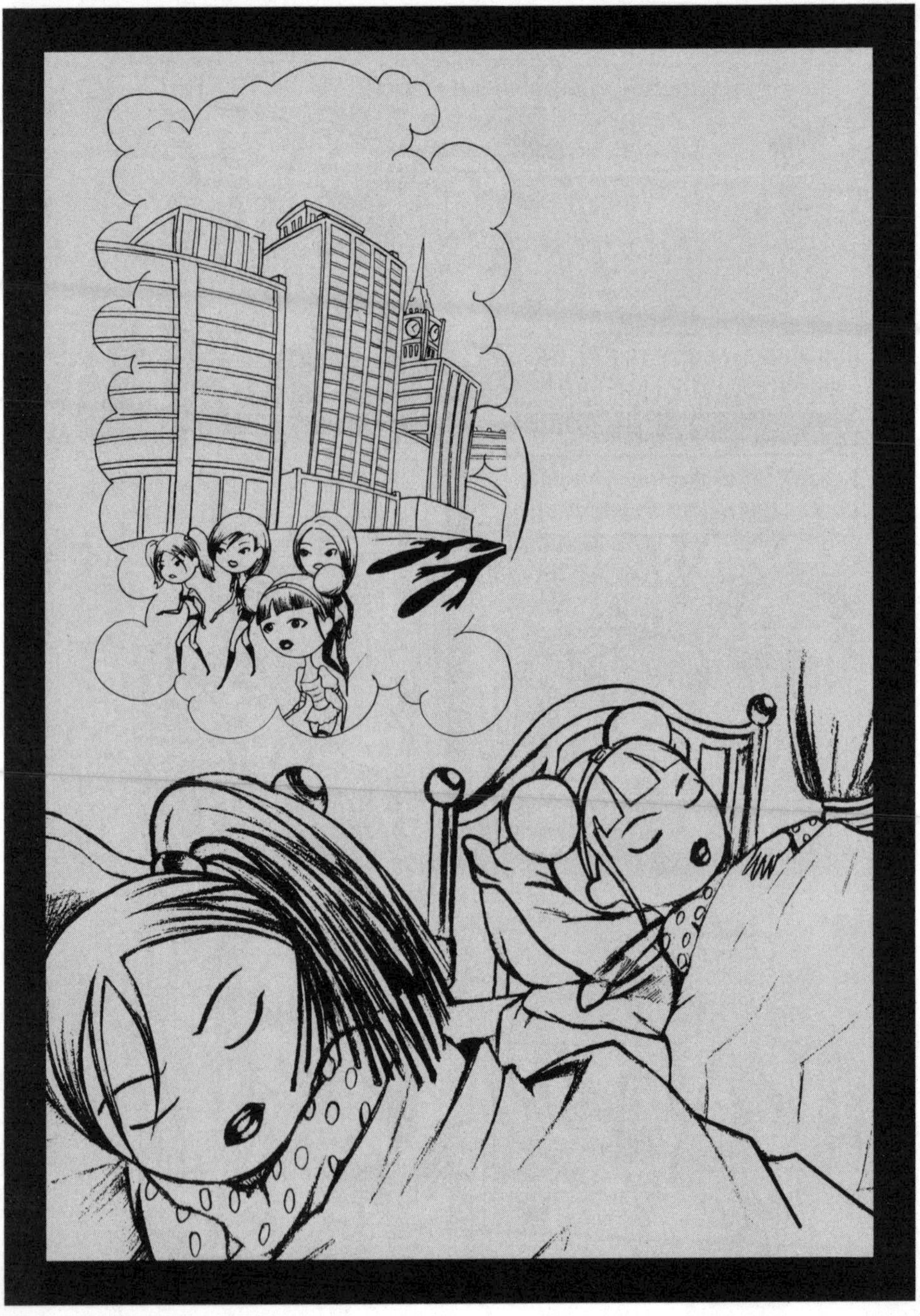

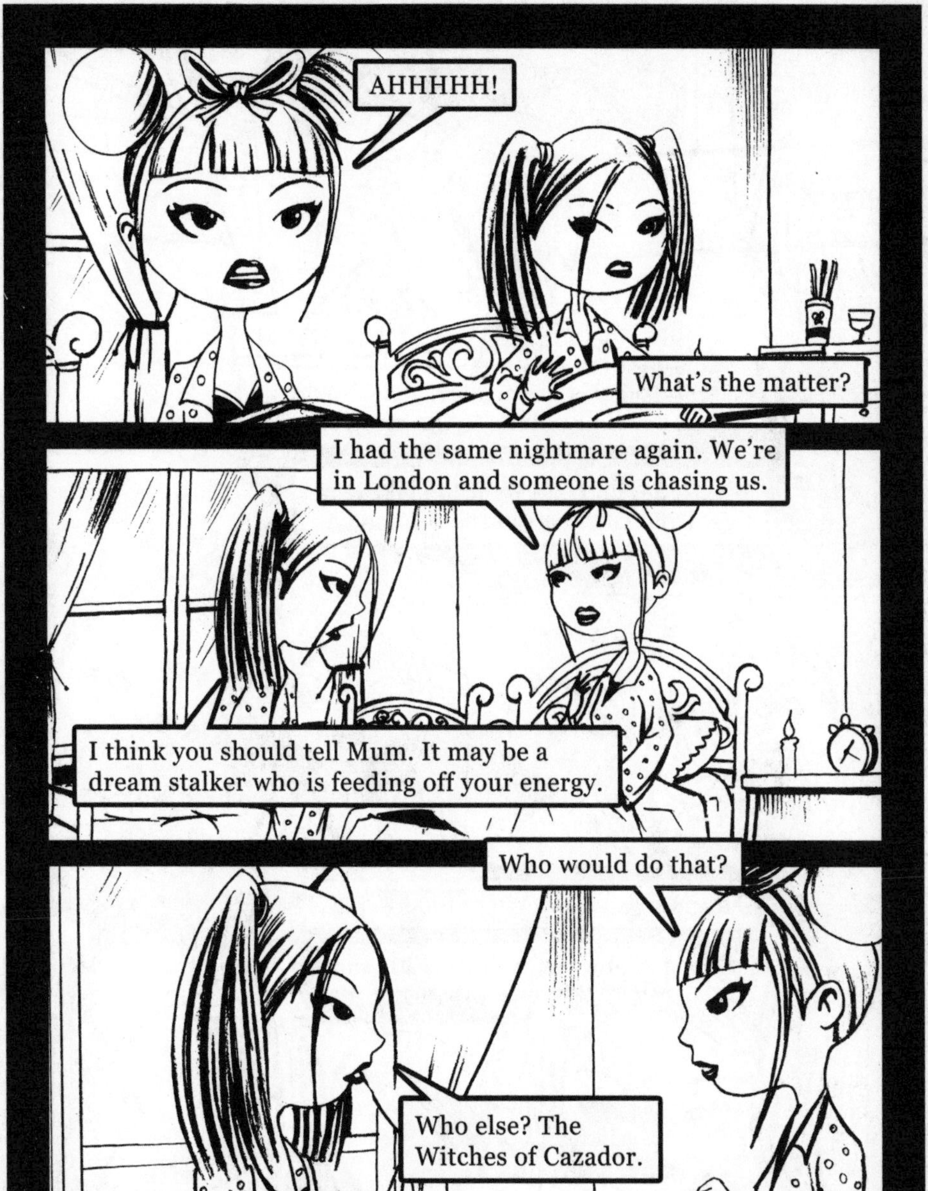
AHHHHH!
What's the matter?
I had the same nightmare again. We're in London and someone is chasing us.
I think you should tell Mum. It may be a dream stalker who is feeding off your energy.
Who would do that?
Who else? The Witches of Cazador.

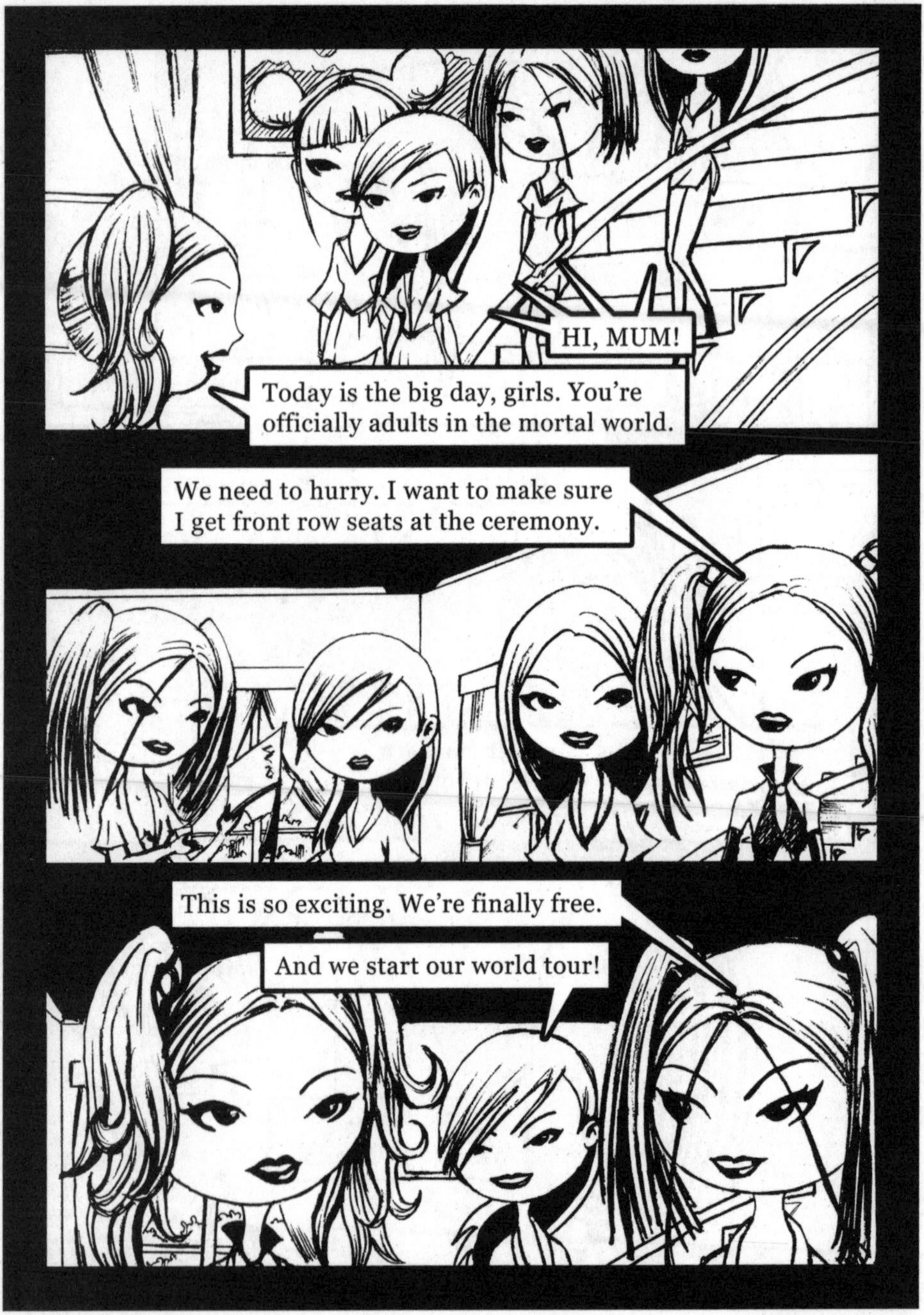
HI, MUM!
Today is the big day, girls. You're officially adults in the mortal world.
We need to hurry. I want to make sure I get front row seats at the ceremony.
This is so exciting. We're finally free.
And we start our world tour!

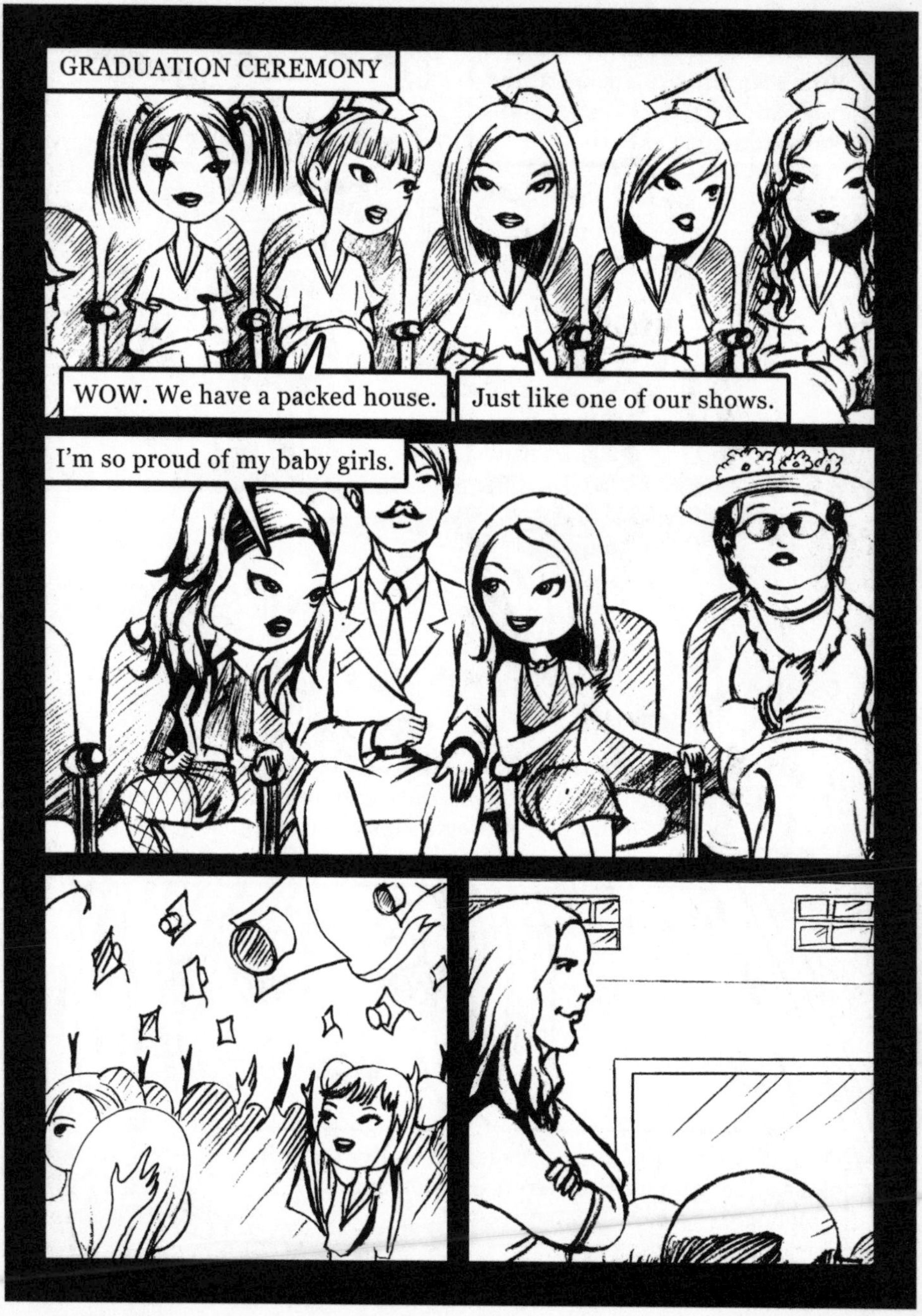
GRADUATION CEREMONY
WOW. We have a packed house.
Just like one of our shows.
I'm so proud of my baby girls.

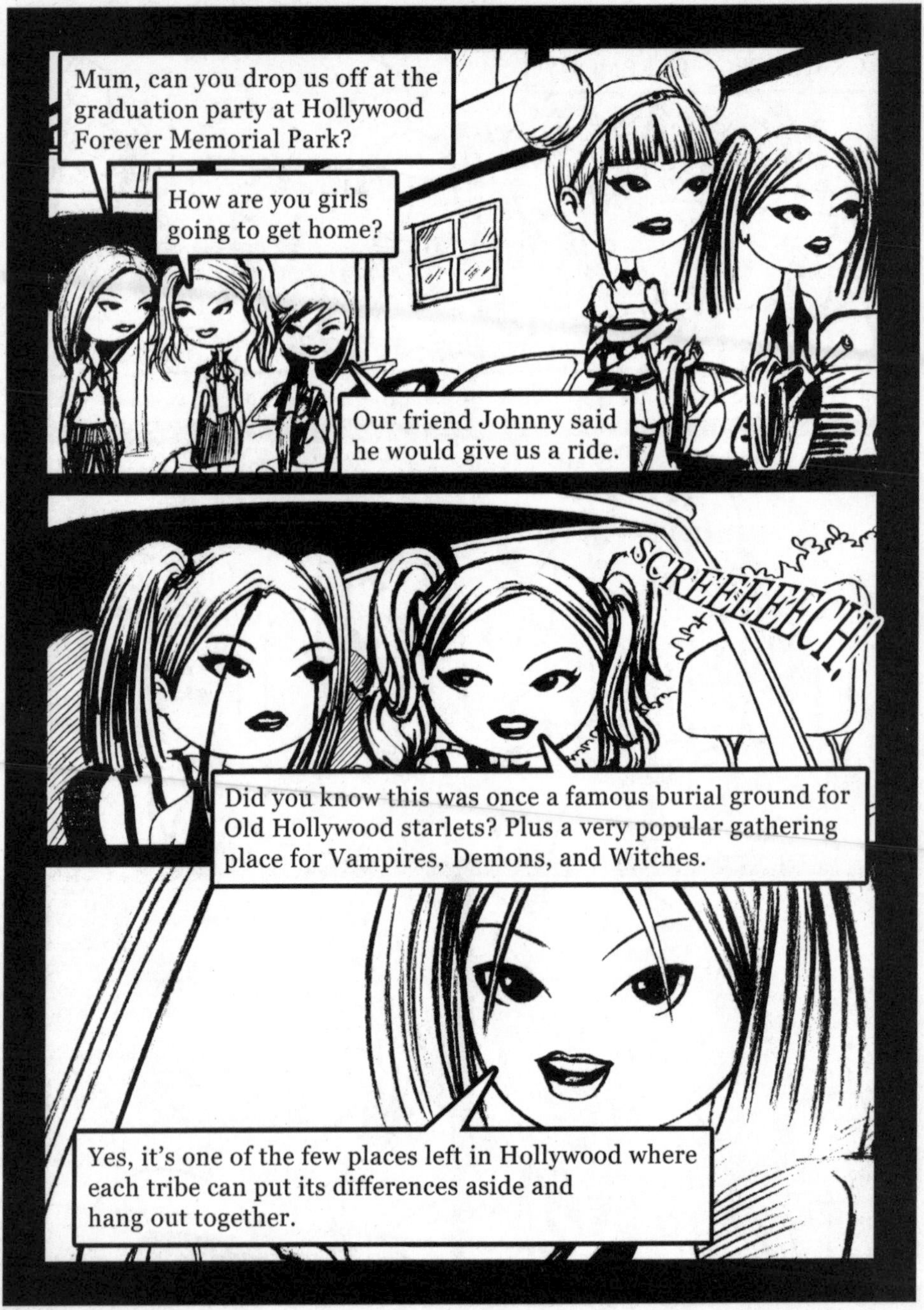
Mum, can you drop us off at the graduation party at Hollywood Forever Memorial Park?
How are you girls going to get home?
Our friend Johnny said he would give us a ride.
SCREEEEEECH!
Did you know this was once a famous burial ground for Old Hollywood starlets? Plus a very popular gathering place for Vampires, Demons, and Witches.
Yes, it's one of the few places left in Hollywood where each tribe can put its differences aside and hang out together.

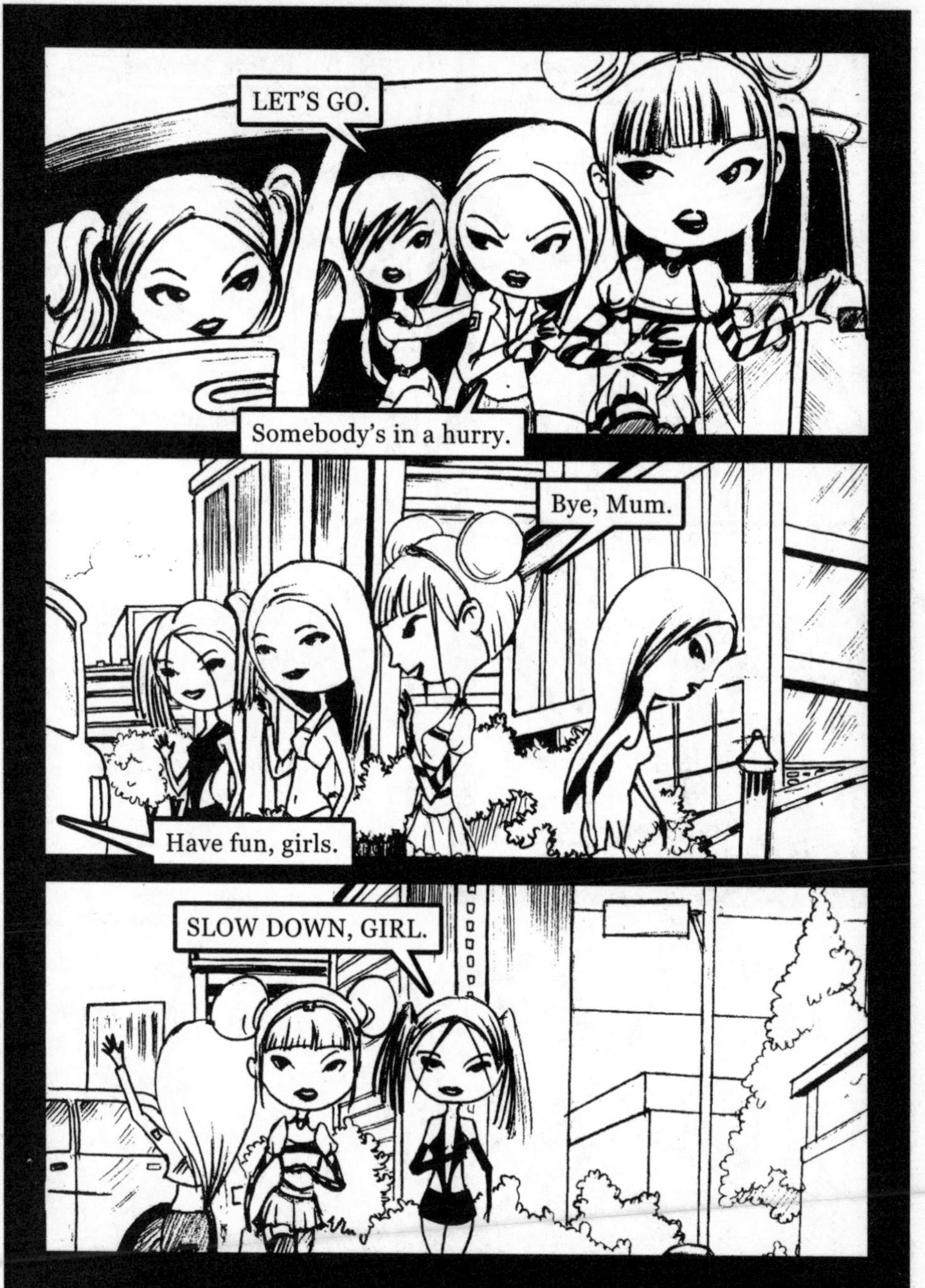
LET'S GO.
Somebody's in a hurry.
Bye, Mum.
Have fun, girls.
SLOW DOWN, GIRL.

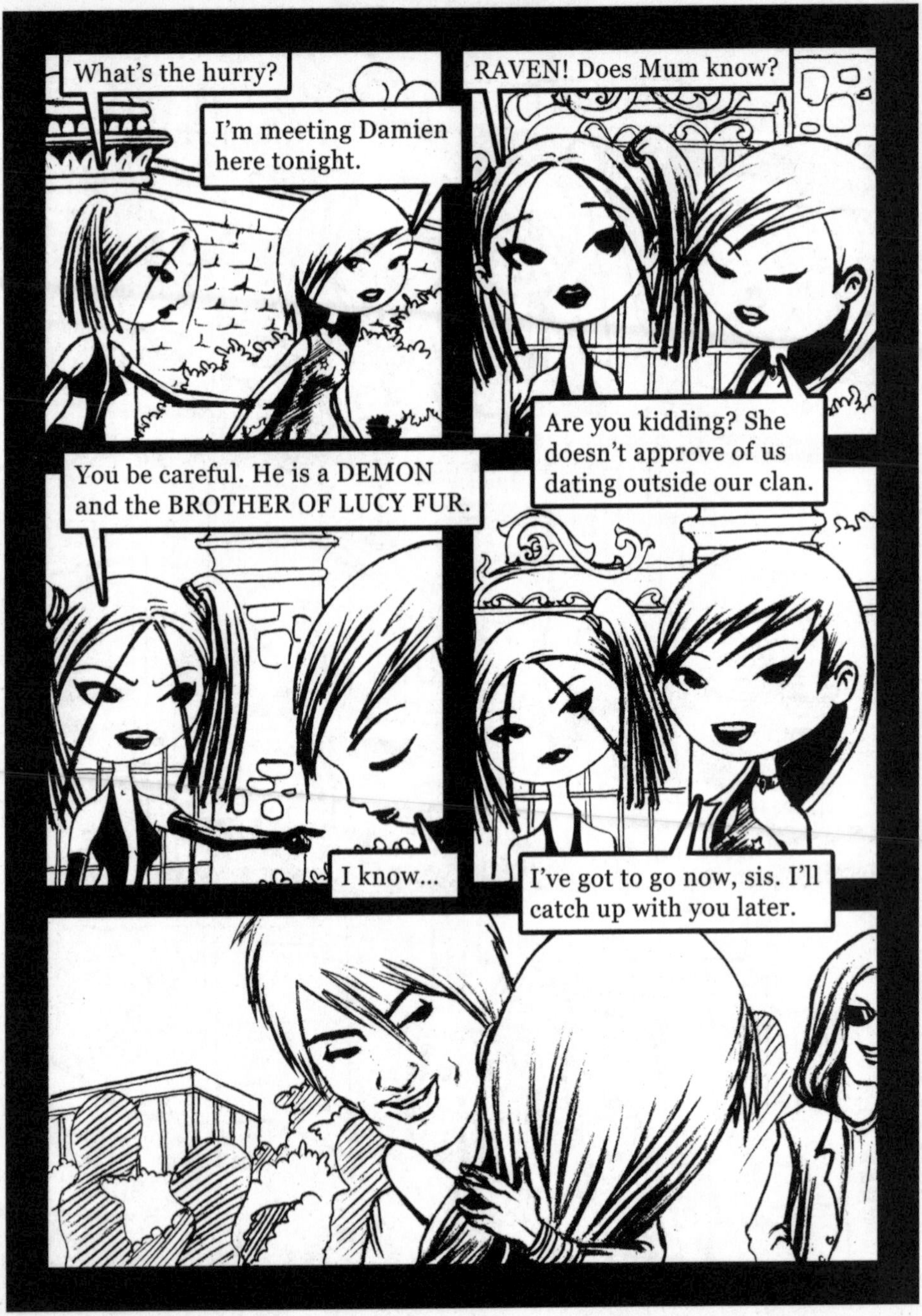
What's the hurry?
I'm meeting Damien here tonight.
RAVEN! Does Mum know?
Are you kidding? She doesn't approve of us dating outside our clan.
You be careful. He is a DEMON and the BROTHER OF LUCY FUR.
I know...
I've got to go now, sis. I'll catch up with you later.

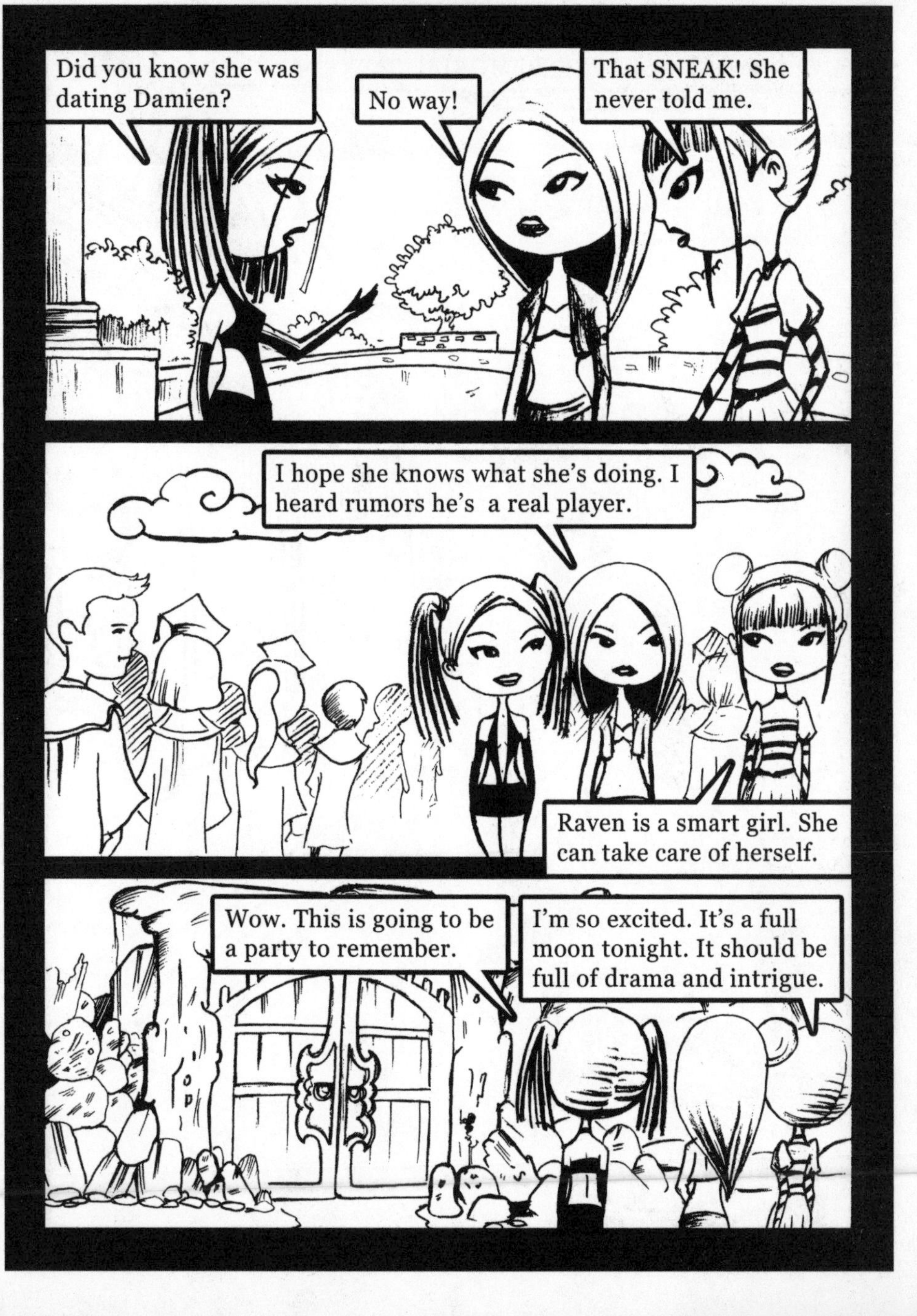
Did you know she was dating Damien?
No way!
That SNEAK! She never told me.
I hope she knows what she's doing. I heard rumors he's a real player.
Raven is a smart girl. She can take care of herself.
Wow. This is going to be a party to remember.
I'm so excited. It's a full moon tonight. It should be full of drama and intrigue.

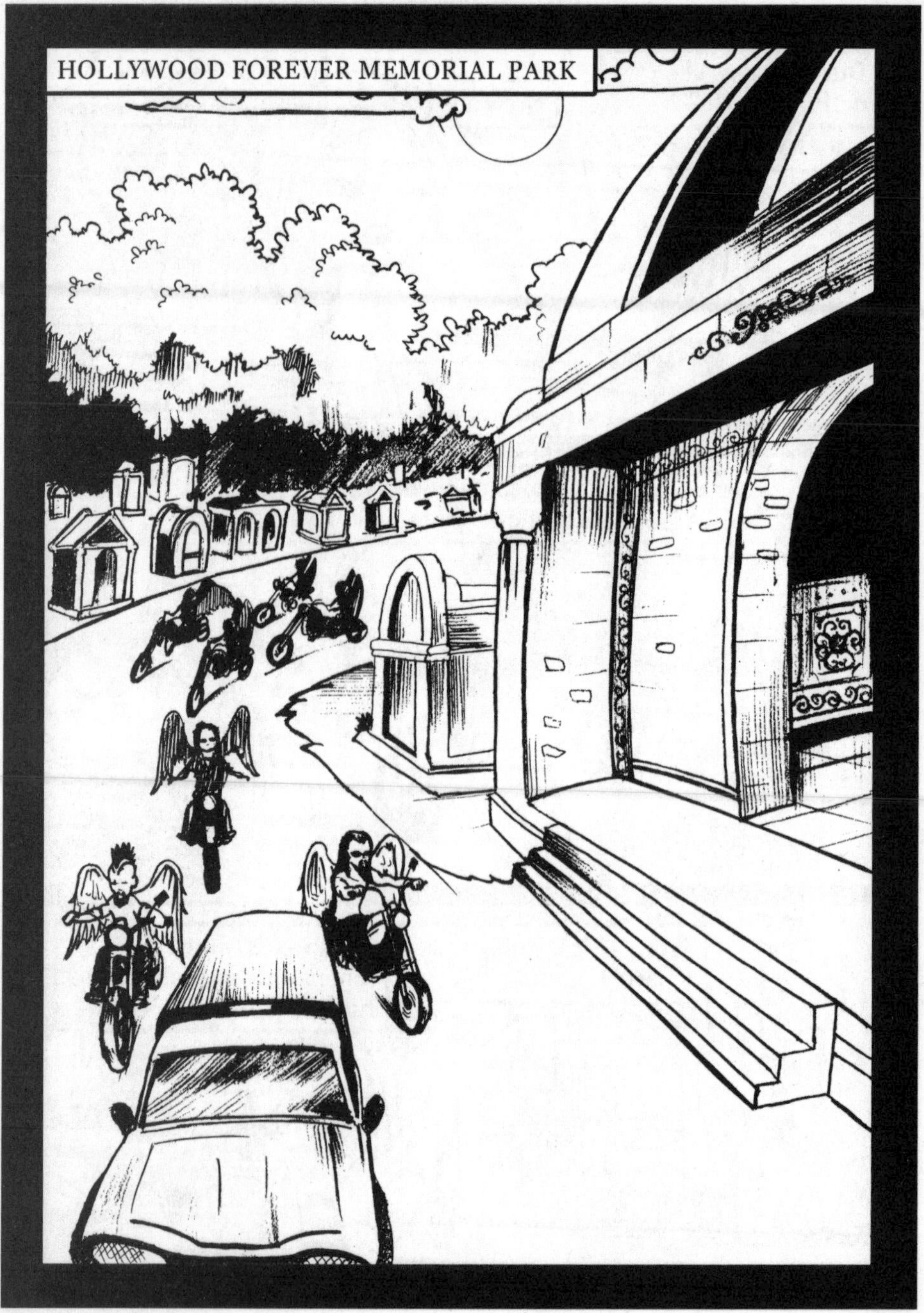
HOLLYWOOD FOREVER MEMORIAL PARK

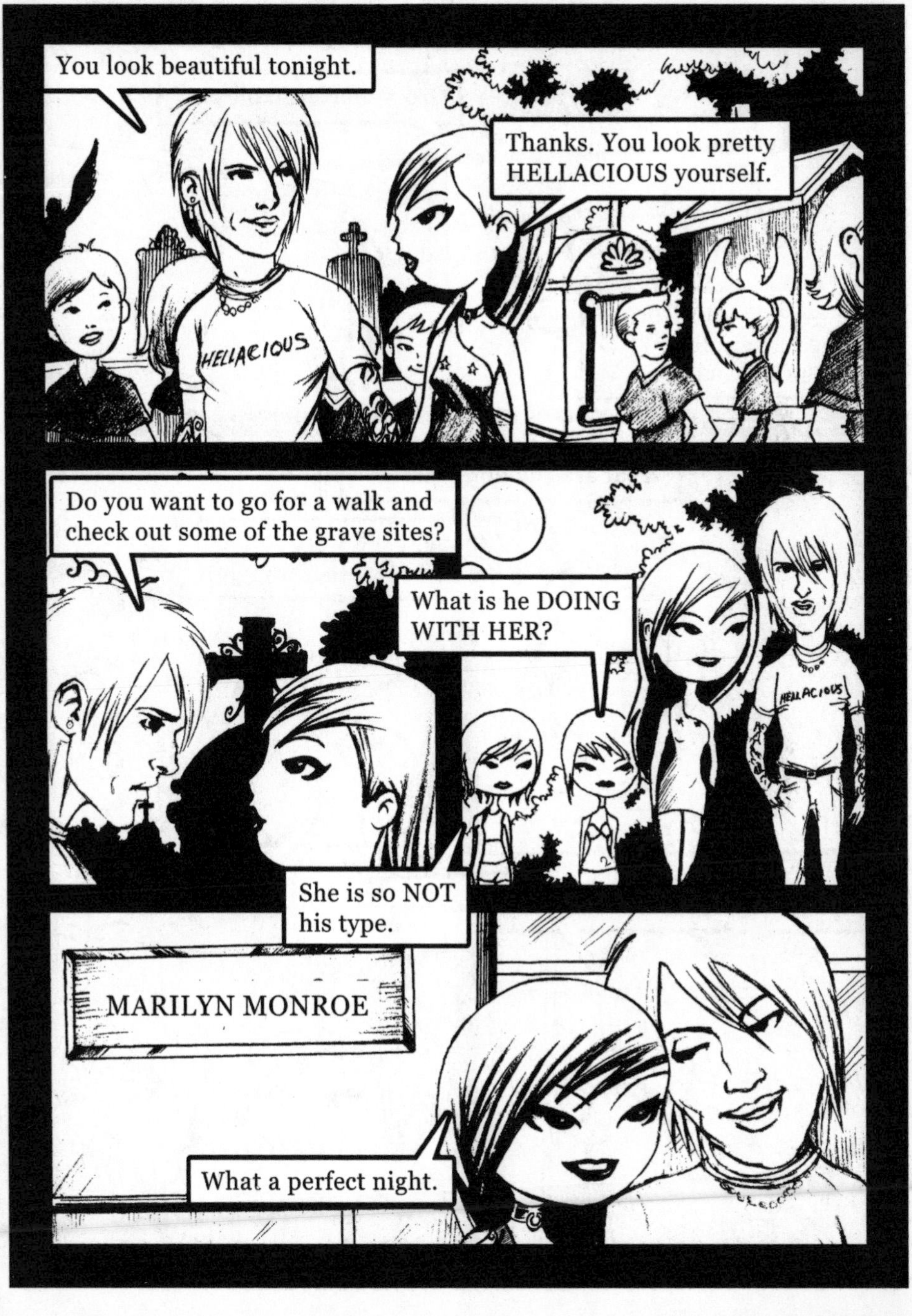
You look beautiful tonight.
Thanks. You look pretty HELLACIOUS yourself.
HELLACIOUS
Do you want to go for a walk and check out some of the grave sites?
What is he DOING WITH HER?
HELLACIOUS
She is so NOT his type.
MARILYN MONROE
What a perfect night.

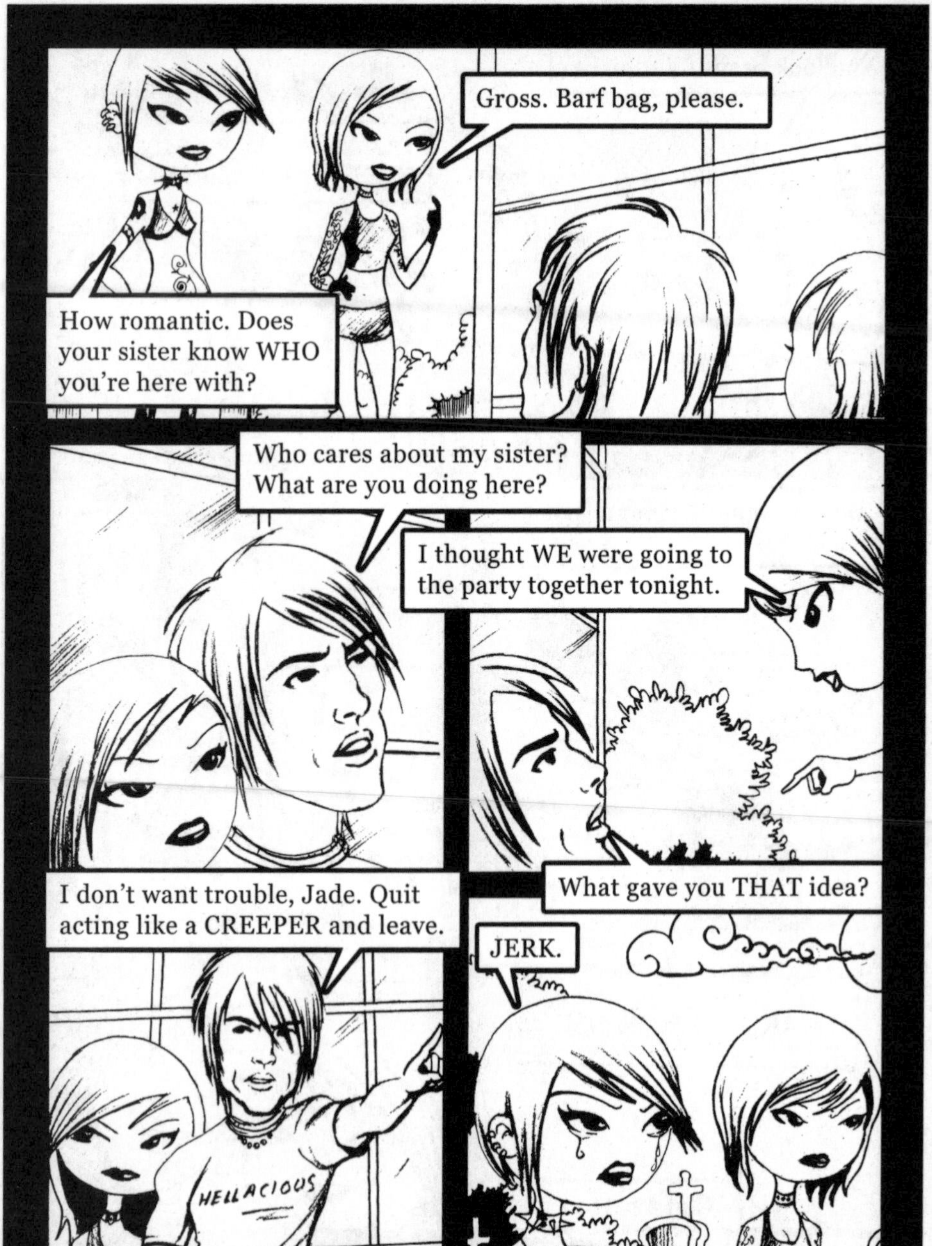

How romantic. Does your sister know WHO you're here with?
Gross. Barf bag, please.
Who cares about my sister? What are you doing here?
I thought WE were going to the party together tonight.
What gave you THAT idea?
I don't want trouble, Jade. Quit acting like a CREEPER and leave.
HELLACIOUS
JERK.

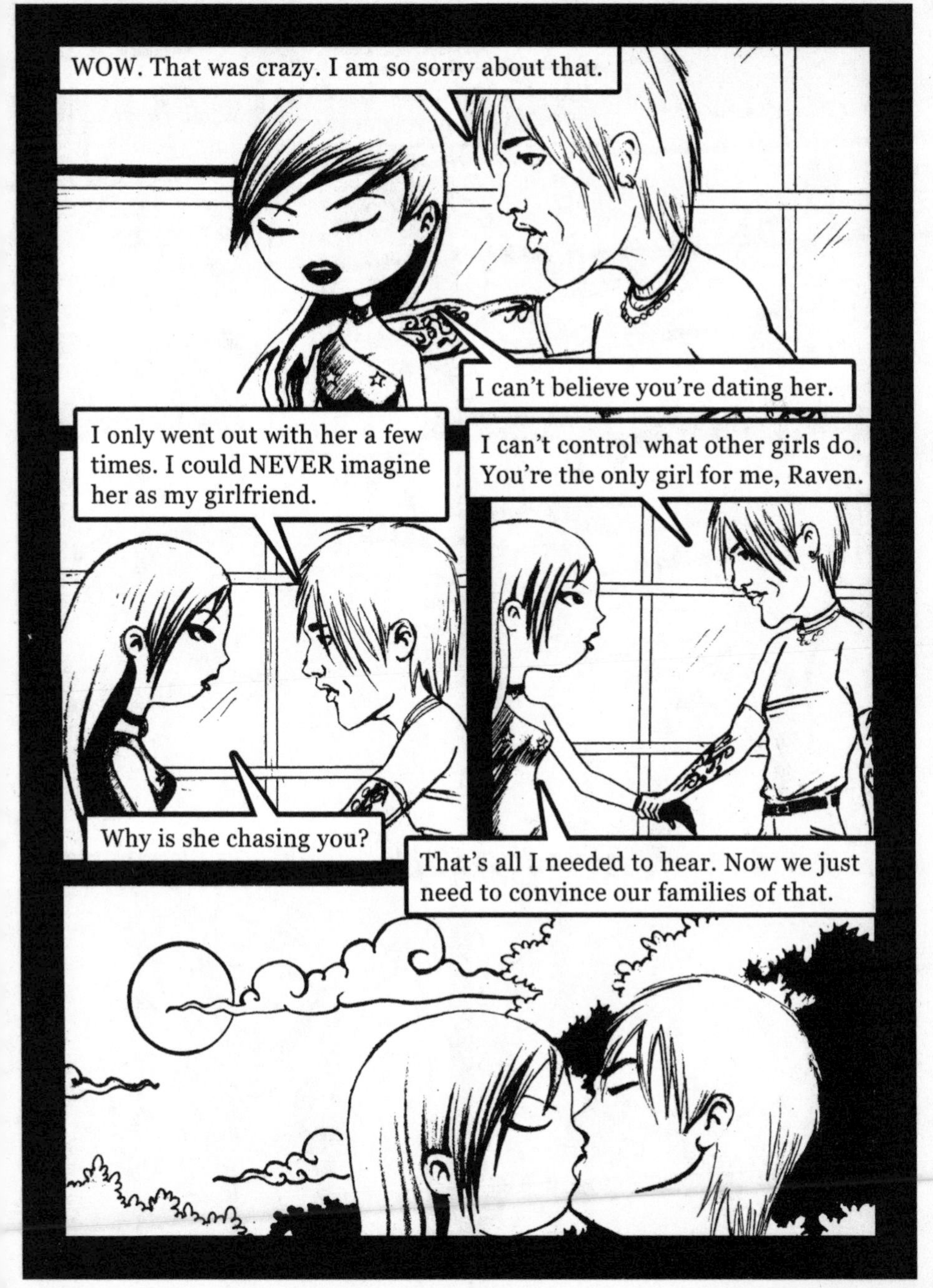
WOW. That was crazy. I am so sorry about that.
I can't believe you're dating her.
I only went out with her a few times. I could NEVER imagine her as my girlfriend.
Why is she chasing you?
I can't control what other girls do. You're the only girl for me, Raven.
That's all I needed to hear. Now we just need to convince our families of that.

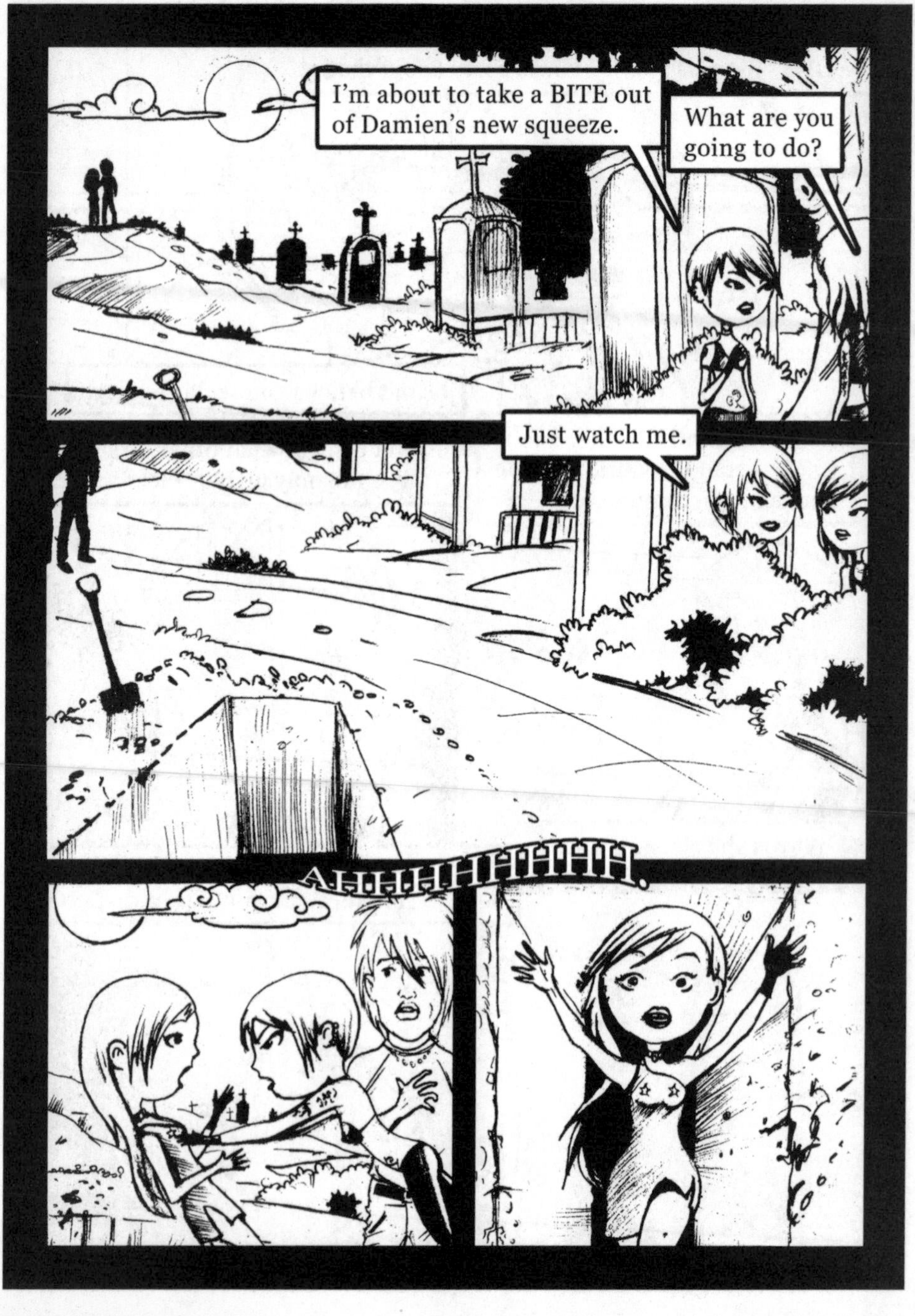
I'm about to take a BITE out of Damien's new squeeze.
What are you going to do?
Just watch me.
AHHHHHHHHH.

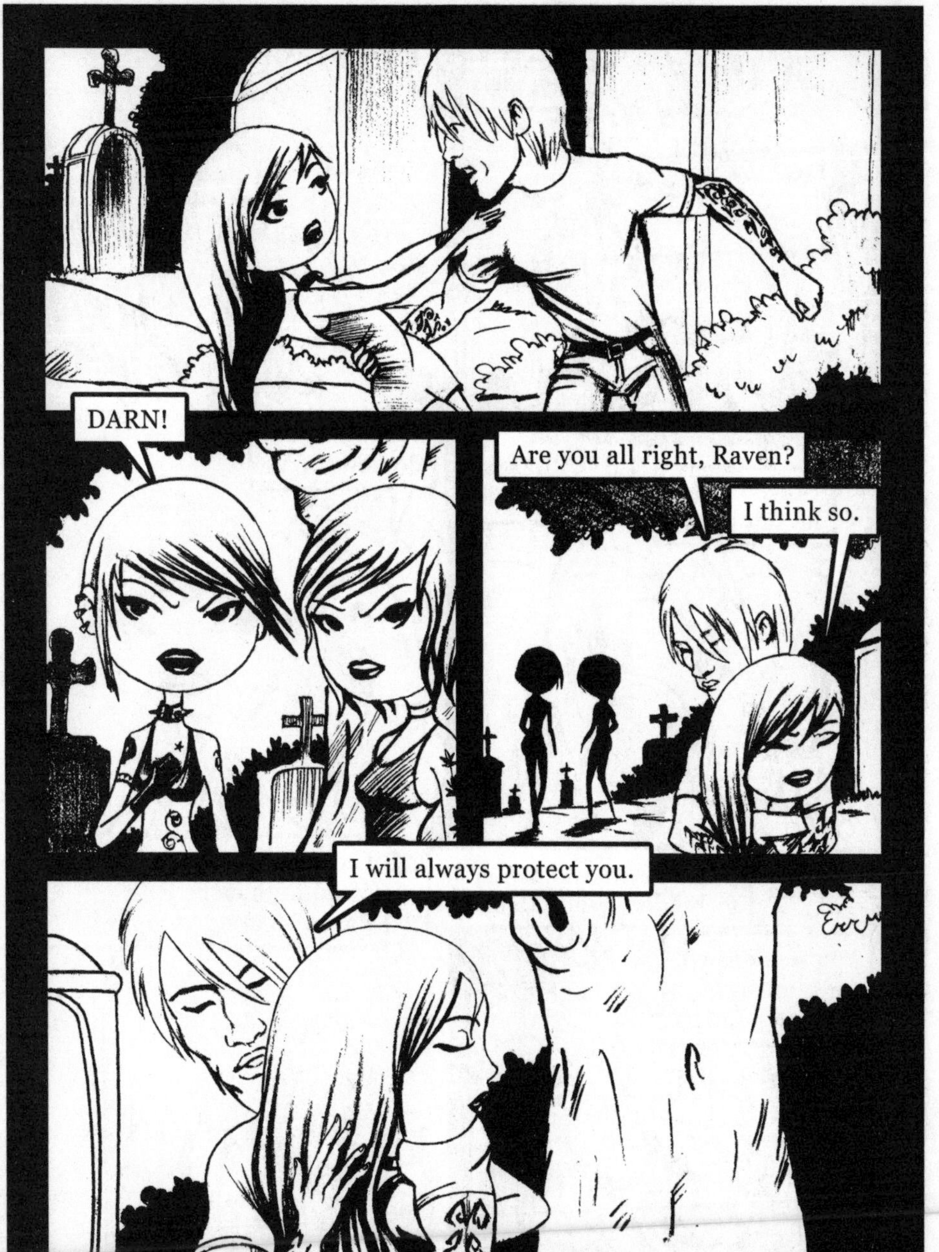
DARN!
Are you all right, Raven?
I think so.
I will always protect you.

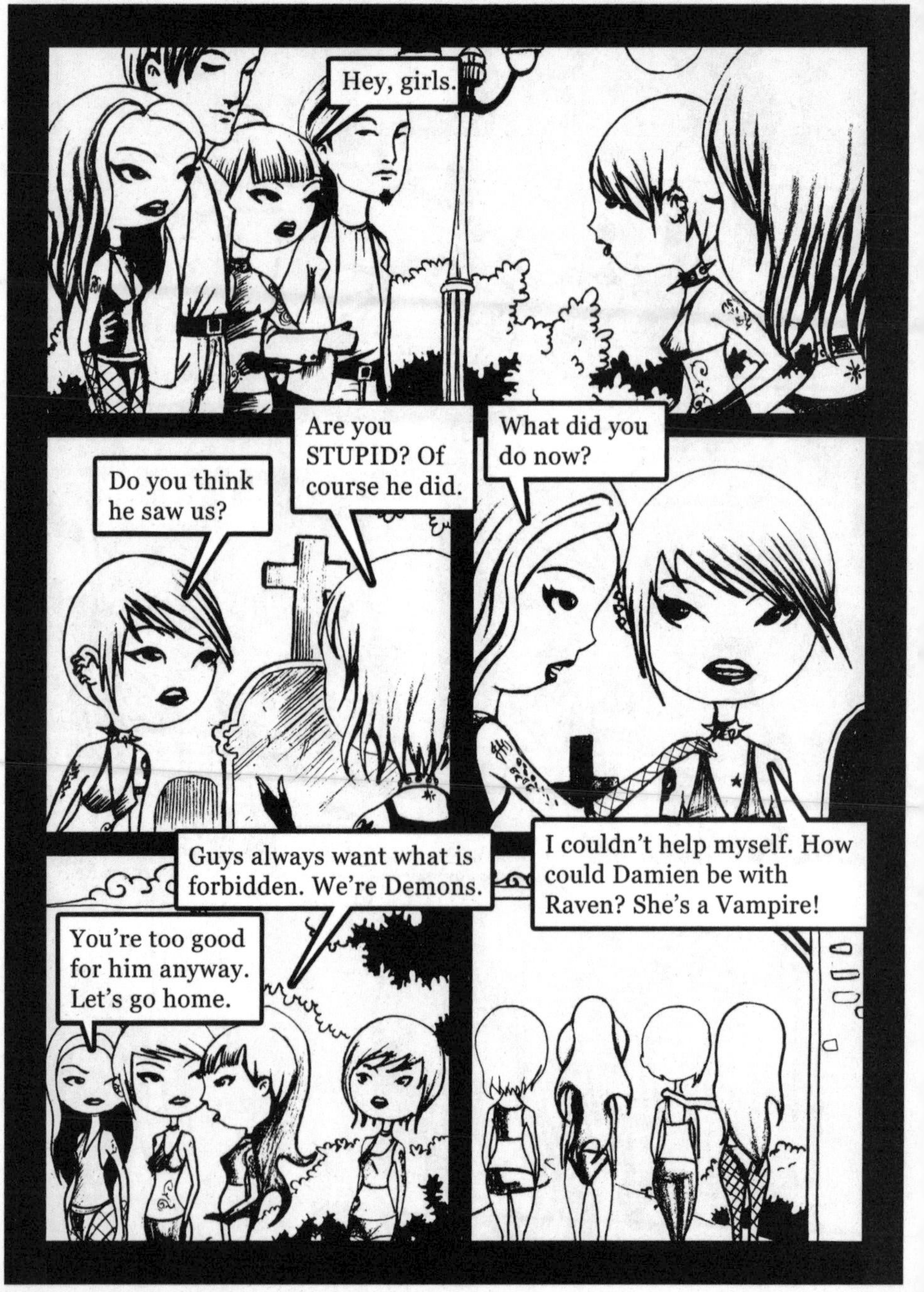
Hey, girls.
Do you think he saw us?
Are you STUPID? Of course he did.
What did you do now?
I couldn't help myself. How could Damien be with Raven? She's a Vampire!
Guys always want what is forbidden. We're Demons.
You're too good for him anyway. Let's go home.

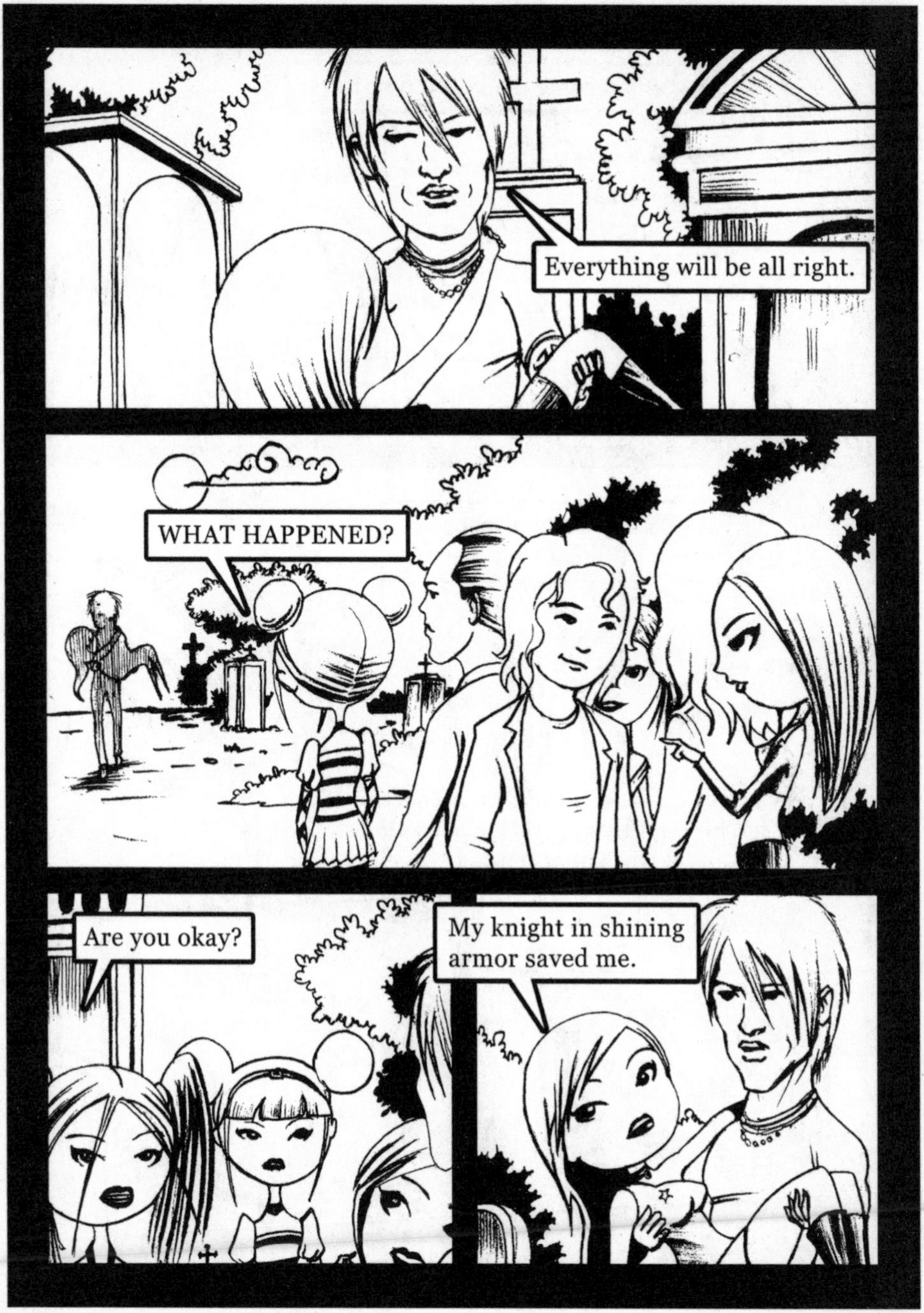
Everything will be all right.
WHAT HAPPENED?
Are you okay?
My knight in shining armor saved me.

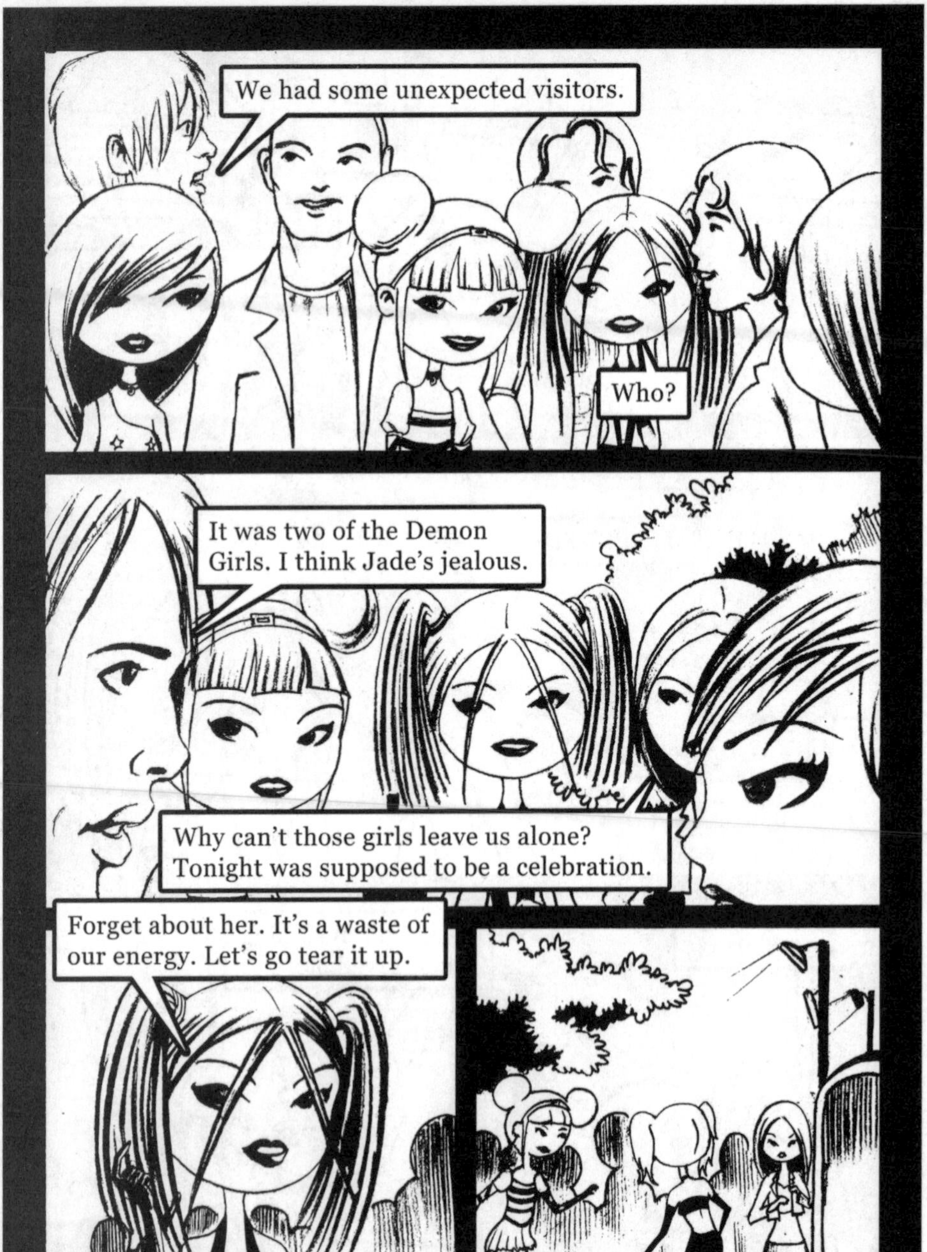
We had some unexpected visitors.
Who?
It was two of the Demon Girls. I think Jade's jealous.
Why can't those girls leave us alone? Tonight was supposed to be a celebration.
Forget about her. It's a waste of our energy. Let's go tear it up.

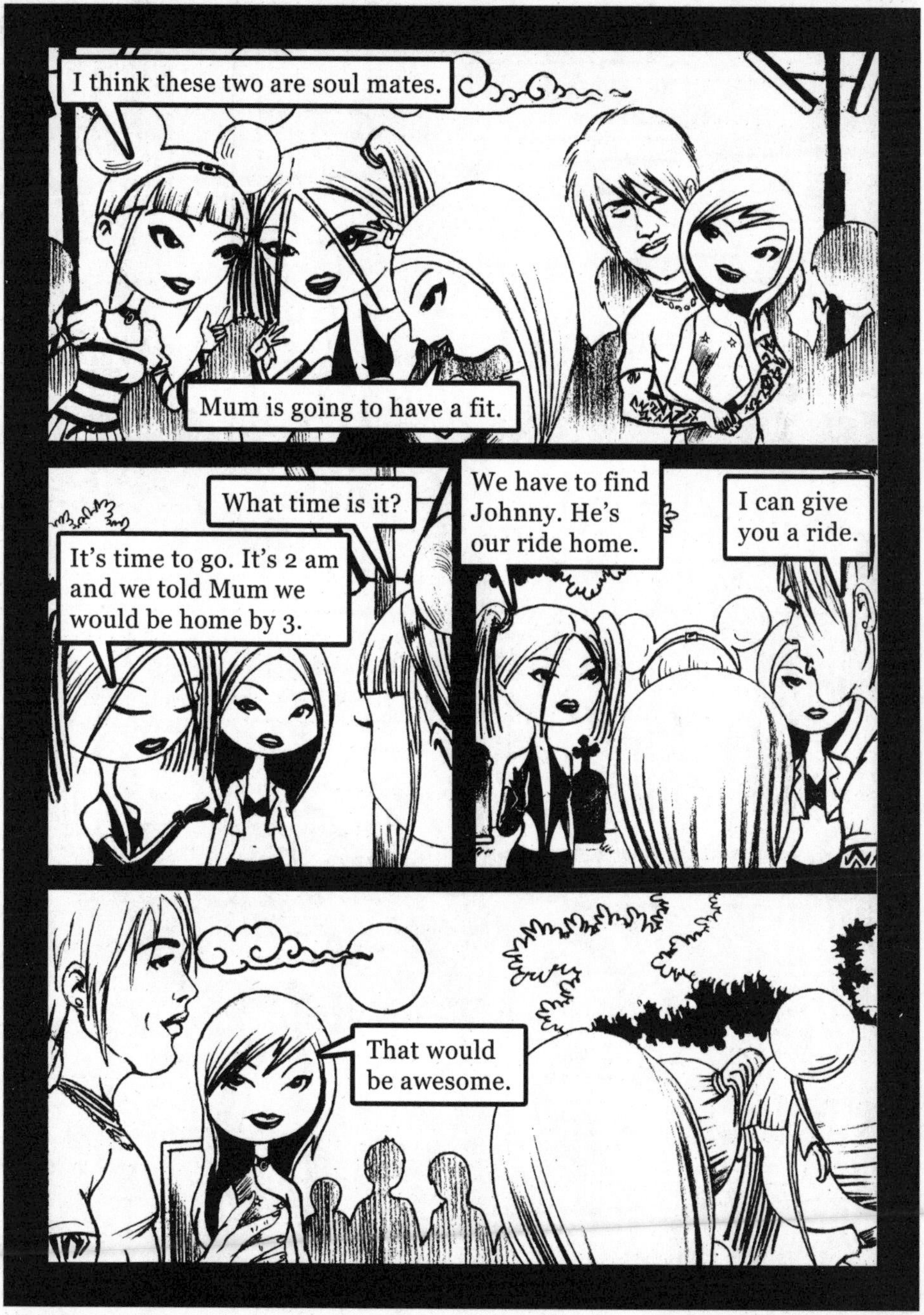
I think these two are soul mates.
Mum is going to have a fit.
What time is it?
It's time to go. It's 2 am and we told Mum we would be home by 3.
We have to find Johnny. He's our ride home.
I can give you a ride.
That would be awesome.

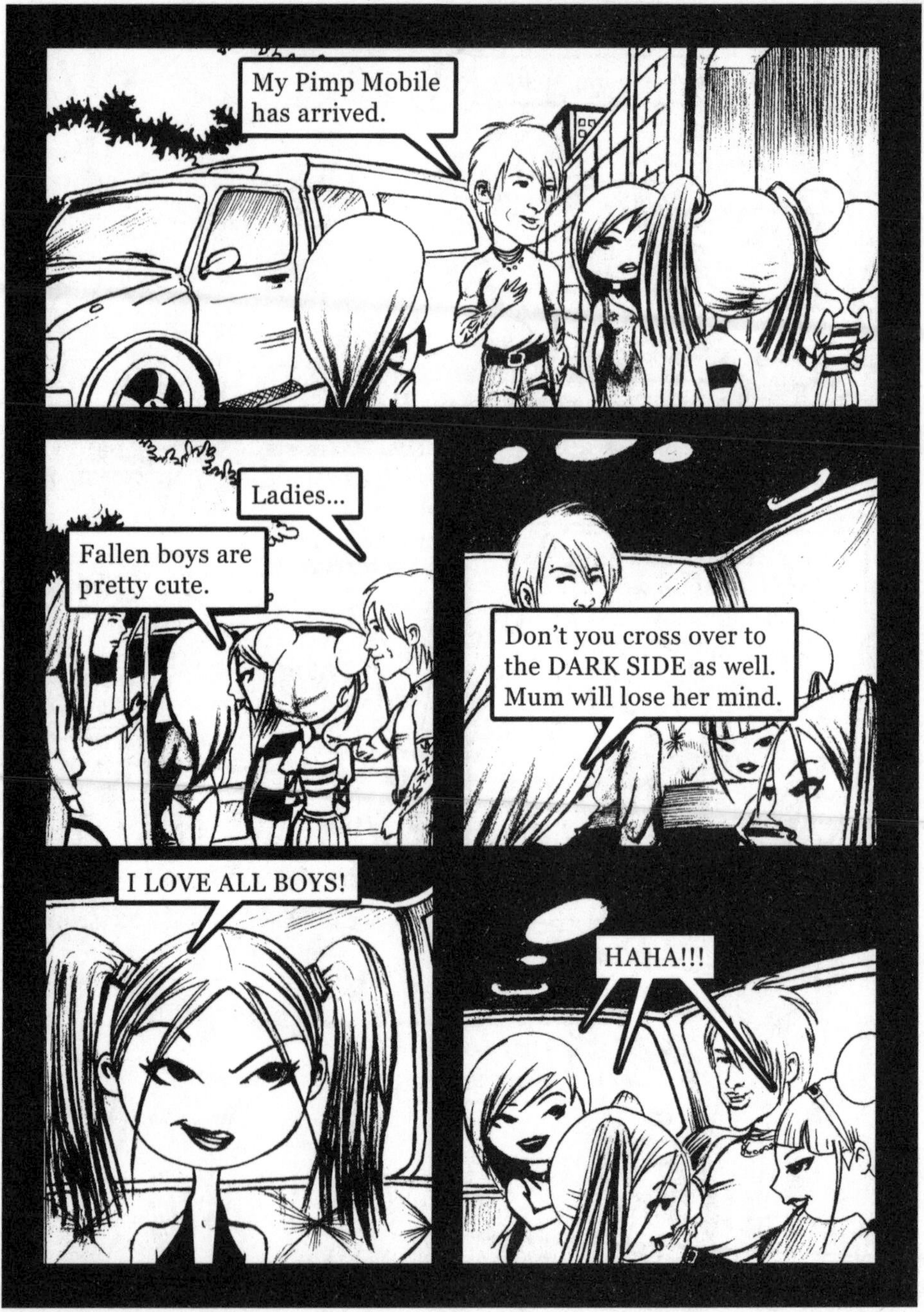
My Pimp Mobile has arrived.
Ladies...
Fallen boys are pretty cute.
Don't you cross over to the DARK SIDE as well. Mum will lose her mind.
I LOVE ALL BOYS!
HAHA!!!

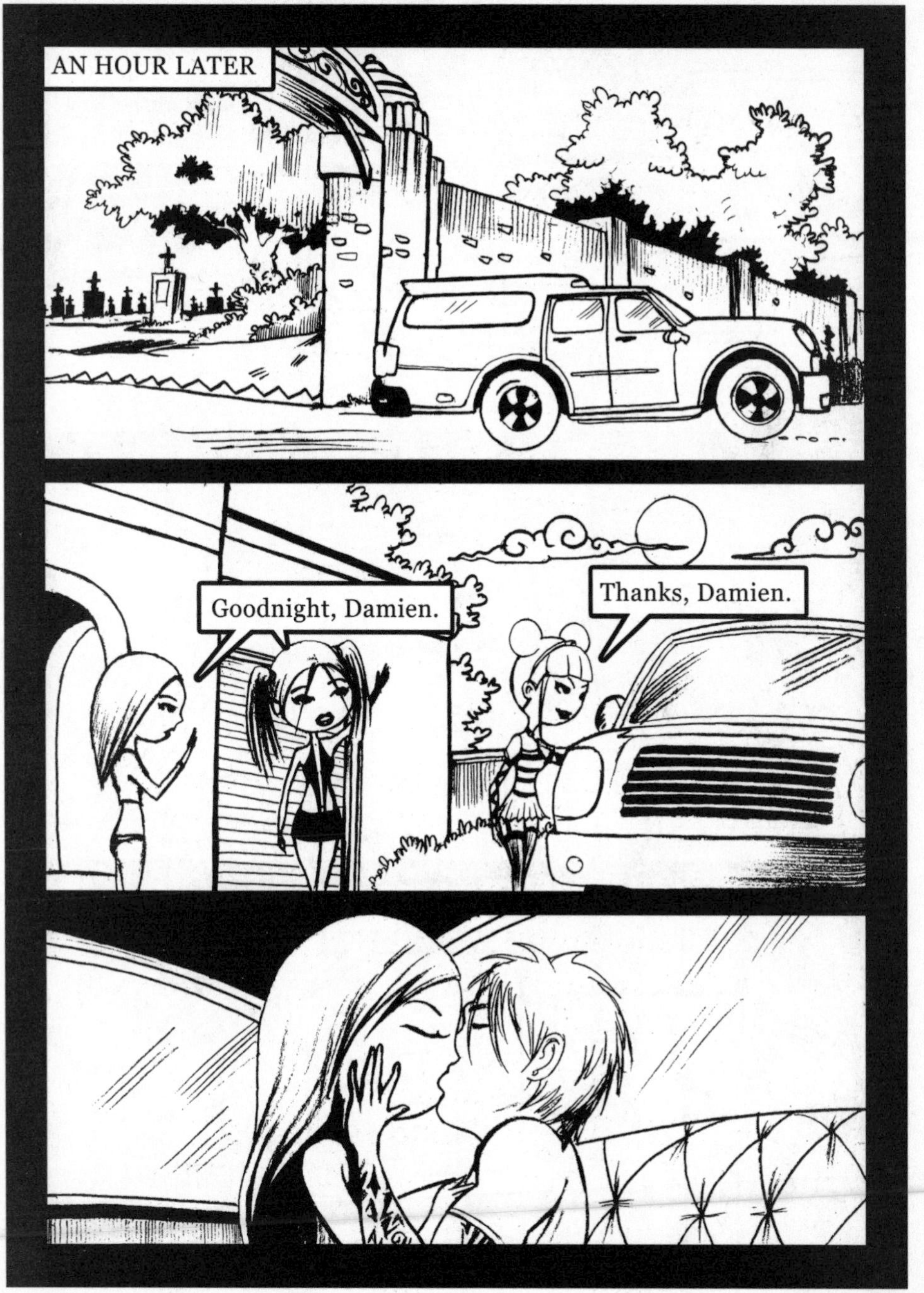
AN HOUR LATER
Goodnight, Damien.
Thanks, Damien.

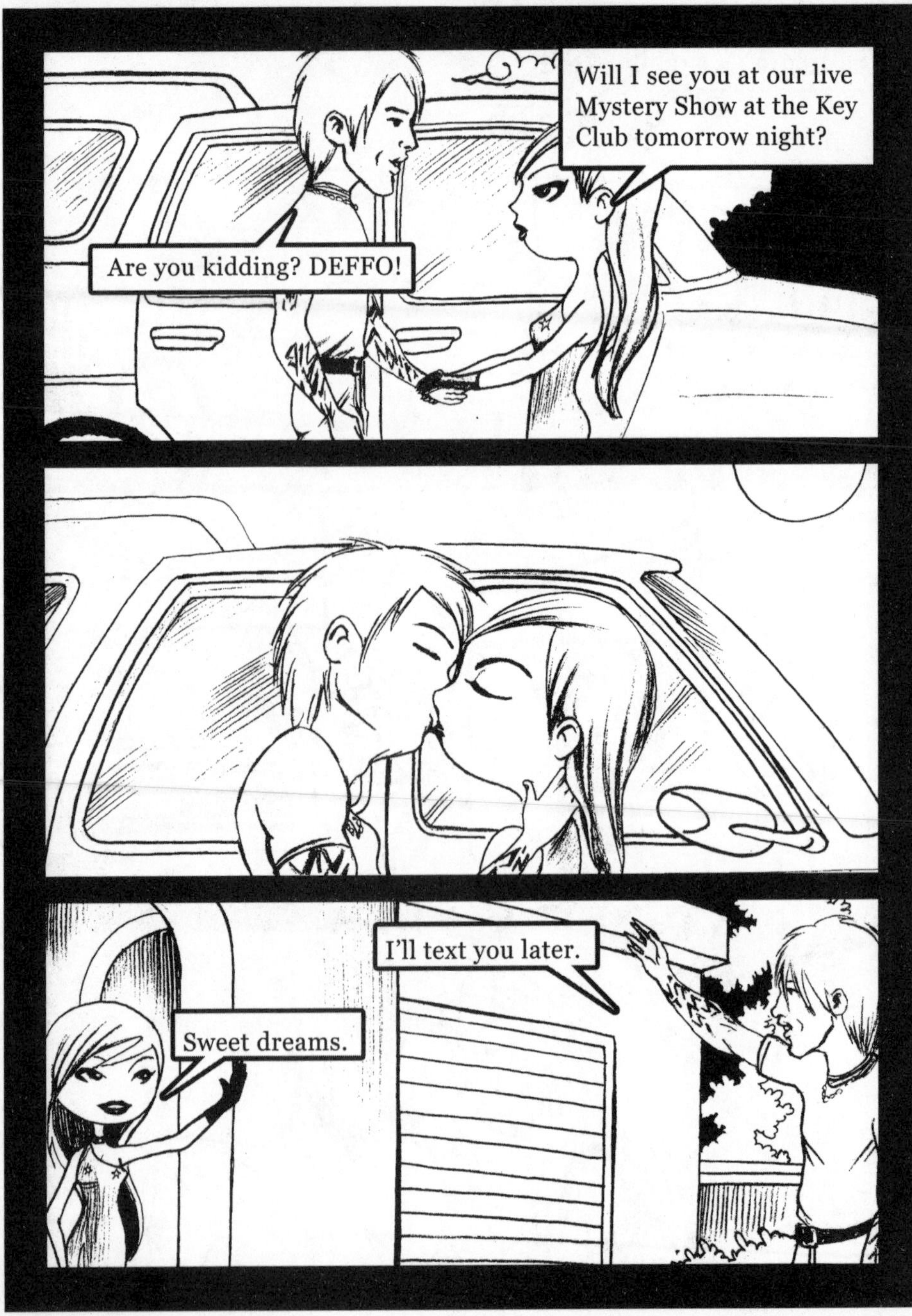
Will I see you at our live Mystery Show at the Key Club tomorrow night?
Are you kidding? DEFFO!
Sweet dreams.
I'll text you later.

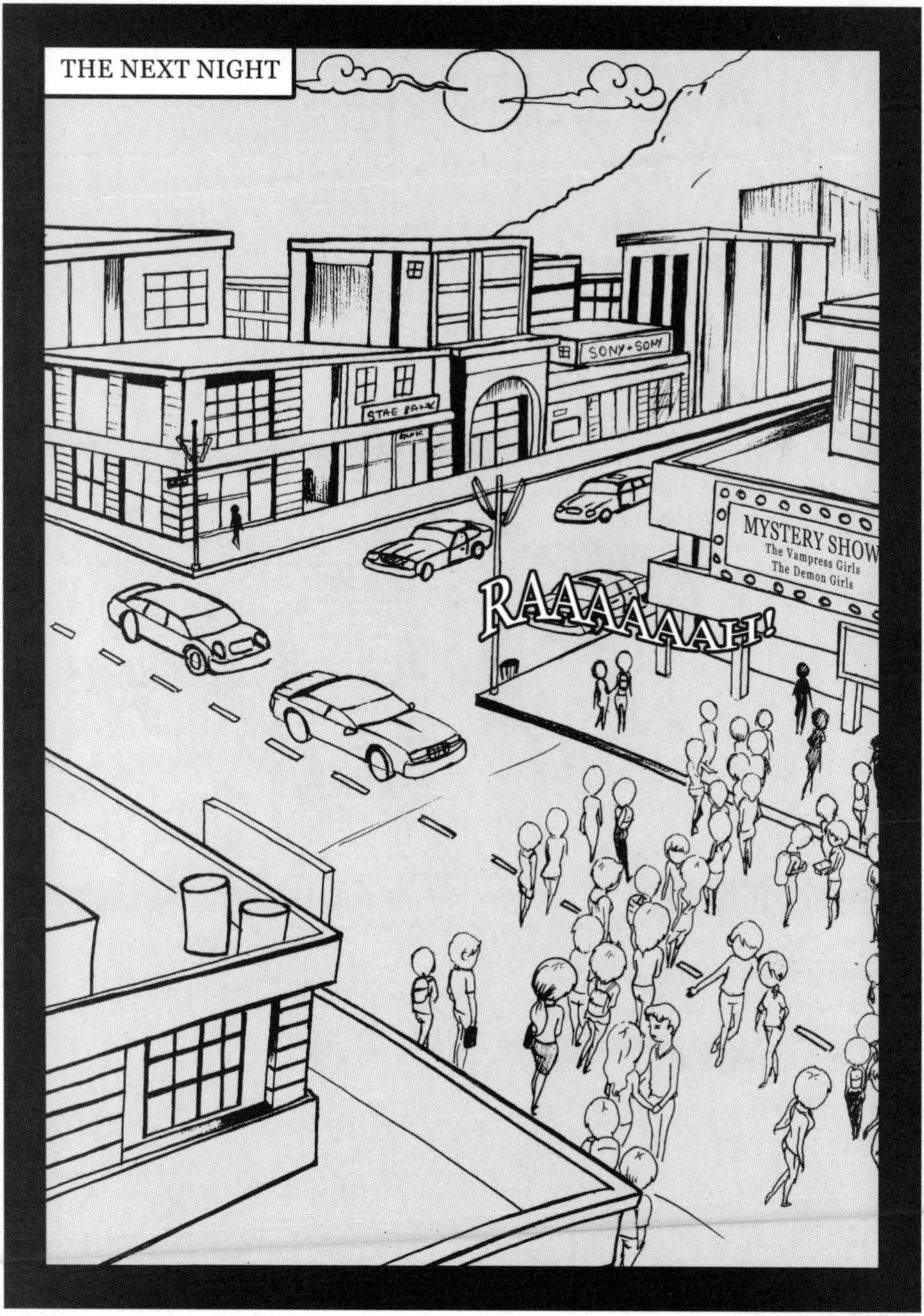
THE NEXT NIGHT
STAE BANK
SONY + SONY
MYSTERY SHOW
The Vampress Girls
The Demon Girls
RAAAAAAH!

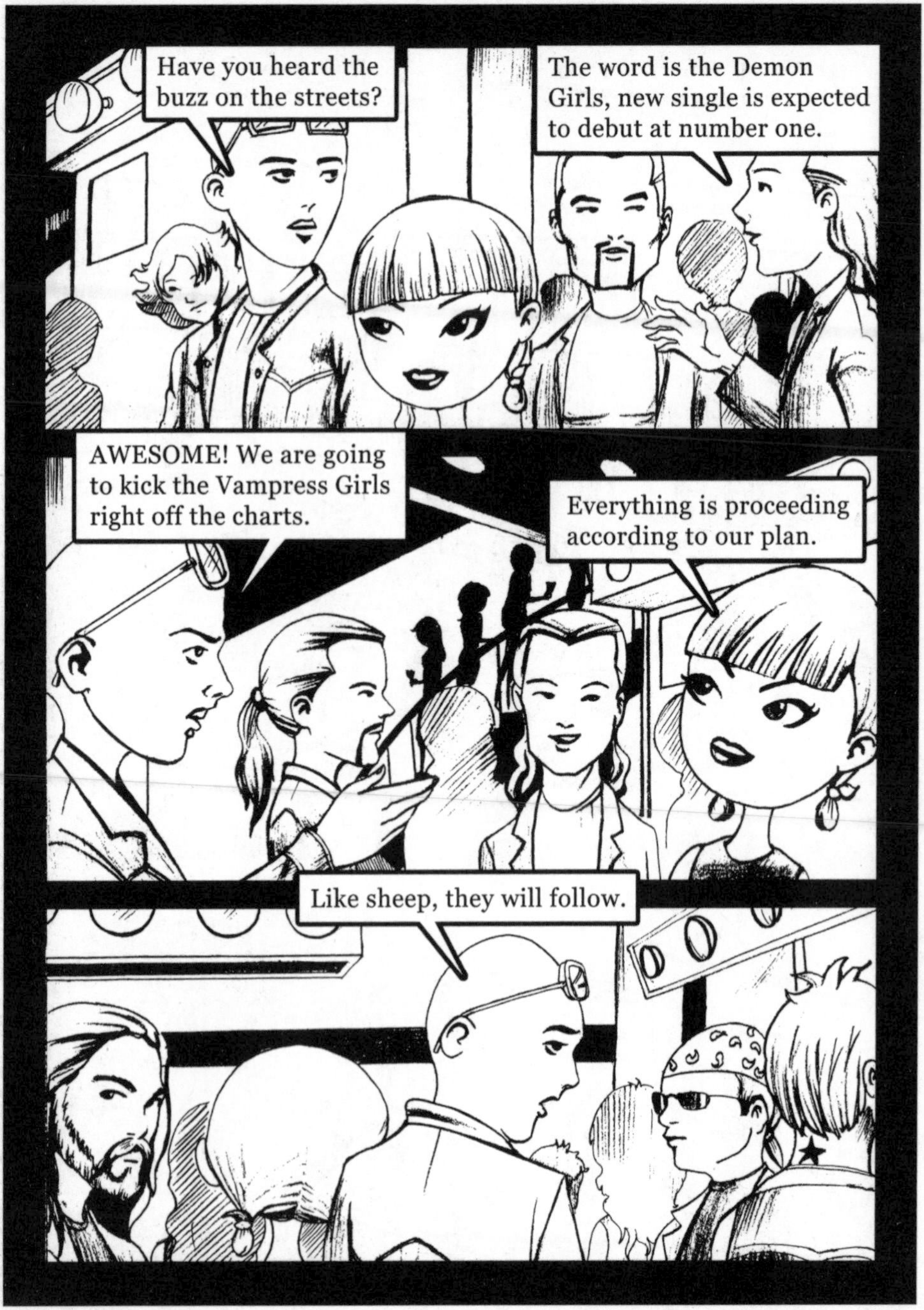
Have you heard the buzz on the streets?
The word is the Demon Girls, new single is expected to debut at number one.
AWESOME! We are going to kick the Vampress Girls right off the charts.
Everything is proceeding according to our plan.
Like sheep, they will follow.

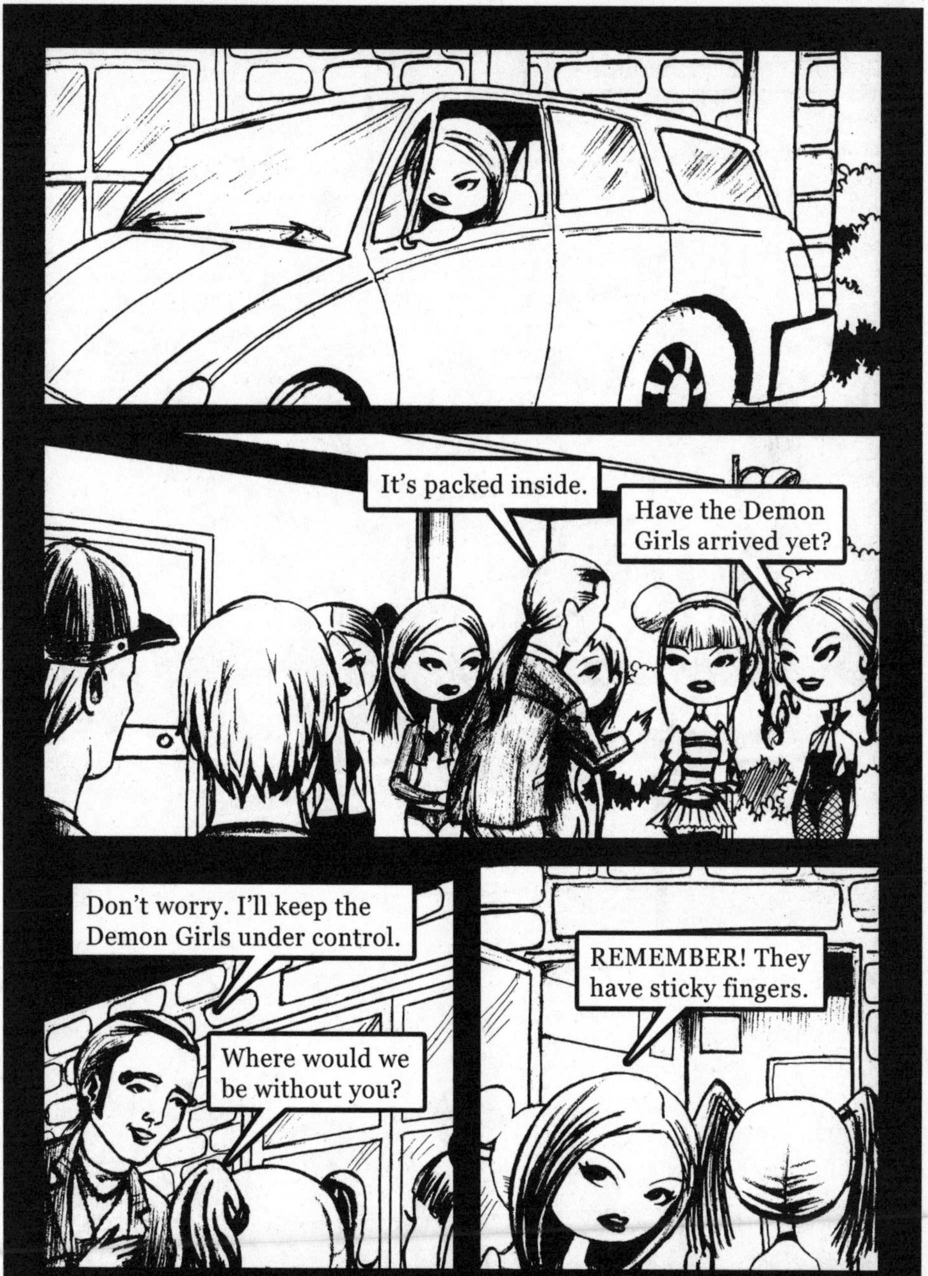
It's packed inside.
Have the Demon Girls arrived yet?
Don't worry. I'll keep the Demon Girls under control.
Where would we be without you?
REMEMBER! They have sticky fingers.

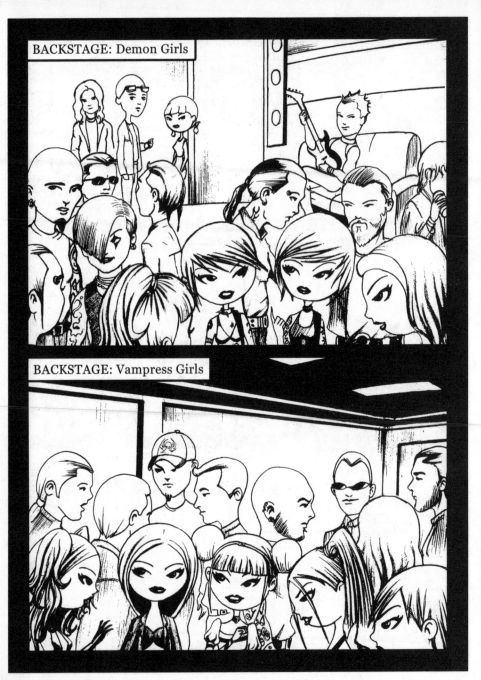

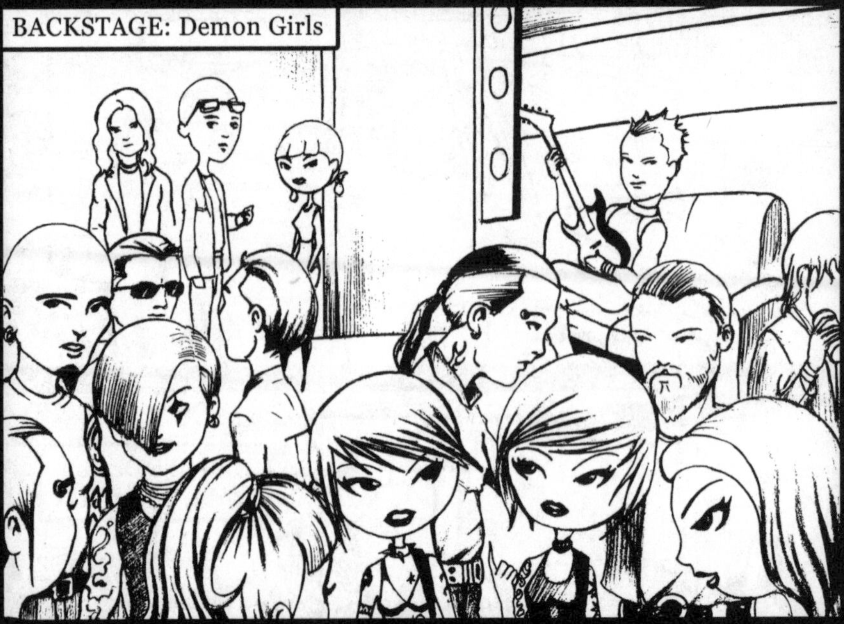
BACKSTAGE: Demon Girls

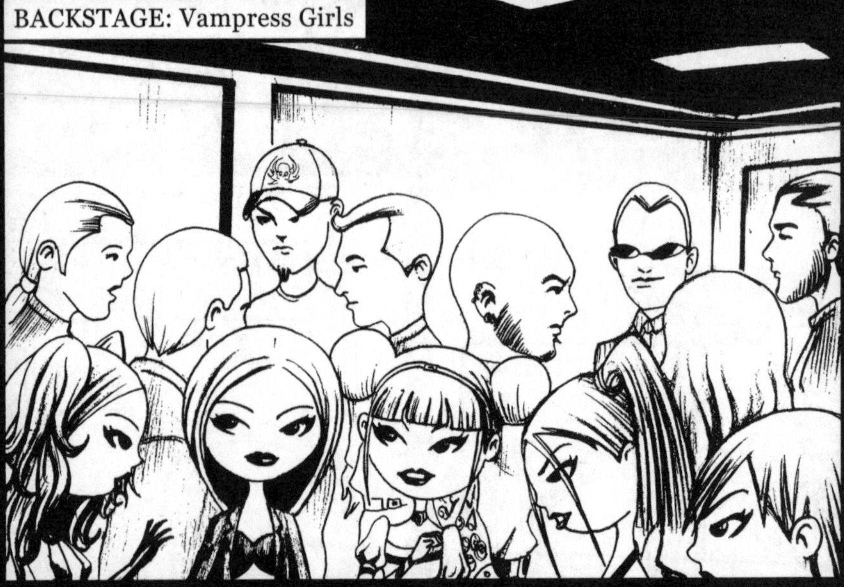
BACKSTAGE: Vampress Girls

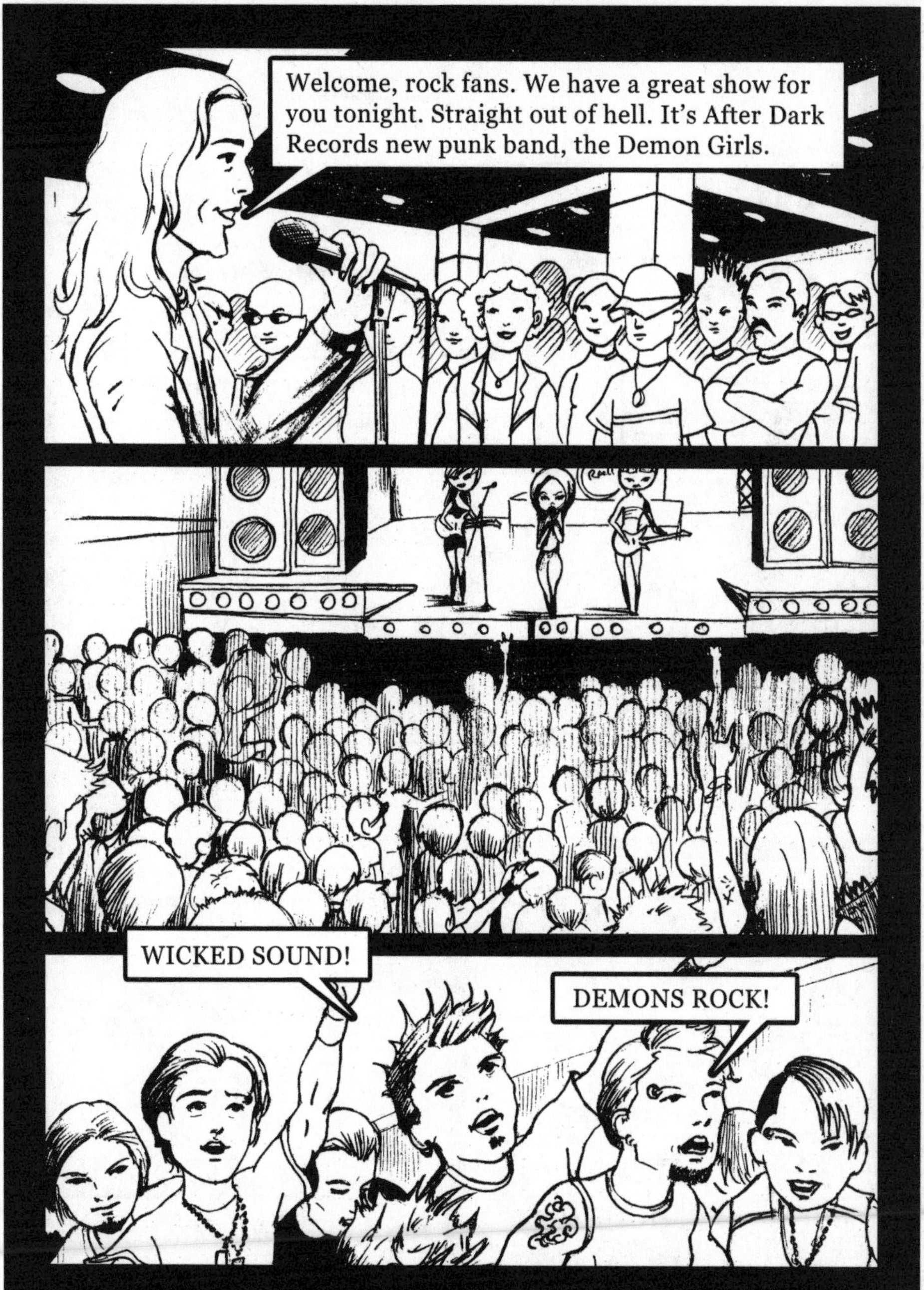
Welcome, rock fans. We have a great show for you tonight. Straight out of hell. It's After Dark Records new punk band, the Demon Girls.
WICKED SOUND!
DEMONS ROCK!

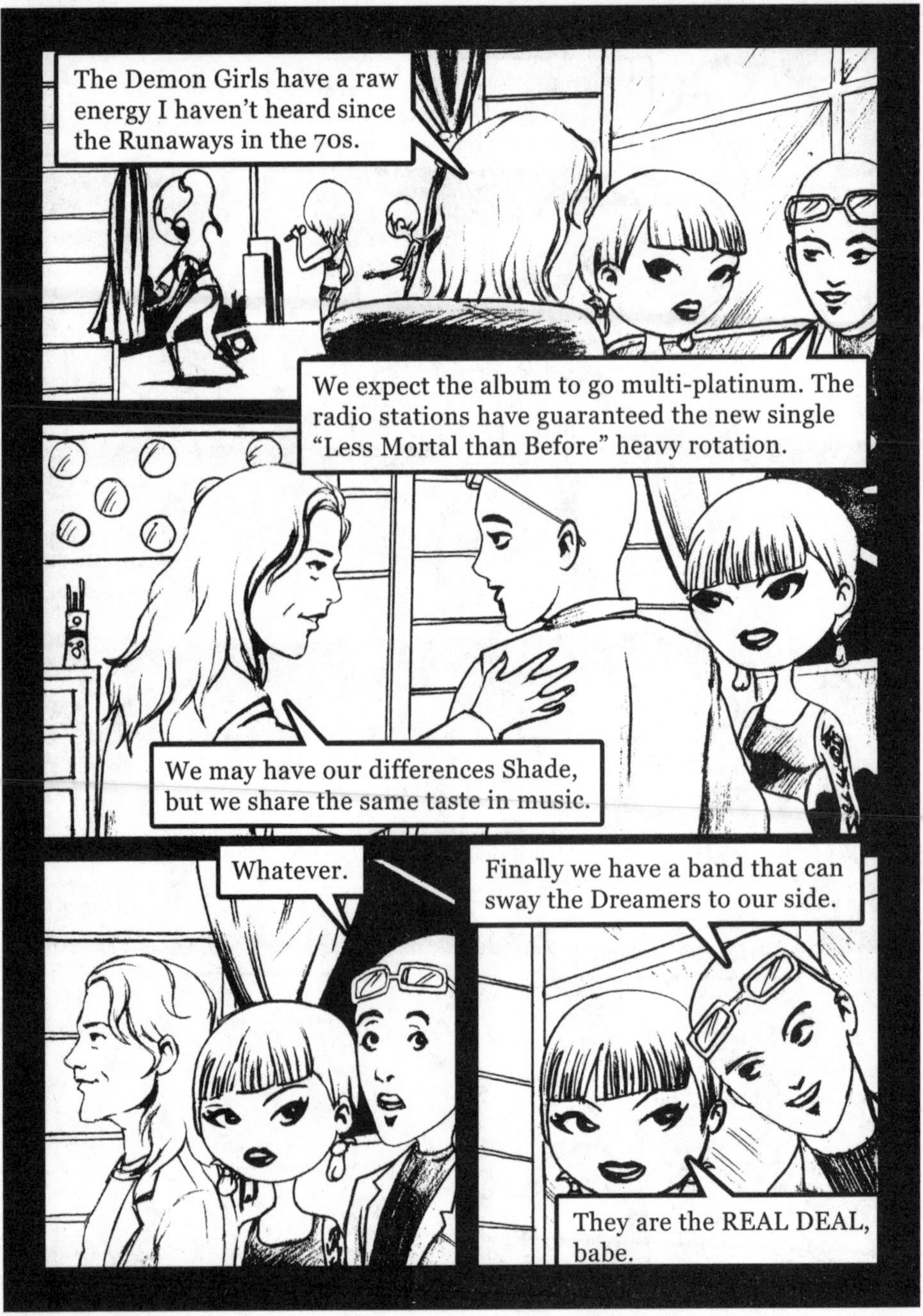
The Demon Girls have a raw energy I haven't heard since the Runaways in the 70s.
We expect the album to go multi-platinum. The radio stations have guaranteed the new single "Less Mortal than Before" heavy rotation.
We may have our differences Shade, but we share the same taste in music.
Whatever.
Finally we have a band that can sway the Dreamers to our side.
They are the REAL DEAL, babe.

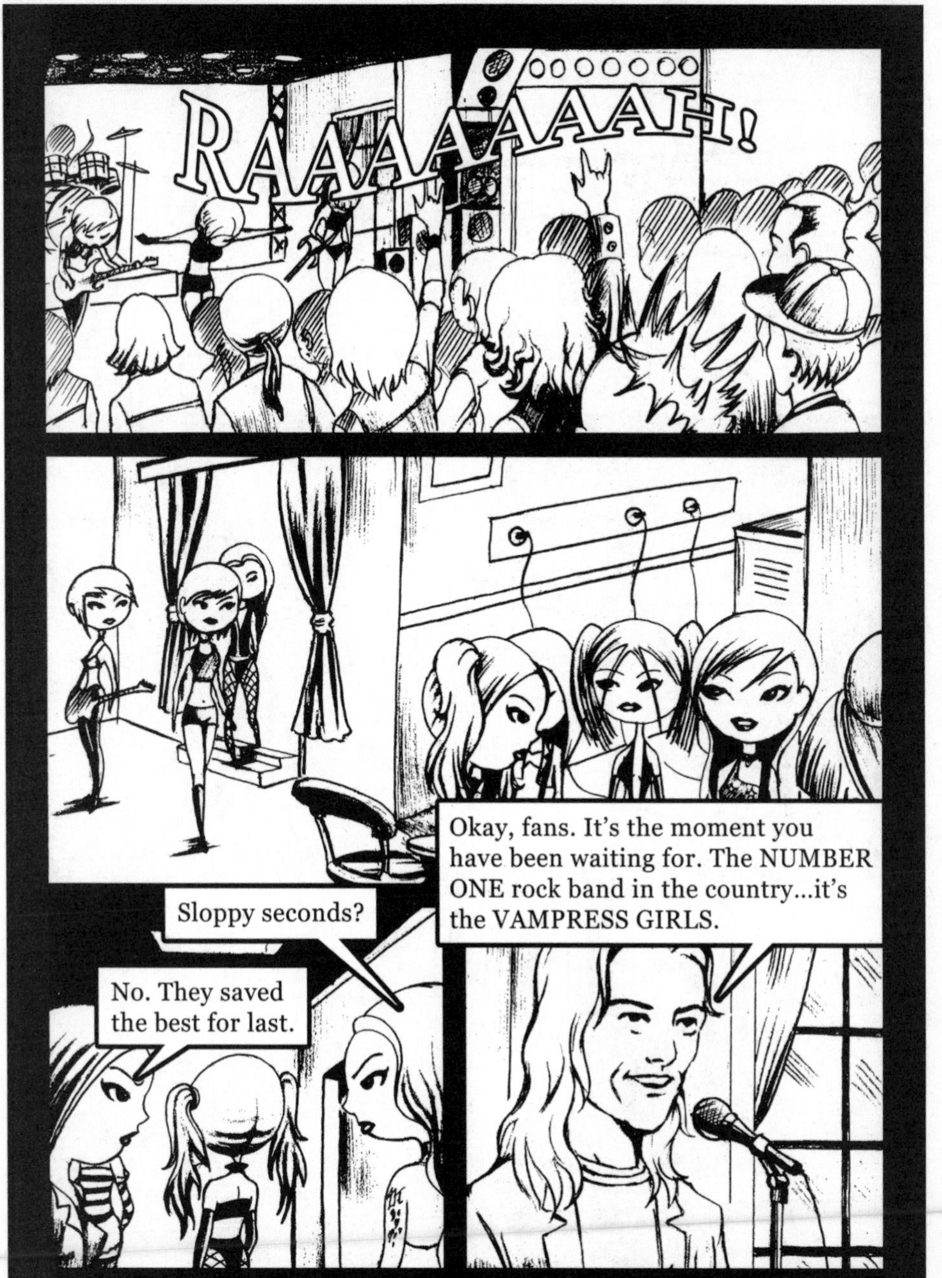
RAAAAAAAAH!
Okay, fans. It's the moment you have been waiting for. The NUMBER ONE rock band in the country...it's the VAMPRESS GIRLS.
Sloppy seconds?
No. They saved the best for last.

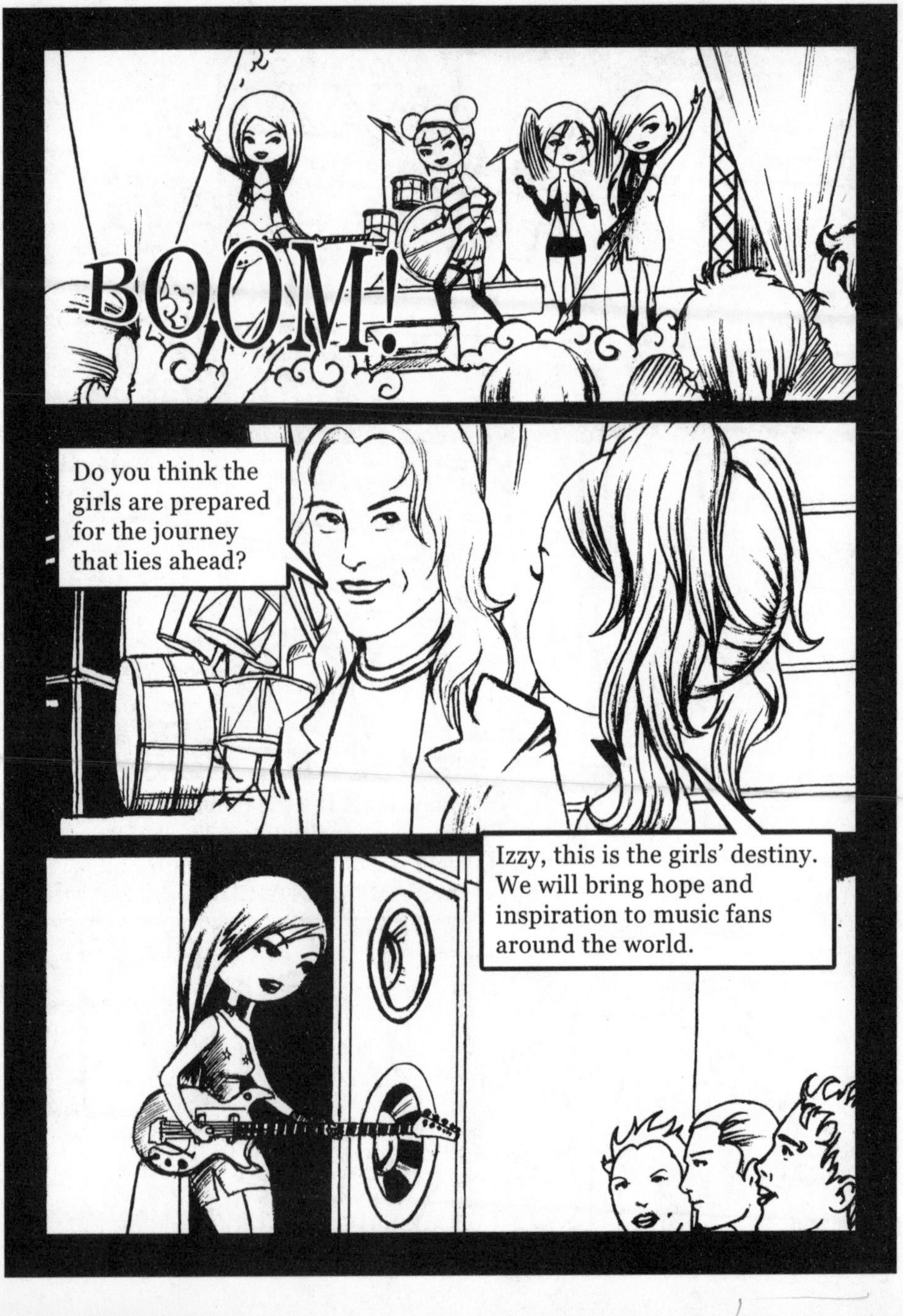
BOOM!
Do you think the girls are prepared for the journey that lies ahead?
Izzy, this is the girls' destiny. We will bring hope and inspiration to music fans around the world.

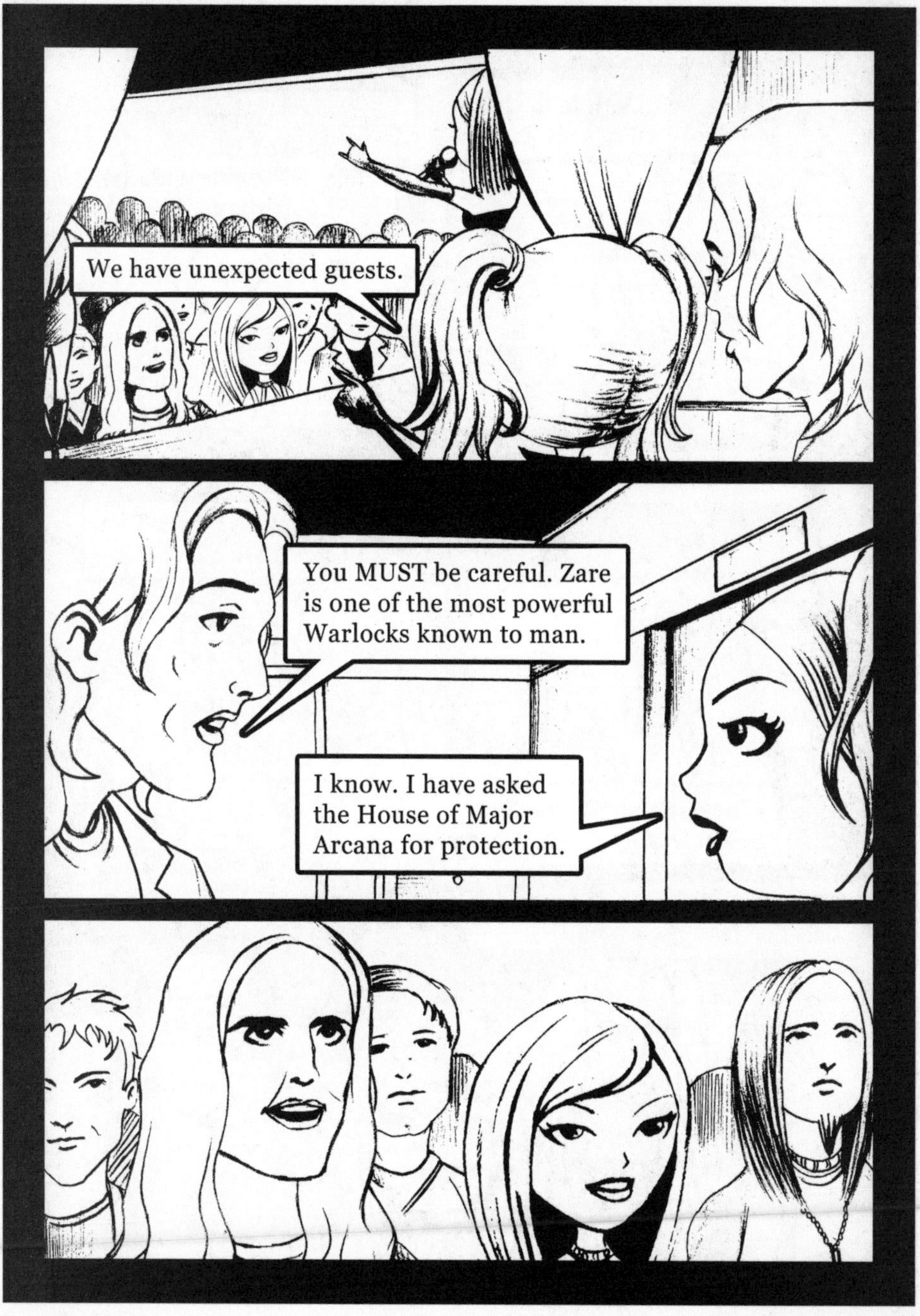
We have unexpected guests.
You MUST be careful. Zare is one of the most powerful Warlocks known to man.
I know. I have asked the House of Major Arcana for protection.

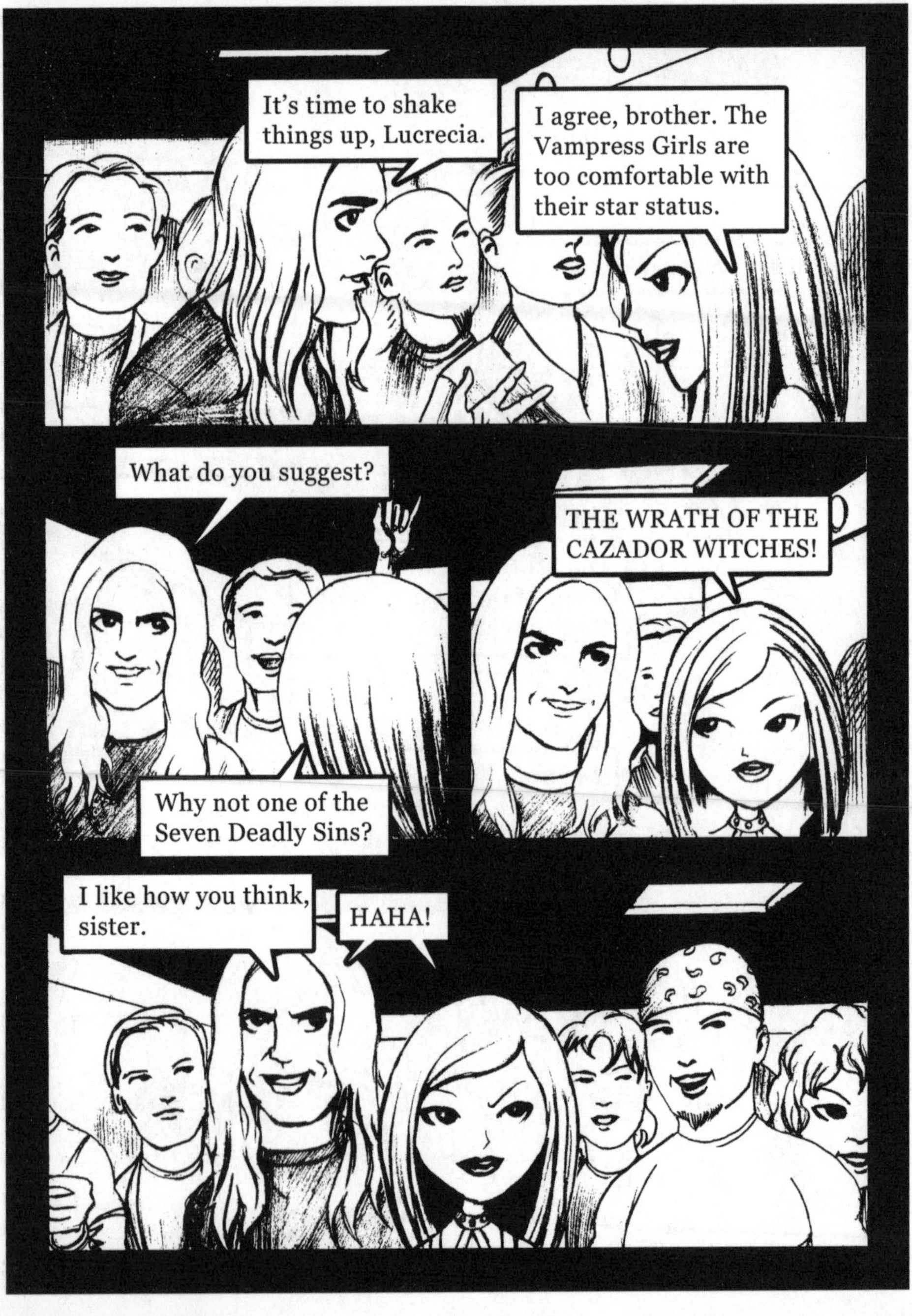
It's time to shake things up, Lucrecia.
I agree, brother. The Vampress Girls are too comfortable with their star status.
What do you suggest?
Why not one of the Seven Deadly Sins?
THE WRATH OF THE CAZADOR WITCHES!
I like how you think, sister.
HAHA!

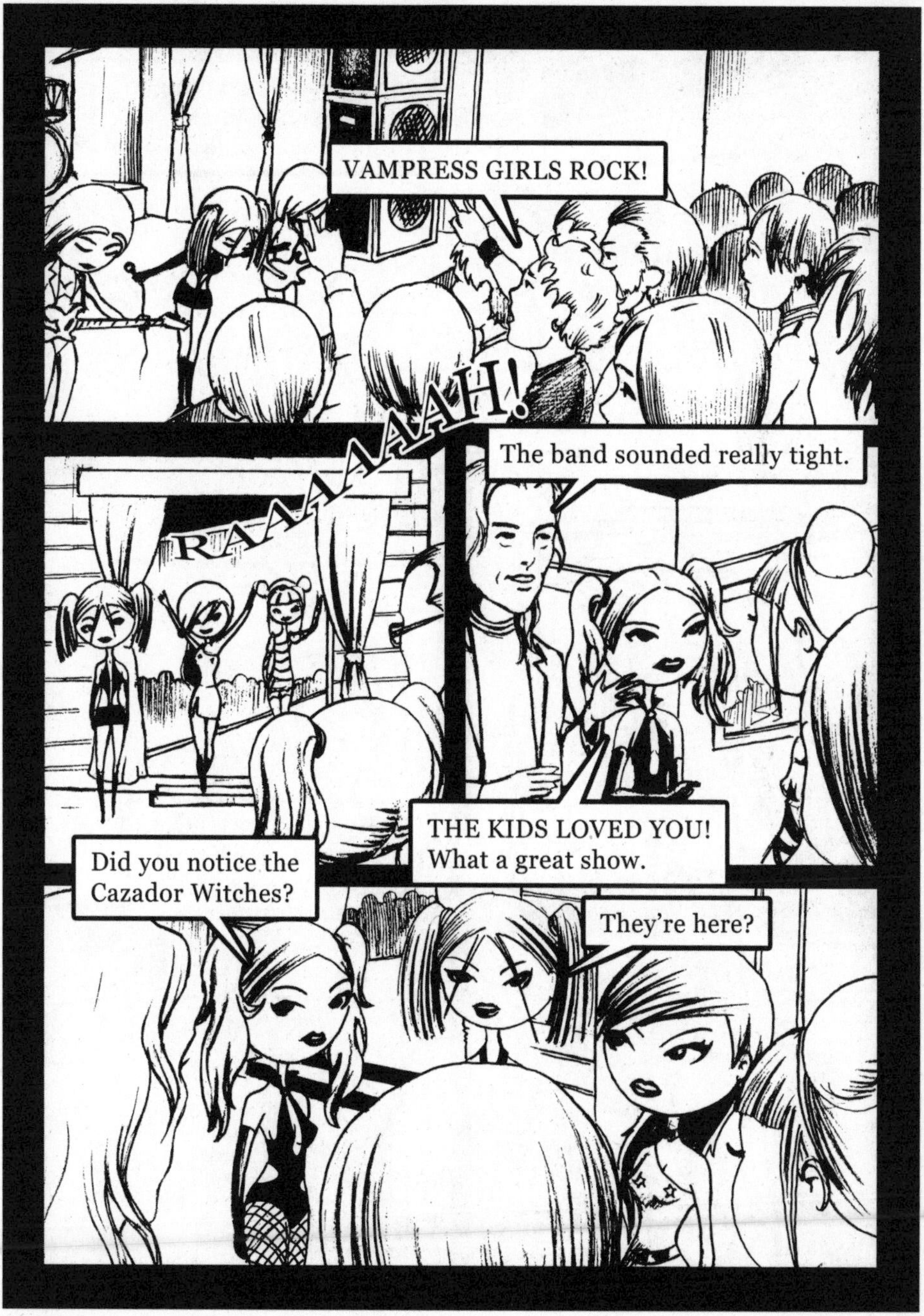

VAMPRESS GIRLS ROCK!
RAAAAAAAH!
The band sounded really tight.
THE KIDS LOVED YOU!
What a great show.
Did you notice the
Cazador Witches?
They're here?

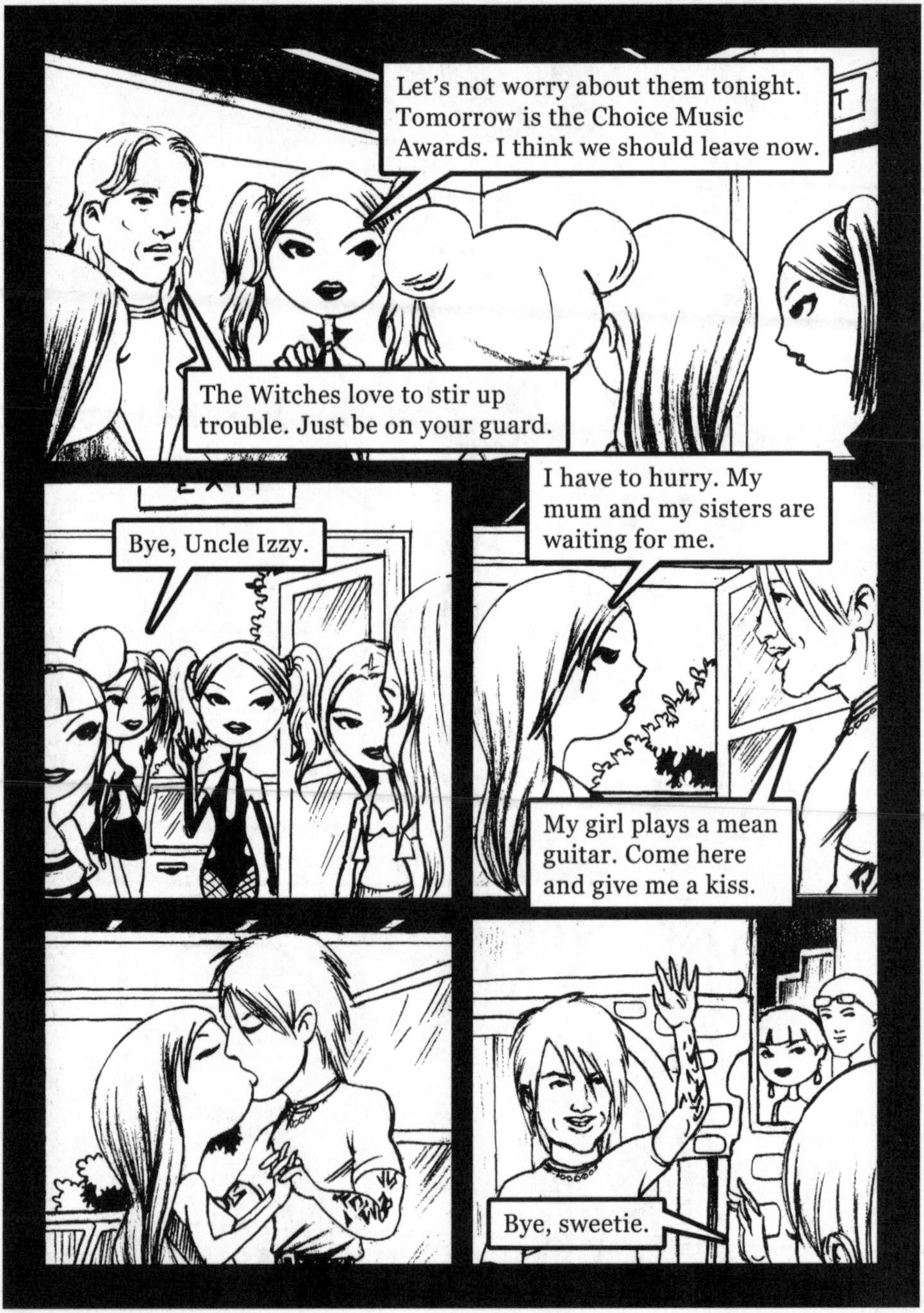
Let's not worry about them tonight. Tomorrow is the Choice Music Awards. I think we should leave now.
The Witches love to stir up trouble. Just be on your guard.
Bye, Uncle Izzy.
I have to hurry. My mum and my sisters are waiting for me.
My girl plays a mean guitar. Come here and give me a kiss.
Bye, sweetie.

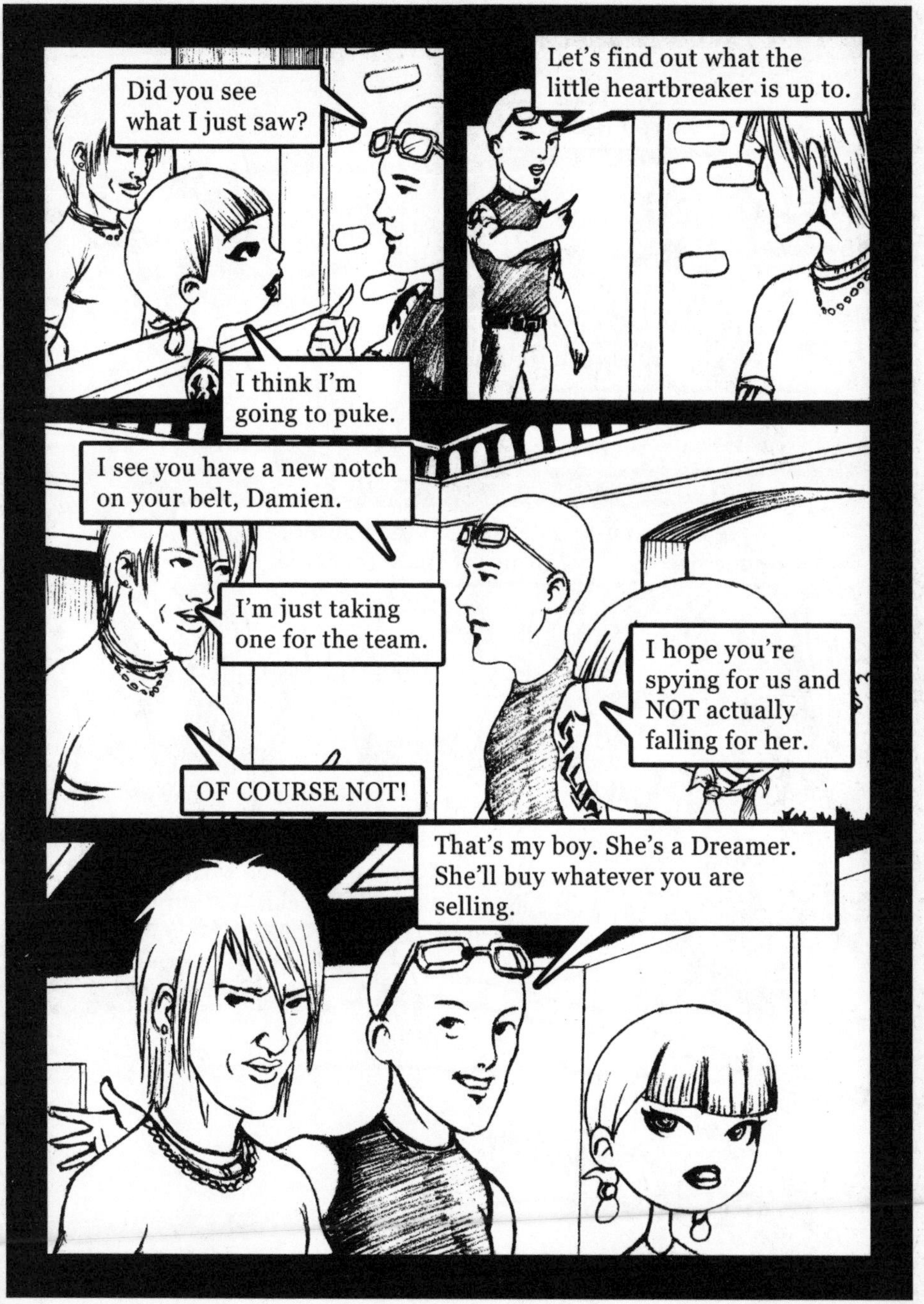
Did you see what I just saw?
I think I'm going to puke.
Let's find out what the little heartbreaker is up to.
I see you have a new notch on your belt, Damien.
I'm just taking one for the team.
OF COURSE NOT!
I hope you're spying for us and NOT actually falling for her.
That's my boy. She's a Dreamer. She'll buy whatever you are selling.

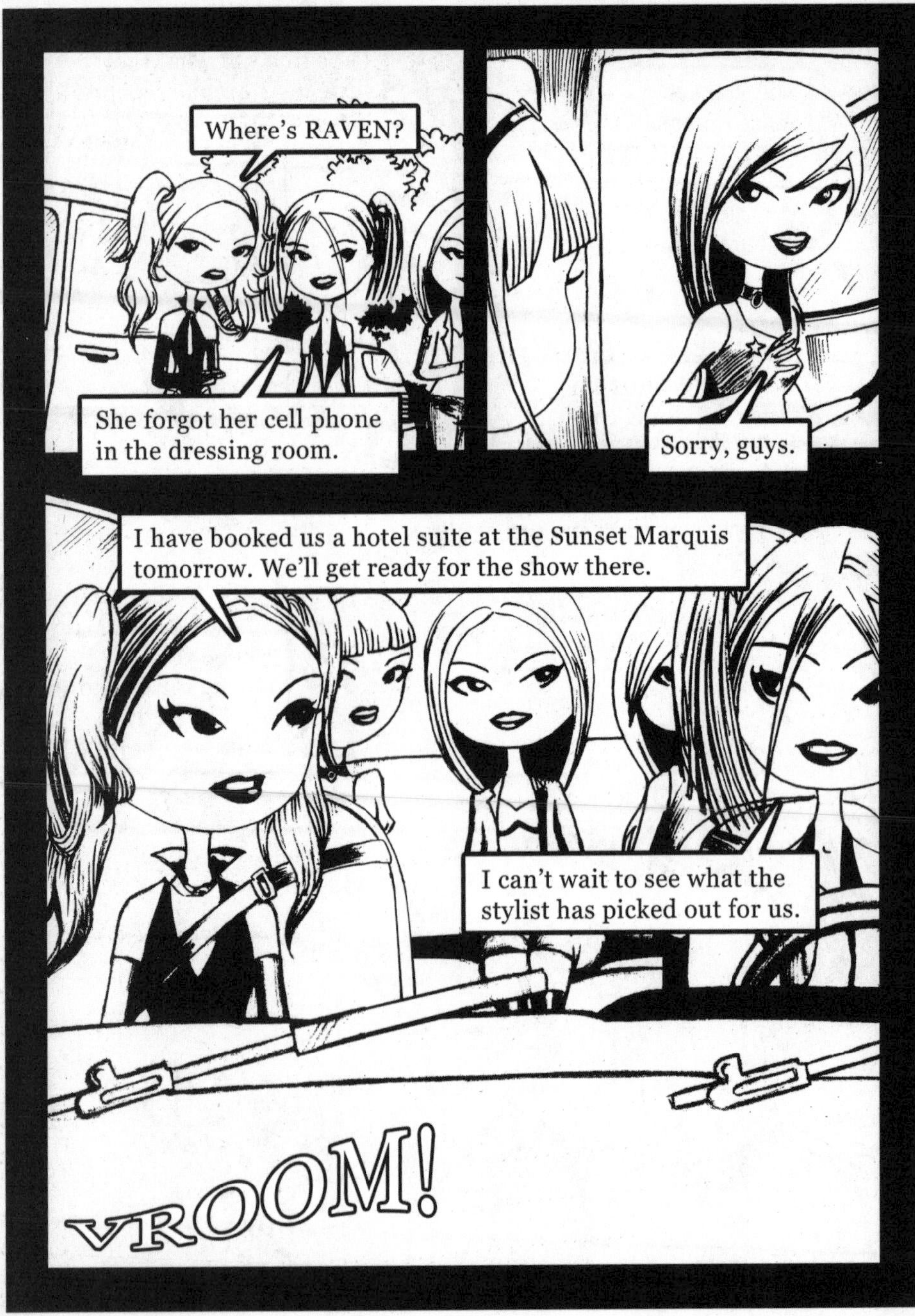
Where's RAVEN?
She forgot her cell phone in the dressing room.
Sorry, guys.
I have booked us a hotel suite at the Sunset Marquis tomorrow. We'll get ready for the show there.
I can't wait to see what the stylist has picked out for us.
VROOM!

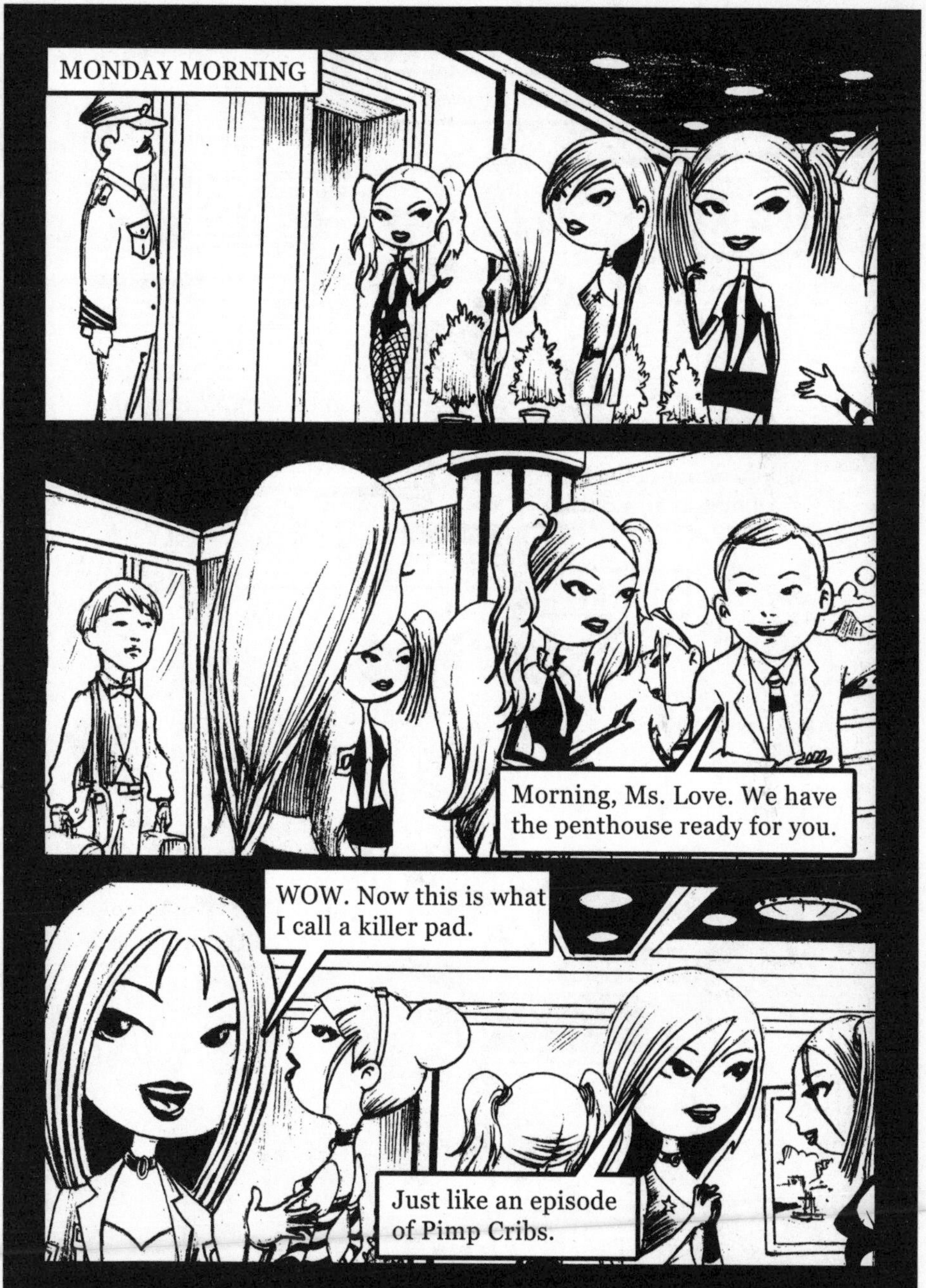
MONDAY MORNING
Morning, Ms. Love. We have the penthouse ready for you.
WOW. Now this is what I call a killer pad.
Just like an episode of Pimp Cribs.

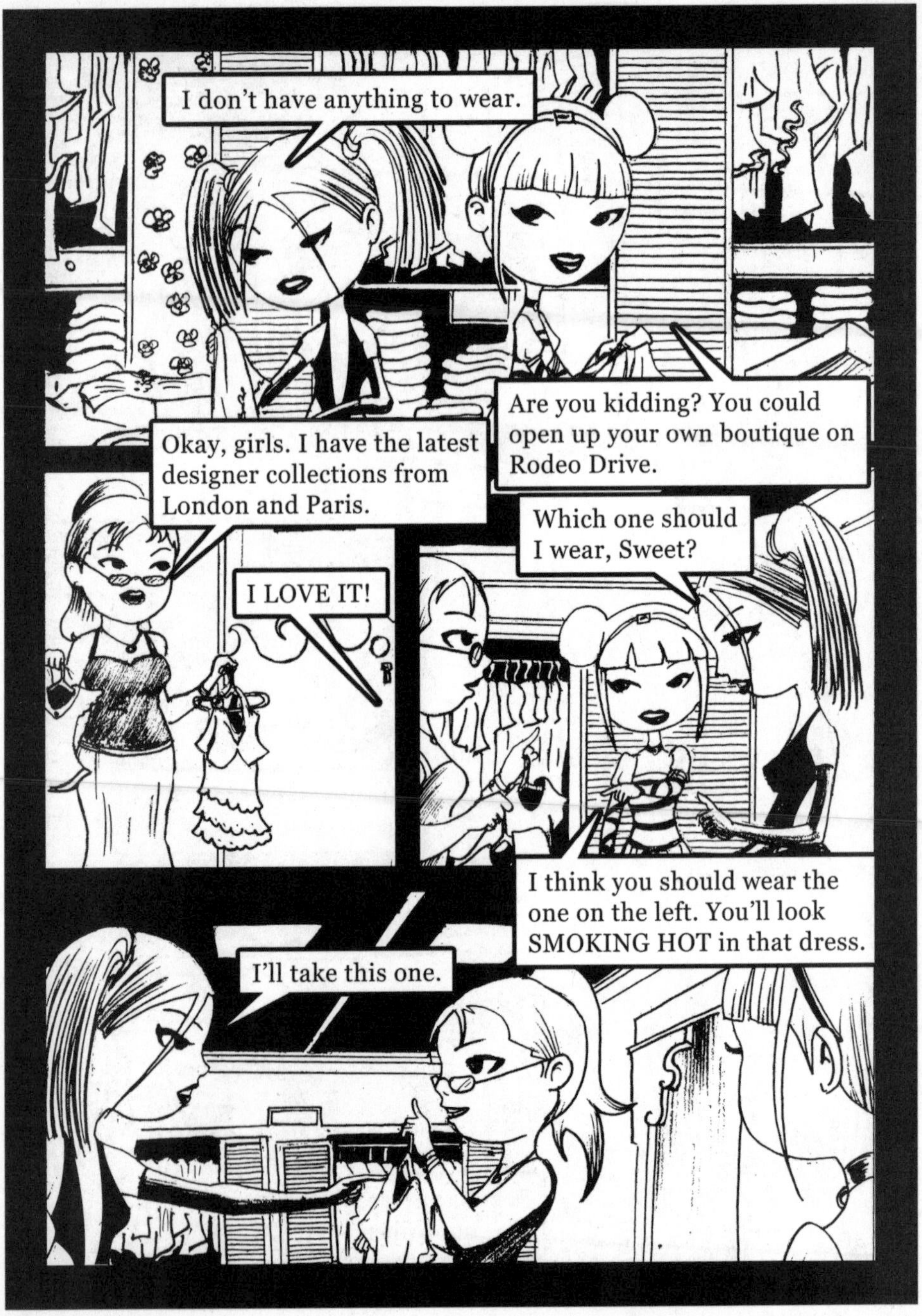
I don't have anything to wear.
Are you kidding? You could open up your own boutique on Rodeo Drive.
Okay, girls. I have the latest designer collections from London and Paris.
I LOVE IT!
Which one should I wear, Sweet?
I think you should wear the one on the left. You'll look SMOKING HOT in that dress.
I'll take this one.

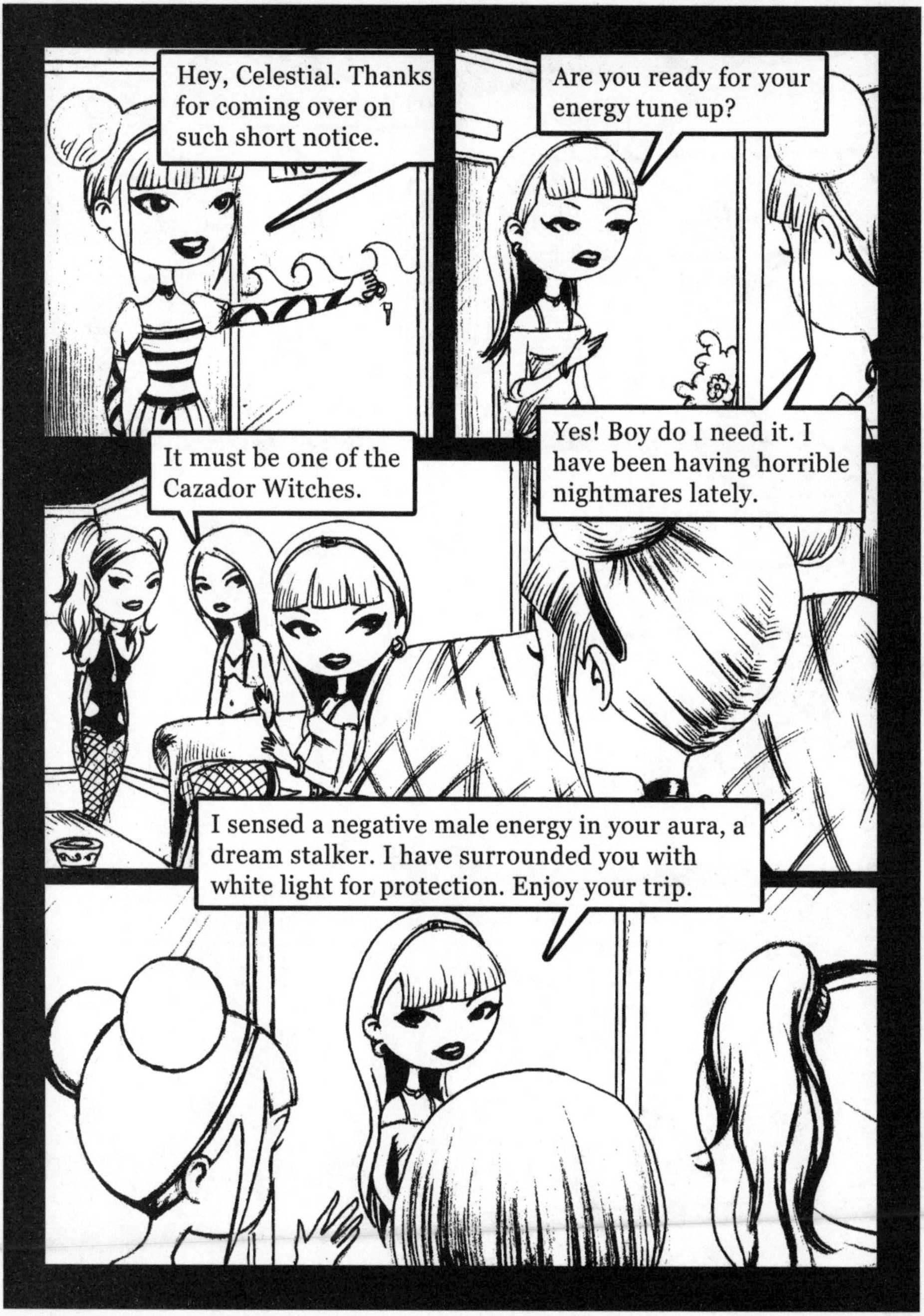
Hey, Celestial. Thanks for coming over on such short notice.
Are you ready for your energy tune up?
Yes! Boy do I need it. I have been having horrible nightmares lately.
It must be one of the Cazador Witches.
I sensed a negative male energy in your aura, a dream stalker. I have surrounded you with white light for protection. Enjoy your trip.

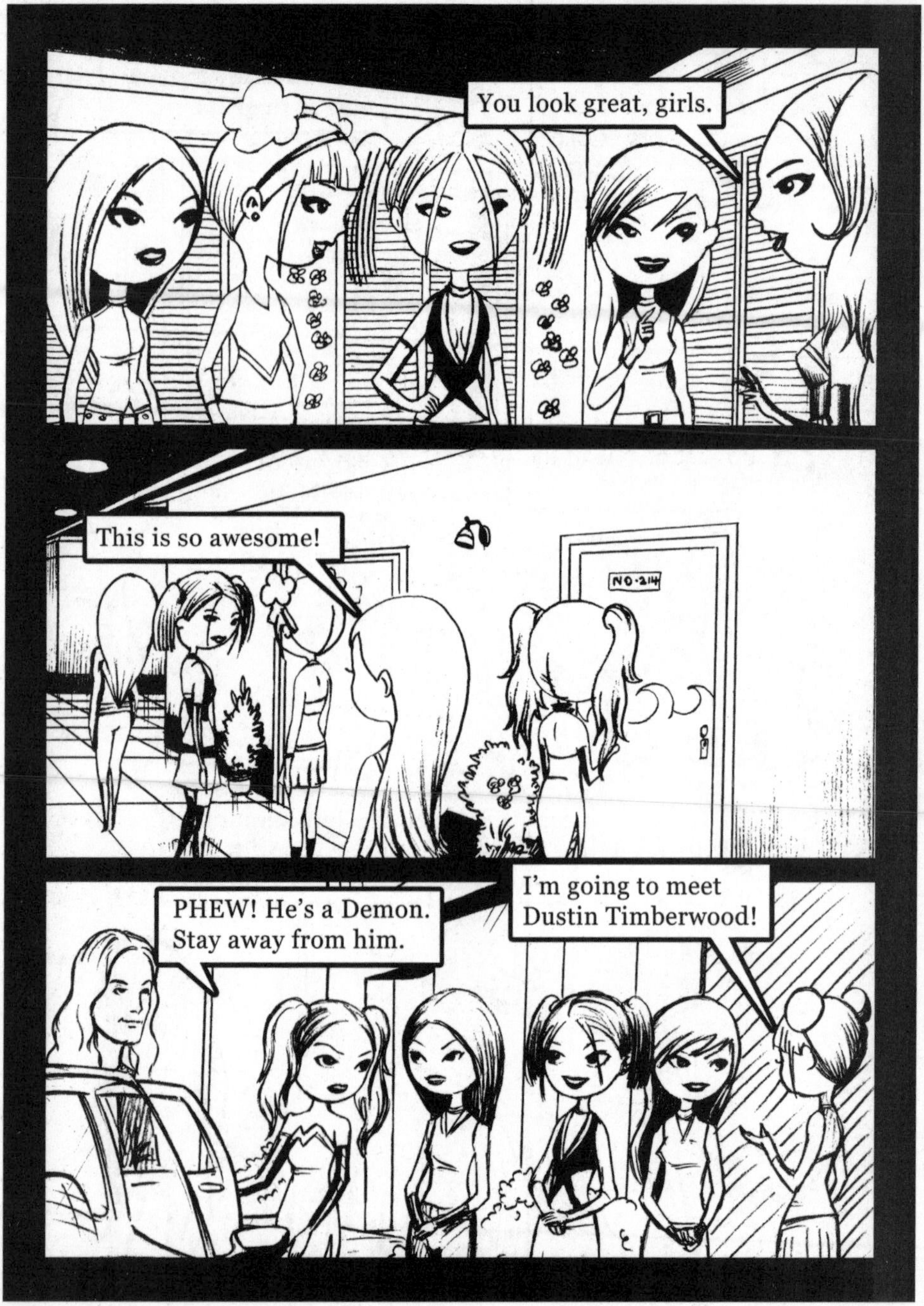
You look great, girls.
This is so awesome!
NO·214
PHEW! He's a Demon. Stay away from him.
I'm going to meet Dustin Timberwood!

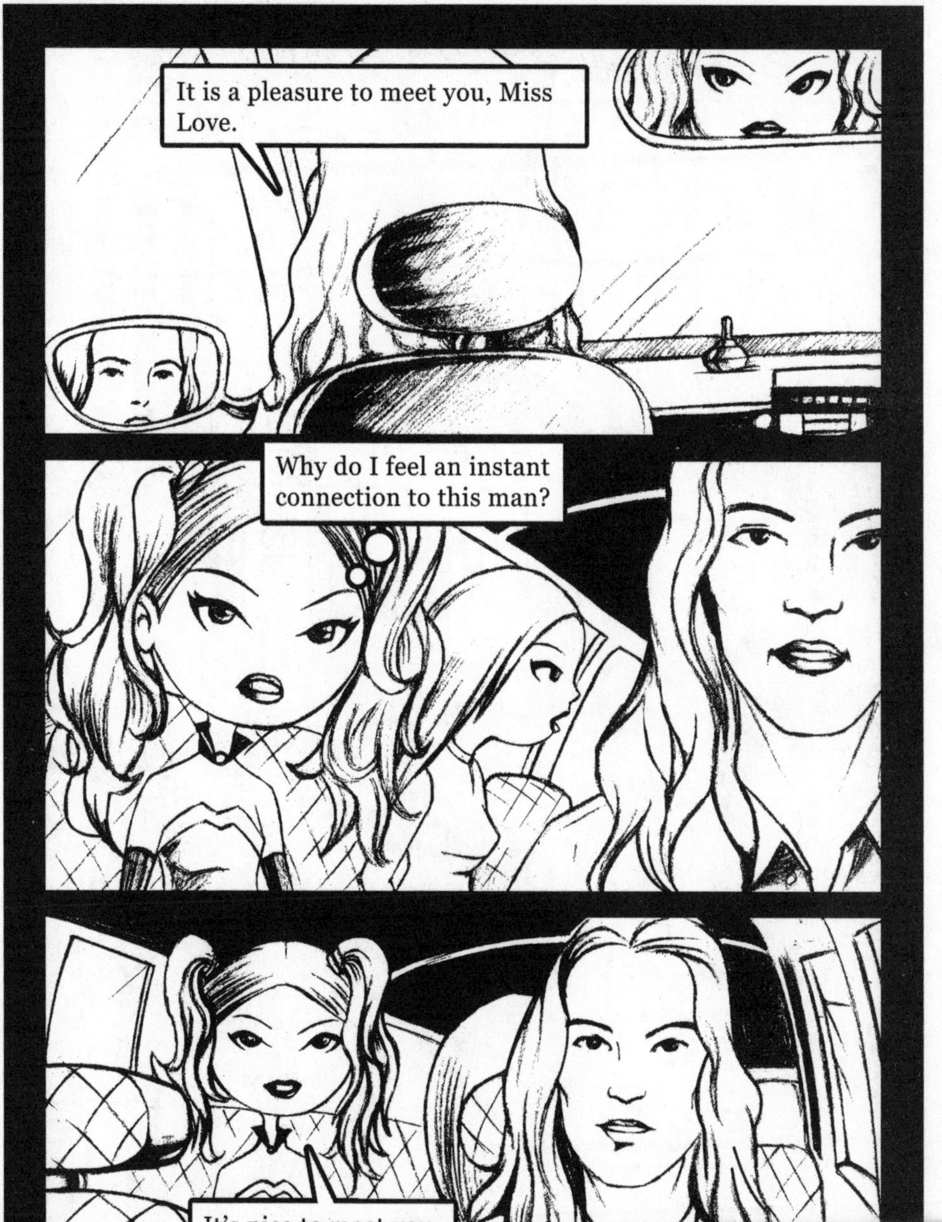
It is a pleasure to meet you, Miss Love.
Why do I feel an instant connection to this man?
It's nice to meet you.

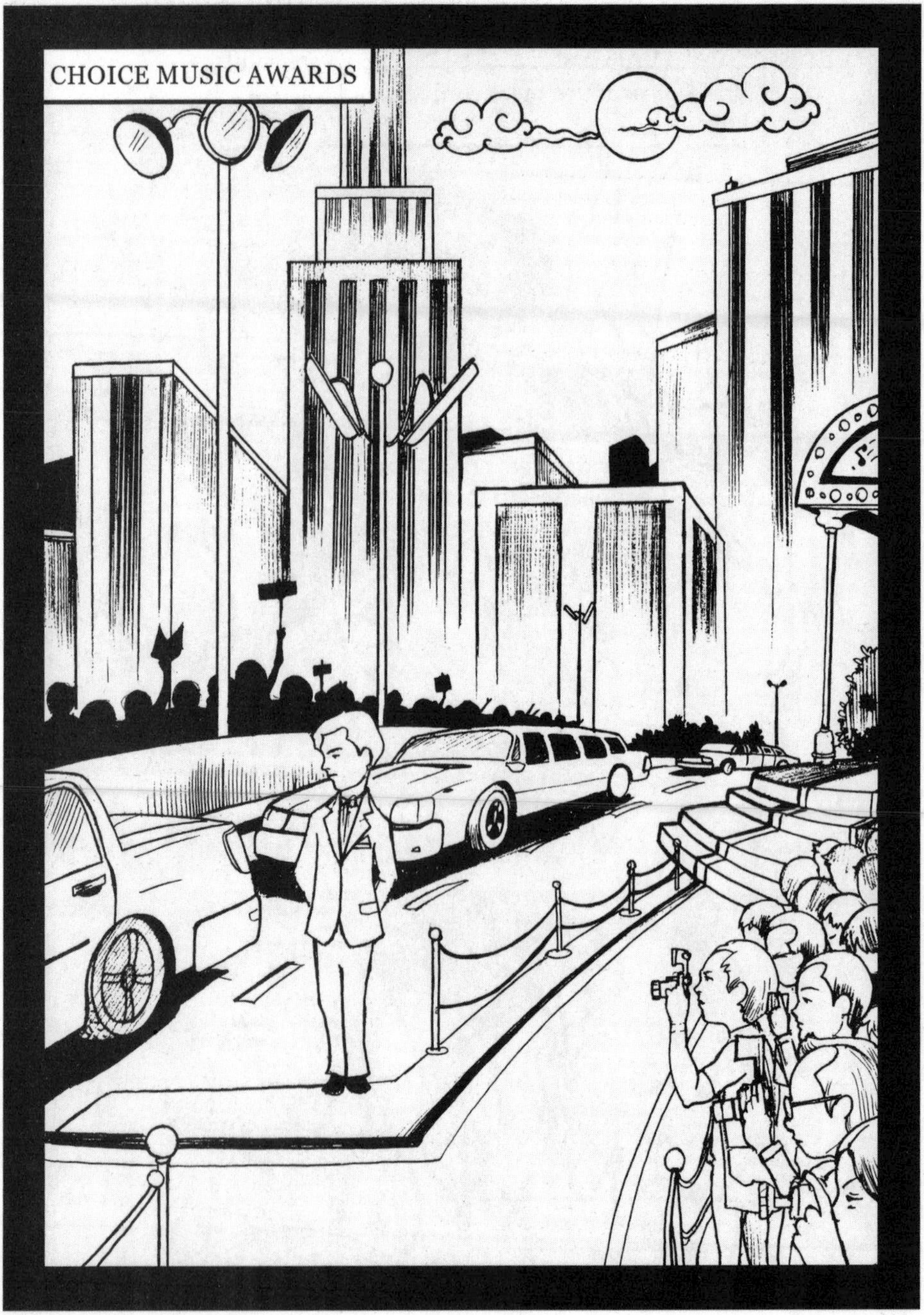
CHOICE MUSIC AWARDS

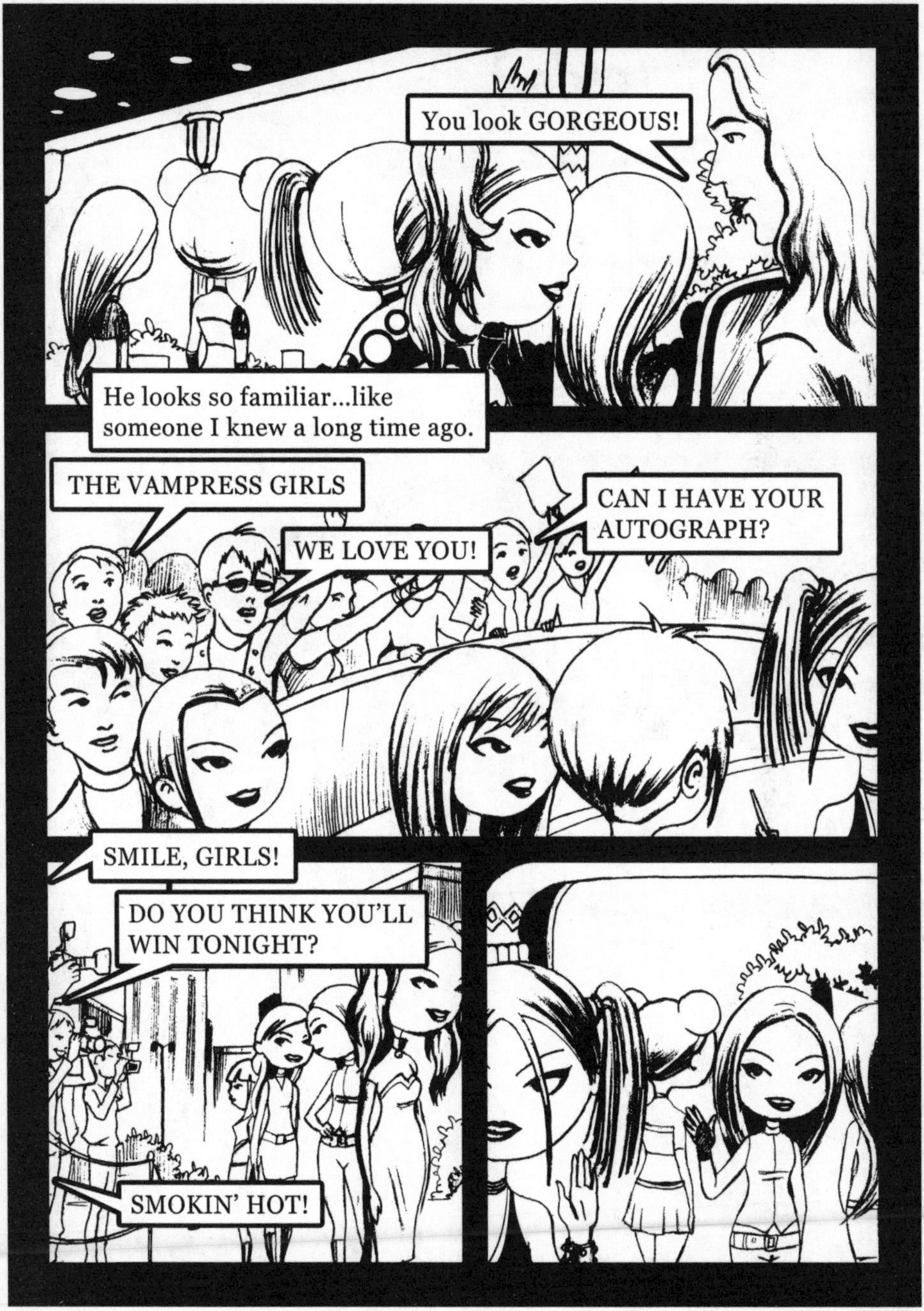
You look GORGEOUS!
He looks so familiar...like someone I knew a long time ago.
THE VAMPRESS GIRLS
WE LOVE YOU!
CAN I HAVE YOUR AUTOGRAPH?
SMILE, GIRLS!
DO YOU THINK YOU'LL WIN TONIGHT?
SMOKIN' HOT!

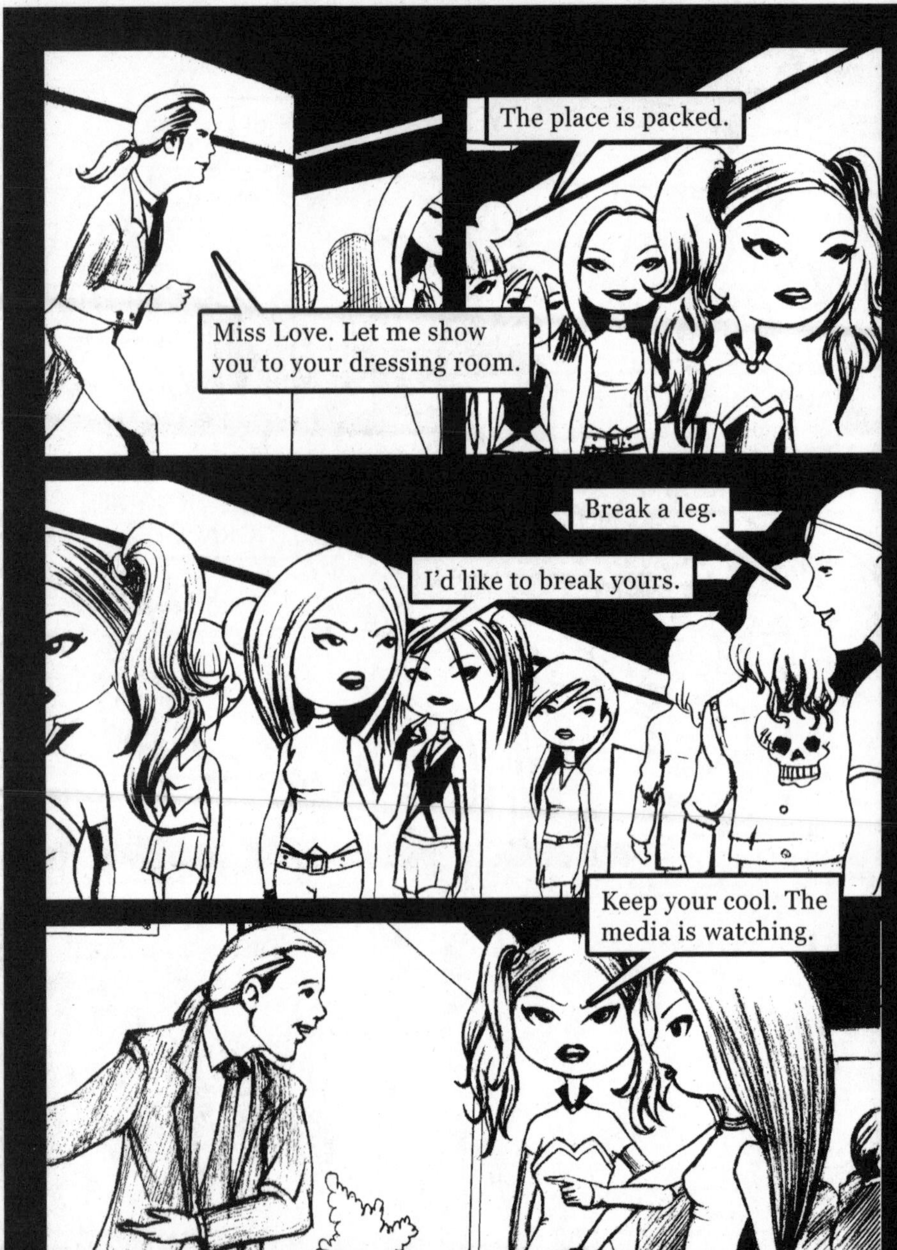
Miss Love. Let me show you to your dressing room.
The place is packed.
Break a leg.
I'd like to break yours.
Keep your cool. The media is watching.

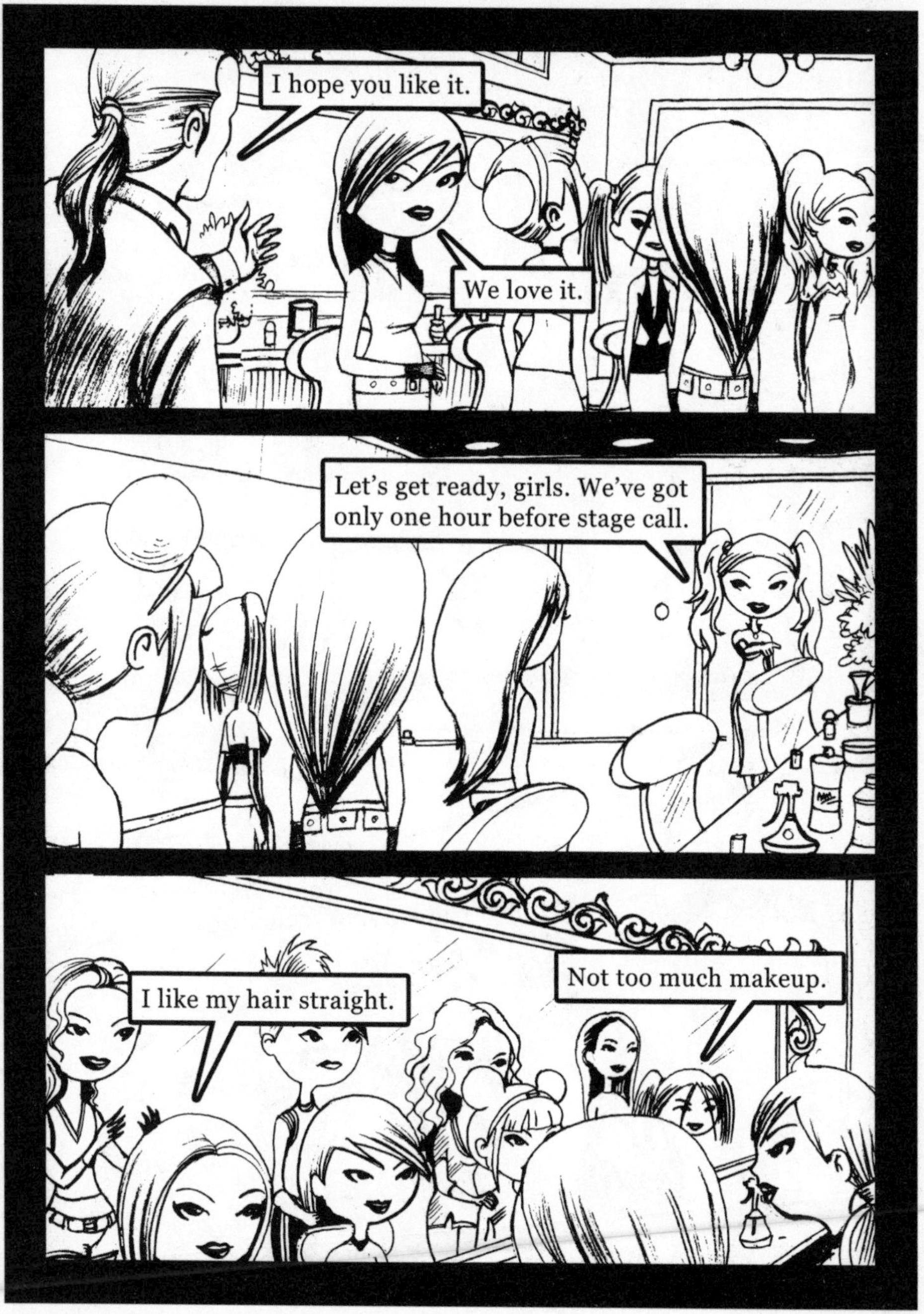
I hope you like it.
We love it.
Let's get ready, girls. We've got only one hour before stage call.
I like my hair straight.
Not too much makeup.

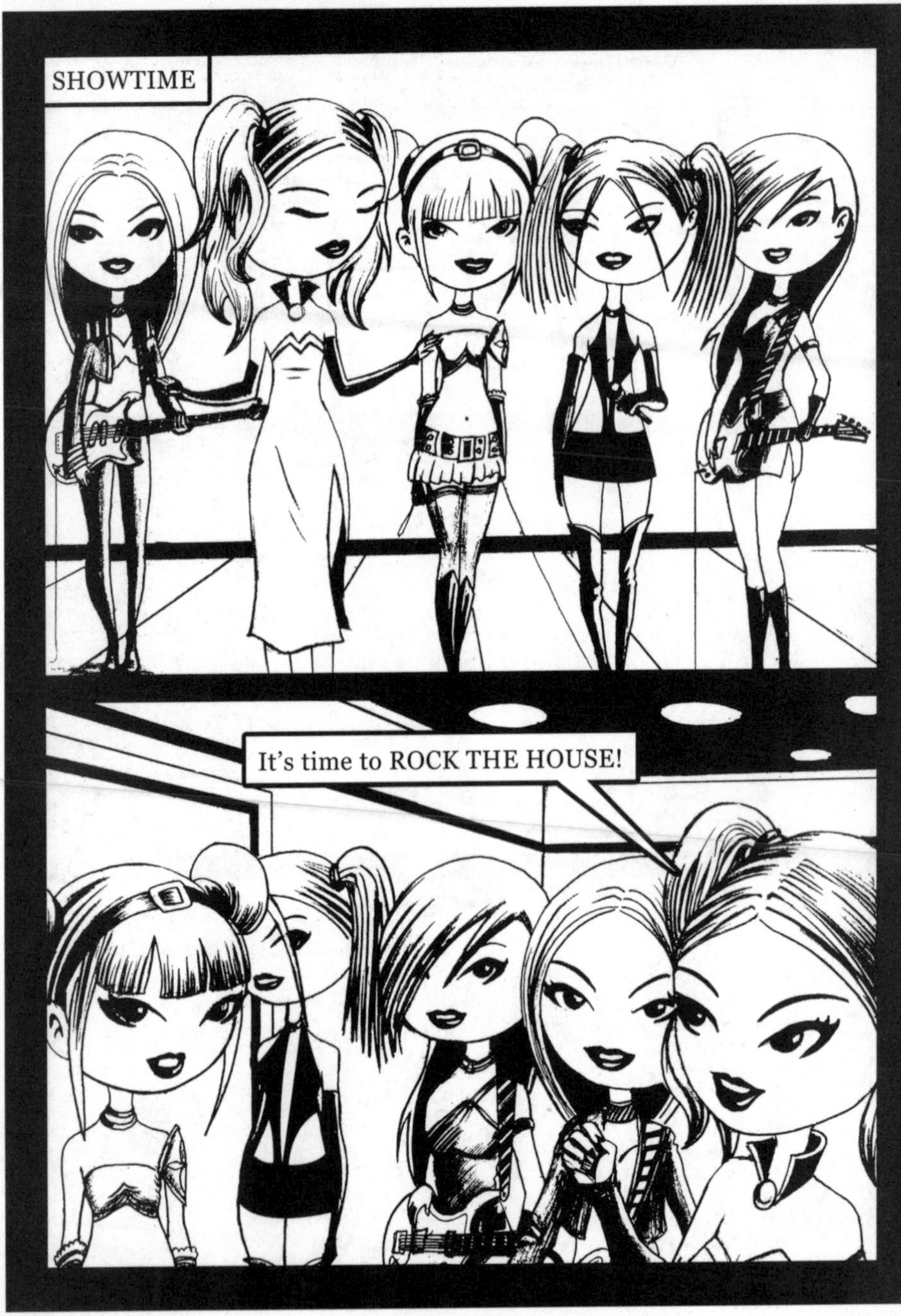
SHOWTIME
It's time to ROCK THE HOUSE!

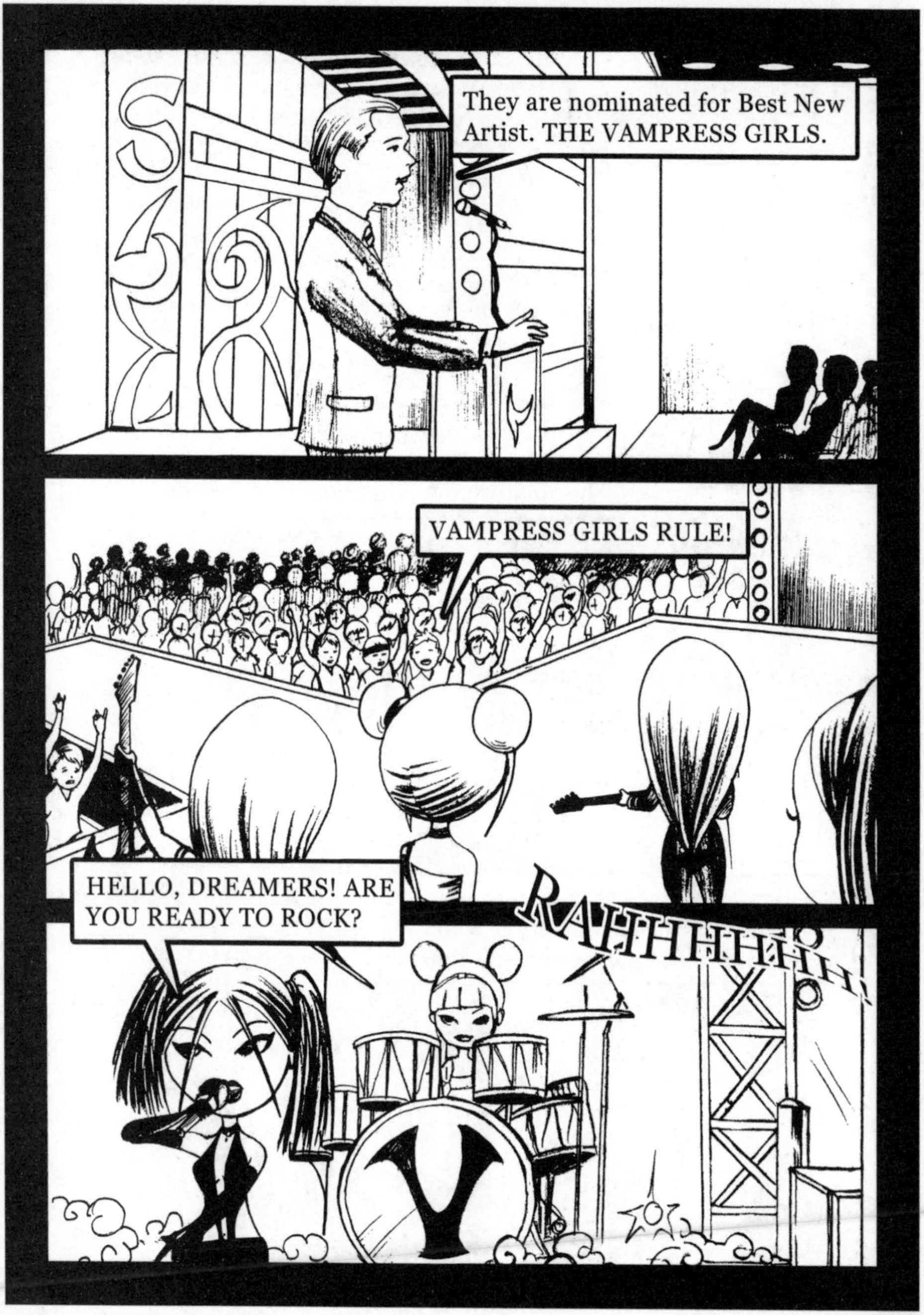
They are nominated for Best New Artist. THE VAMPRESS GIRLS.
VAMPRESS GIRLS RULE!
HELLO, DREAMERS! ARE YOU READY TO ROCK?
RAHHHHHHH!

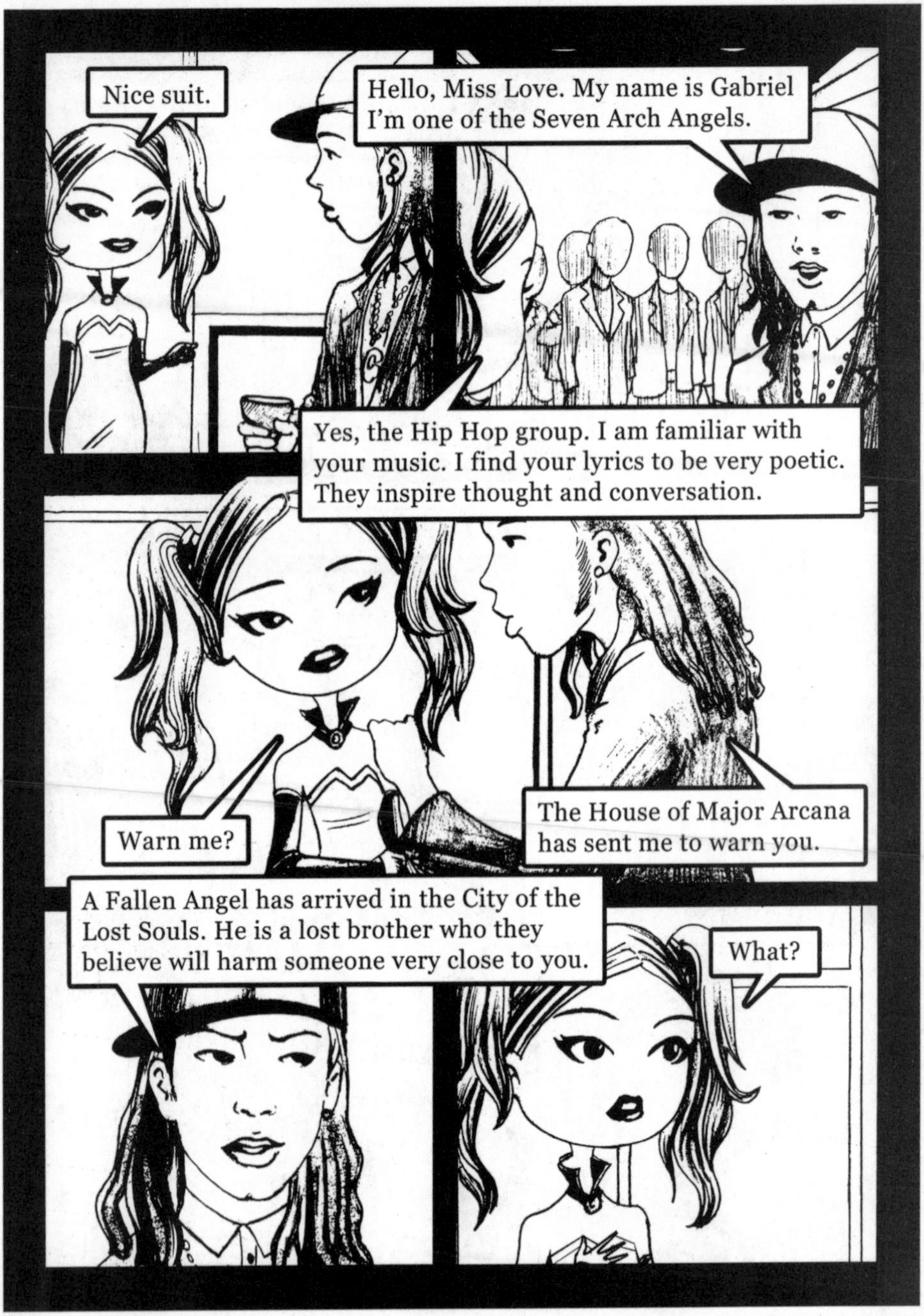

Nice suit.
Hello, Miss Love. My name is Gabriel I'm one of the Seven Arch Angels.
Yes, the Hip Hop group. I am familiar with your music. I find your lyrics to be very poetic. They inspire thought and conversation.
Warn me?
The House of Major Arcana has sent me to warn you.
A Fallen Angel has arrived in the City of the Lost Souls. He is a lost brother who they believe will harm someone very close to you.
What?

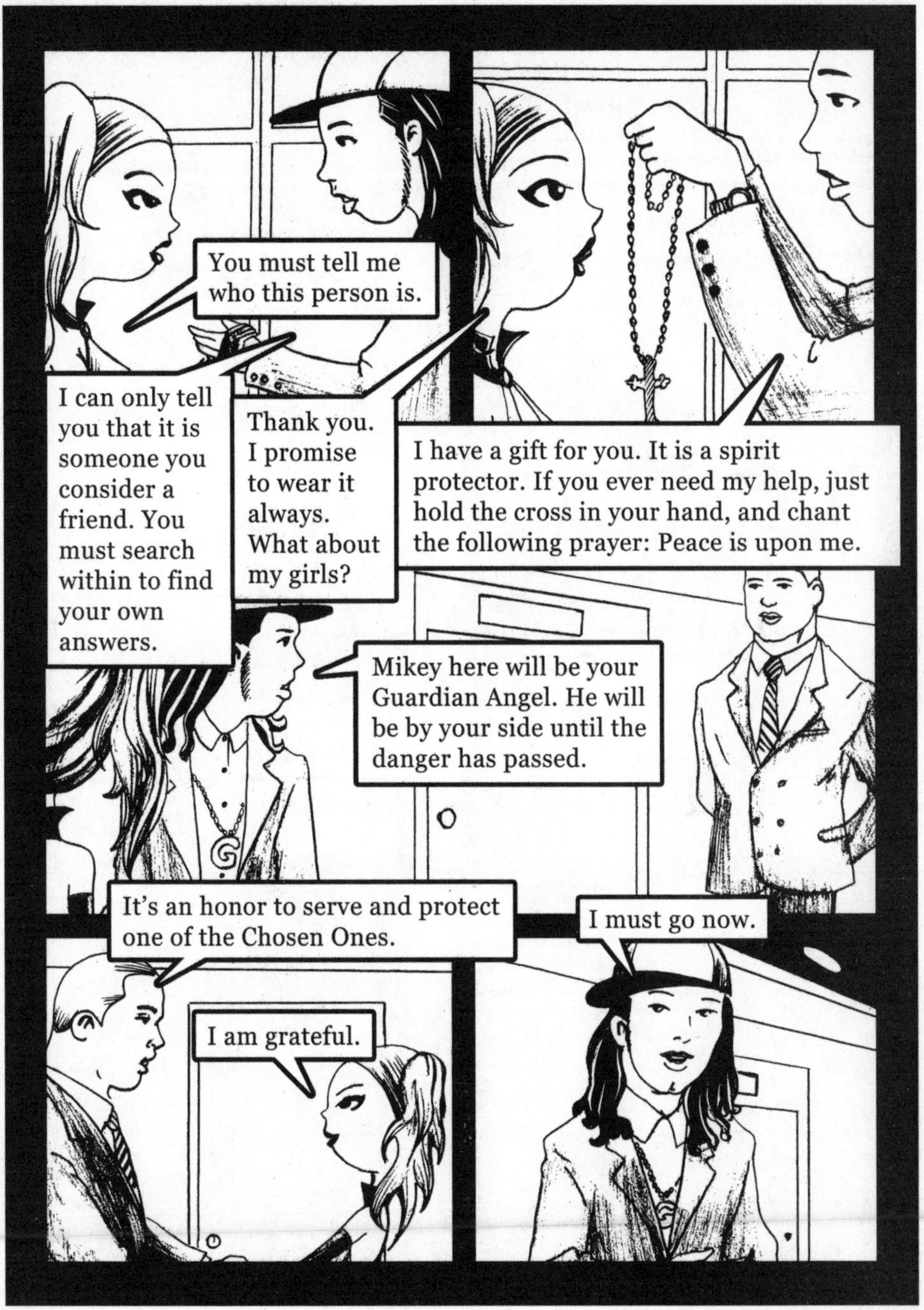
You must tell me who this person is.
I can only tell you that it is someone you consider a friend. You must search within to find your own answers.
Thank you. I promise to wear it always. What about my girls?
I have a gift for you. It is a spirit protector. If you ever need my help, just hold the cross in your hand, and chant the following prayer: Peace is upon me.
Mikey here will be your Guardian Angel. He will be by your side until the danger has passed.
It's an honor to serve and protect one of the Chosen Ones.
I am grateful.
I must go now.

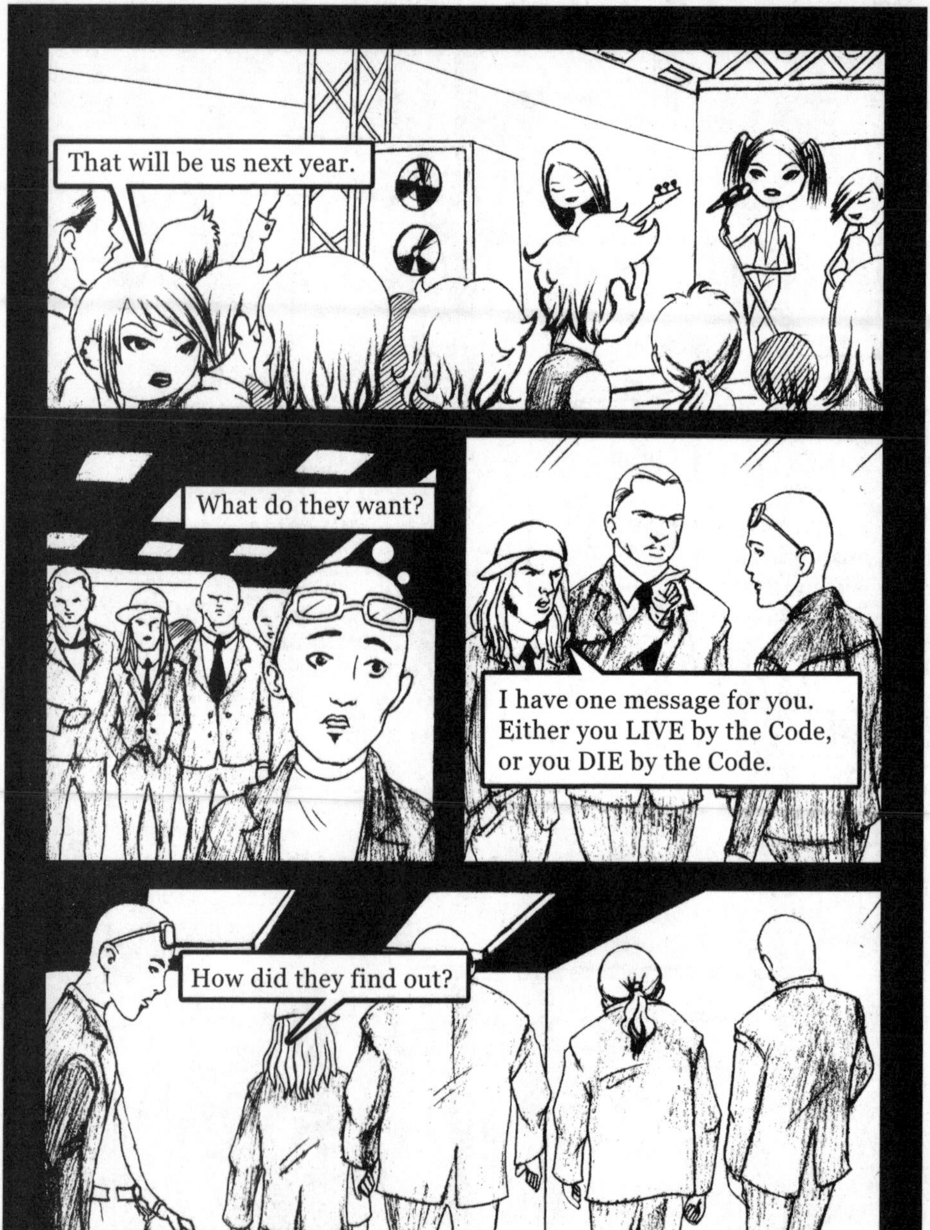
That will be us next year.
What do they want?
I have one message for you. Either you LIVE by the Code, or you DIE by the Code.
How did they find out?

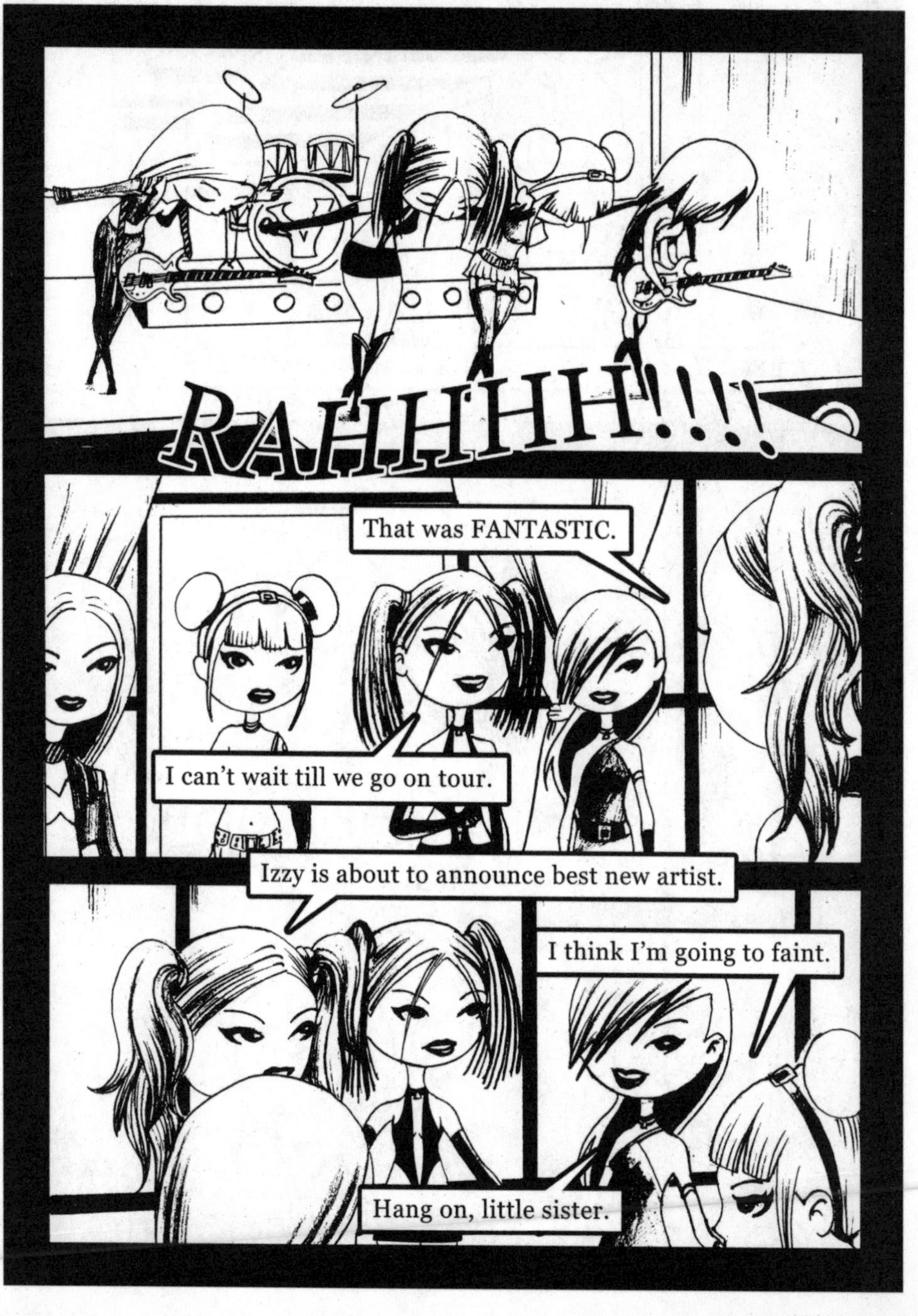
RAHHHH!!!
That was FANTASTIC.
I can't wait till we go on tour.
Izzy is about to announce best new artist.
I think I'm going to faint.
Hang on, little sister.

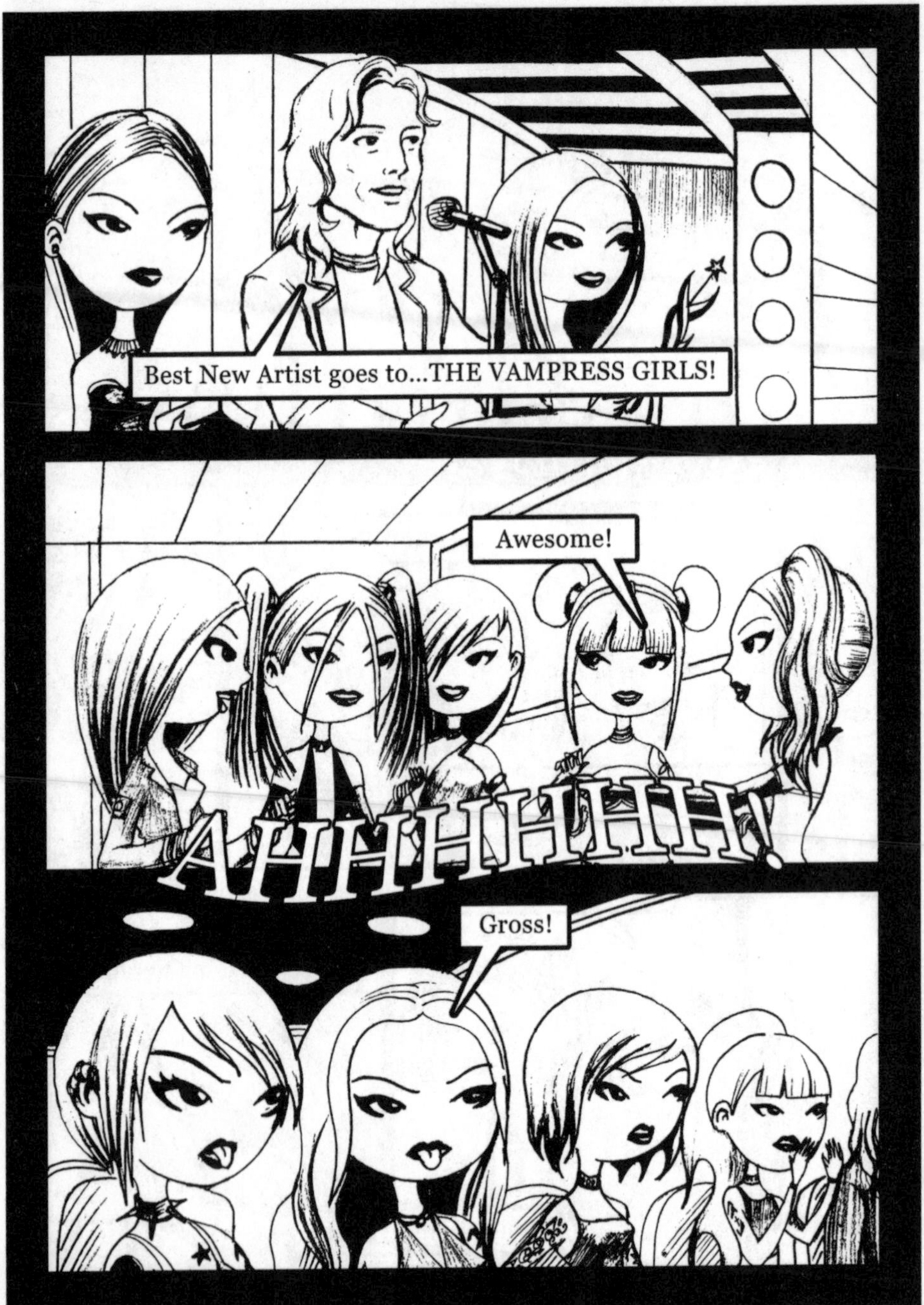
Best New Artist goes to...THE VAMPRESS GIRLS!
Awesome!
AHHHHHHHH!
Gross!

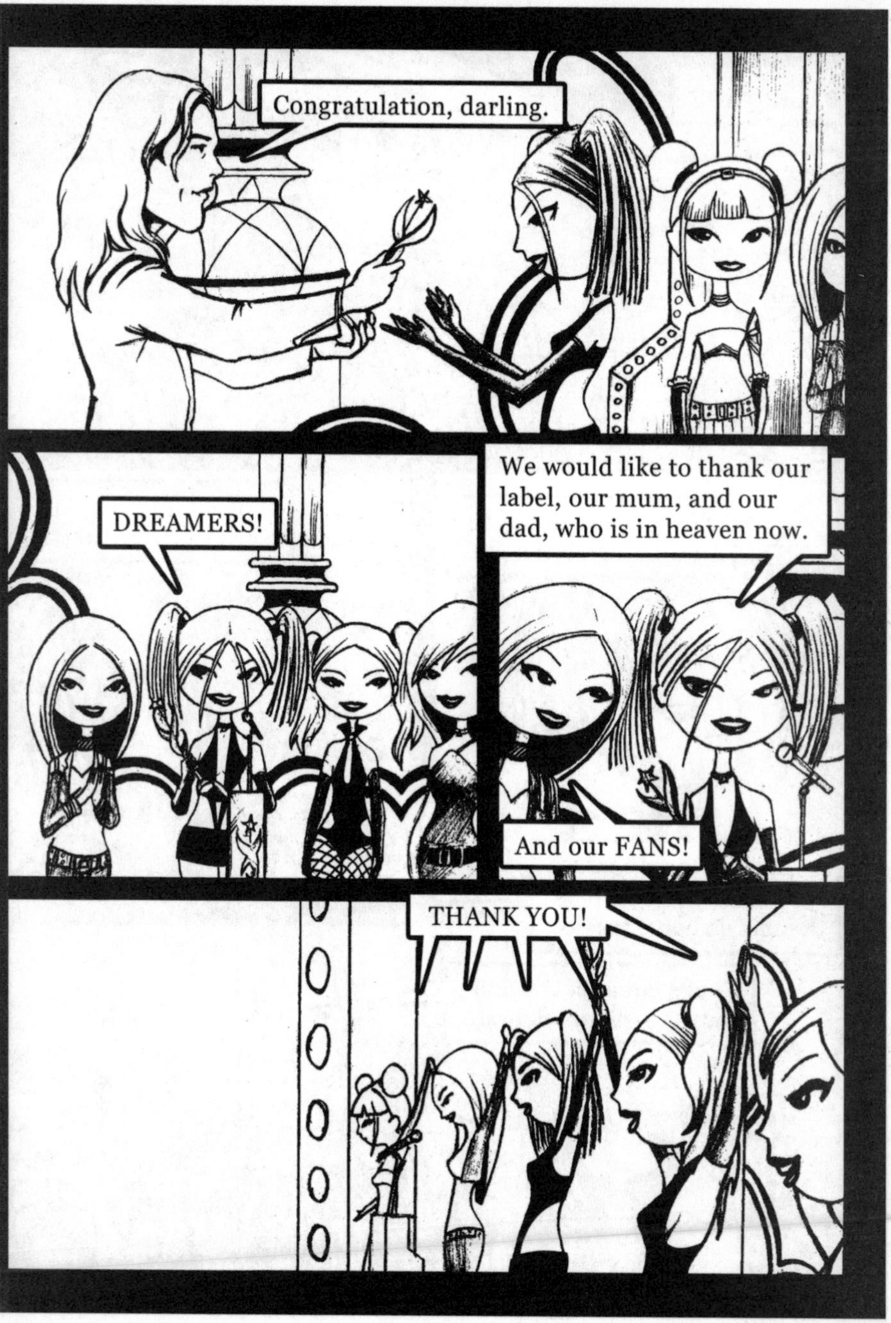
Congratulation, darling.
DREAMERS!
We would like to thank our label, our mum, and our dad, who is in heaven now.
And our FANS!
THANK YOU!

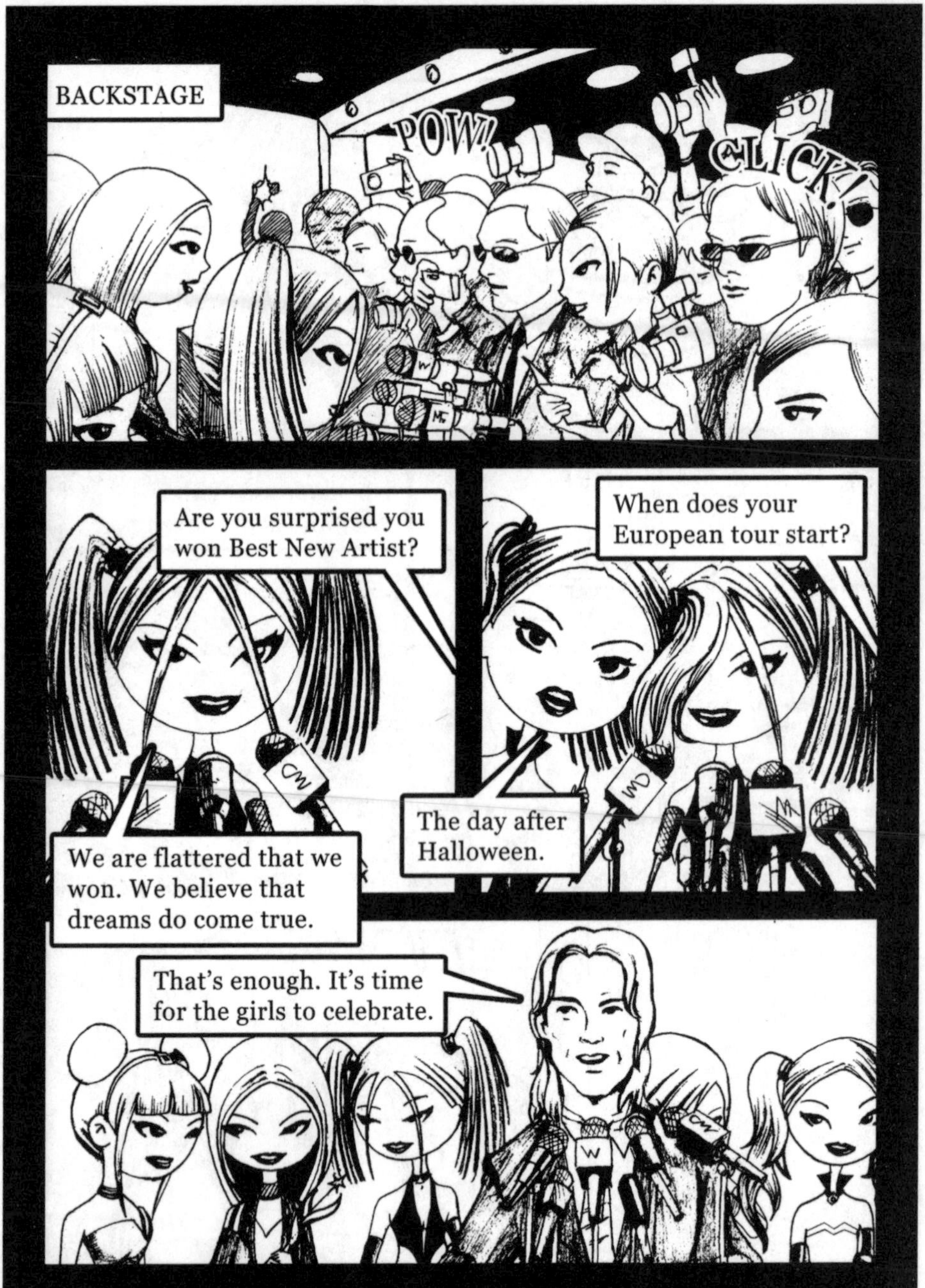
BACKSTAGE
POW!
CLICK!
Are you surprised you won Best New Artist?
We are flattered that we won. We believe that dreams do come true.
When does your European tour start?
The day after Halloween.
That's enough. It's time for the girls to celebrate.

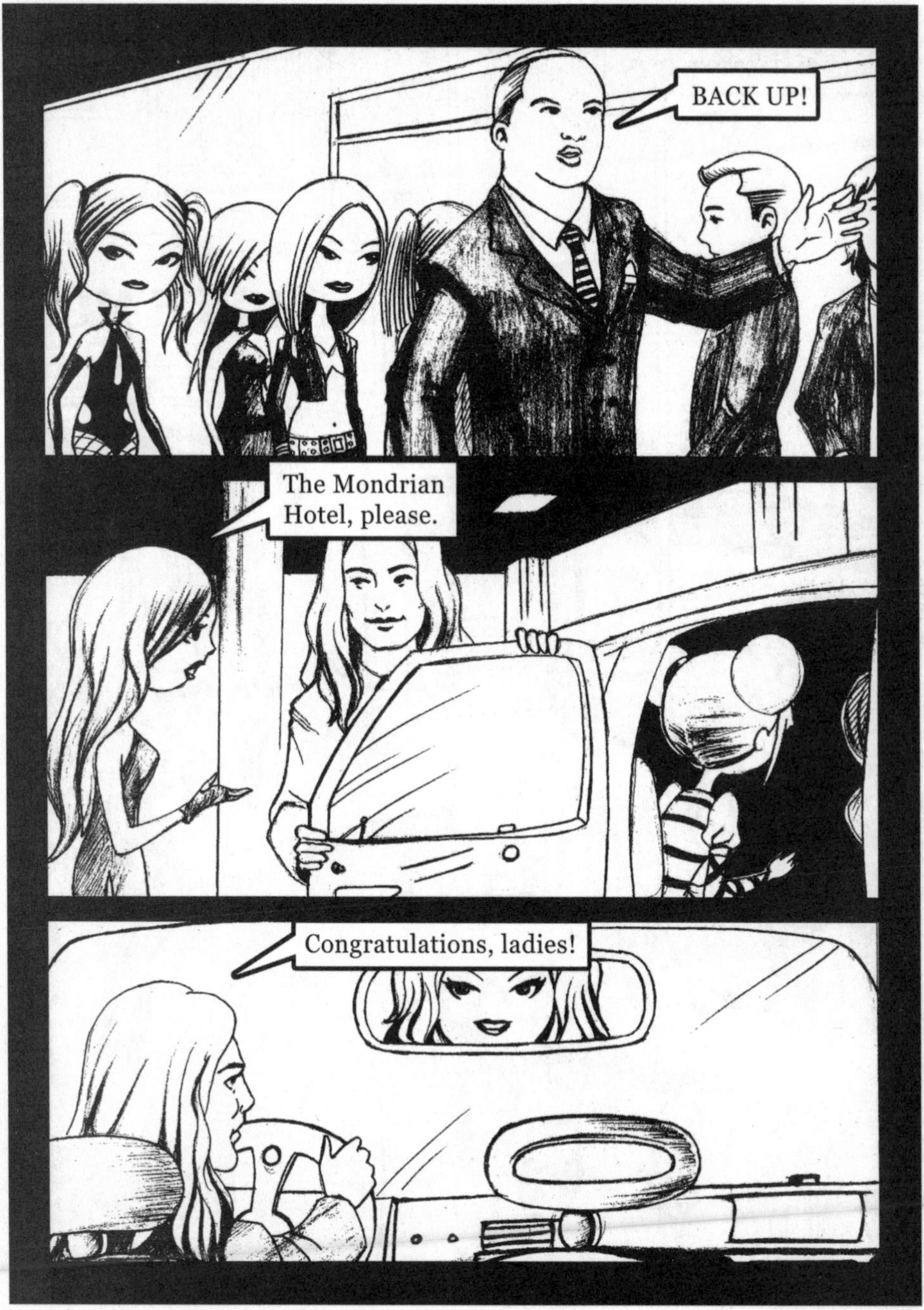
BACK UP!
The Mondrian Hotel, please.
Congratulations, ladies!

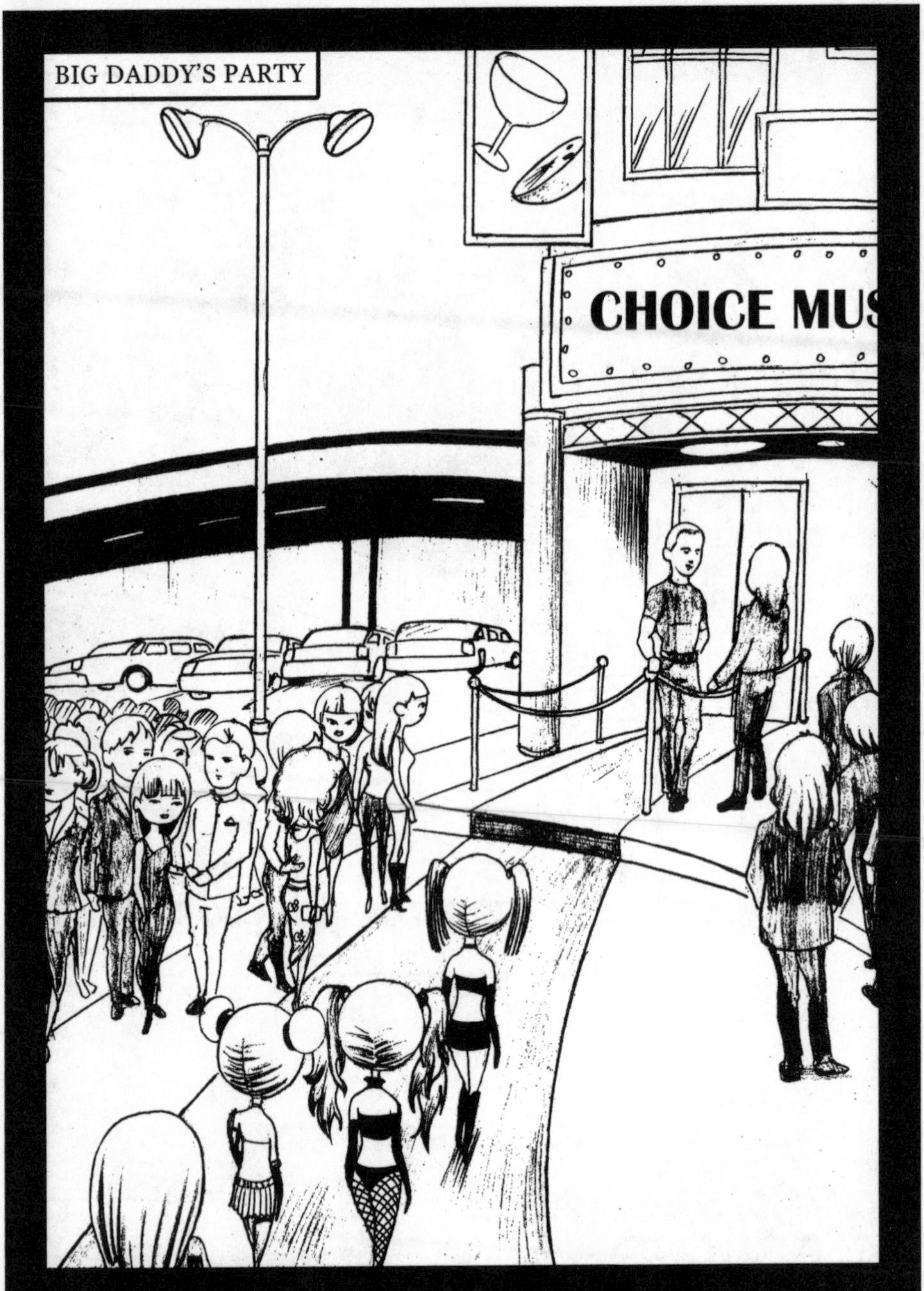
BIG DADDY'S PARTY
CHOICE MUS

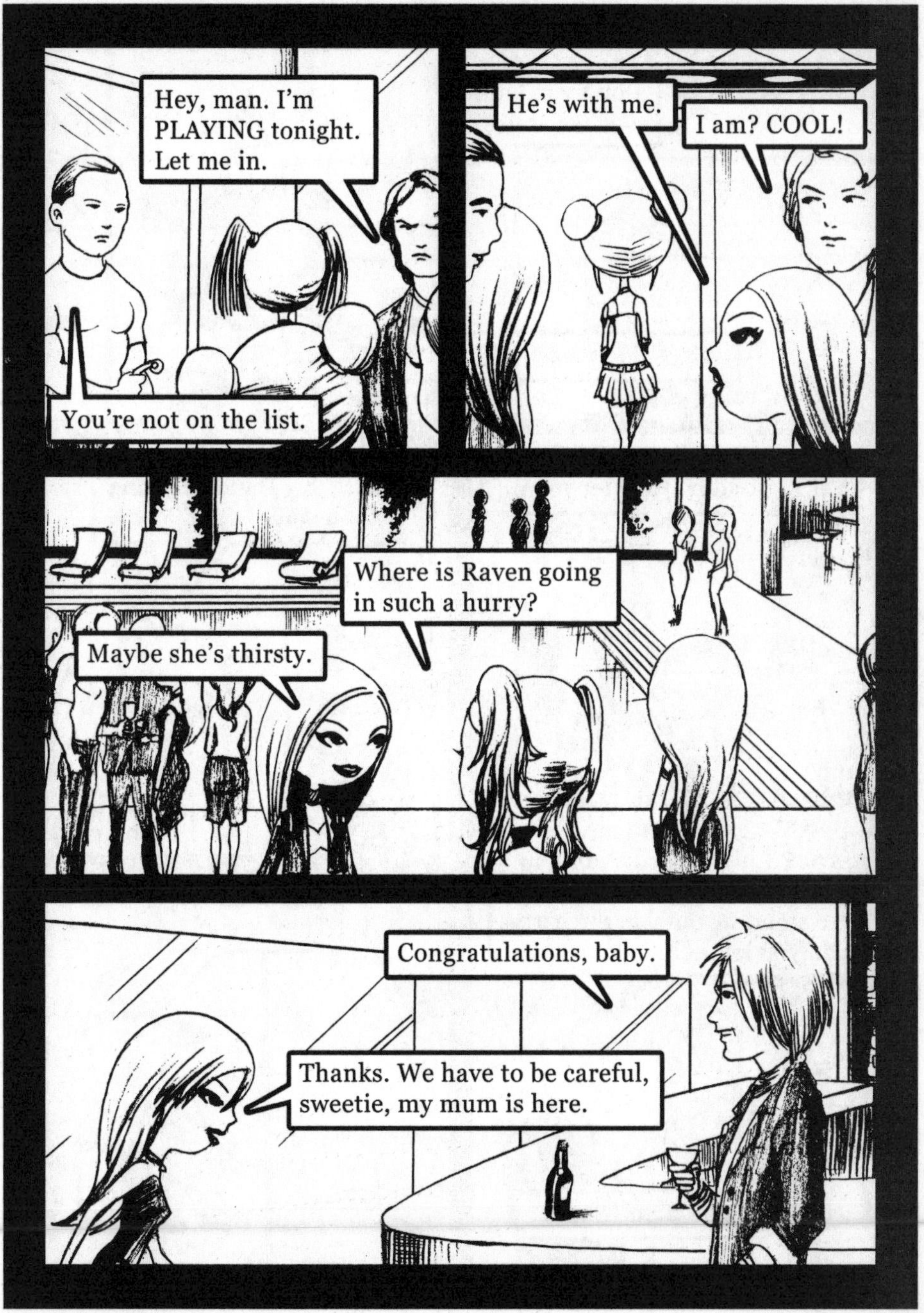
Hey, man. I'm PLAYING tonight. Let me in.
You're not on the list.
He's with me.
I am? COOL!
Where is Raven going in such a hurry?
Maybe she's thirsty.
Congratulations, baby.
Thanks. We have to be careful, sweetie, my mum is here.

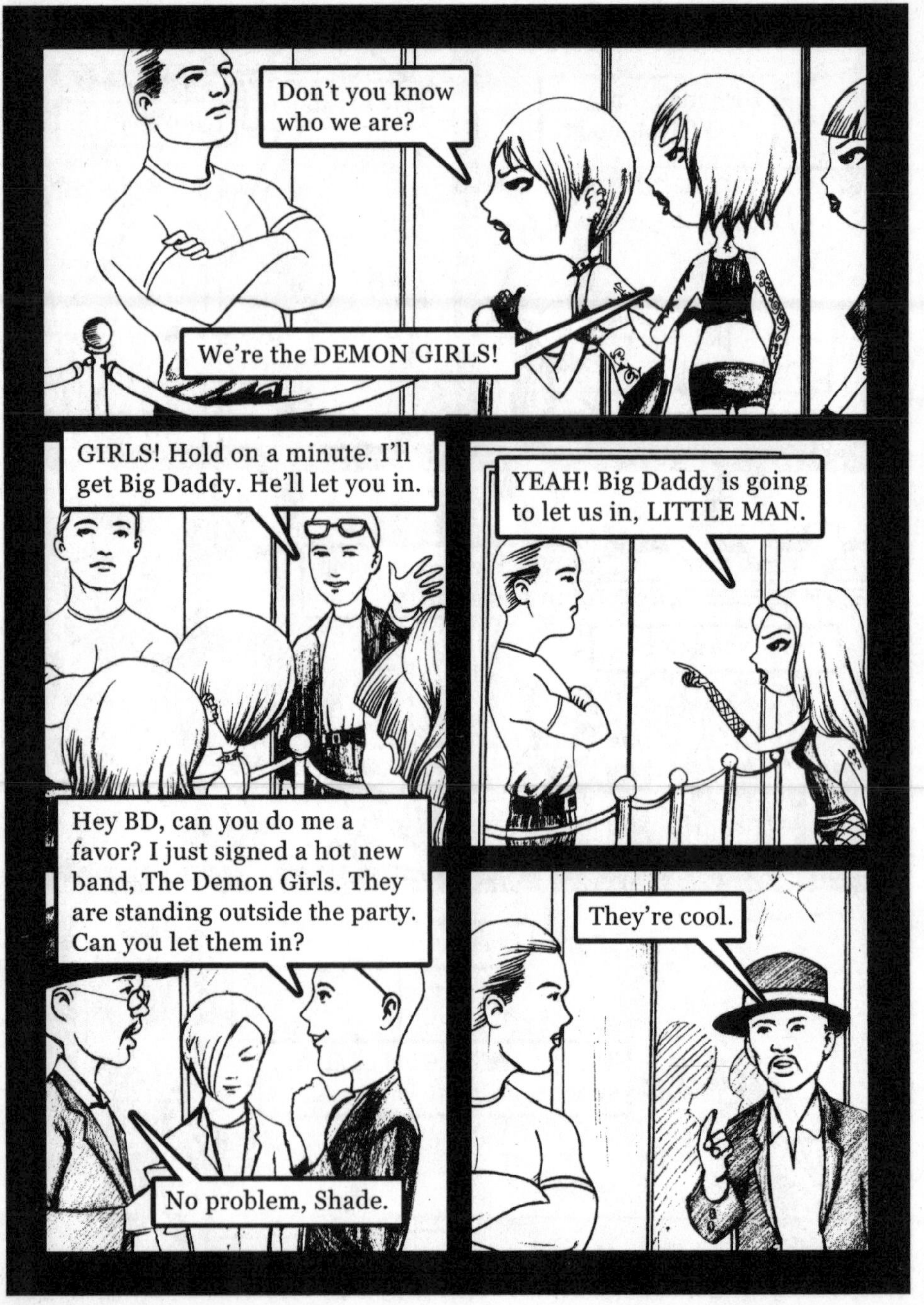
Don't you know who we are?
We're the DEMON GIRLS!
GIRLS! Hold on a minute. I'll get Big Daddy. He'll let you in.
YEAH! Big Daddy is going to let us in, LITTLE MAN.
Hey BD, can you do me a favor? I just signed a hot new band, The Demon Girls. They are standing outside the party. Can you let them in?
No problem, Shade.
They're cool.

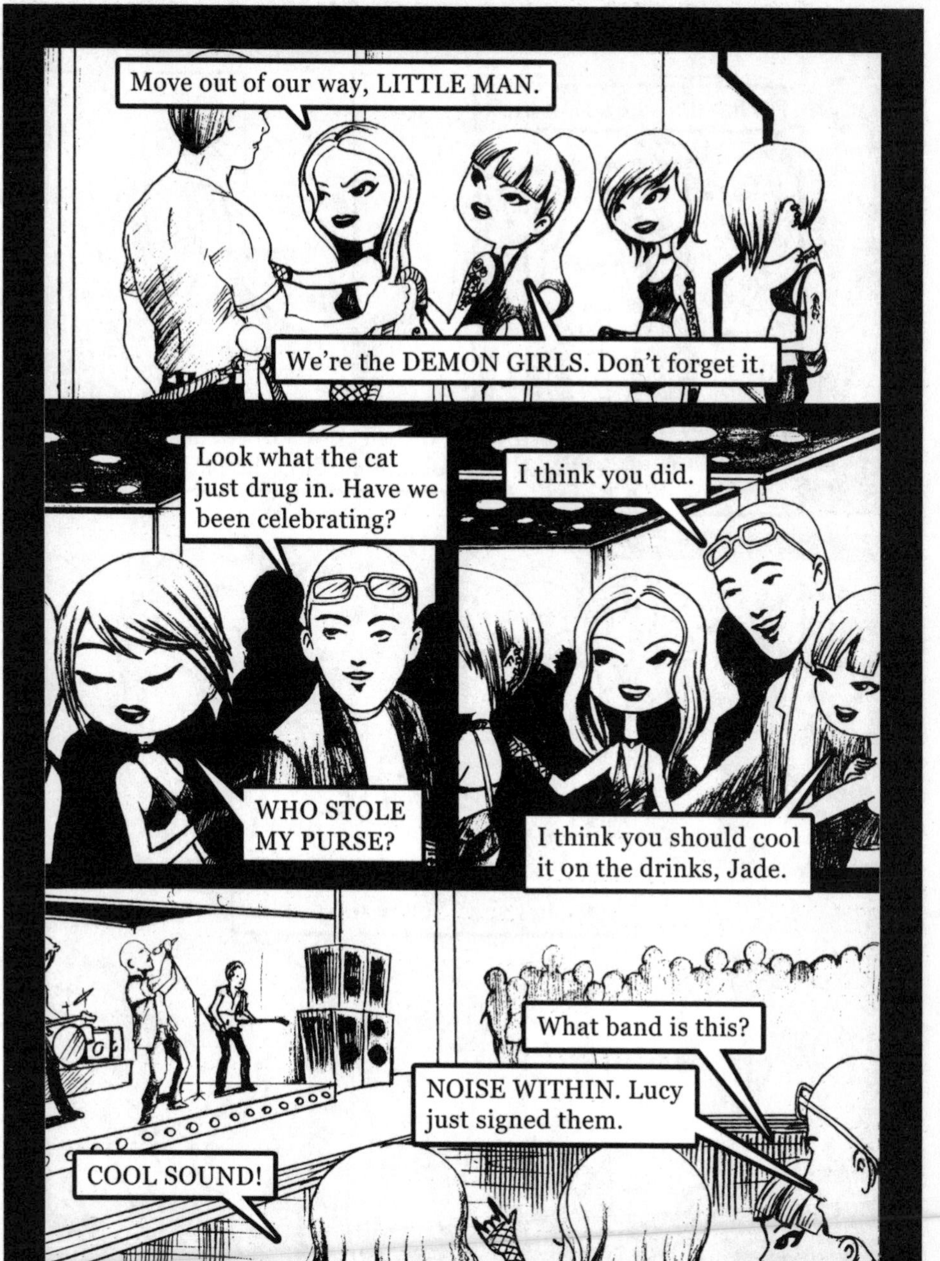
Move out of our way, LITTLE MAN.
We're the DEMON GIRLS. Don't forget it.
Look what the cat just drug in. Have we been celebrating?
WHO STOLE MY PURSE?
I think you did.
I think you should cool it on the drinks, Jade.
What band is this?
NOISE WITHIN. Lucy just signed them.
COOL SOUND!

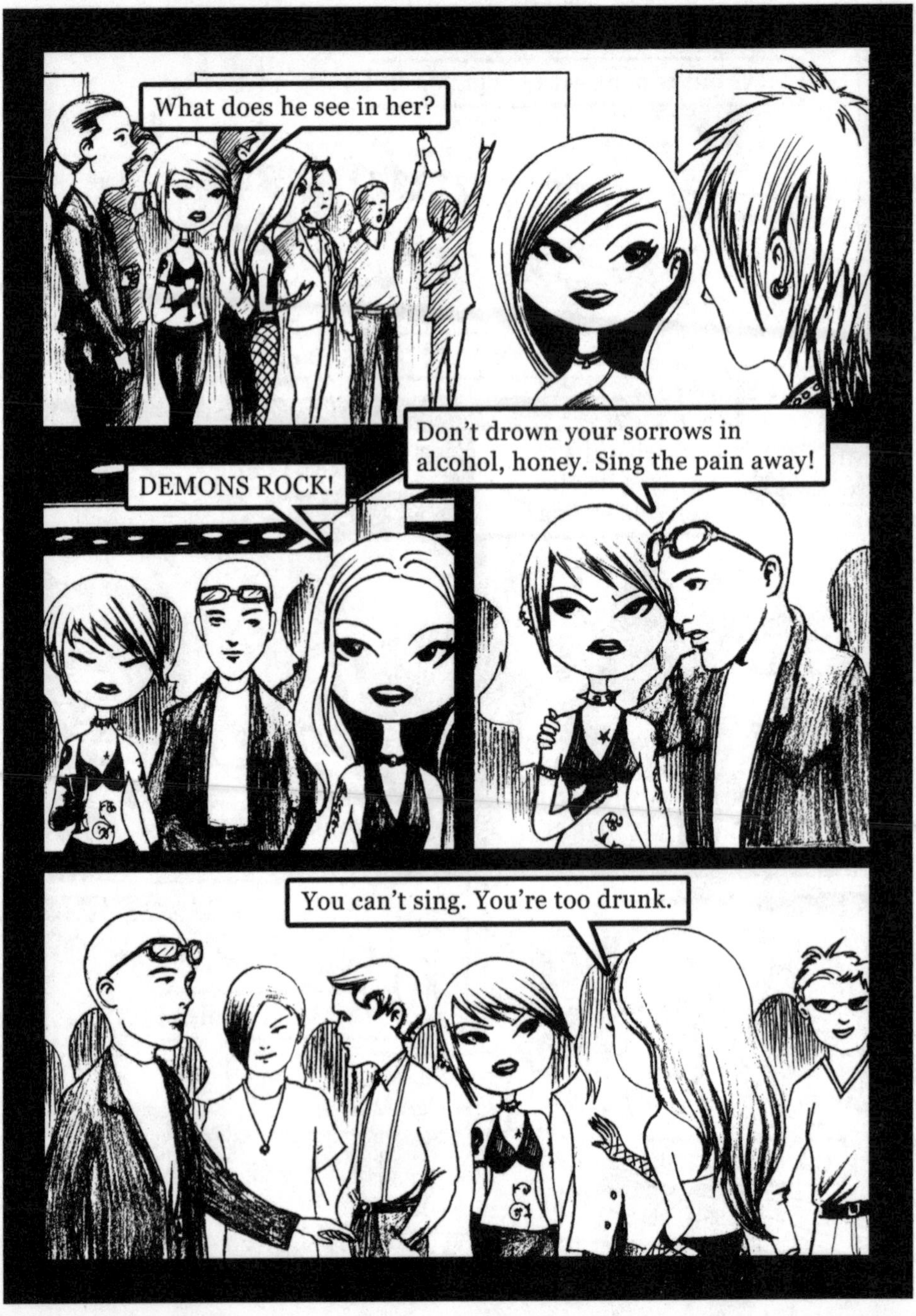
What does he see in her?
DEMONS ROCK!
Don’t drown your sorrows in alcohol, honey. Sing the pain away!
You can’t sing. You’re too drunk.

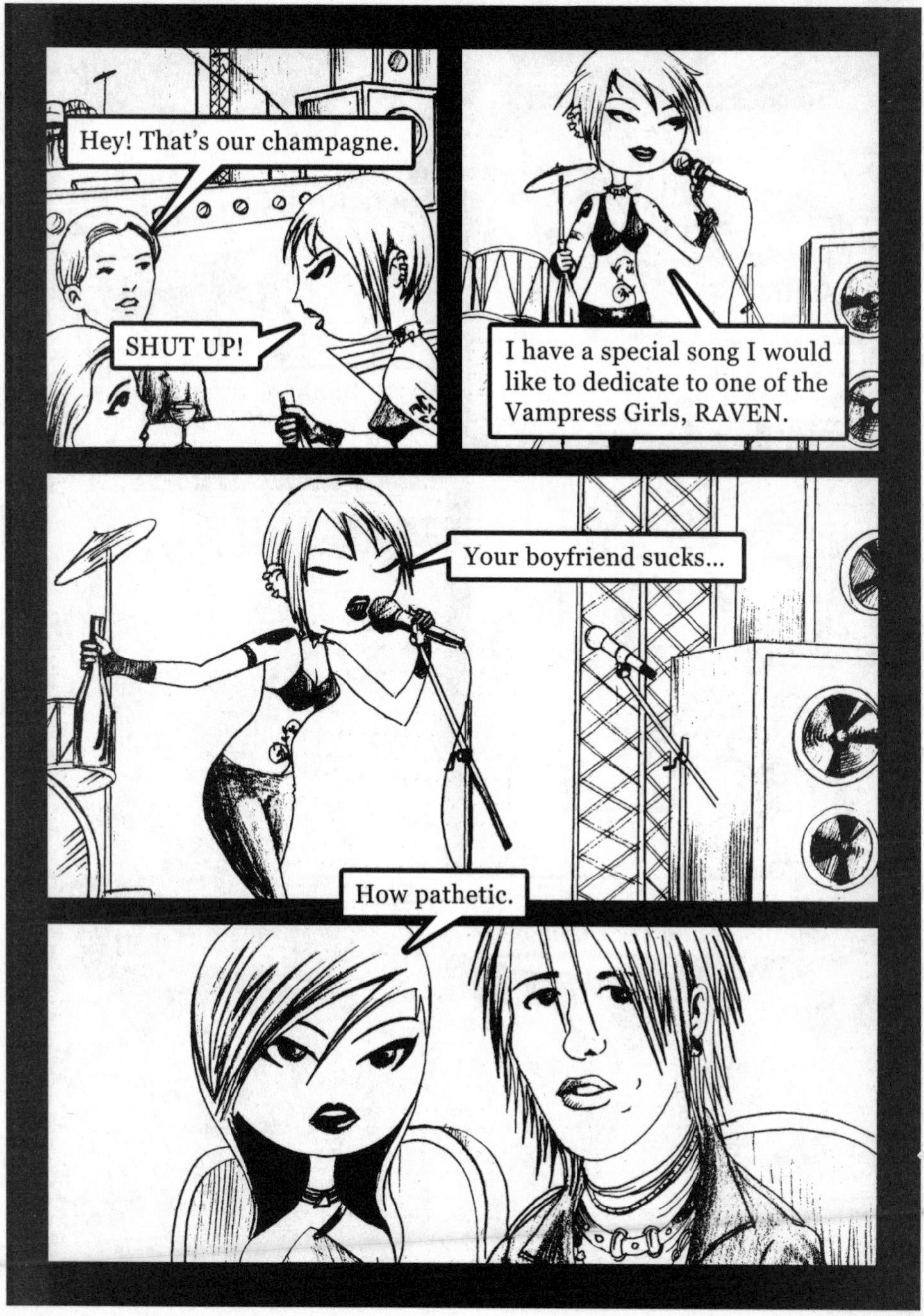
Hey! That's our champagne.
SHUT UP!
I have a special song I would like to dedicate to one of the Vampress Girls, RAVEN.
Your boyfriend sucks...
How pathetic.

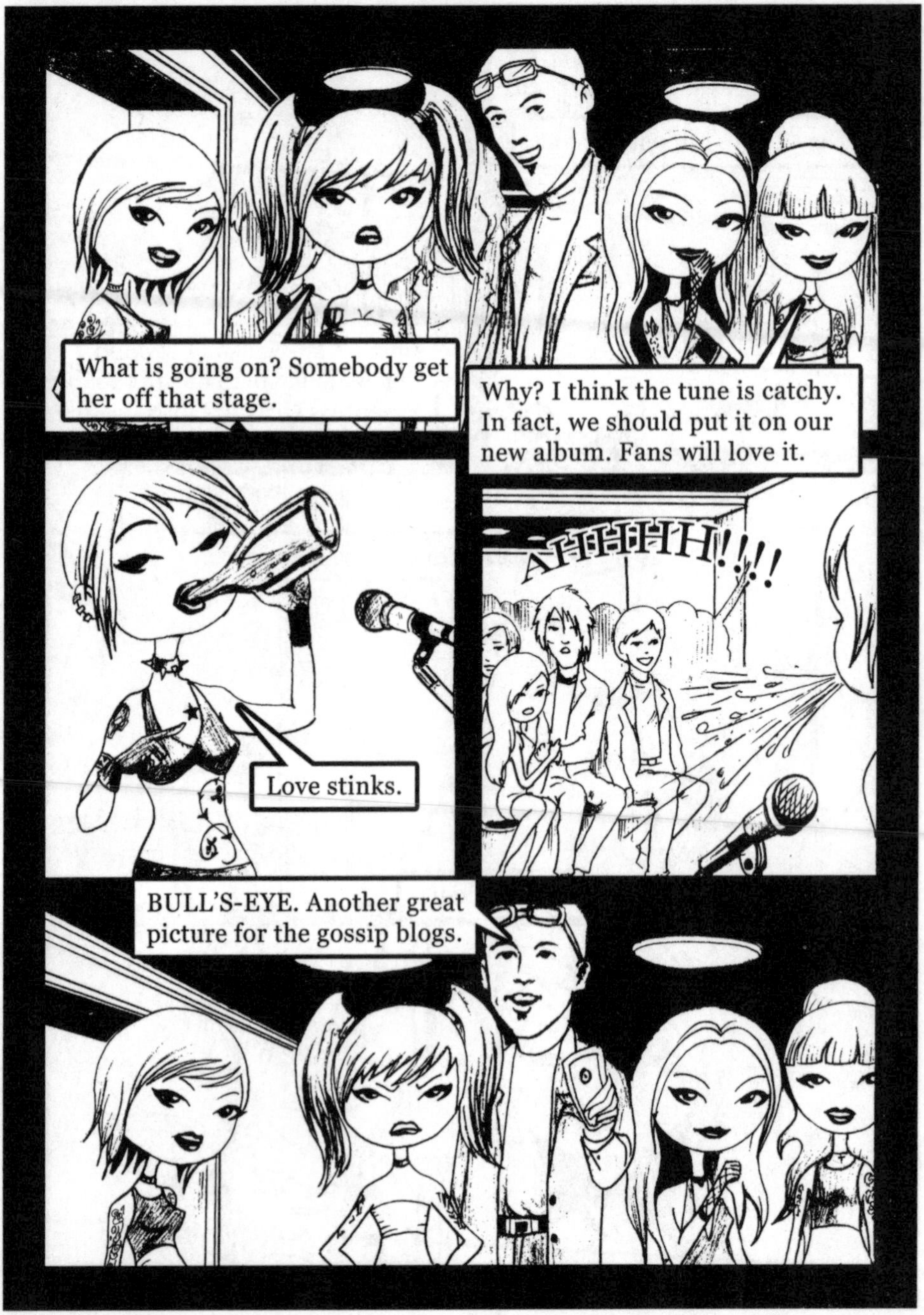
What is going on? Somebody get her off that stage.
Why? I think the tune is catchy. In fact, we should put it on our new album. Fans will love it.
Love stinks.
AHHHHH!!!!
BULL'S-EYE. Another great picture for the gossip blogs.

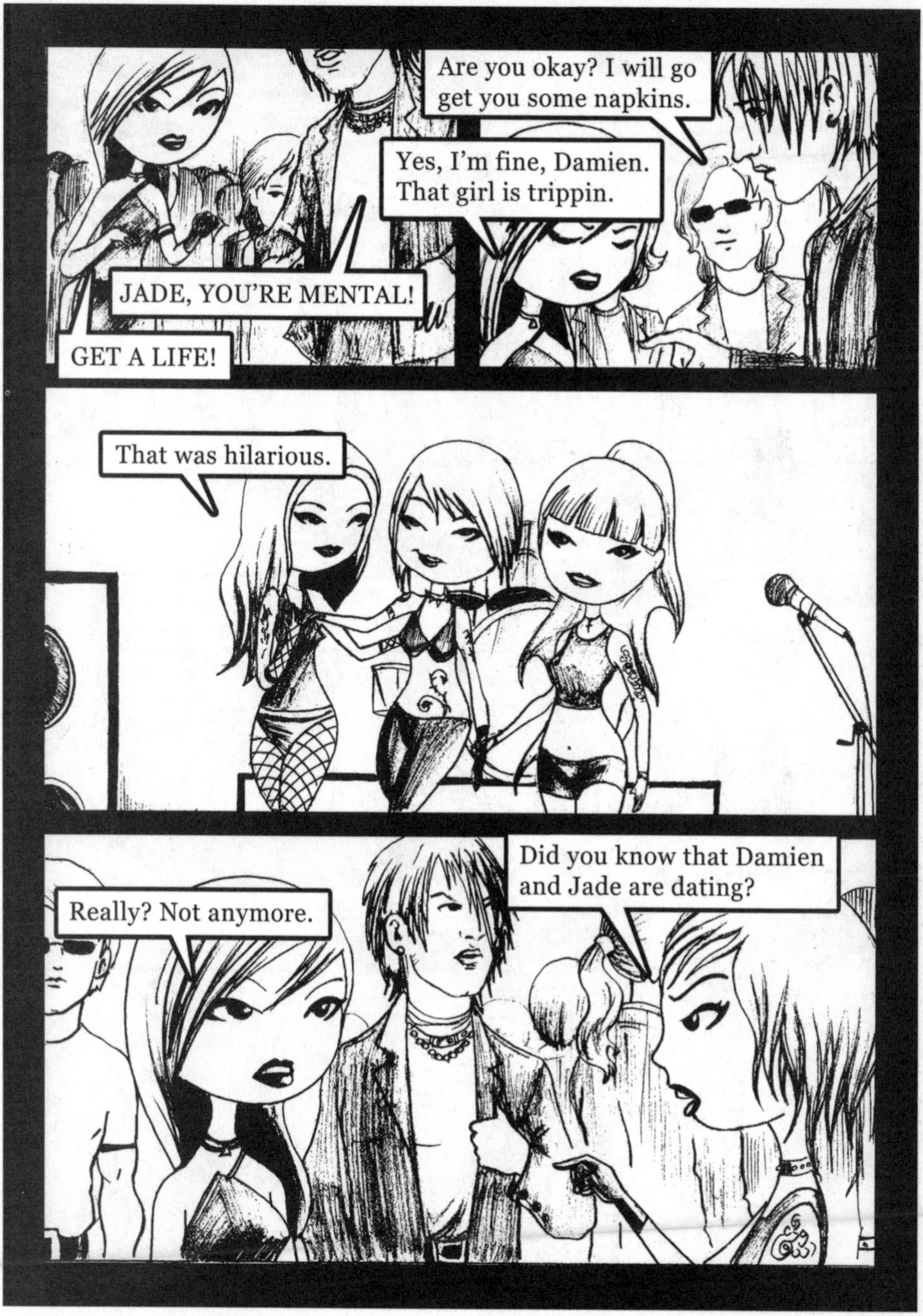
JADE, YOU'RE MENTAL!
GET A LIFE!
Are you okay? I will go get you some napkins.
Yes, I'm fine, Damien. That girl is trippin.
That was hilarious.
Did you know that Damien and Jade are dating?
Really? Not anymore.

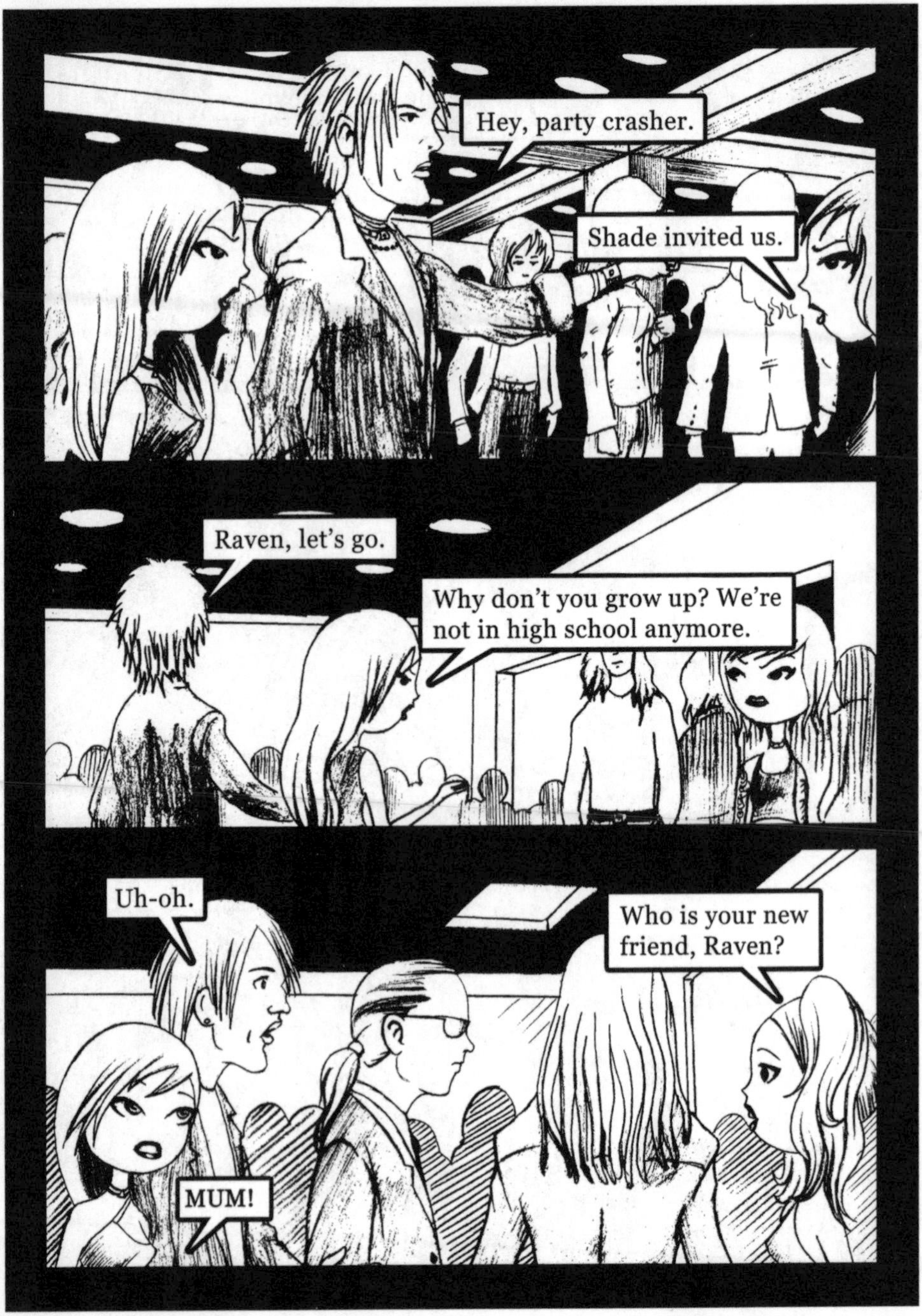
Hey, party crasher.
Shade invited us.
Raven, let's go.
Why don't you grow up? We're not in high school anymore.
Uh-oh.
Who is your new friend, Raven?
MUM!

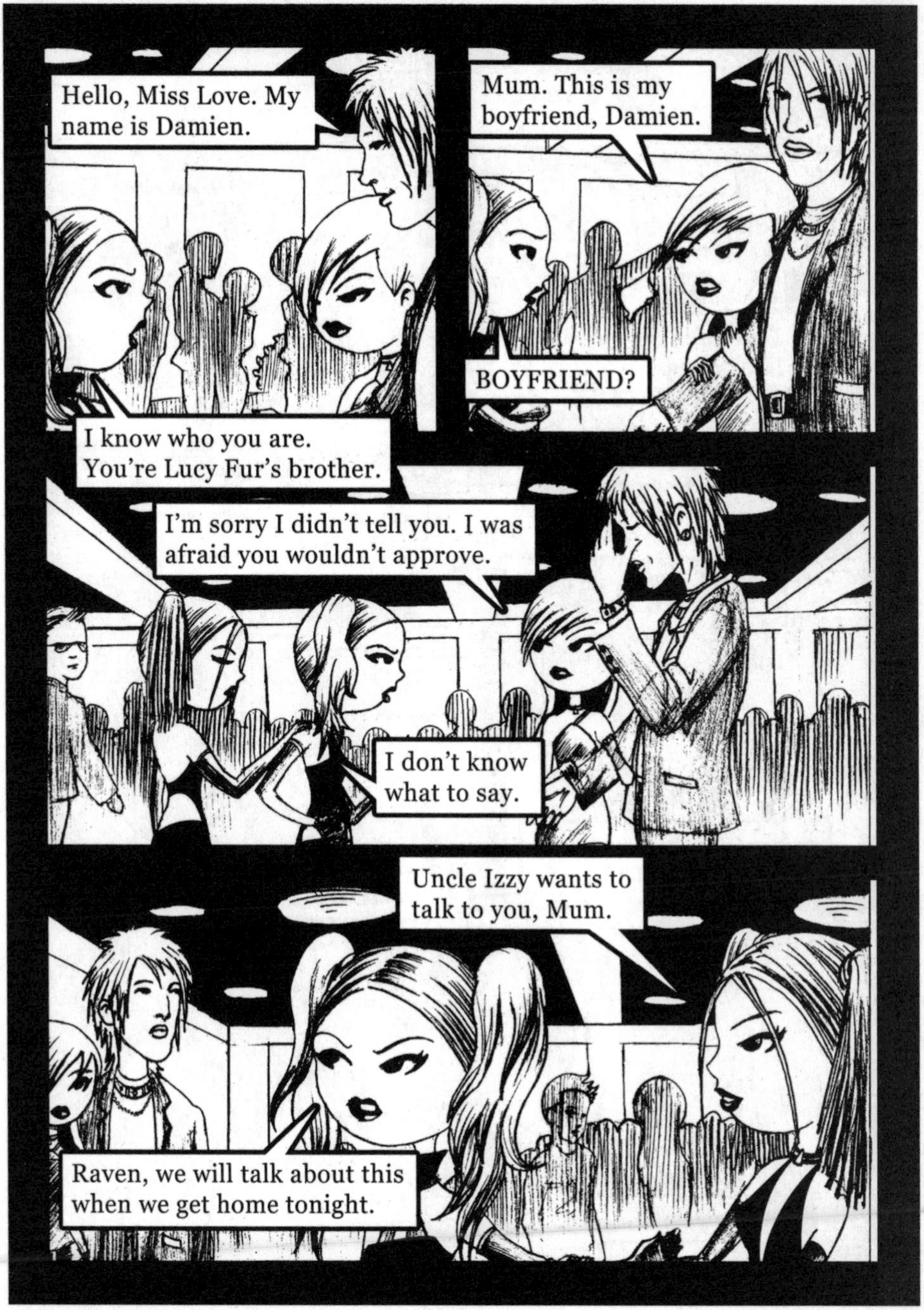
Hello, Miss Love. My name is Damien.
I know who you are. You're Lucy Fur's brother.
Mum. This is my boyfriend, Damien.
BOYFRIEND?
I'm sorry I didn't tell you. I was afraid you wouldn't approve.
I don't know what to say.
Uncle Izzy wants to talk to you, Mum.
Raven, we will talk about this when we get home tonight.

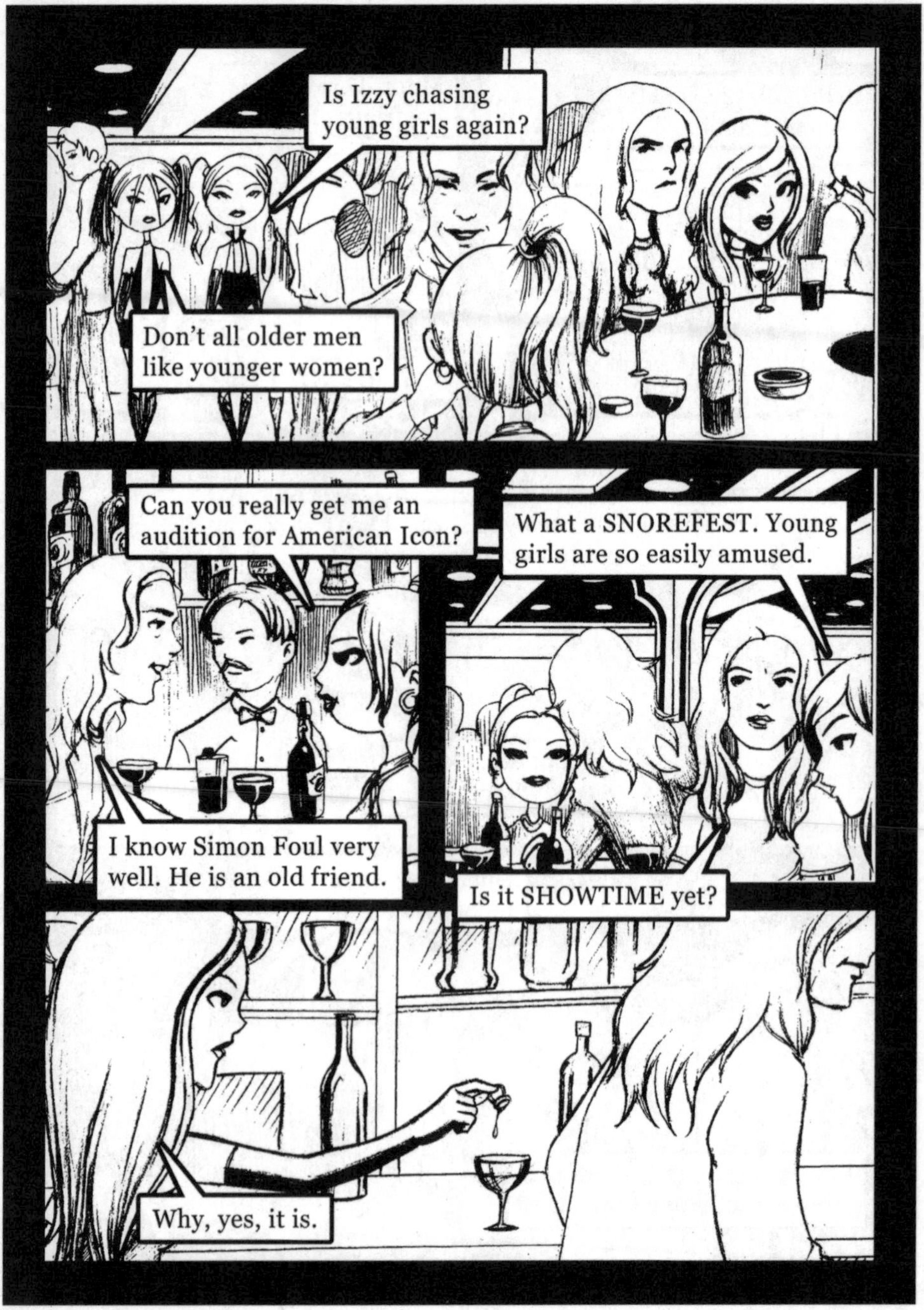
Is Izzy chasing young girls again?
Don't all older men like younger women?
Can you really get me an audition for American Icon?
I know Simon Foul very well. He is an old friend.
What a SNOREFEST. Young girls are so easily amused.
Is it SHOWTIME yet?
Why, yes, it is.

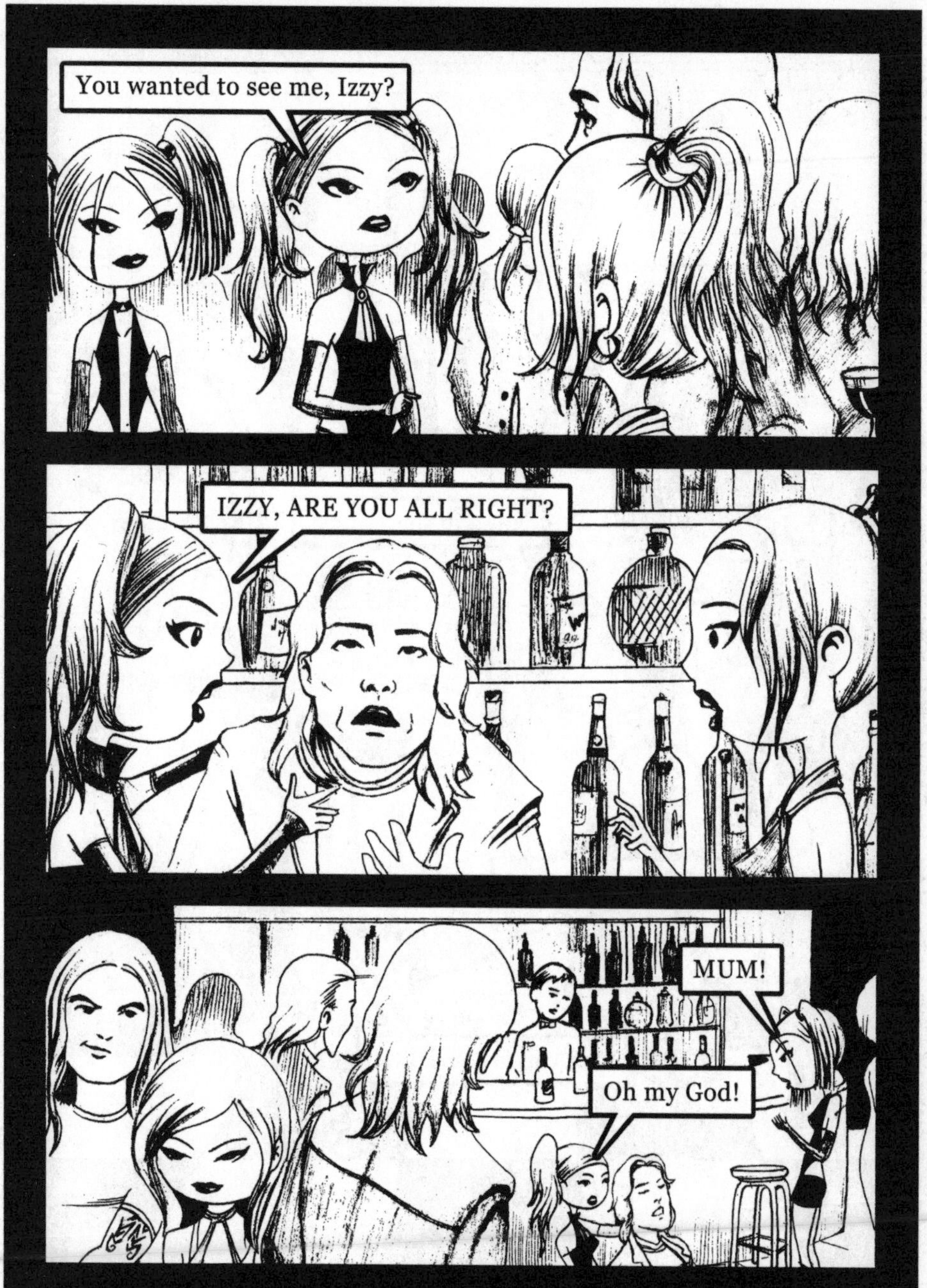
You wanted to see me, Izzy?
IZZY, ARE YOU ALL RIGHT?
MUM!
Oh my God!

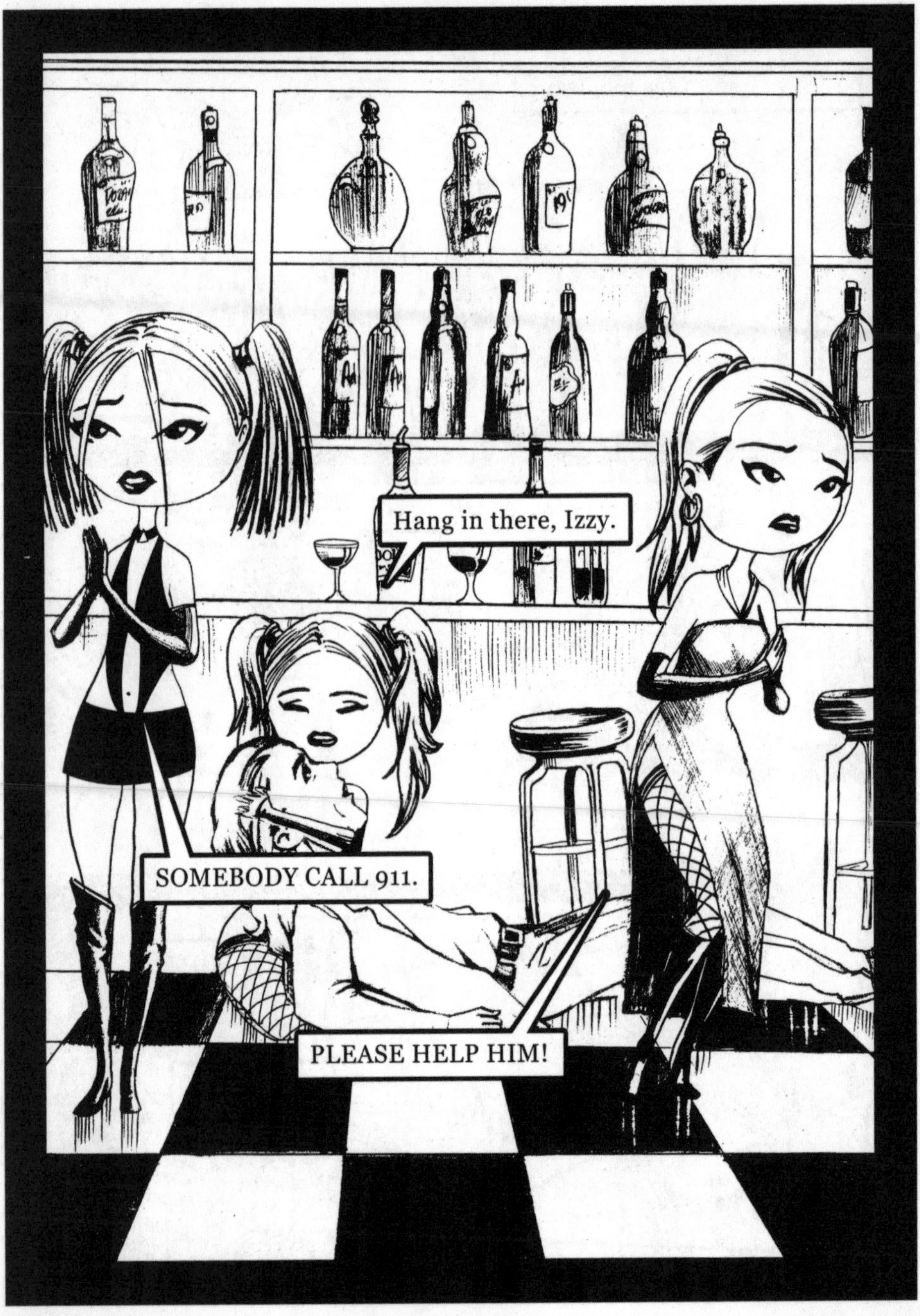
Hang in there, Izzy.
SOMEBODY CALL 911.
PLEASE HELP HIM!

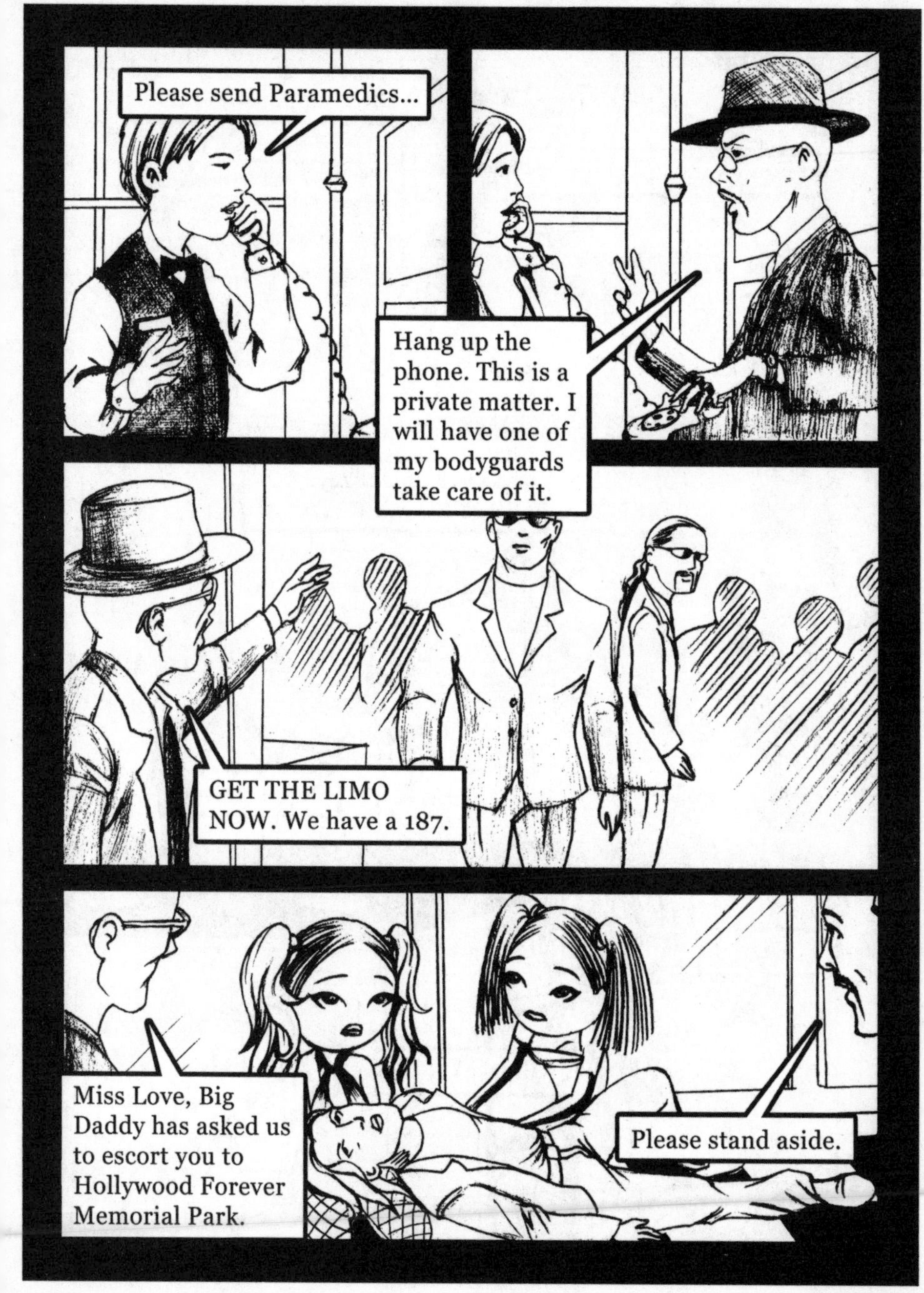
Please send Paramedics...
Hang up the phone. This is a private matter. I will have one of my bodyguards take care of it.
GET THE LIMO NOW. We have a 187.
Miss Love, Big Daddy has asked us to escort you to Hollywood Forever Memorial Park.
Please stand aside.

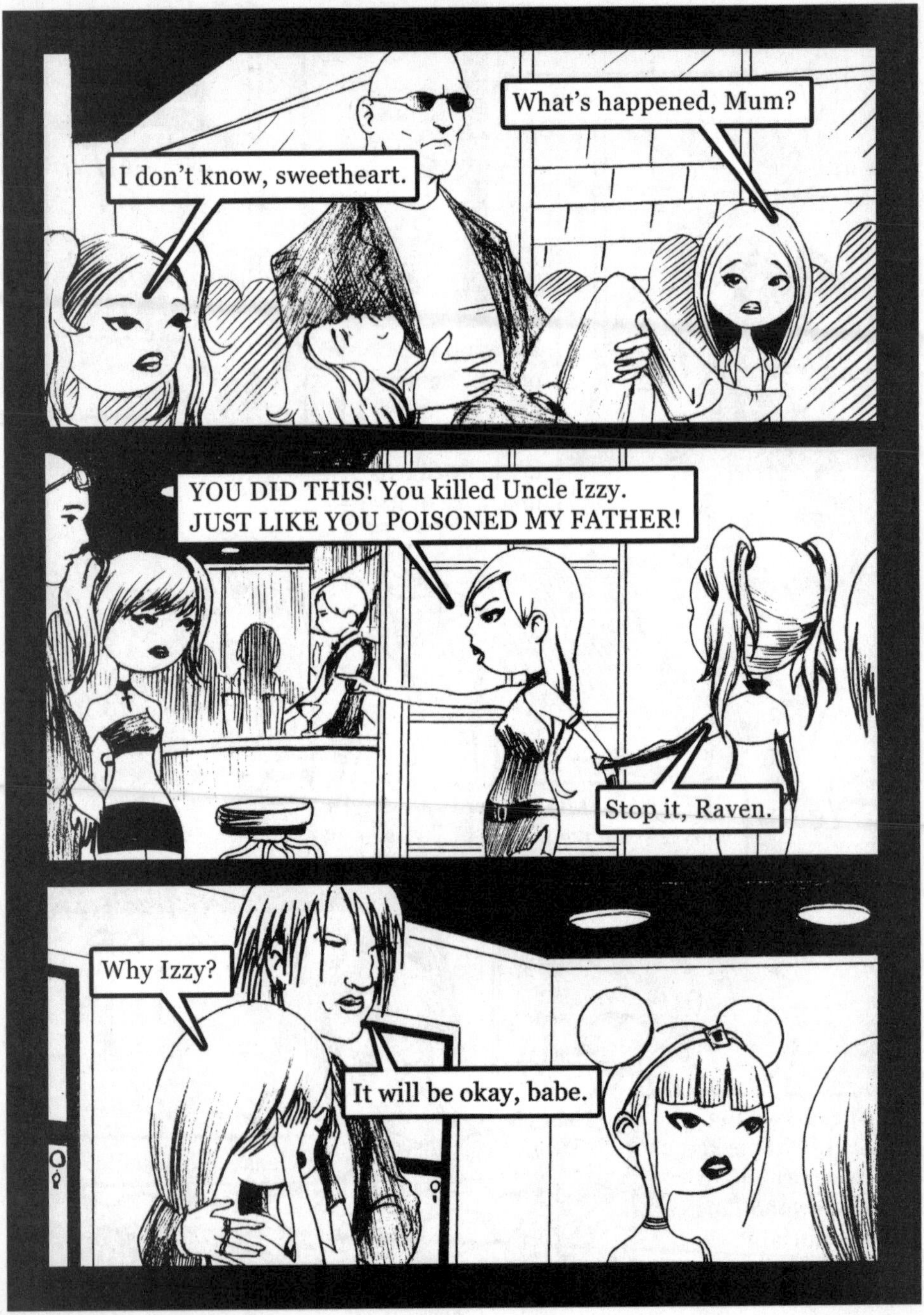
What's happened, Mum?
I don't know, sweetheart.
YOU DID THIS! You killed Uncle Izzy. JUST LIKE YOU POISONED MY FATHER!
Stop it, Raven.
Why Izzy?
It will be okay, babe.

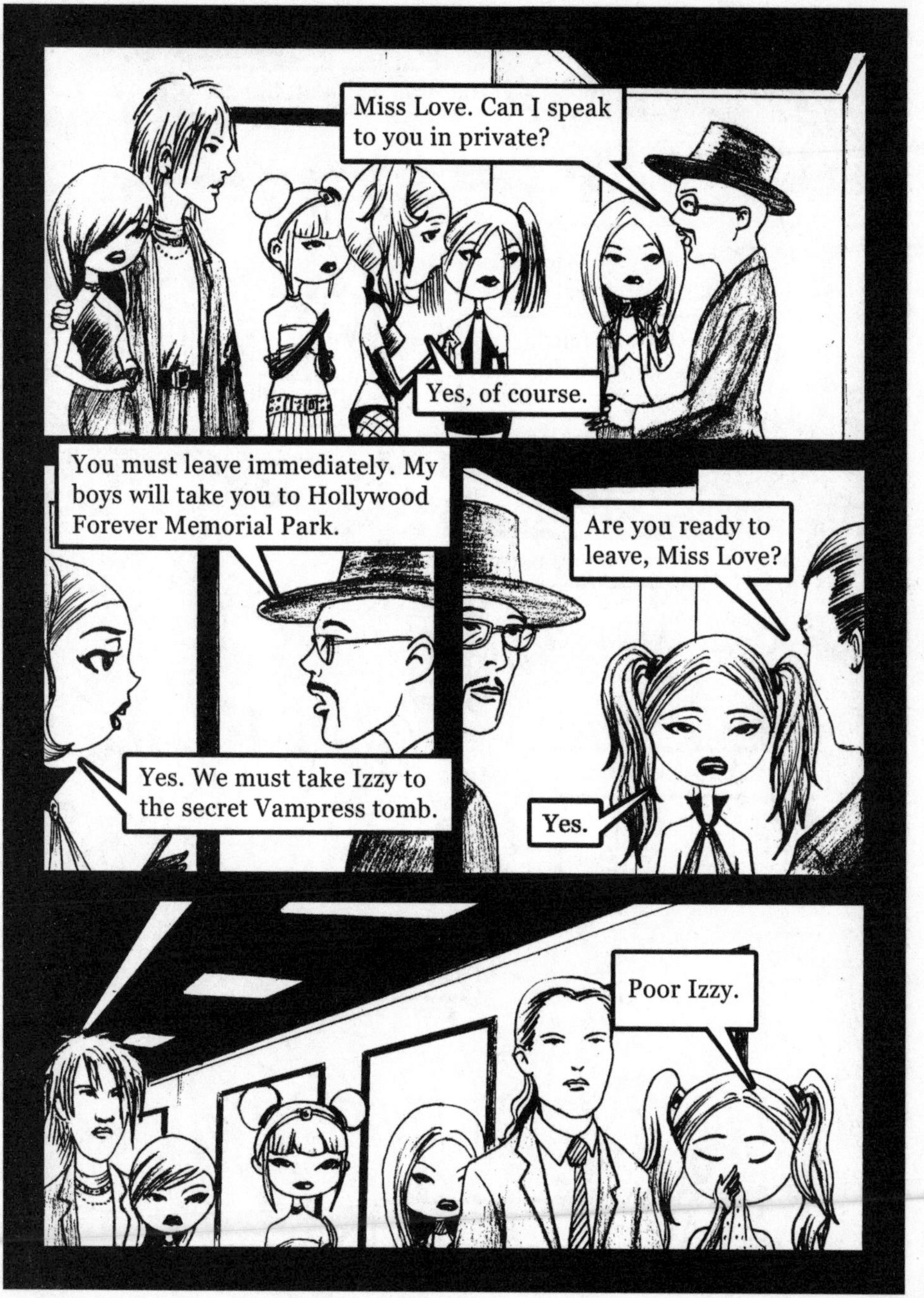
Miss Love. Can I speak to you in private?
Yes, of course.
You must leave immediately. My boys will take you to Hollywood Forever Memorial Park.
Yes. We must take Izzy to the secret Vampress tomb.
Are you ready to leave, Miss Love?
Yes.
Poor Izzy.

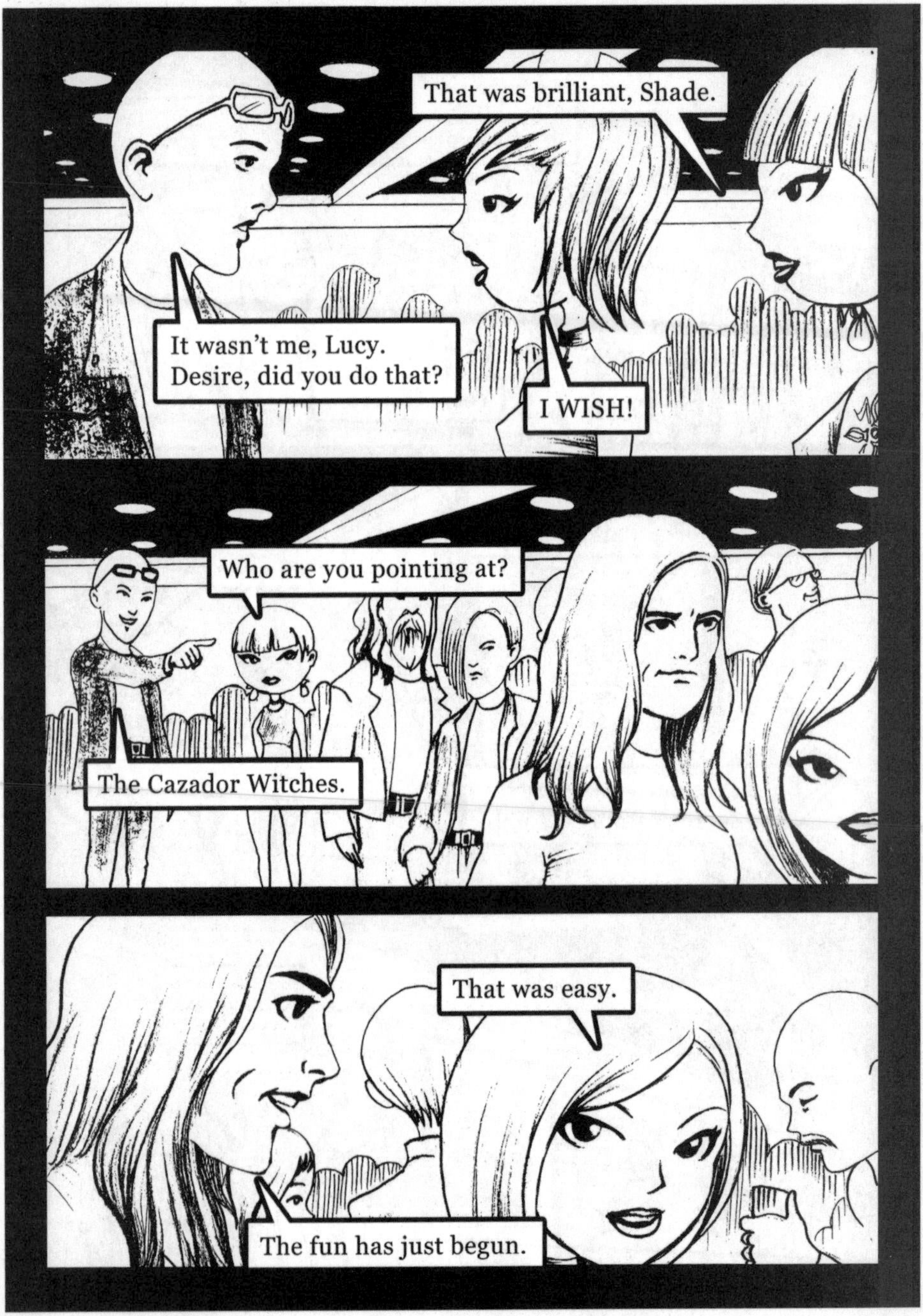
That was brilliant, Shade.
It wasn't me, Lucy. Desire, did you do that?
I WISH!
Who are you pointing at?
The Cazador Witches.
That was easy.
The fun has just begun.

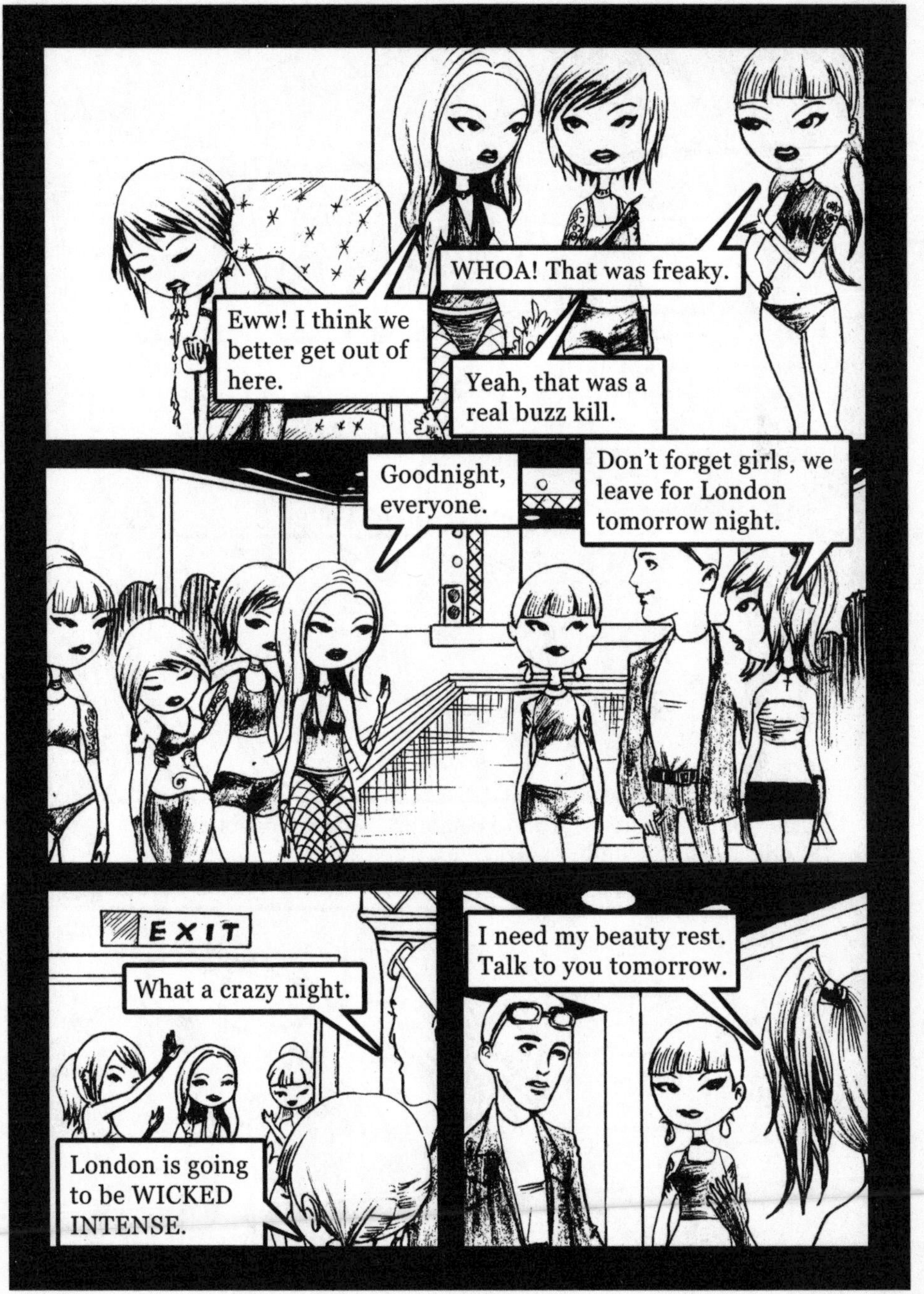
Eww! I think we better get out of here.
WHOA! That was freaky.
Yeah, that was a real buzz kill.
Goodnight, everyone.
Don't forget girls, we leave for London tomorrow night.
EXIT
What a crazy night.
London is going to be WICKED INTENSE.
I need my beauty rest. Talk to you tomorrow.

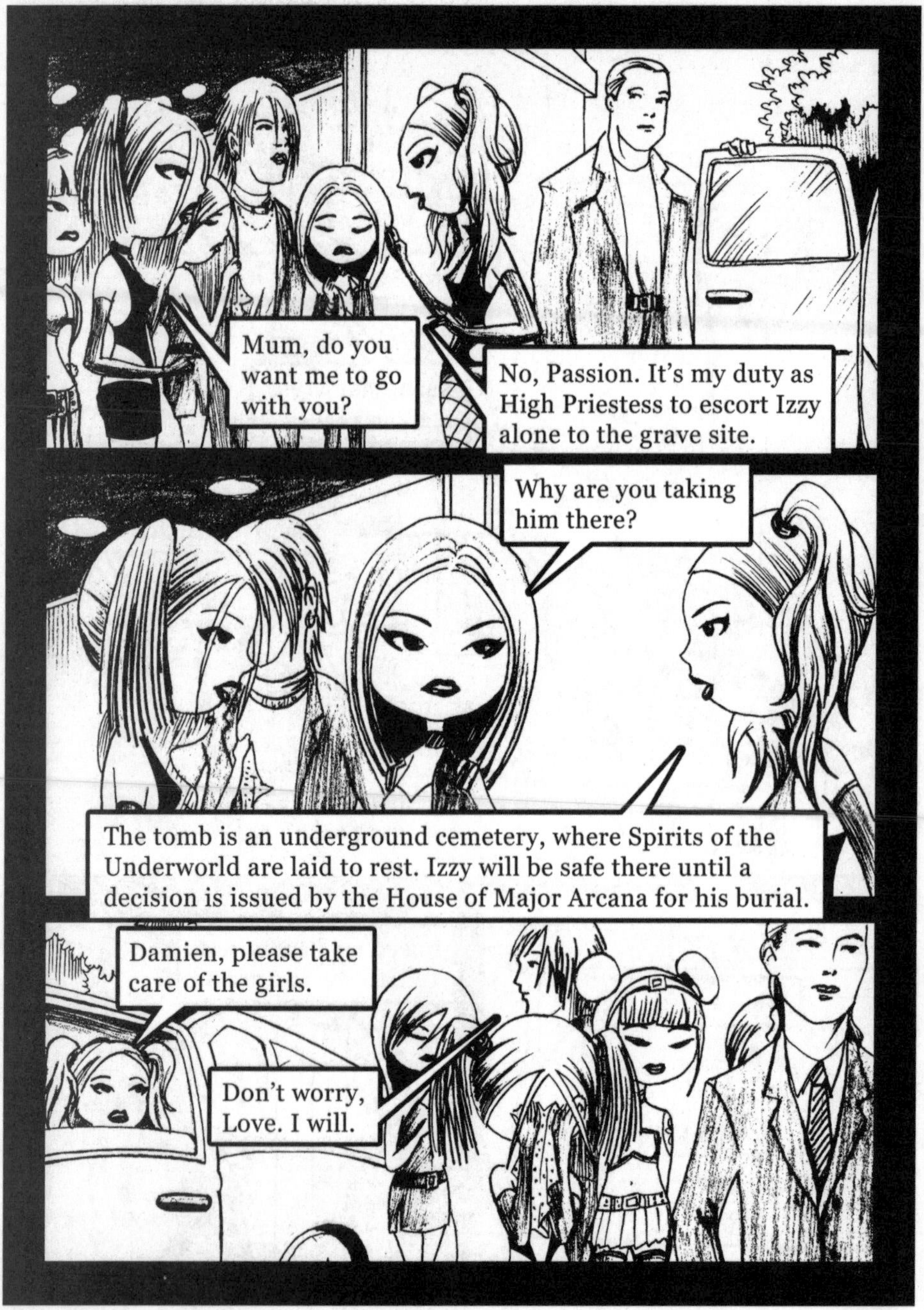
Mum, do you want me to go with you?
No, Passion. It's my duty as High Priestess to escort Izzy alone to the grave site.
Why are you taking him there?
The tomb is an underground cemetery, where Spirits of the Underworld are laid to rest. Izzy will be safe there until a decision is issued by the House of Major Arcana for his burial.
Damien, please take care of the girls.
Don't worry, Love. I will.

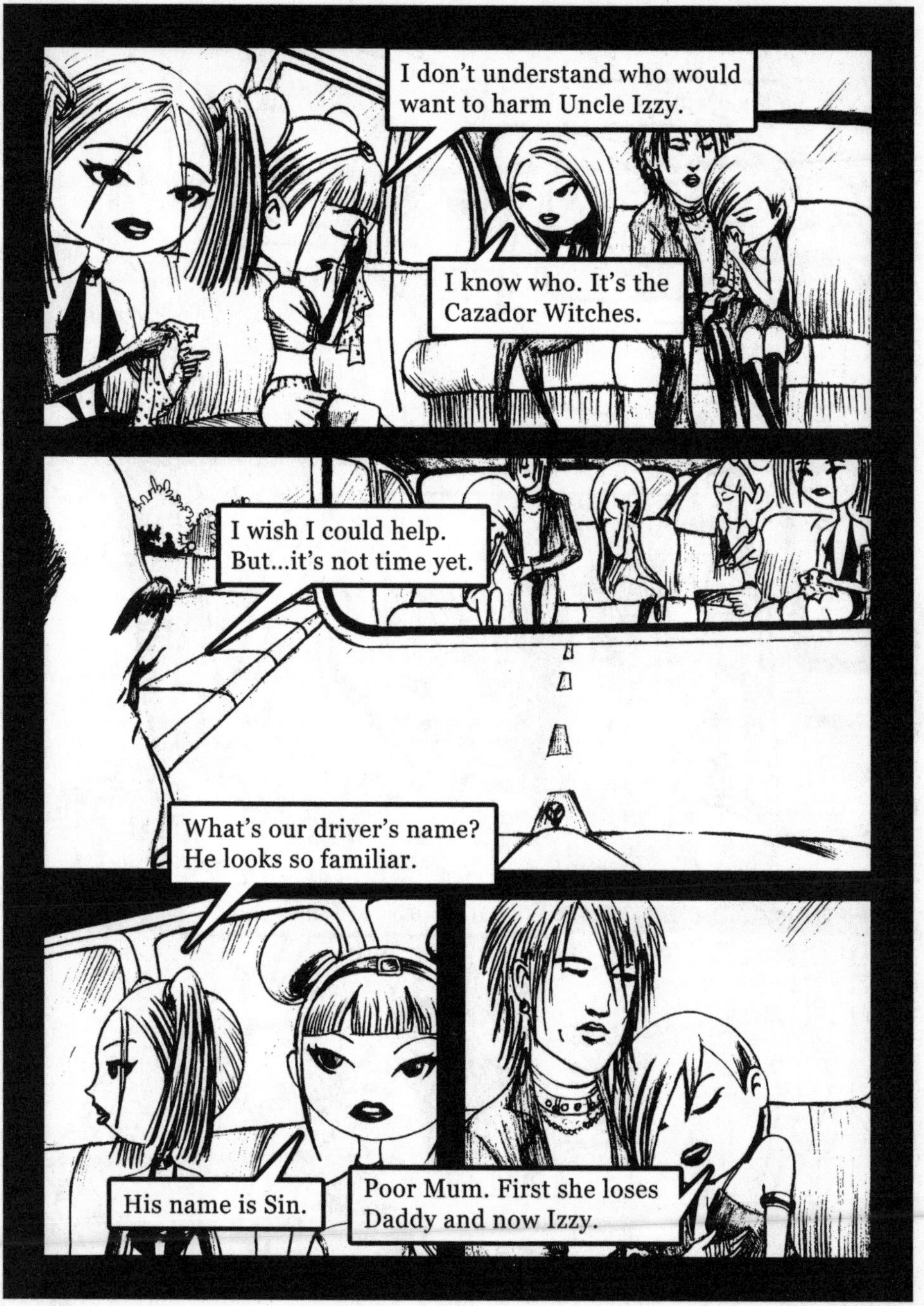
I don't understand who would want to harm Uncle Izzy.
I know who. It's the Cazador Witches.
I wish I could help. But...it's not time yet.
What's our driver's name? He looks so familiar.
His name is Sin.
Poor Mum. First she loses Daddy and now Izzy.

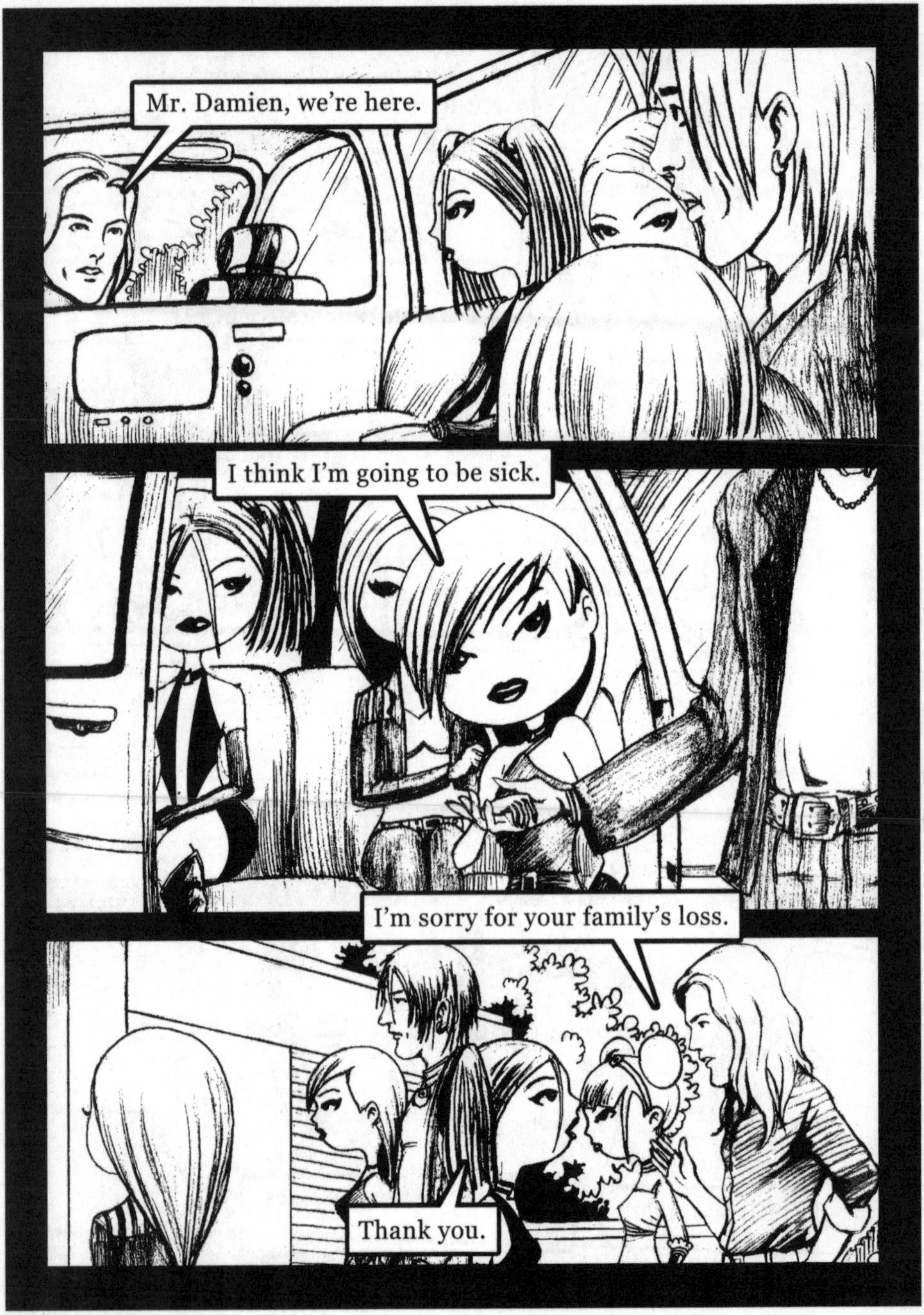
Mr. Damien, we're here.
I think I'm going to be sick.
I'm sorry for your family's loss.
Thank you.

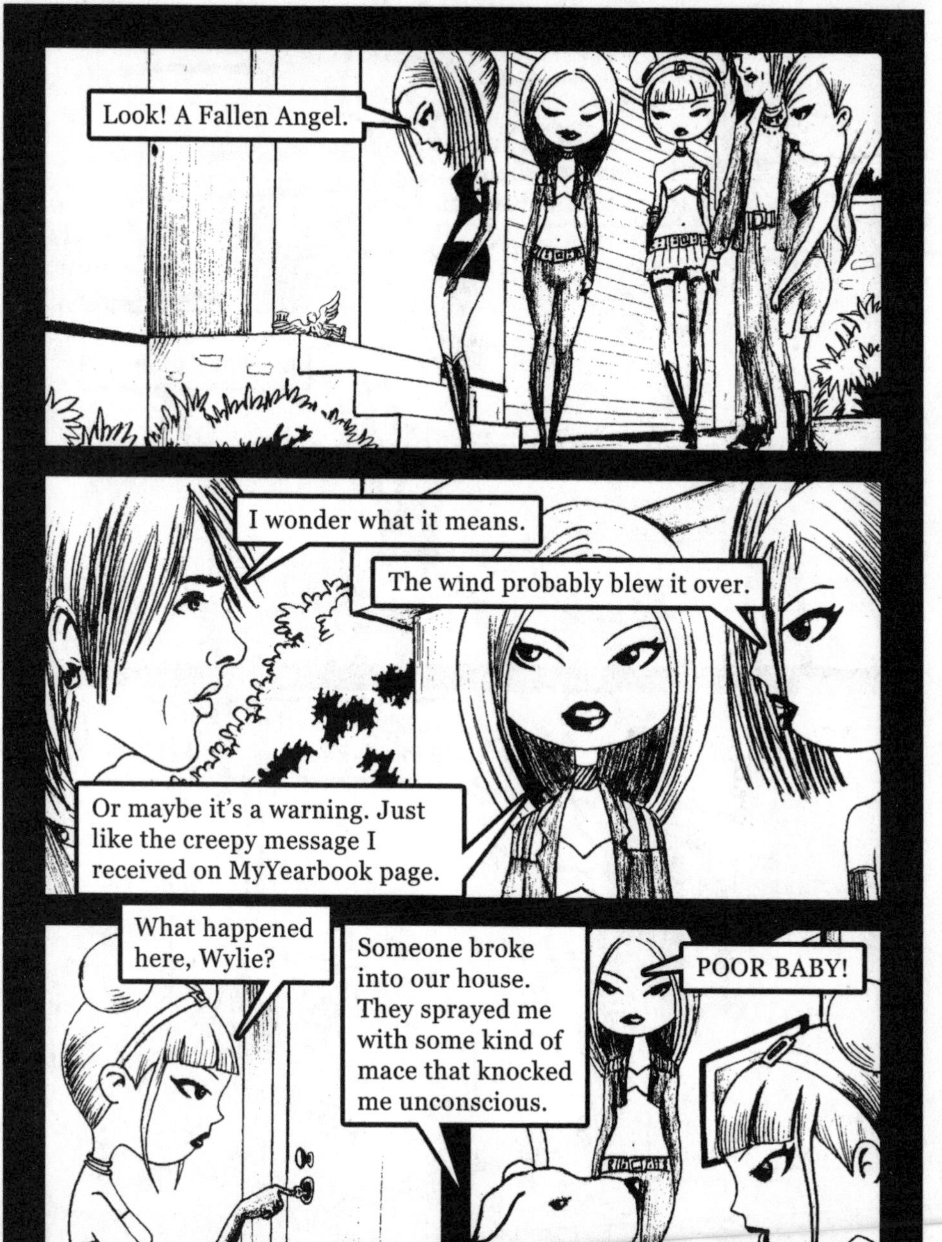
Look! A Fallen Angel.
I wonder what it means.
The wind probably blew it over.
Or maybe it's a warning. Just like the creepy message I received on MyYearbook page.
What happened here, Wylie?
Someone broke into our house. They sprayed me with some kind of mace that knocked me unconscious.
POOR BABY!

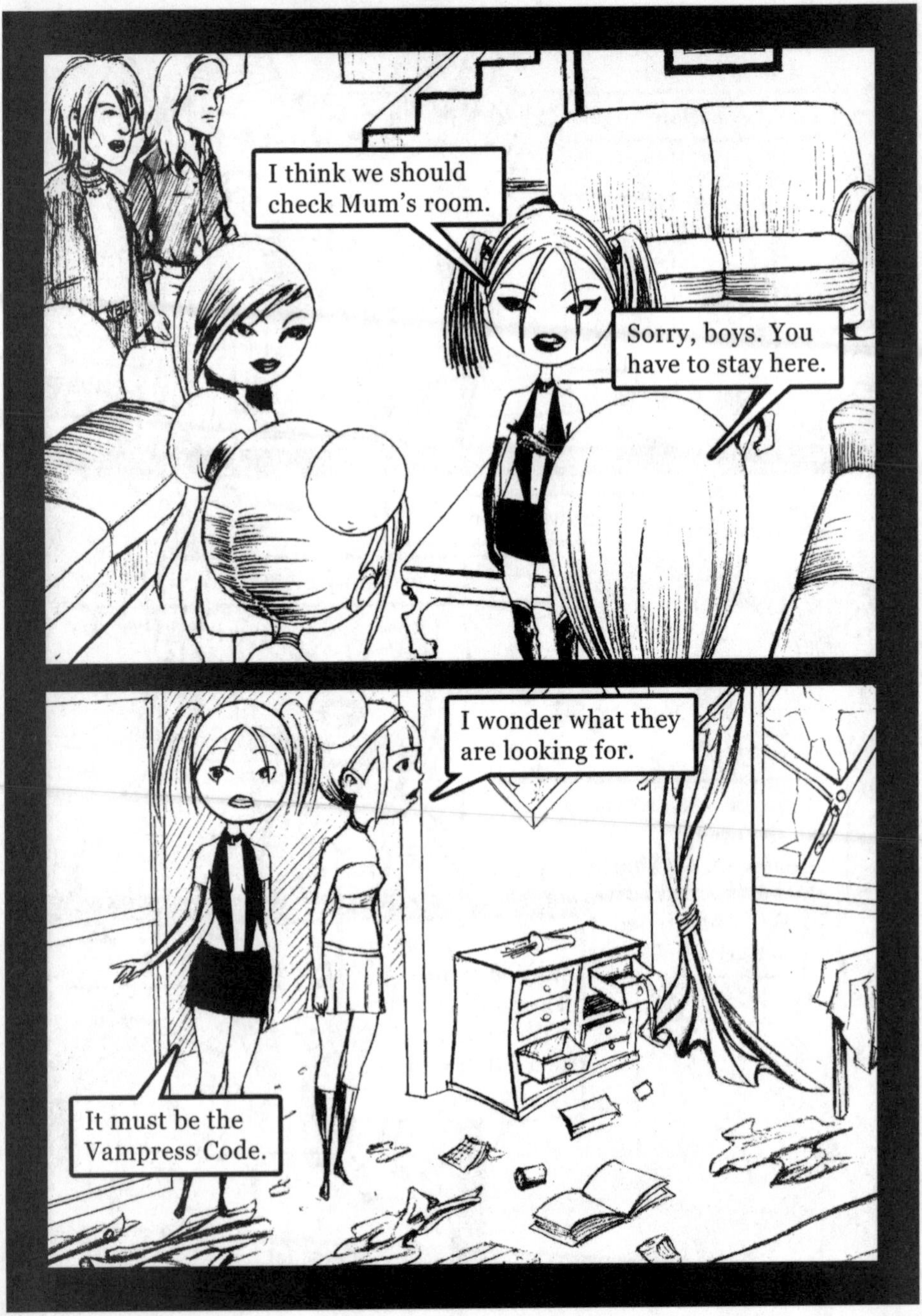
I think we should check Mum's room.
Sorry, boys. You have to stay here.
I wonder what they are looking for.
It must be the Vampress Code.

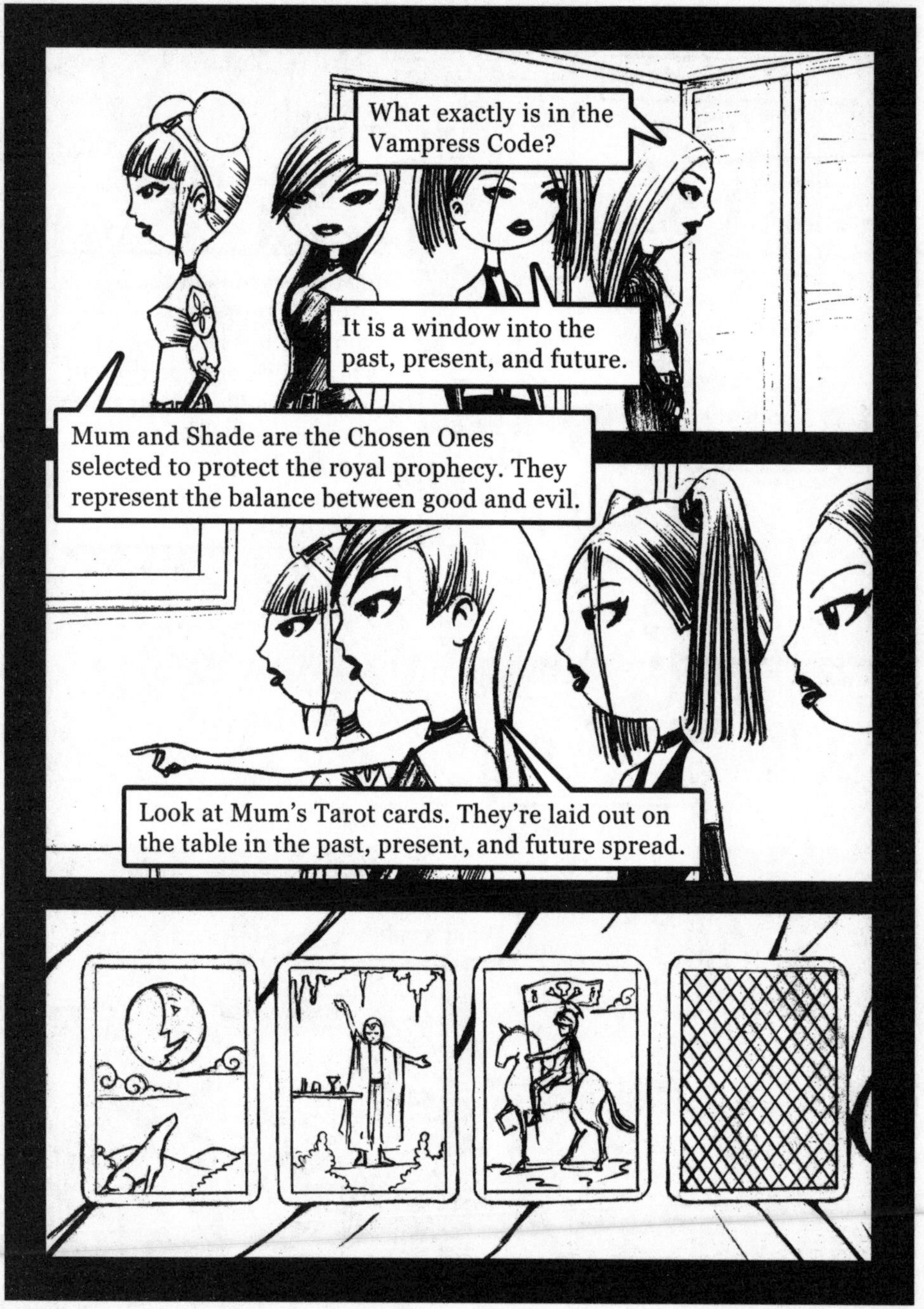
What exactly is in the Vampress Code?
It is a window into the past, present, and future.
Mum and Shade are the Chosen Ones selected to protect the royal prophecy. They represent the balance between good and evil.
Look at Mum's Tarot cards. They're laid out on the table in the past, present, and future spread.

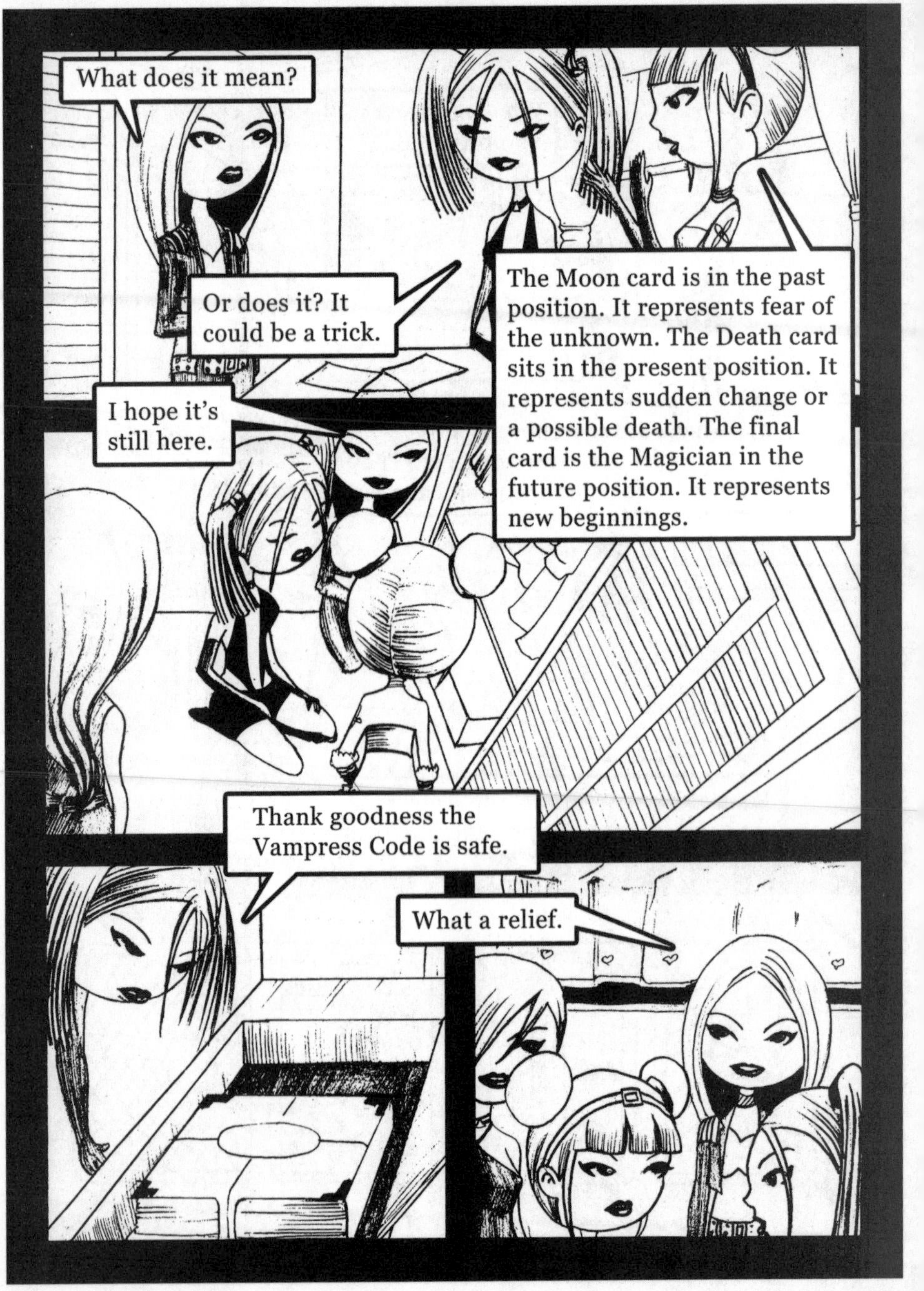
What does it mean?
The Moon card is in the past position. It represents fear of the unknown. The Death card sits in the present position. It represents sudden change or a possible death. The final card is the Magician in the future position. It represents new beginnings.
Or does it? It could be a trick.
I hope it's still here.
Thank goodness the Vampress Code is safe.
What a relief.

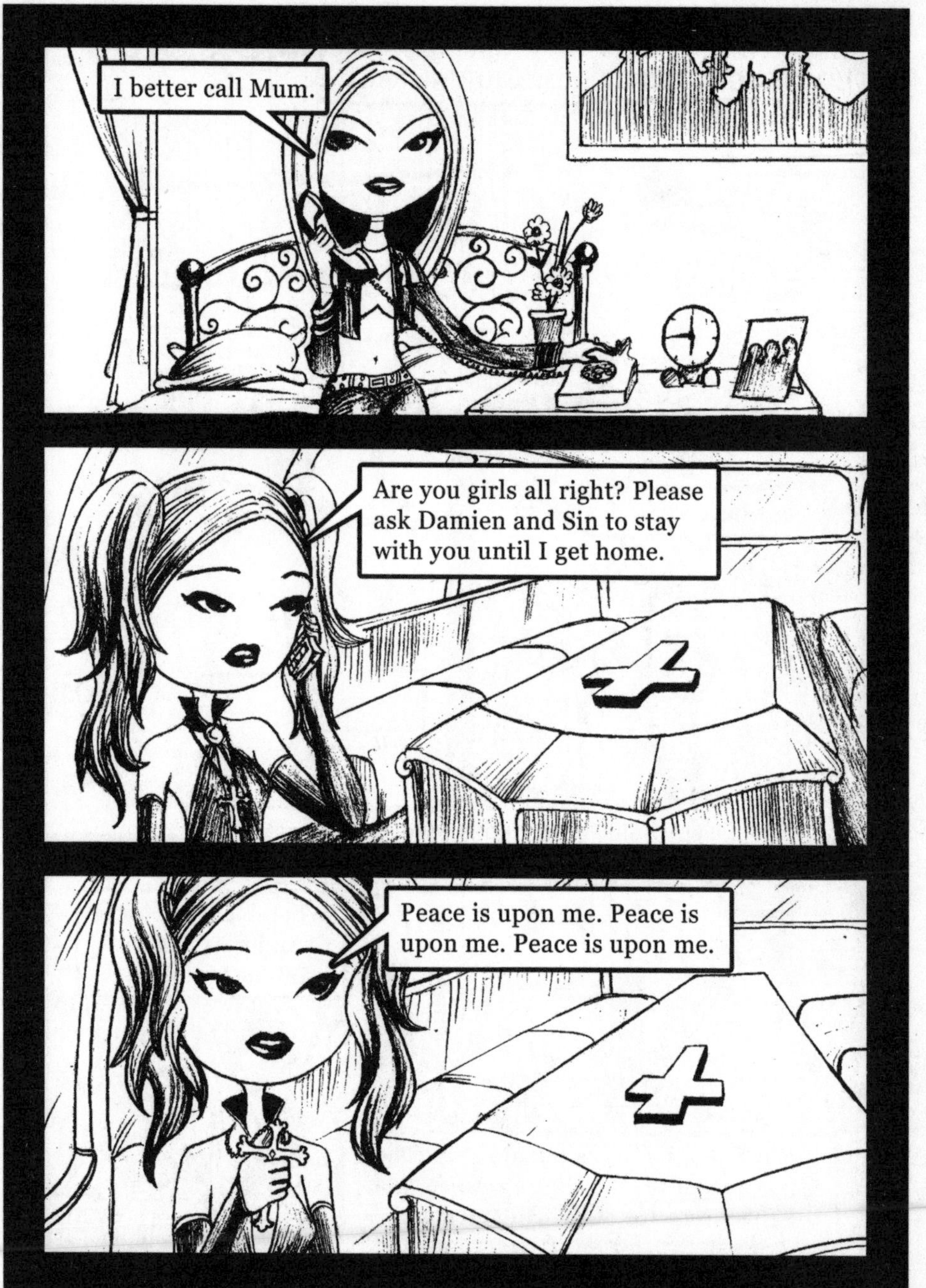
I better call Mum.
Are you girls all right? Please ask Damien and Sin to stay with you until I get home.
Peace is upon me. Peace is upon me. Peace is upon me.

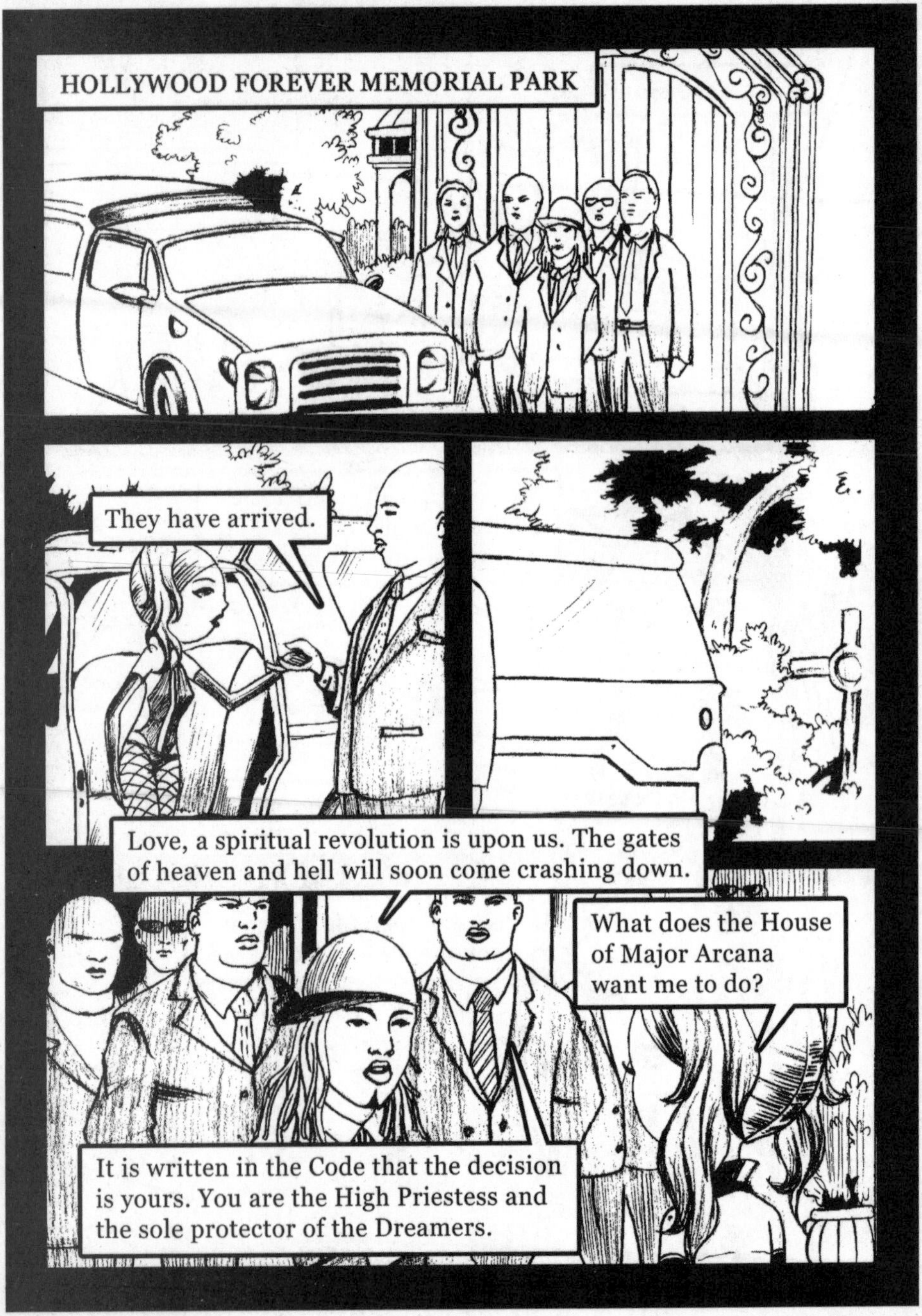
HOLLYWOOD FOREVER MEMORIAL PARK
They have arrived.
Love, a spiritual revolution is upon us. The gates of heaven and hell will soon come crashing down.
What does the House of Major Arcana want me to do?
It is written in the Code that the decision is yours. You are the High Priestess and the sole protector of the Dreamers.

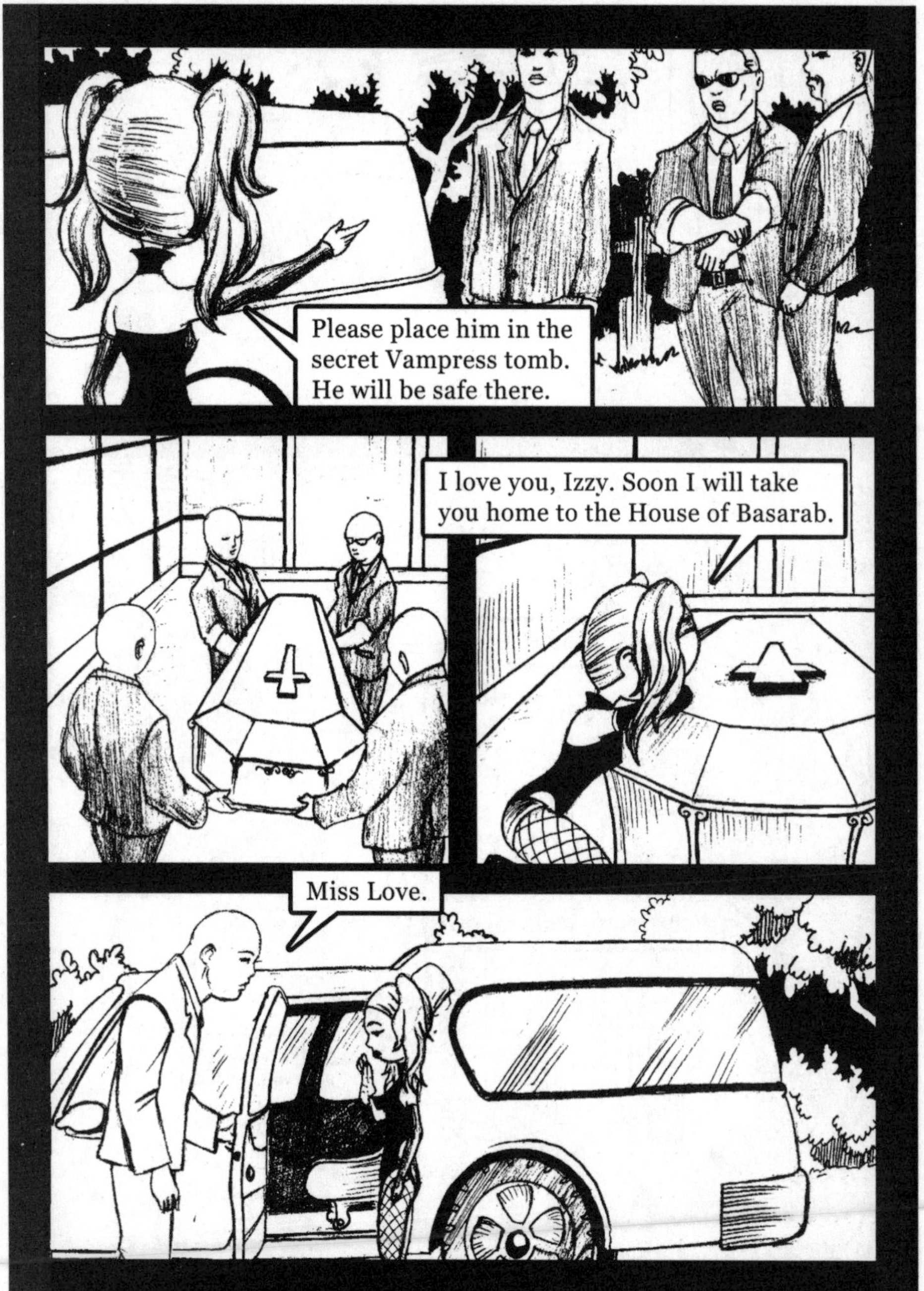
Please place him in the secret Vampress tomb. He will be safe there.
I love you, Izzy. Soon I will take you home to the House of Basarab.
Miss Love.

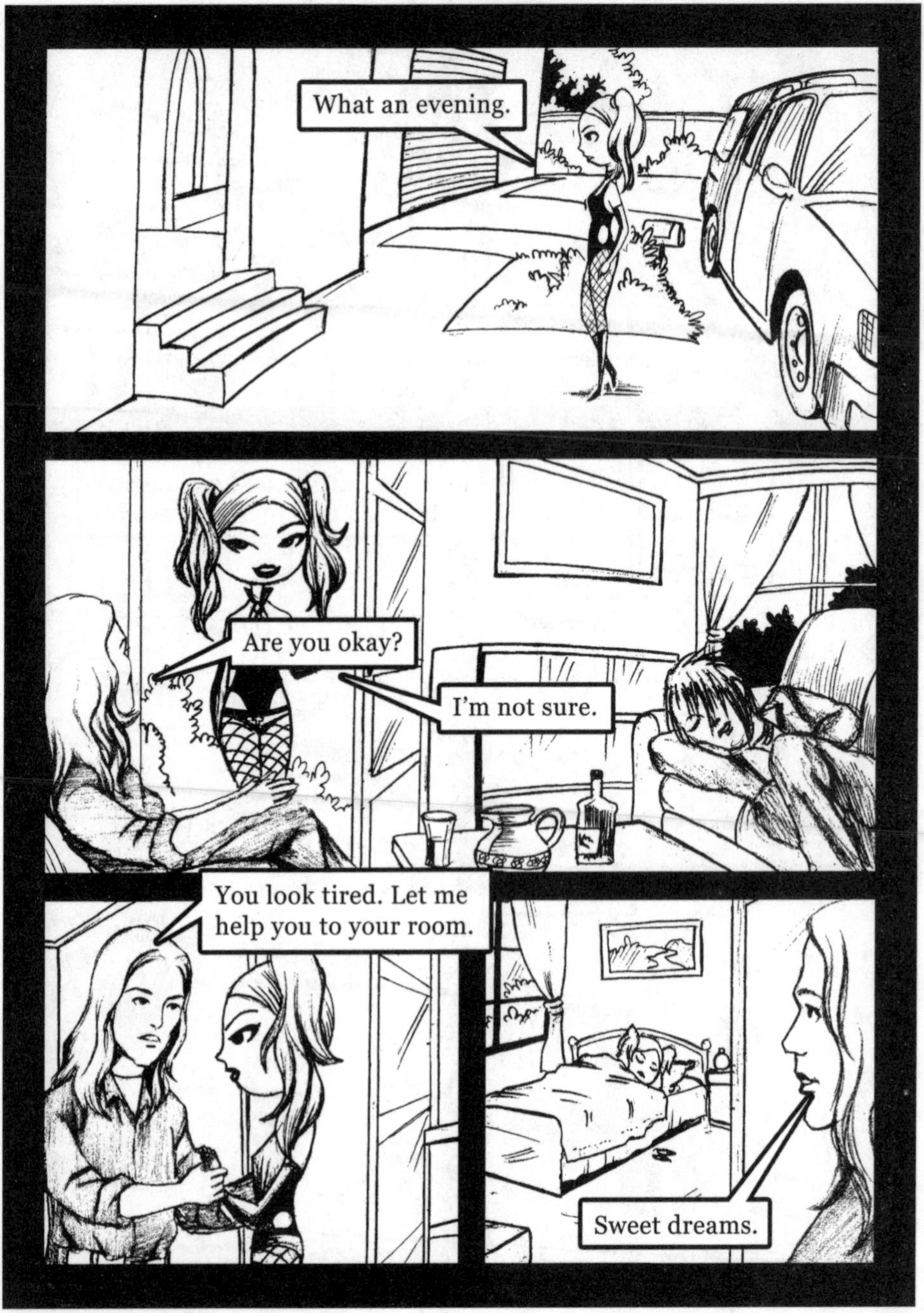
What an evening.
Are you okay?
I'm not sure.
You look tired. Let me help you to your room.
Sweet dreams.

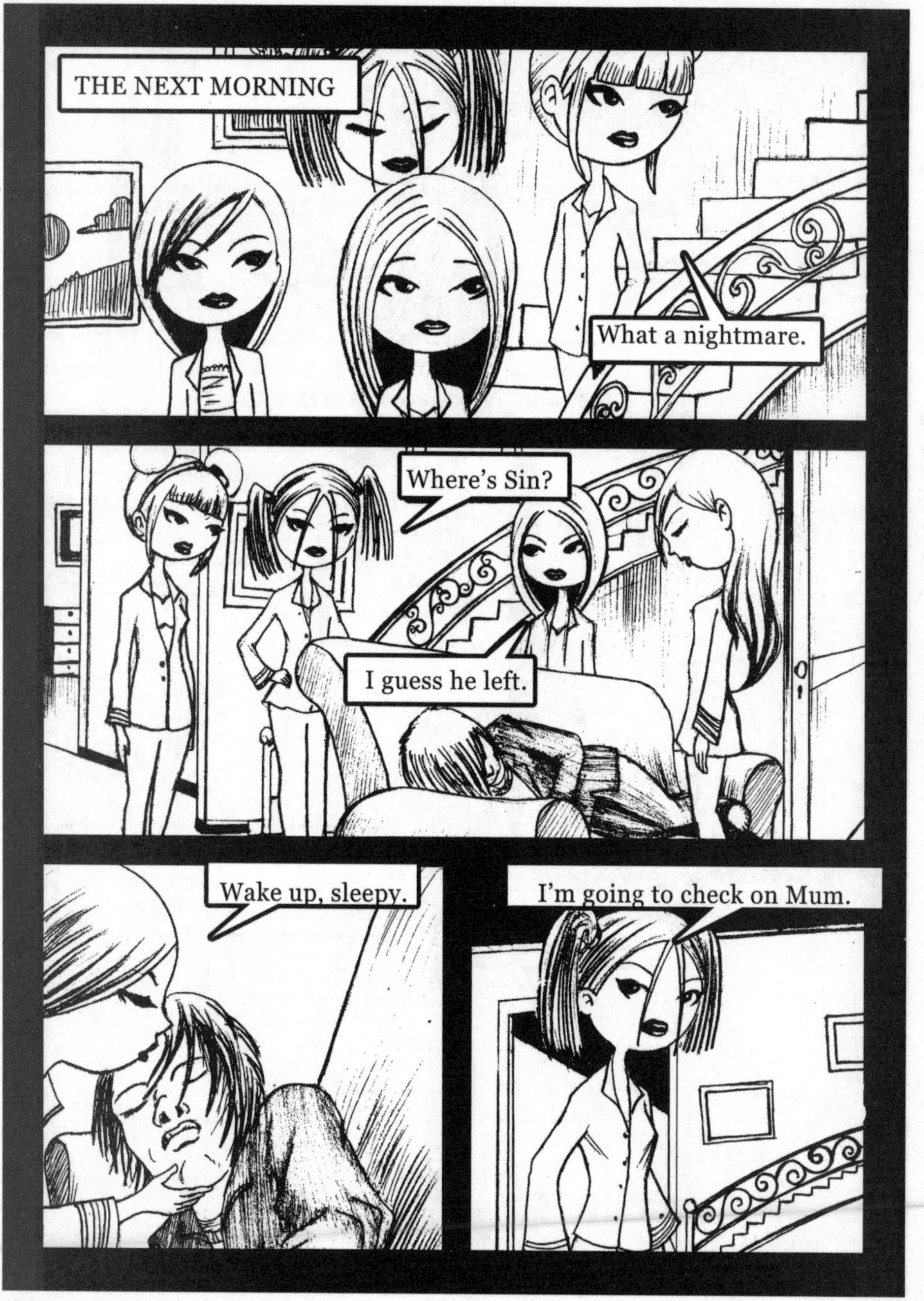
THE NEXT MORNING
What a nightmare.
Where's Sin?
I guess he left.
Wake up, sleepy.
I'm going to check on Mum.

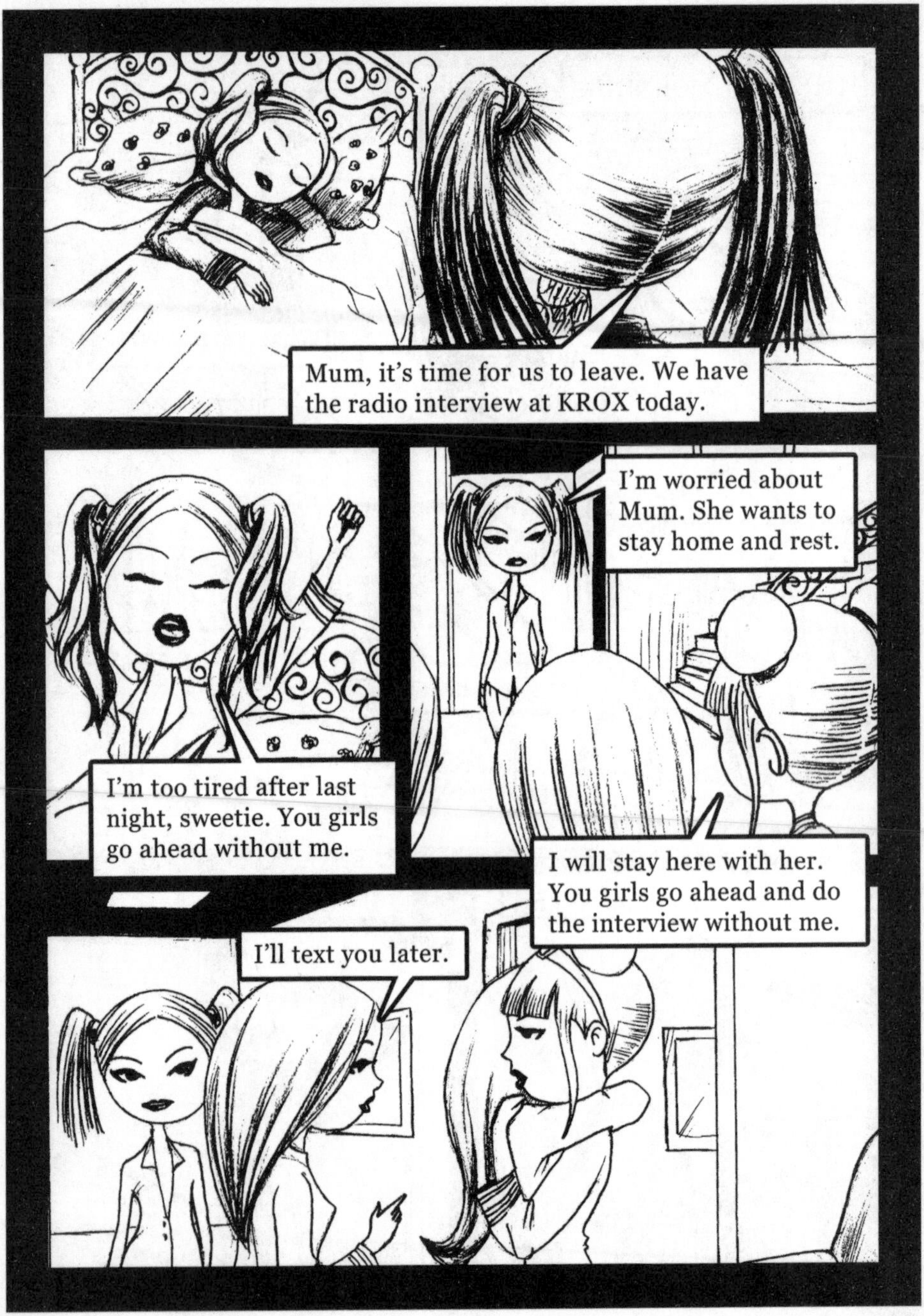

Mum, it's time for us to leave. We have the radio interview at KROX today.
I'm too tired after last night, sweetie. You girls go ahead without me.
I'm worried about Mum. She wants to stay home and rest.
I will stay here with her. You girls go ahead and do the interview without me.
I'll text you later.

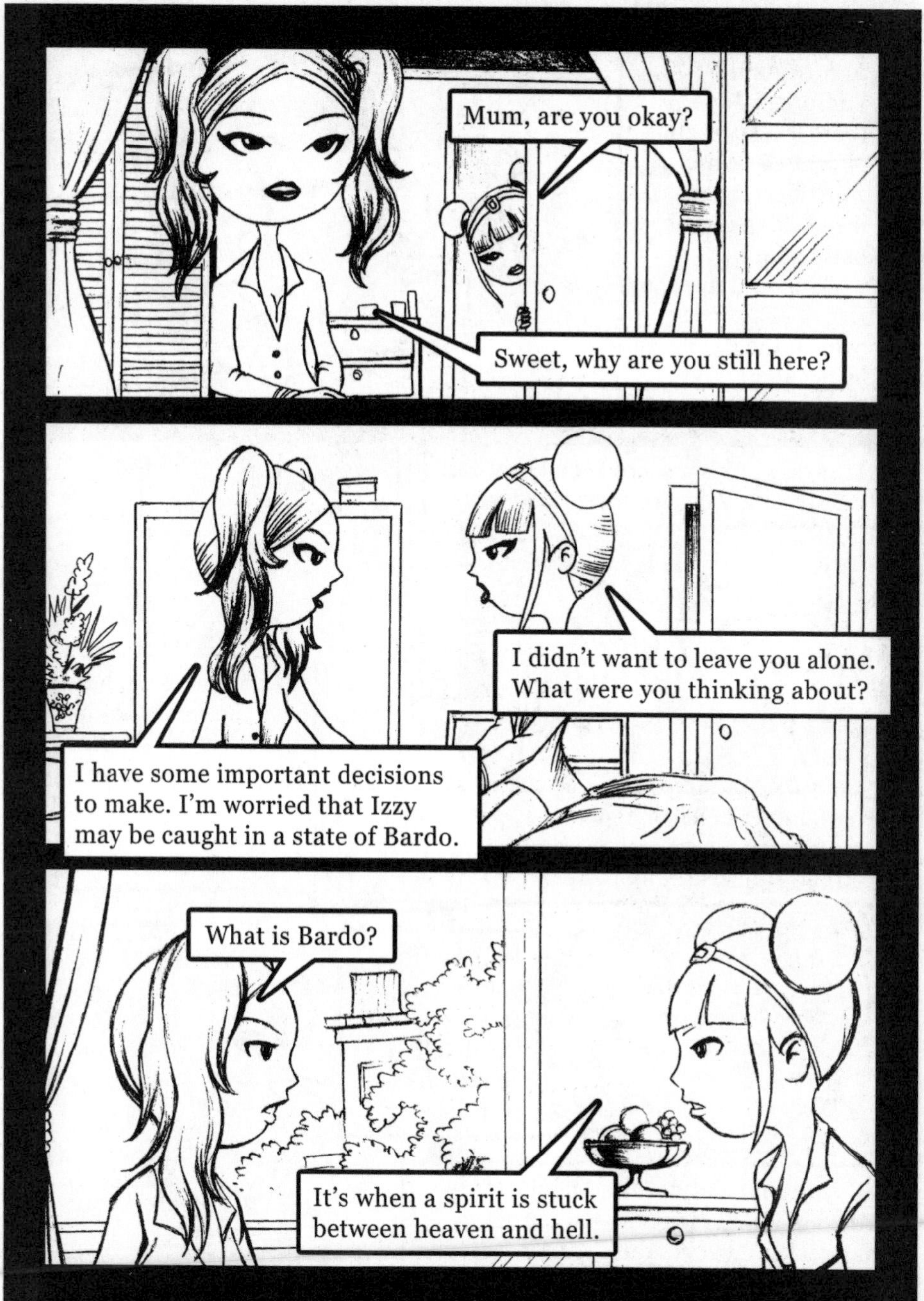
Mum, are you okay?
Sweet, why are you still here?
I didn't want to leave you alone. What were you thinking about?
I have some important decisions to make. I'm worried that Izzy may be caught in a state of Bardo.
What is Bardo?
It's when a spirit is stuck between heaven and hell.

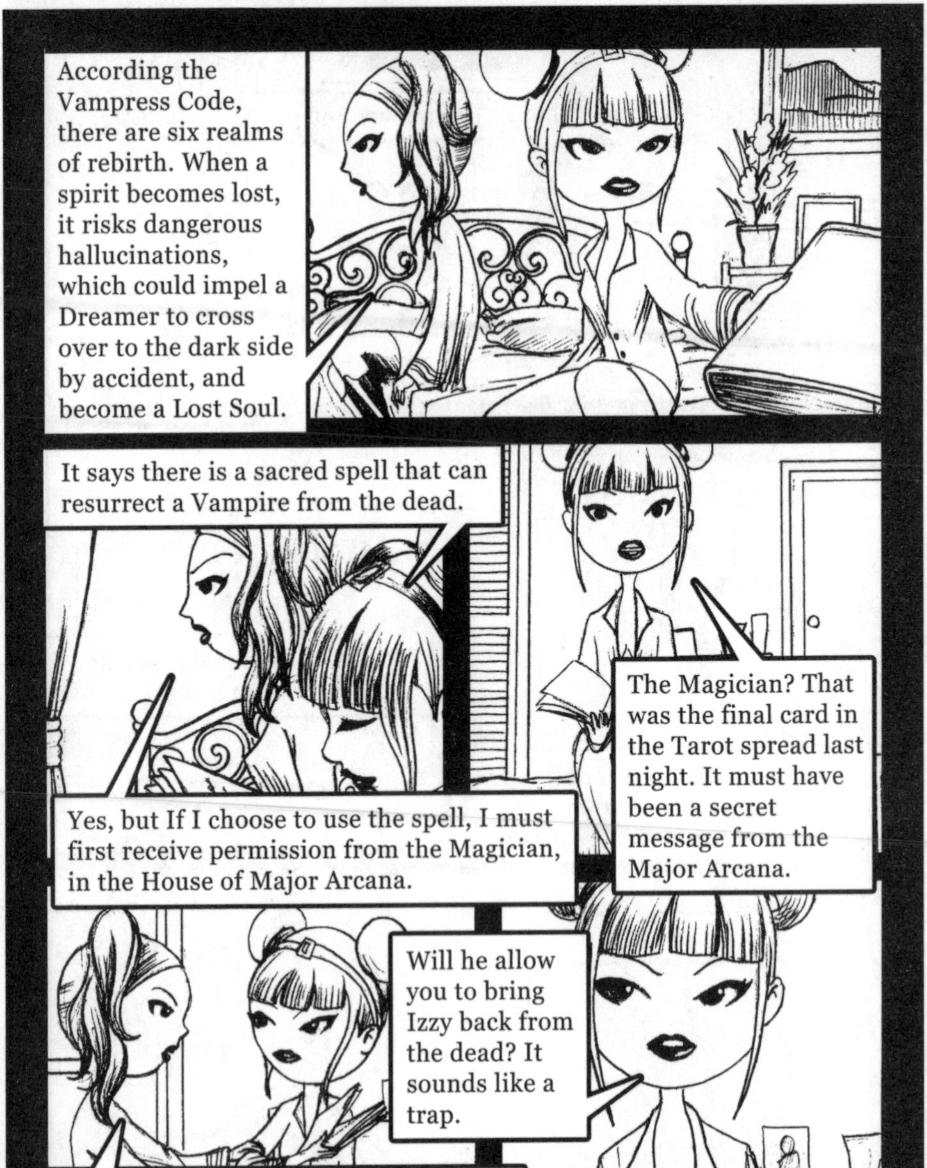
According the Vampress Code, there are six realms of rebirth. When a spirit becomes lost, it risks dangerous hallucinations, which could impel a Dreamer to cross over to the dark side by accident, and become a Lost Soul.
It says there is a sacred spell that can resurrect a Vampire from the dead.
Yes, but If I choose to use the spell, I must first receive permission from the Magician, in the House of Major Arcana.
The Magician? That was the final card in the Tarot spread last night. It must have been a secret message from the Major Arcana.
Will he allow you to bring Izzy back from the dead? It sounds like a trap.
It's not that simple. The Magician is Alexander VI. He is the Father of Lucrecia and Zare, the Cazador Witches.

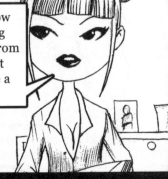

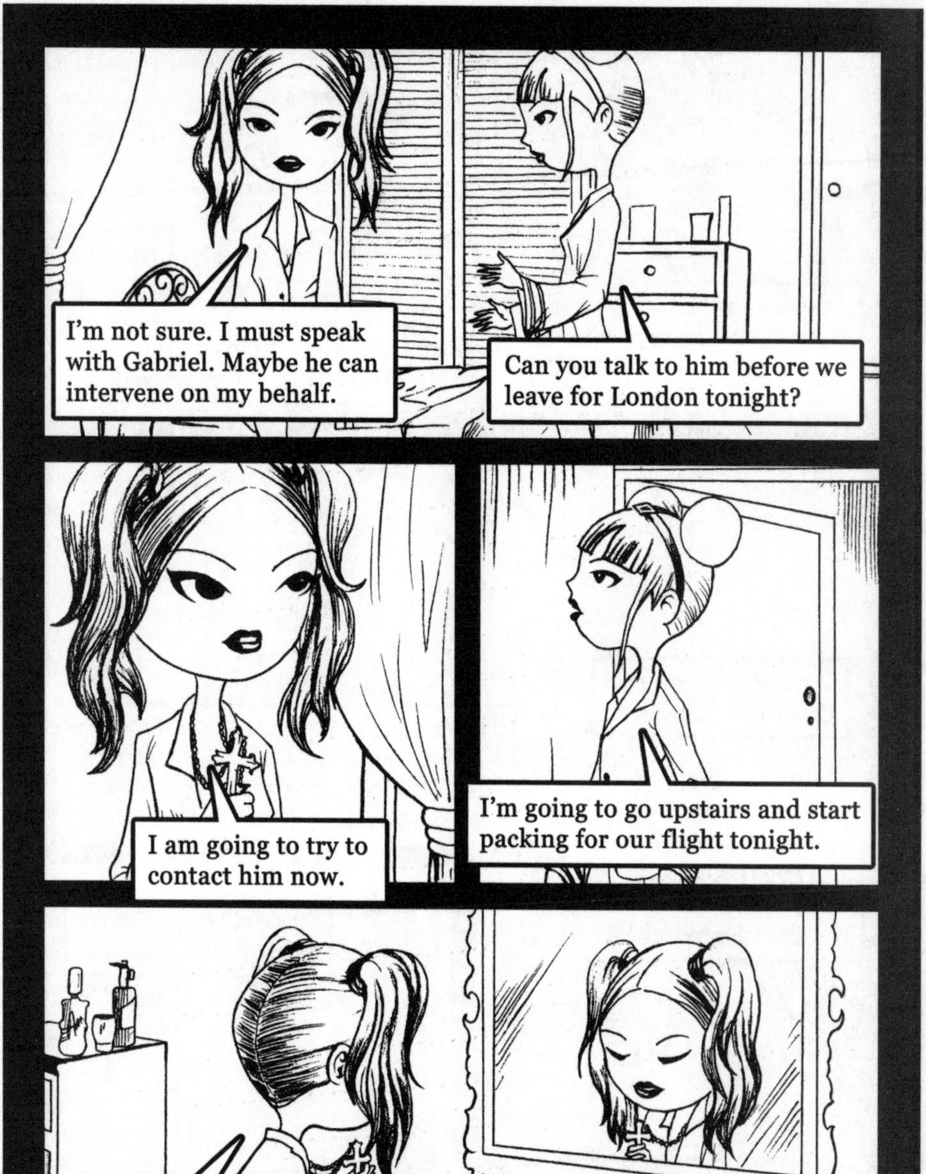
I'm not sure. I must speak with Gabriel. Maybe he can intervene on my behalf.
Can you talk to him before we leave for London tonight?
I am going to try to contact him now.
I'm going to go upstairs and start packing for our flight tonight.
Peace is upon me. Peace is upon me. Peace is upon me.

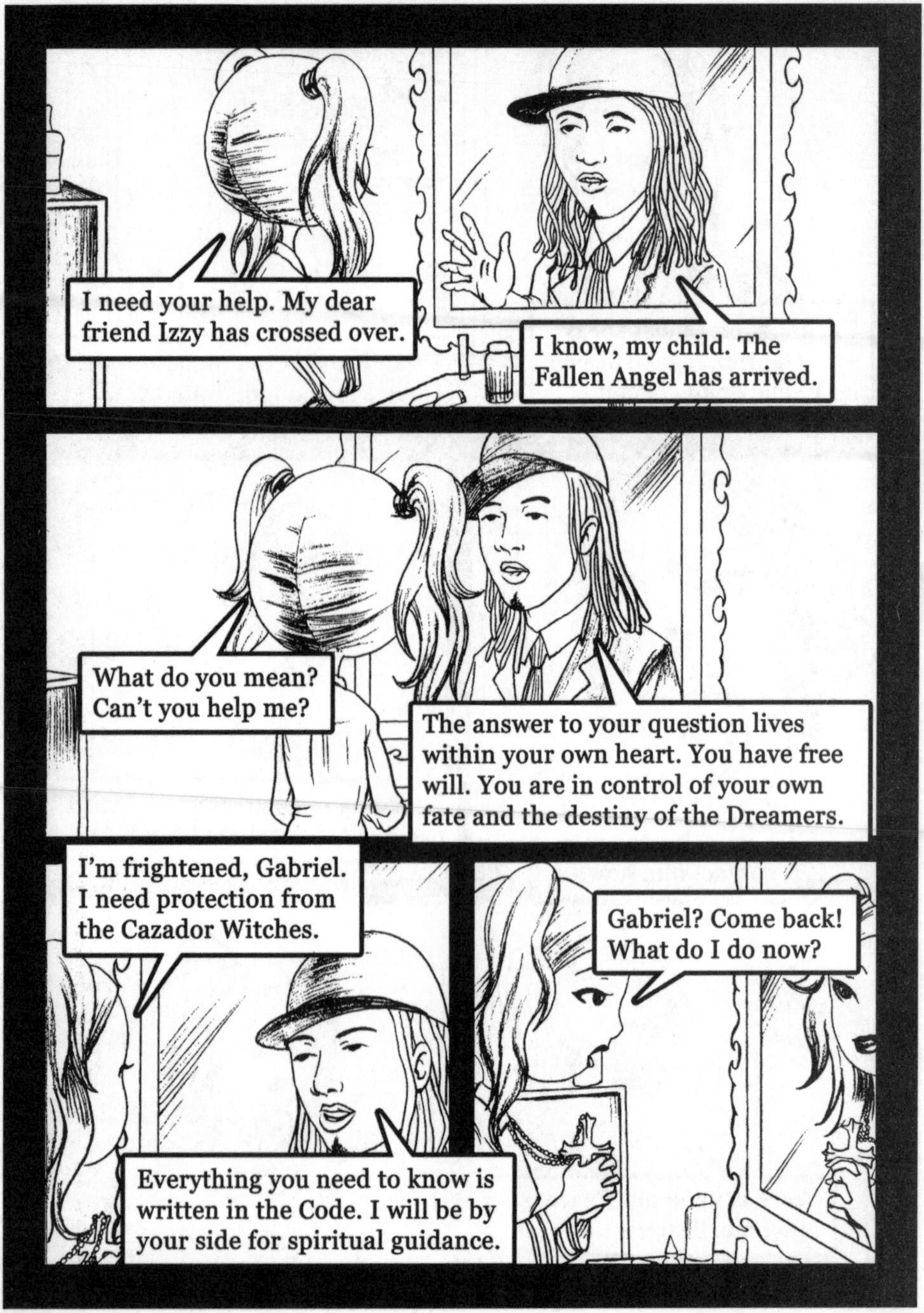
I need your help. My dear friend Izzy has crossed over.
I know, my child. The Fallen Angel has arrived.
What do you mean? Can't you help me?
The answer to your question lives within your own heart. You have free will. You are in control of your own fate and the destiny of the Dreamers.
I'm frightened, Gabriel. I need protection from the Cazador Witches.
Everything you need to know is written in the Code. I will be by your side for spiritual guidance.
Gabriel? Come back! What do I do now?

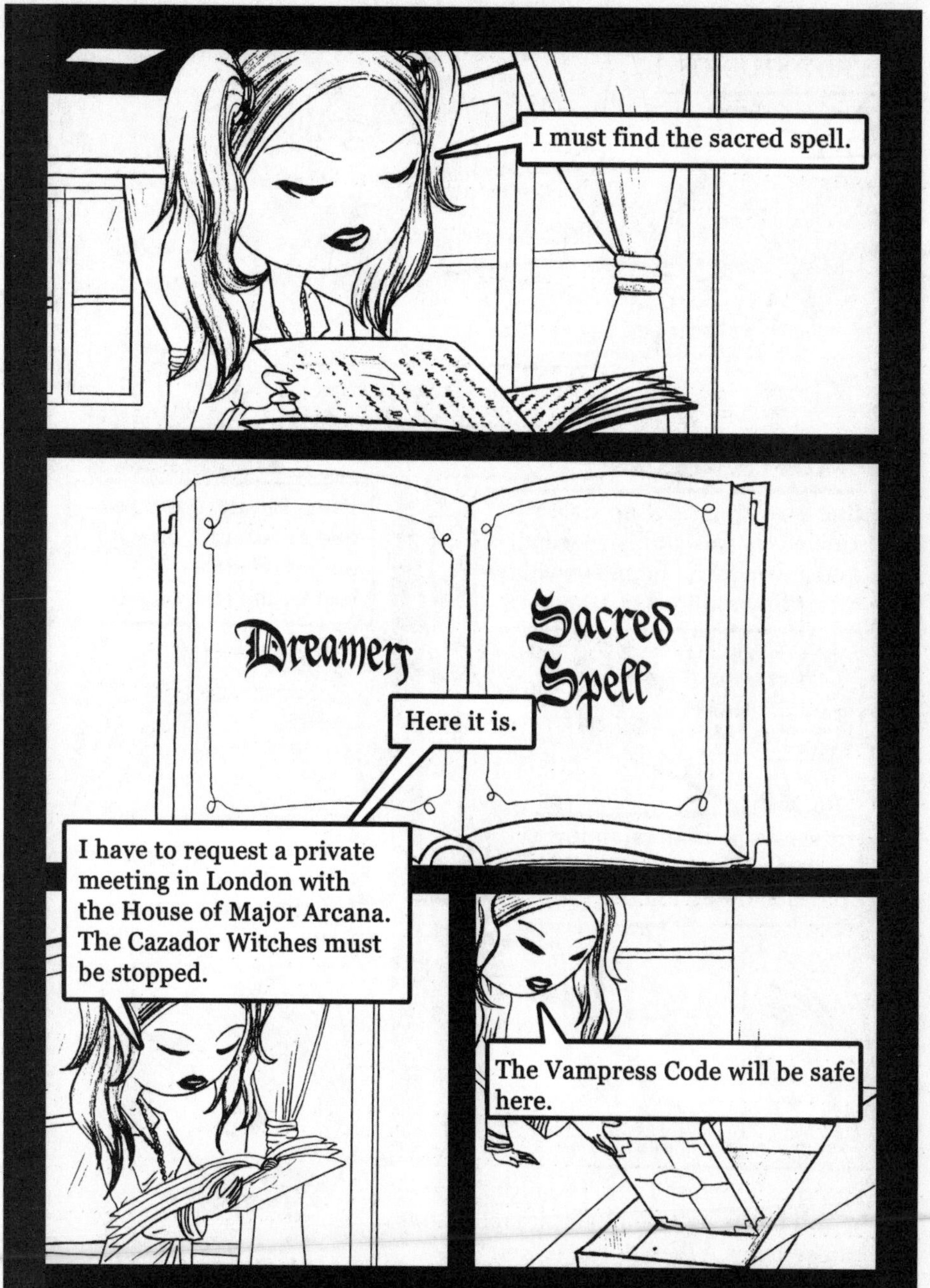
I must find the sacred spell.
Dreamers
Sacred Spell
Here it is.
I have to request a private meeting in London with the House of Major Arcana. The Cazador Witches must be stopped.
The Vampress Code will be safe here.

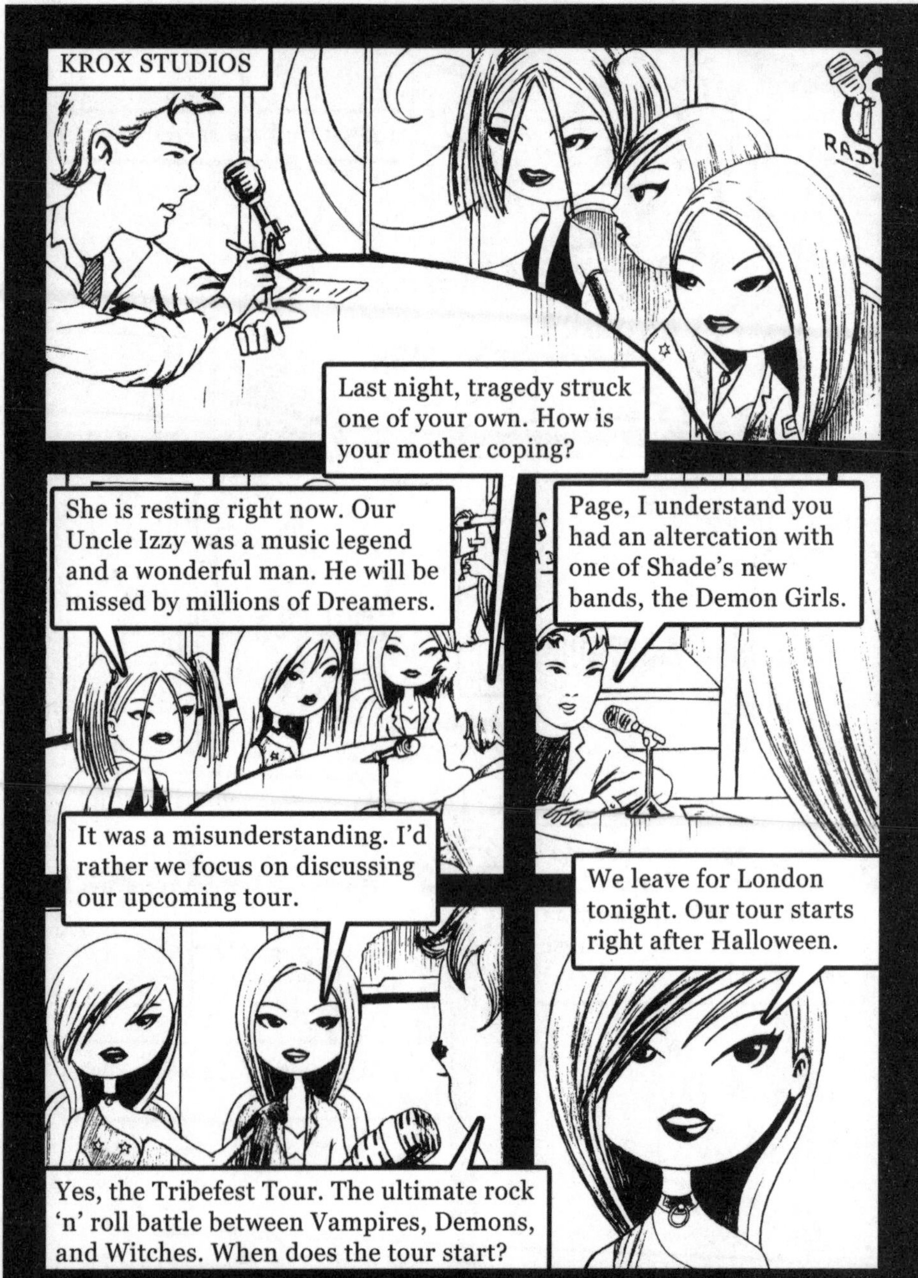
KROX STUDIOS
RADI
Last night, tragedy struck one of your own. How is your mother coping?
She is resting right now. Our Uncle Izzy was a music legend and a wonderful man. He will be missed by millions of Dreamers.
Page, I understand you had an altercation with one of Shade's new bands, the Demon Girls.
It was a misunderstanding. I'd rather we focus on discussing our upcoming tour.
Yes, the Tribefest Tour. The ultimate rock 'n' roll battle between Vampires, Demons, and Witches. When does the tour start?
We leave for London tonight. Our tour starts right after Halloween.

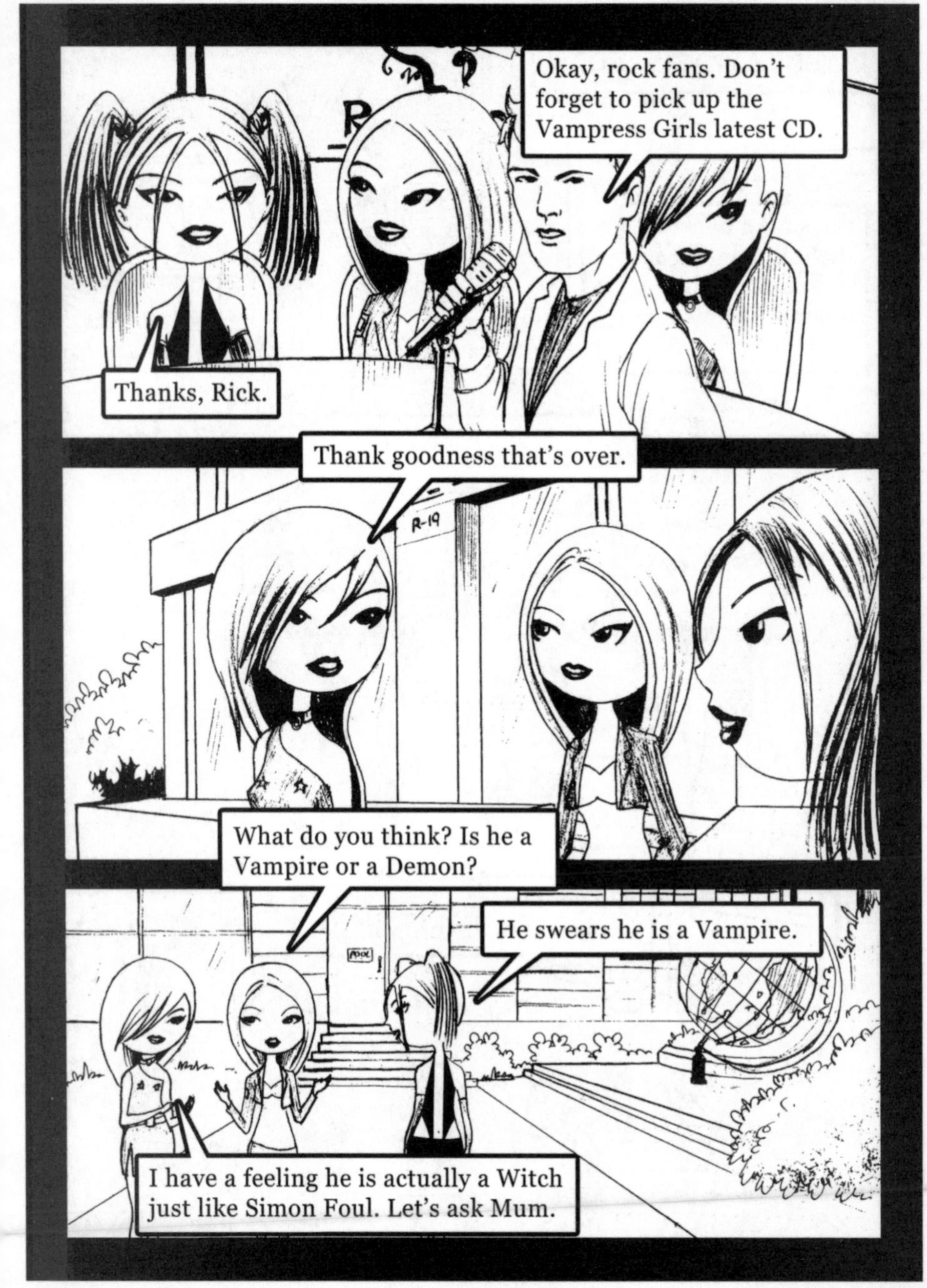
Okay, rock fans. Don't forget to pick up the Vampress Girls latest CD.
Thanks, Rick.
Thank goodness that's over.
R-19
What do you think? Is he a Vampire or a Demon?
He swears he is a Vampire.
I have a feeling he is actually a Witch just like Simon Foul. Let's ask Mum.

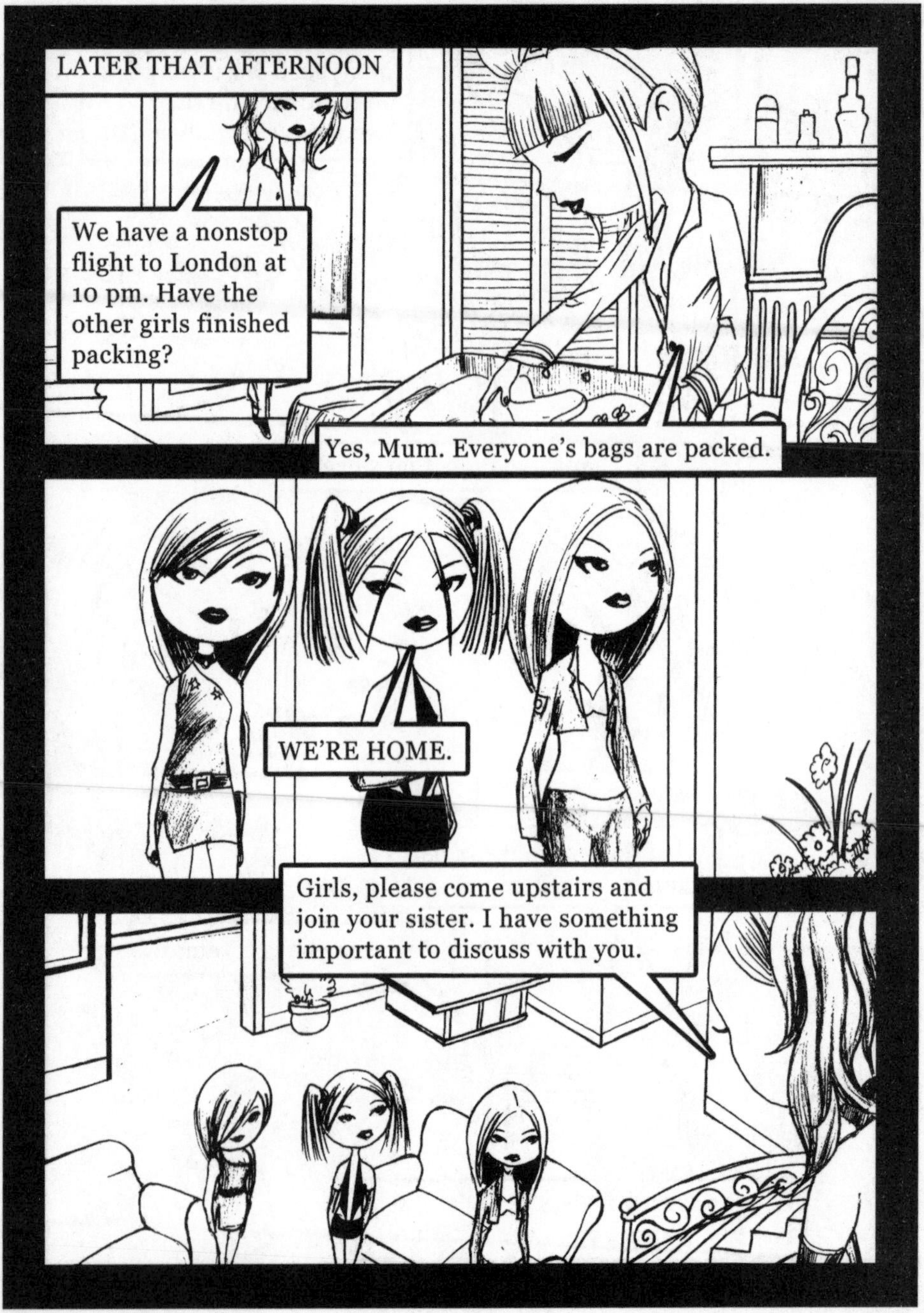
LATER THAT AFTERNOON
We have a nonstop flight to London at 10 pm. Have the other girls finished packing?
Yes, Mum. Everyone's bags are packed.
WE'RE HOME.
Girls, please come upstairs and join your sister. I have something important to discuss with you.

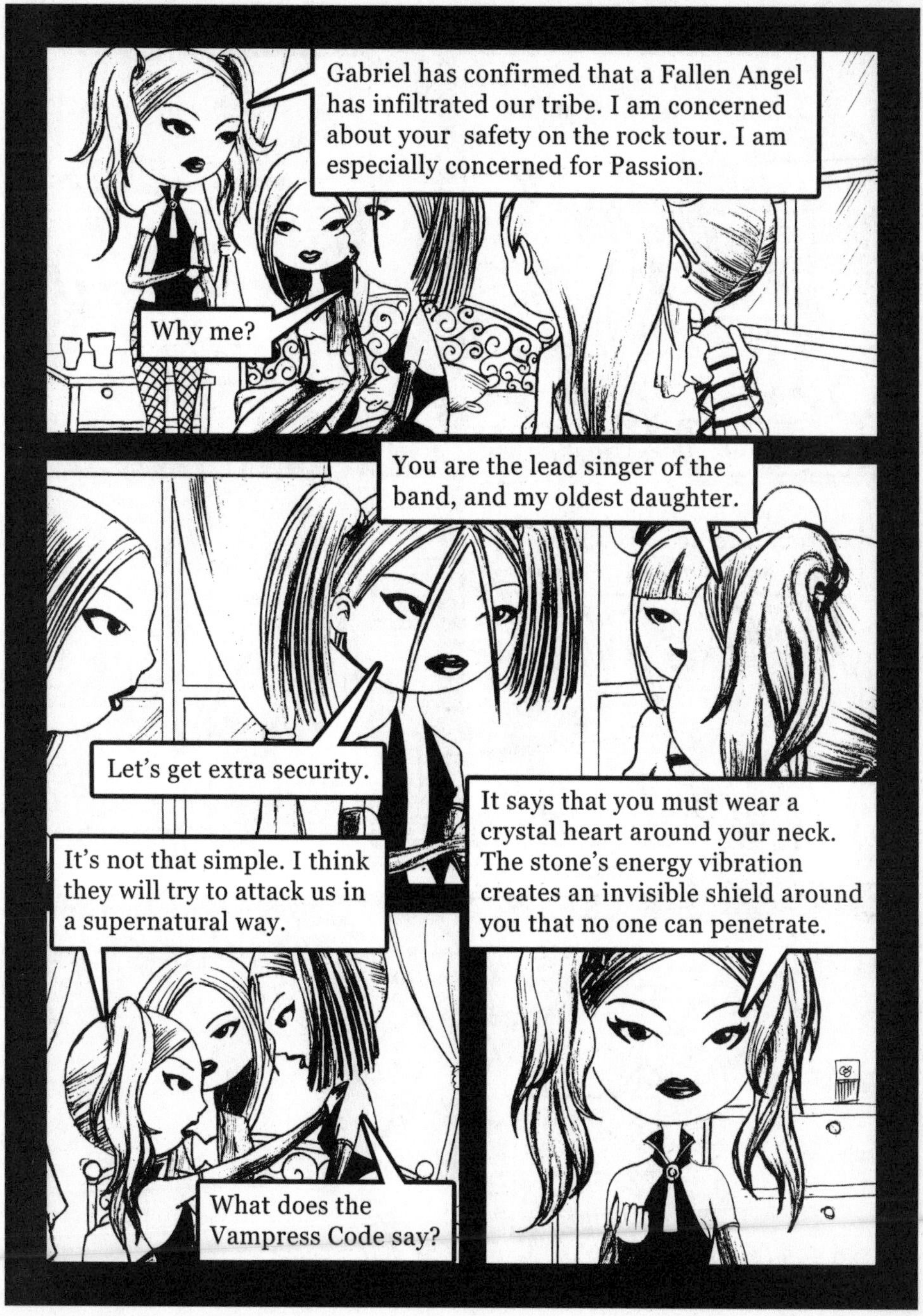
Gabriel has confirmed that a Fallen Angel has infiltrated our tribe. I am concerned about your safety on the rock tour. I am especially concerned for Passion.
Why me?
You are the lead singer of the band, and my oldest daughter.
Let's get extra security.
It's not that simple. I think they will try to attack us in a supernatural way.
What does the Vampress Code say?
It says that you must wear a crystal heart around your neck. The stone's energy vibration creates an invisible shield around you that no one can penetrate.

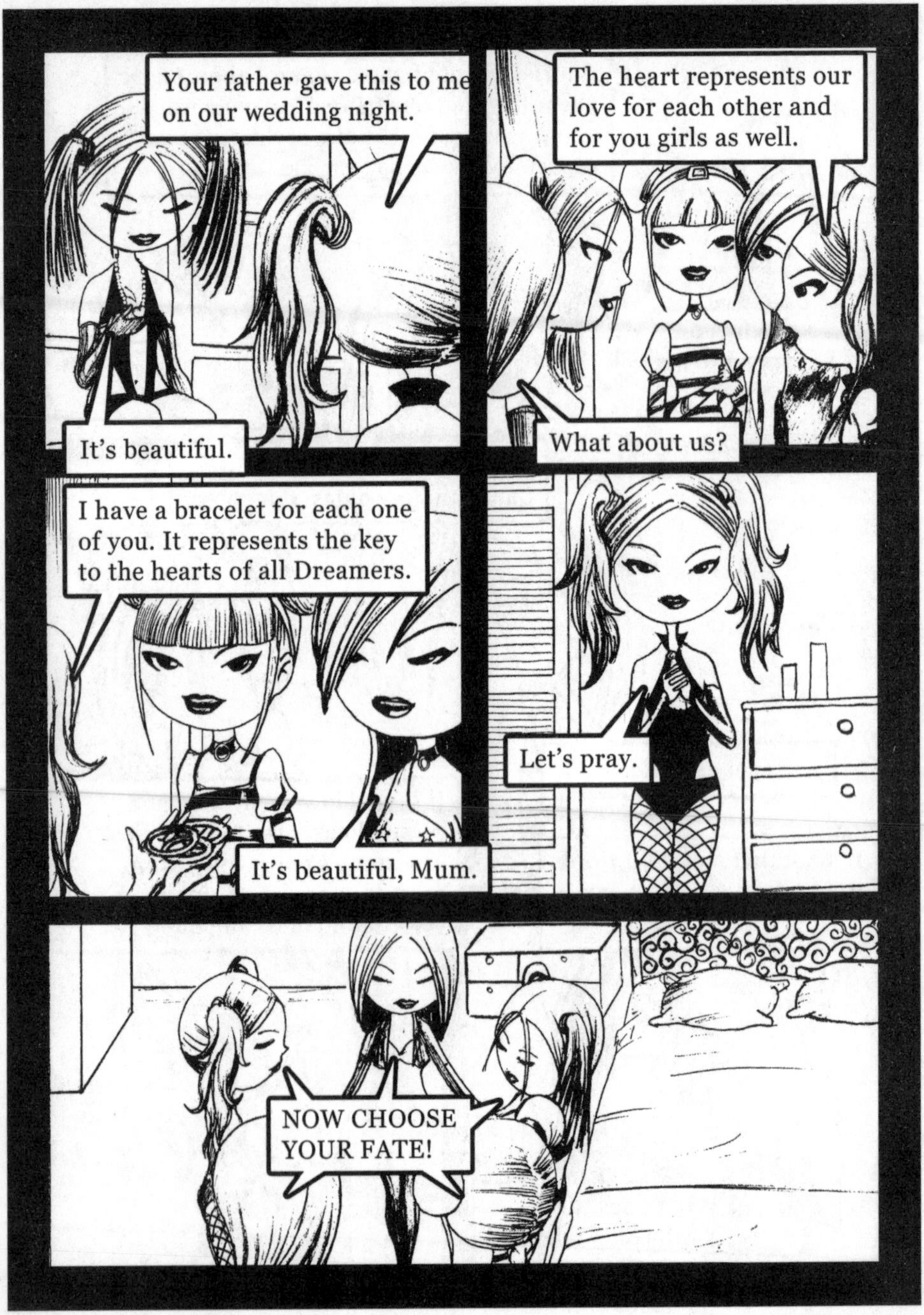
Your father gave this to me on our wedding night.
It's beautiful.
The heart represents our love for each other and for you girls as well.
What about us?
I have a bracelet for each one of you. It represents the key to the hearts of all Dreamers.
It's beautiful, Mum.
Let's pray.
NOW CHOOSE YOUR FATE!

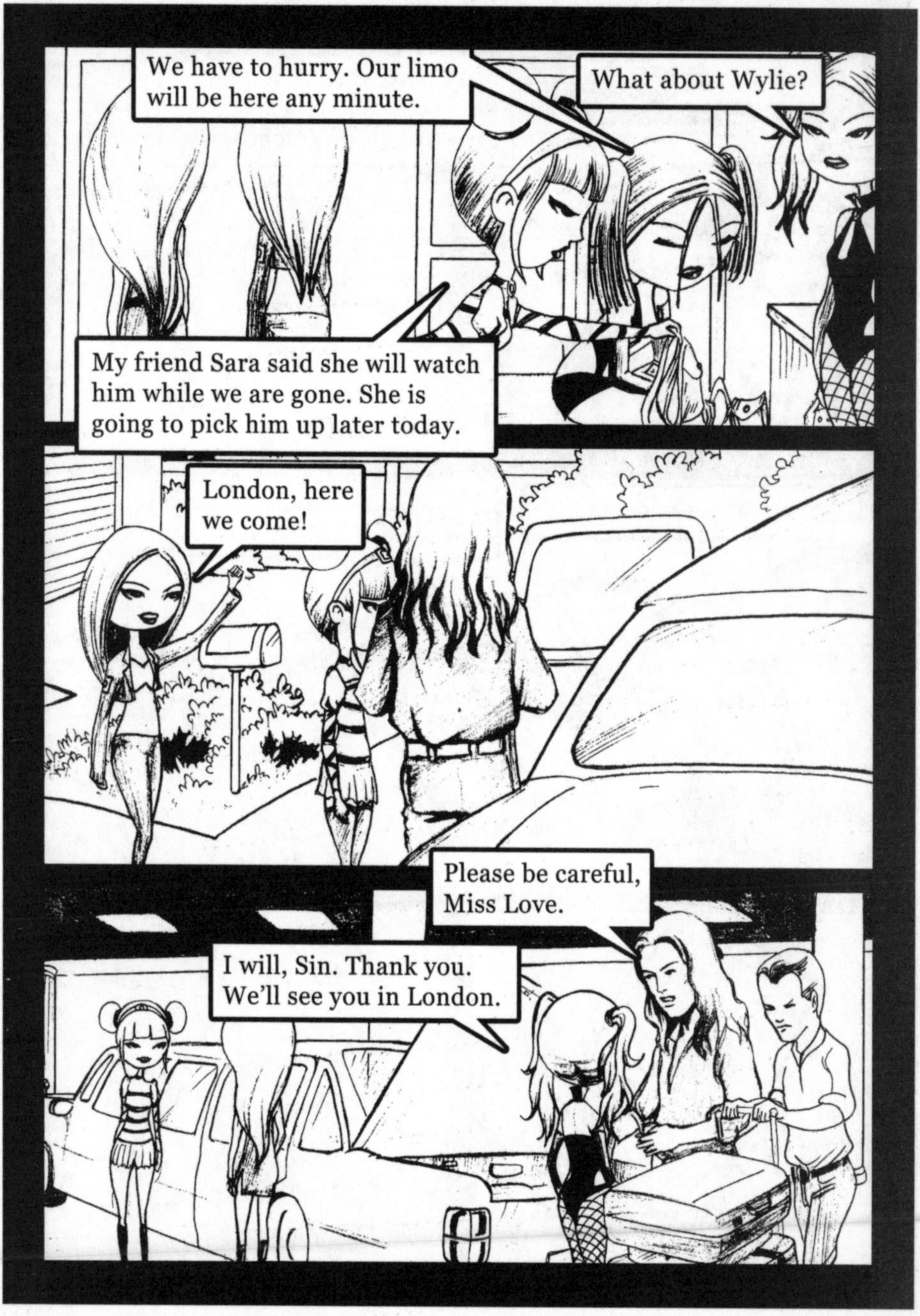
We have to hurry. Our limo will be here any minute.
What about Wylie?
My friend Sara said she will watch him while we are gone. She is going to pick him up later today.
London, here we come!
Please be careful, Miss Love.
I will, Sin. Thank you. We'll see you in London.

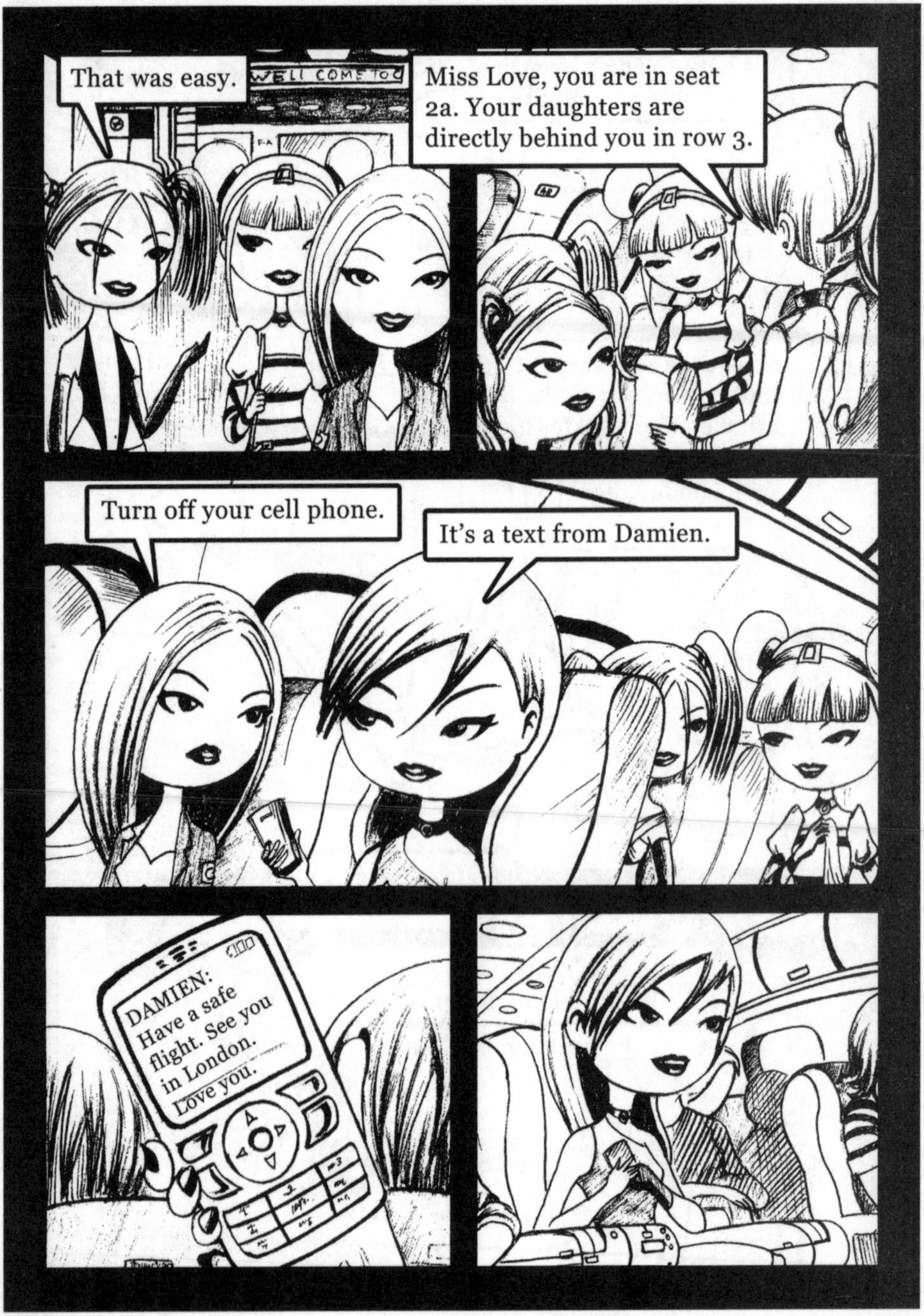
That was easy.
WELL COMETO
Miss Love, you are in seat 2a. Your daughters are directly behind you in row 3.
Turn off your cell phone.
It's a text from Damien.
DAMIEN: Have a safe flight. See you in London. Love you.

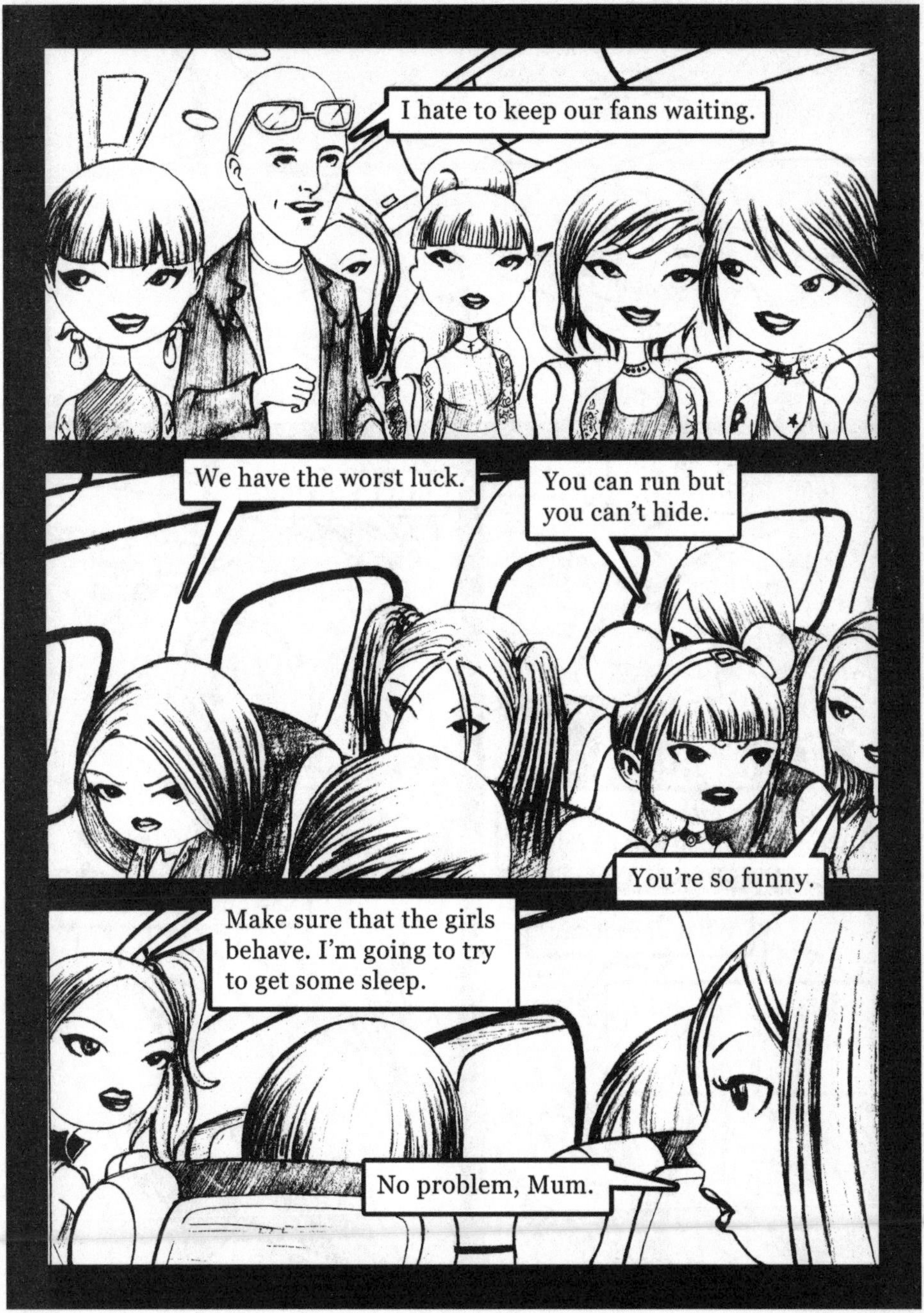
I hate to keep our fans waiting.
We have the worst luck.
You can run but you can't hide.
You're so funny.
Make sure that the girls behave. I'm going to try to get some sleep.
No problem, Mum.

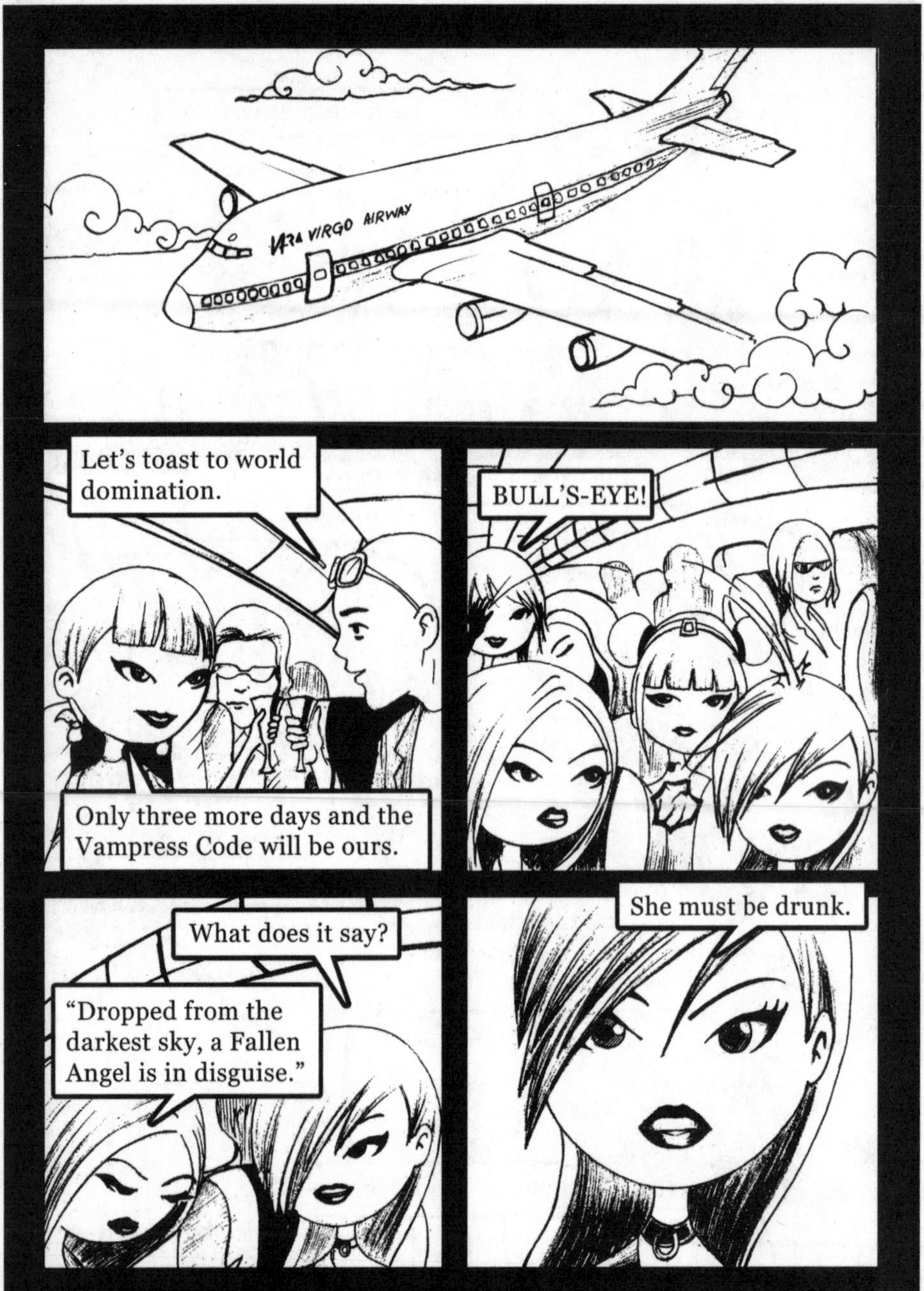
VIRGO AIRWAY
Let's toast to world domination.
Only three more days and the Vampress Code will be ours.
BULL'S-EYE!
What does it say?
"Dropped from the darkest sky, a Fallen Angel is in disguise."
She must be drunk.

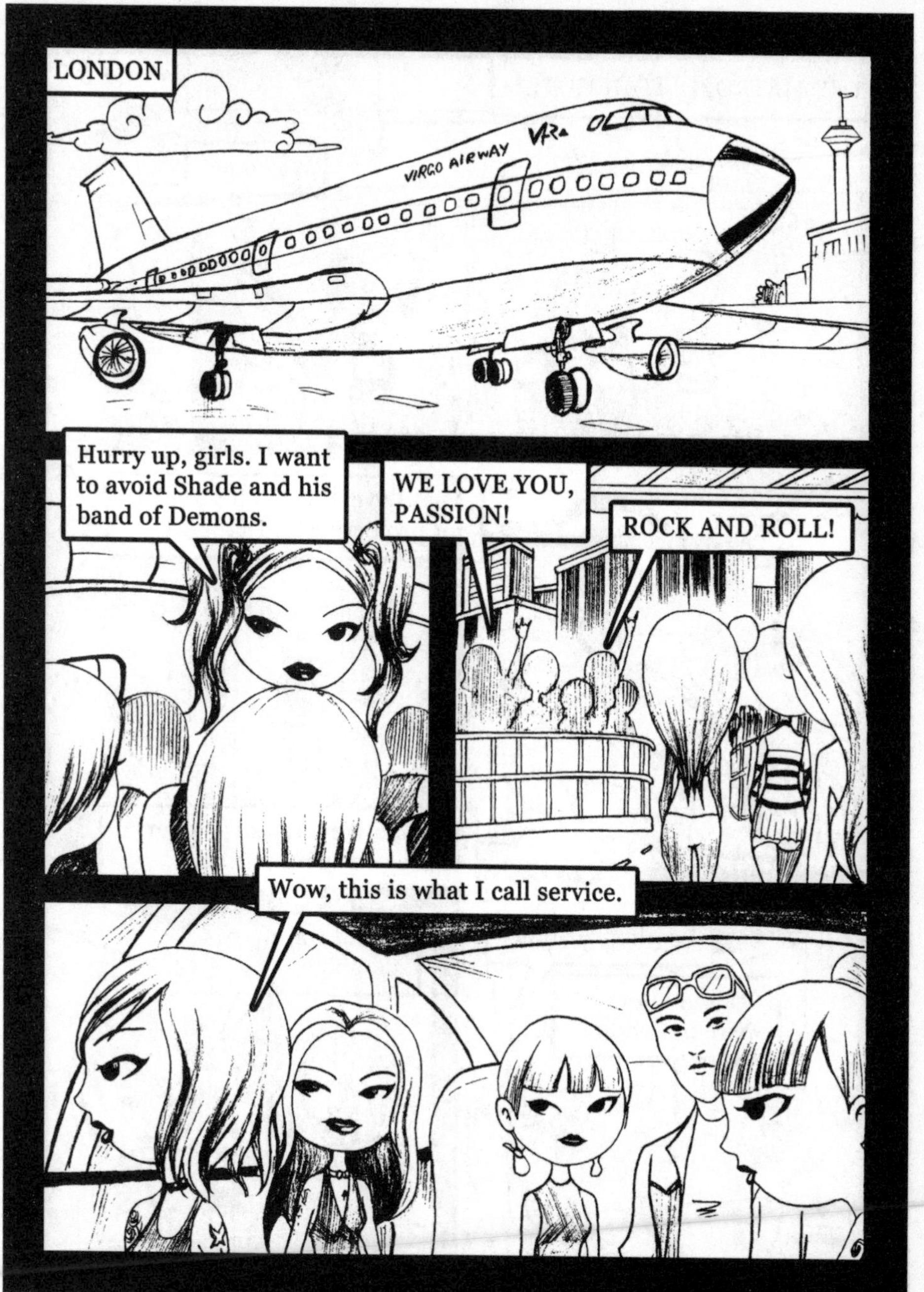
LONDON
VIRGO AIRWAY
Hurry up, girls. I want to avoid Shade and his band of Demons.
WE LOVE YOU, PASSION!
ROCK AND ROLL!
Wow, this is what I call service.

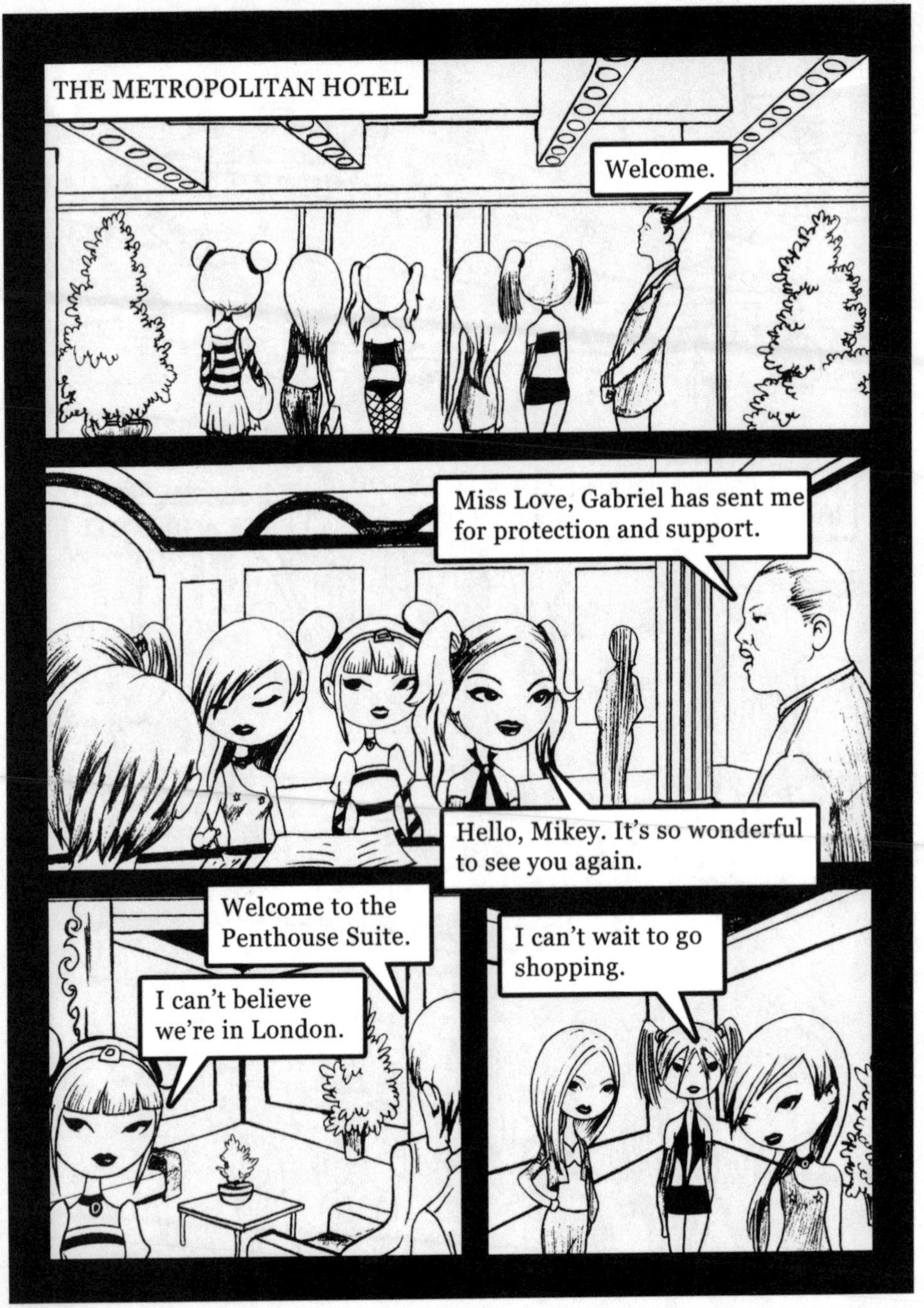
THE METROPOLITAN HOTEL
Welcome.
Miss Love, Gabriel has sent me for protection and support.
Hello, Mikey. It's so wonderful to see you again.
Welcome to the Penthouse Suite.
I can't believe we're in London.
I can't wait to go shopping.

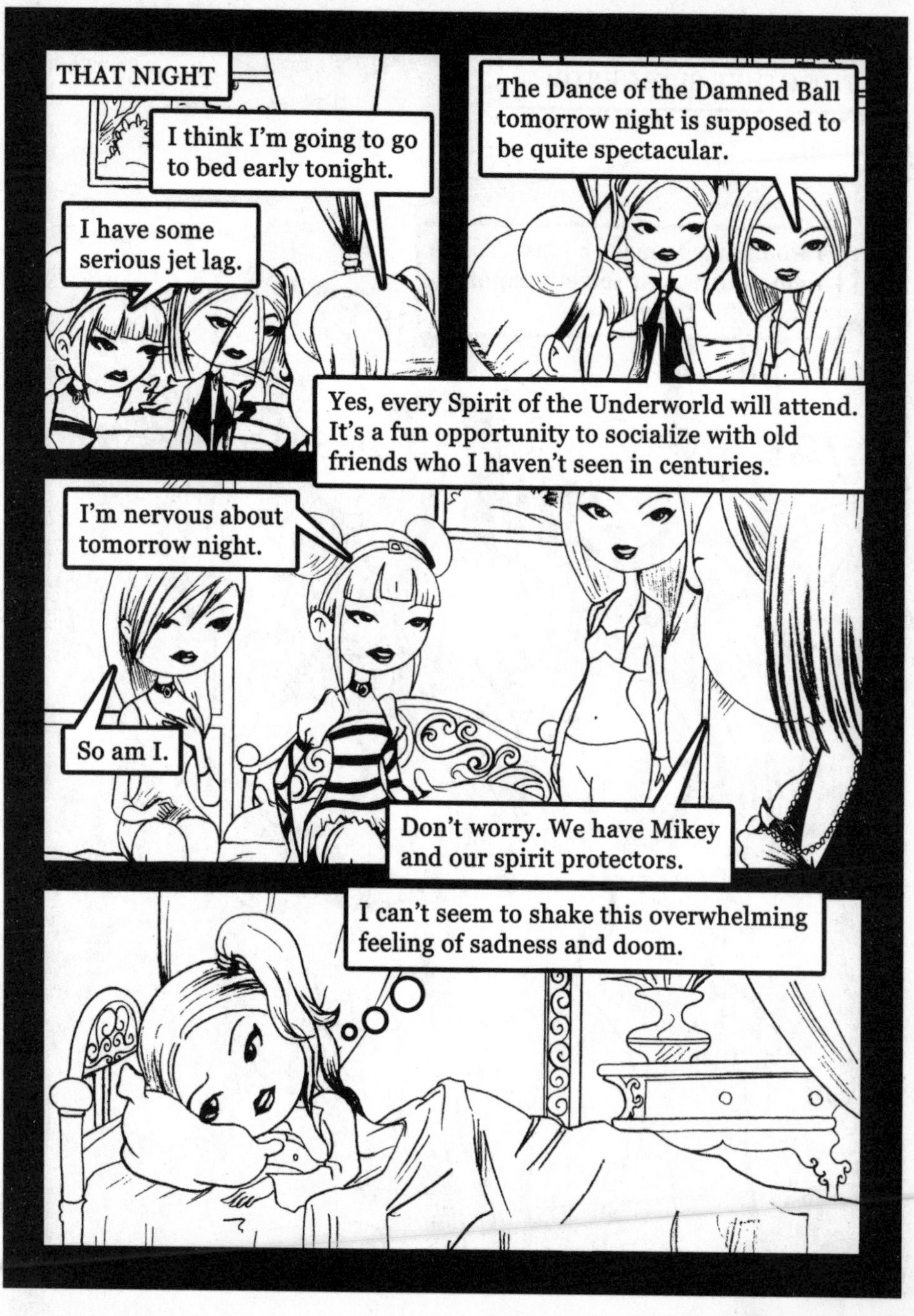
THAT NIGHT
I think I'm going to go to bed early tonight.
I have some serious jet lag.
The Dance of the Damned Ball tomorrow night is supposed to be quite spectacular.
Yes, every Spirit of the Underworld will attend. It's a fun opportunity to socialize with old friends who I haven't seen in centuries.
I'm nervous about tomorrow night.
So am I.
Don't worry. We have Mikey and our spirit protectors.
I can't seem to shake this overwhelming feeling of sadness and doom.

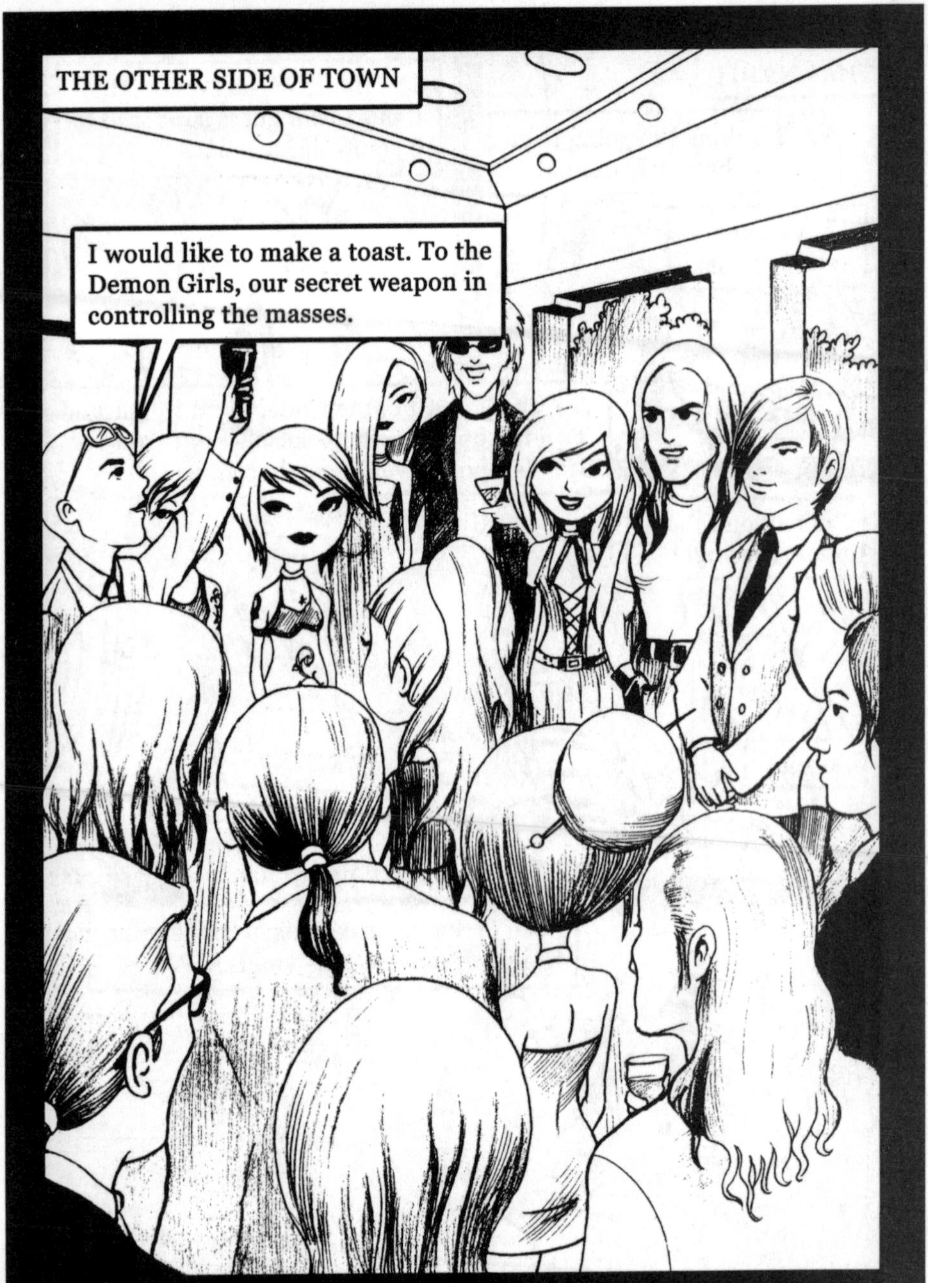
THE OTHER SIDE OF TOWN
I would like to make a toast. To the Demon Girls, our secret weapon in controlling the masses.

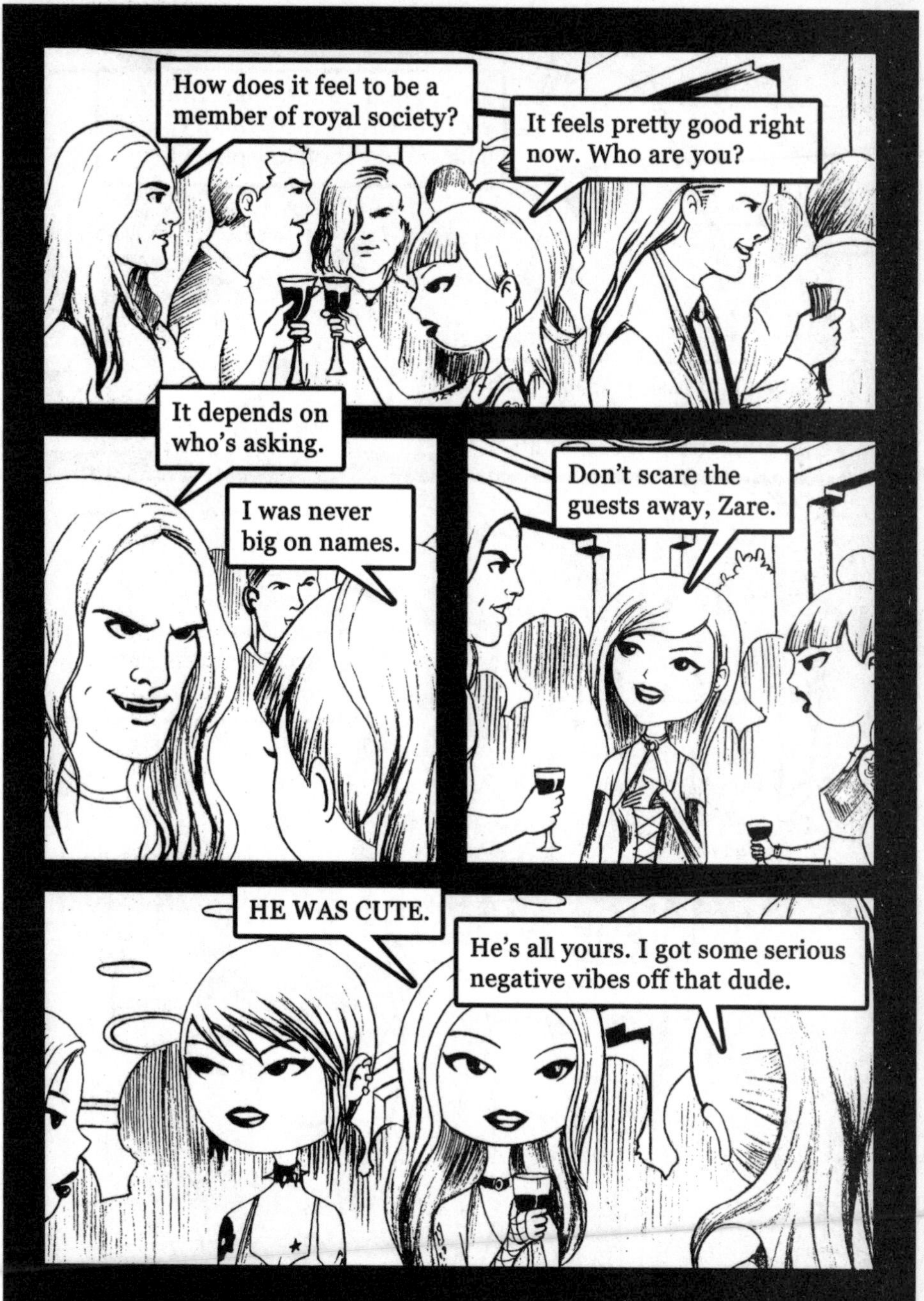
How does it feel to be a member of royal society?
It feels pretty good right now. Who are you?
It depends on who's asking.
I was never big on names.
Don't scare the guests away, Zare.
HE WAS CUTE.
He's all yours. I got some serious negative vibes off that dude.

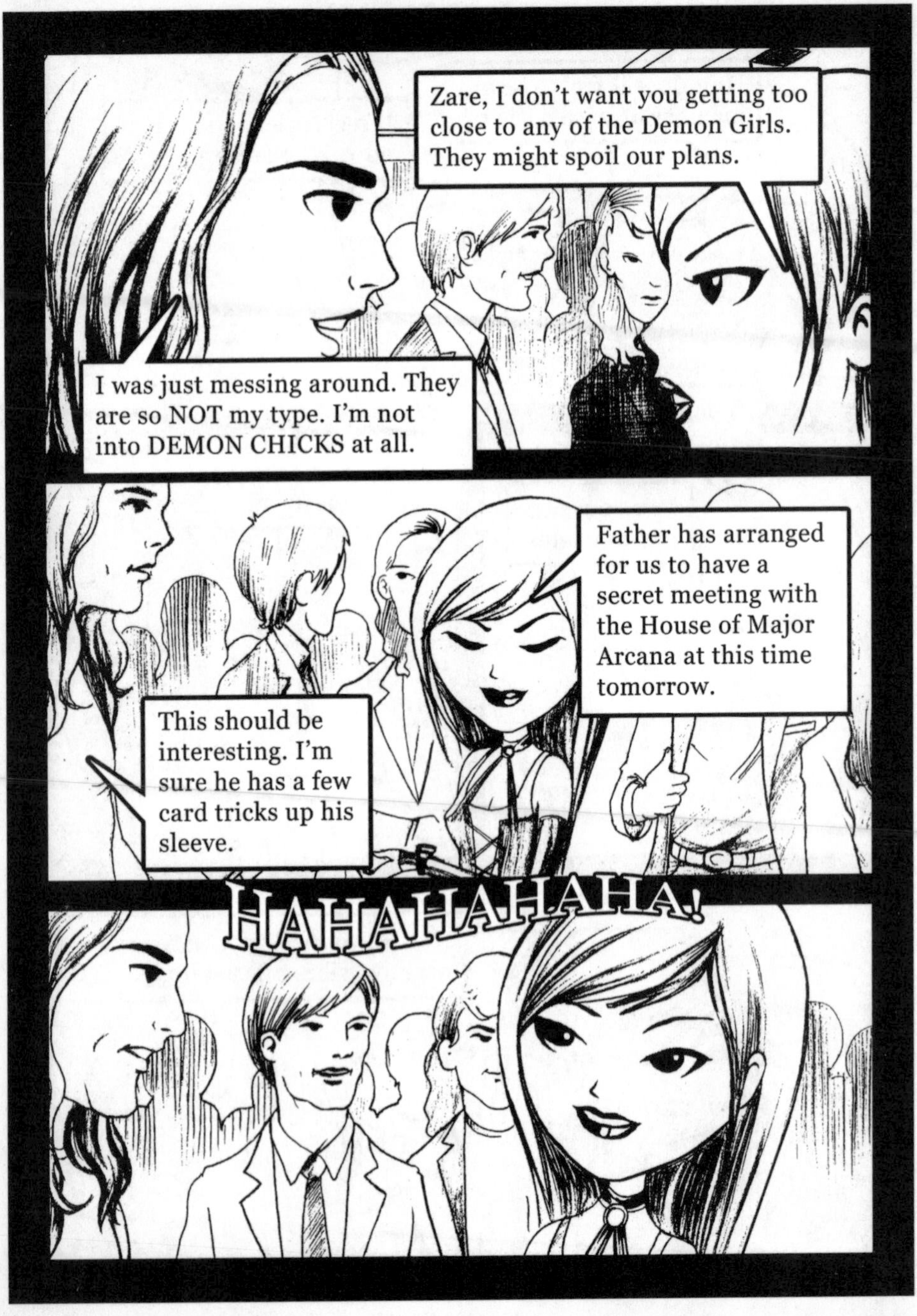
Zare, I don't want you getting too close to any of the Demon Girls. They might spoil our plans.
I was just messing around. They are so NOT my type. I'm not into DEMON CHICKS at all.
This should be interesting. I'm sure he has a few card tricks up his sleeve.
Father has arranged for us to have a secret meeting with the House of Major Arcana at this time tomorrow.
HAHAHAHAHA!

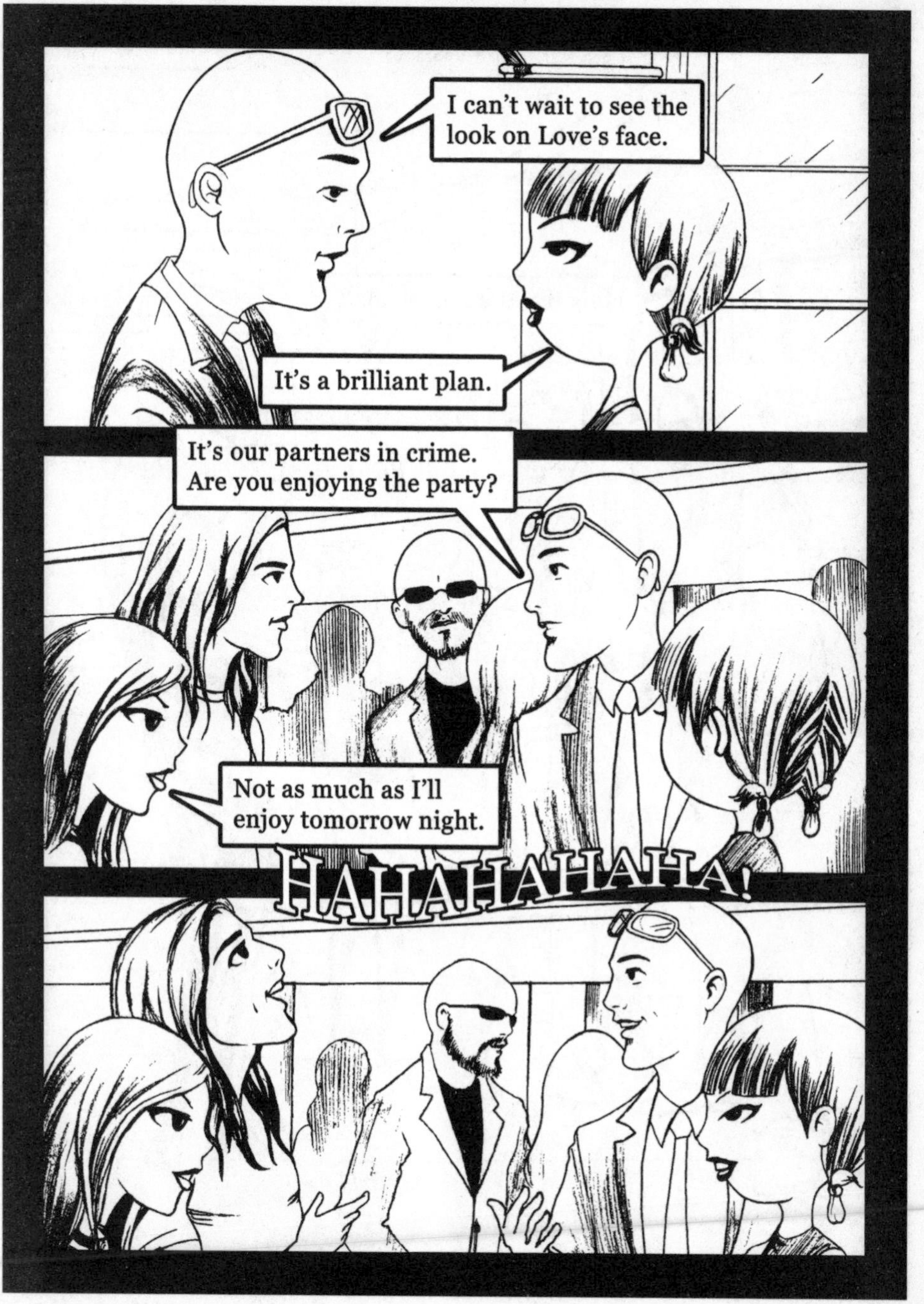
I can't wait to see the look on Love's face.
It's a brilliant plan.
It's our partners in crime. Are you enjoying the party?
Not as much as I'll enjoy tomorrow night.
HAHAHAHAHA!

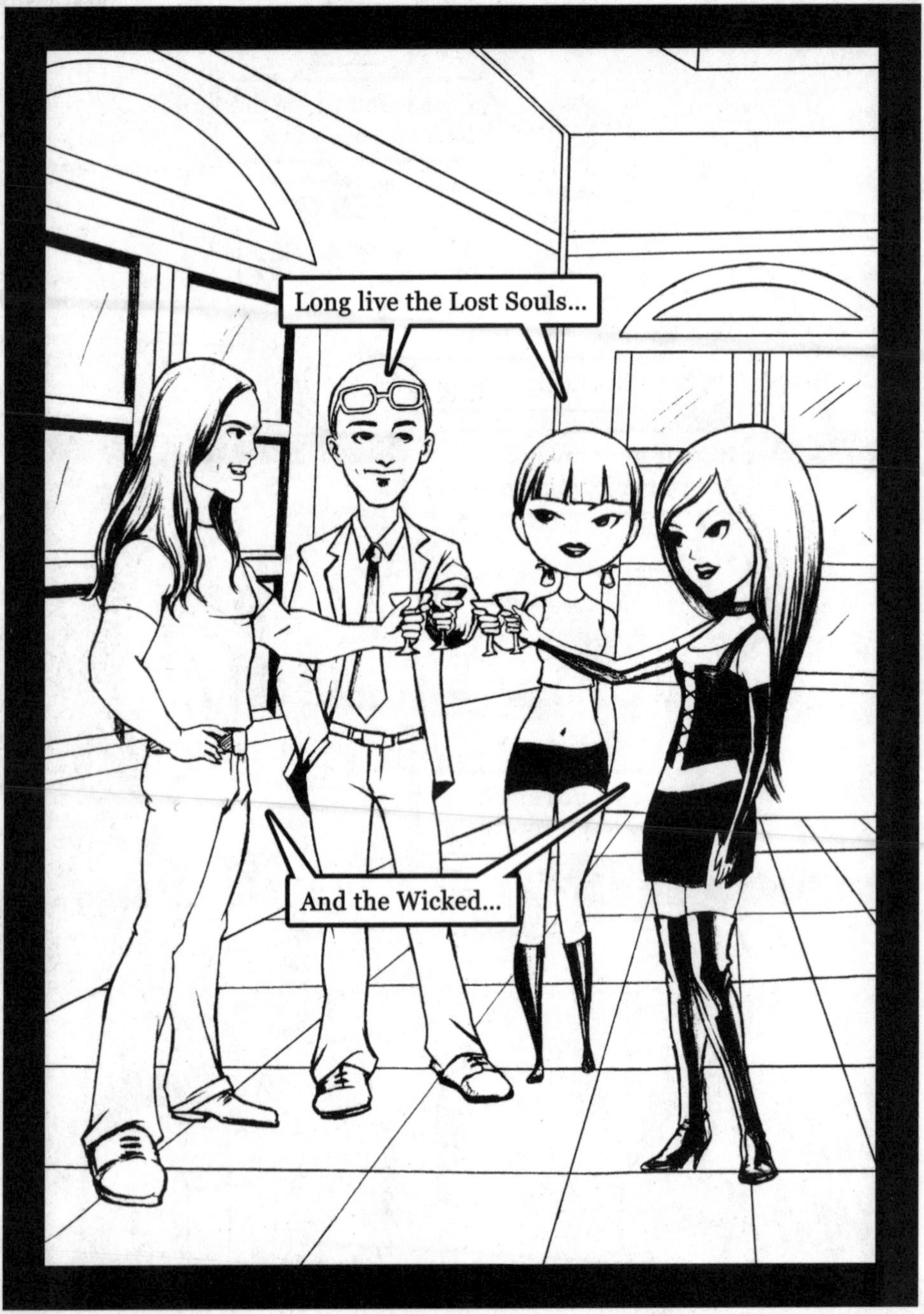
Long live the Lost Souls...
And the Wicked...

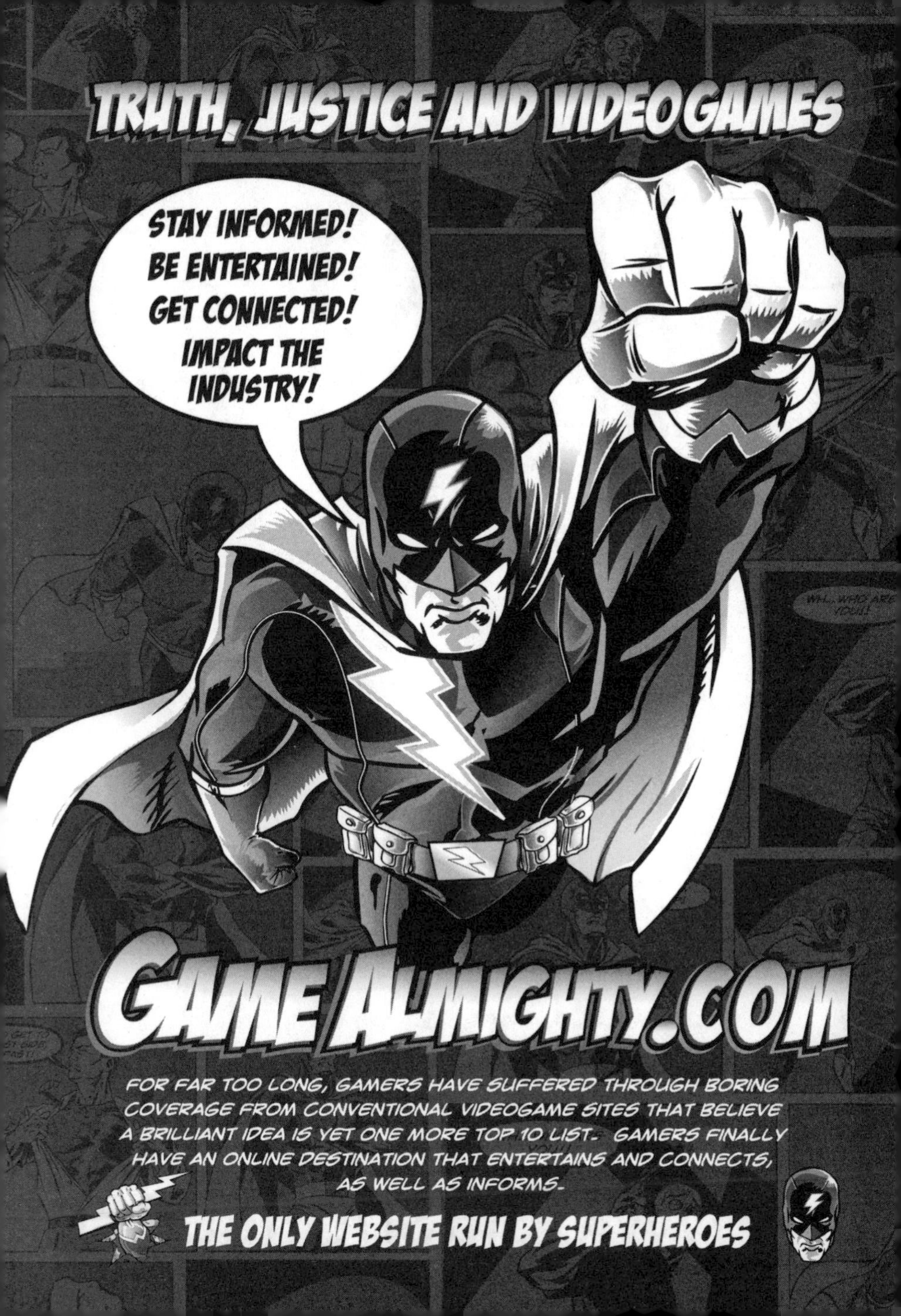
TRUTH, JUSTICE AND VIDEOGAMES
STAY INFORMED! BE ENTERTAINED! GET CONNECTED! IMPACT THE INDUSTRY!
GAME ALMIGHTY.COM
FOR FAR TOO LONG, GAMERS HAVE SUFFERED THROUGH BORING COVERAGE FROM CONVENTIONAL VIDEOGAME SITES THAT BELIEVE A BRILLIANT IDEA IS YET ONE MORE TOP 10 LIST. GAMERS FINALLY HAVE AN ONLINE DESTINATION THAT ENTERTAINS AND CONNECTS, AS WELL AS INFORMS.
THE ONLY WEBSITE RUN BY SUPERHEROES

Grab the
coolest content
for your profile at
www.SplashCast.net

Don't forget to check out our official website at
www.vampressgirls.com.
Free daily horoscopes, tarot card readings, screen savers,
and more. Also, check out The Vampress Girls band page
at myYearbook.com/vampressgirls.